APOCALYPSE

Dean Crawford began writing after his dream of becoming a fighter pilot in the Royal Air Force was curtailed when he failed their stringent sight tests. Fusing his interest in science with a love of fast-paced revelatory thrillers, he soon found a career that he could pursue with as much passion as flying a fighter jet. Now a full-time author, he lives with his partner and daughter in Surrey.

Also by Dean Crawford
Covenant
Immortal

For Terry and Carolyn

You can't own it but you can use it. You can't keep it but you can spend it. Once you've lost it, you can never get it back. Time is free, but it is priceless.

Harvey MacKay

I

CORAL GABLES, MIAMI, FLORIDA

June 27, 19:16

'How many bodies are there?'

Captain Kyle Sears hung one arm out of the Ford Crown Victoria Police Interceptor as it accelerated away from the airport district station. The warm evening breeze rippled the sleeves of his distinctive taupe uniform, the nearby ocean sparkling as the sun set behind the glassy towers of the city skyline.

The warbled tones of a despatch officer replied to his question across the radio waves.

'Two victims, both confirmed deceased from gunshot wounds. We got a tip-off from an unknown male caller. A forensics team is on their way and we've got a witness on the scene.'

Sears grimaced behind his sunglasses. The motion twisted his neat gray mustache as he glanced at his fellow officer, Lieutenant José Rodriquez, who shrugged as he drove. 'A witness doesn't necessarily lead to a conviction.'

Sears flicked a switch on the dashboard that sent sirens wailing as they raced along the boulevard, the interceptor's flashing lights reflecting off the windows of other vehicles that swerved to get out of the way. Southbound on the Expressway, Sears could see the metallic sprawl of Miami International Airport nearby, the navigation lights of airliners blinking as they climbed into a spectacular sunset striped with tattered ribbons of black cloud.

Rodriquez, a 30-year-old Latino out of Westchester, turned away from the palms of SW 40th and Ponce de Leon Boulevard and down onto Sistina Avenue, a shady tree-lined residential street where most all the homes were two-story colonials with manicured lawns. A far cry, Sears recognized, from the usual homicide call-ups on the north side, where ranks of shabby clapperboard houses ringed with chain-link fences faced sidewalks littered with junk.

'There it is.'

Half a dozen squad cars lined the street in a blaze of hazard lights outside one of the elaborate homes, police cordons blocking access to the sidewalk and gardens. A television crew from a local station was already hovering around, a reporter jawing into a camera as she gestured to the mansion behind her. Rodriquez pulled in and killed the engine as Sears climbed out and ducked under the cordon, flashing his badge at a beat cop who waved him through.

'Forensics arrived yet?'

'Inside,' the cop replied. 'Got here a few minutes ago.'

Sears strode up to the front door as he donned a set of blue rubber gloves and surveyed the exterior of the property. To his right, a middle-aged woman cradling a small poodle in her arms was being questioned by two uniformed officers. Sears strolled over and the senior of the two cops, a portly officer with heavy jowls, filled him in.

'This is Madeleine Ford, Captain,' the officer informed him. 'She observed the home-owner leaving the property in a real hurry about two hours ago, a man named Charles Purcell. We're just waiting to find out who he is.'

Sears nodded and looked at the woman, her white hair immaculately styled and her movements precise and controlled. Probably retired years before, most likely widowed with nothing better to do than watch the street outside.

'What exactly did you see, ma'am?' he asked with an easy smile as he removed his sunglasses.

Madeleine stroked the dog in her arms and glanced at the television crews nearby with their hefty cameras.

'Mr. Purcell came through here about two hours ago, officer,' she said, clearly enjoying the attention. 'Looked like he was in a real hurry. He went inside, and then about twenty minutes later he took off in his car like he was fleeing the devil himself.'

Sears nodded.

'Did you hear any gunshots or any kind of fracas from the home?'

Madeleine shook her head.

'Not that I recall. They seemed such a nice family, always polite, although he wasn't about much.'

'Purcell?' Rodriquez asked.

'He was always working out at sea,' Madeleine replied. 'Or so his wife said.'

Sears made a mental note and then left Madeleine with the uniforms and strode with Rodriquez toward the Purcell family home.

'Professional hit?' Rodriquez hazarded. 'Silenced weapons?'

'Maybe,' Sears replied thoughtfully as they walked into the house.

A bespectacled forensics expert, Hickling, guarded the entrance hall and waved them forward with a nod.

'The hall's clear but don't handle anything. We haven't dusted down yet.'

Sears headed toward the lounge at the end of a long corridor, where he could see periodic flashes from a crime-scene officer's camera. He heard a cheerful voice followed by a burst of laughter and applause, bizarrely out of place at a crime scene. Hickling rested a hand on Sears' shoulder as he passed.

'It's a bad one, Kyle.'

The captain slowed. Despite years of experience, the cautioning hand of a forensics expert was enough to make even Sears apprehensive. He took a breath and walked into the lounge, then paused at the doorway to take in the scene before him as a tight acidic ball lodged in his throat.

The lounge was large and well organized, two double leather couches lining the back and side walls, both within view of a large plasma screen that dominated the longest wall above a faux mantelpiece. French doors to his left. Bay windows to his right looking out over the lawns to the street. Sears looked at the plasma screen to see a re-run of *Everybody Loves Raymond* playing, incongruous with the somber mood. He couldn't see what Raymond was doing because of the thick blood splatter sprayed across the screen.

A woman lay slumped against the mantelpiece. Blond, mid-thirties, and dressed in a beige two-piece power suit. Maybe a lawyer or a banker. Her hair had once been carefully piled high on her delicate head but was now matted with thick blood, whilst most of the rear of her skull was embedded in chunks in the walls of the lounge and smeared across the mantelpiece beside her. She stared with her one remaining eye at the lounge door.

'Surprise attack,' Rodriquez said. 'Last thing she saw was her killer.'

Sears moved forward and looked down to his left, where, on one of the couches, lay the second body. The acidic ball in his throat threatened to leap out and he forced himself to keep breathing as he looked at the second corpse.

A girl, maybe nine years old, like a miniature carbon copy of her mother. Right down to the bloodied cavity where the back of her head had once been. Her hair, delicately swept back on one side over a tiny ear, lay in thick tresses on the other side across a congealing mass of blood and bone that had stained the couch. Spilled bodily fluids caked her bare legs. What was left of one side of her face stared up at them, locked in a gruesome rigor of shock.

Rodriquez's voice was tight as he surveyed the scene.

'Same MO. She never had a chance to react. Probably saw her mother die before she was shot.'

When it came to homicide, like most all detectives with the Miami-Dade Police Department, Sears had seen it all; fourteen years of shootings, stabbings and poisonings; gangs, drugs and racial hatred. He had seen corpses sliced, punctured, maimed and decomposed. But every now and again he bore witness to something approaching true evil – a murderer who killed for no other reason than the goddamn hell of it. If the killer had a beef with the woman, that was one thing. But shooting the kid too?

The flash of the CSI team's cameras jerked him out of his grim reverie.

'Any sign of forced entry?' Sears asked, mastering his rage and revulsion.

'Nothing,' came the response. 'Whoever did this was either a real pro or they walked right in.'

'Burglary gone wrong?' he asked, already knowing the answer.

'You kidding?' one of the CSI guys responded, a small but studious-looking man who, like Sears, was struggling to contain his rage at the carnage surrounding them. 'Nothing's missing that we know of. Matter of fact, there's no sign the killer even went anywhere else in the house. This was a hit, plain and simple.'

Sears glanced at the mantelpiece, where a row of family photographs stood. Images of happiness. A smiling wife, the daughter at junior high, grandparents, friends. The whole nine yards. All of them splattered with blood. Sears was about to turn away when one of the frames caught his eye. So thick was the mess upon it that nobody had noticed that the frame was empty. Sears pointed to it.

'Fingerprints, right now,' he snapped. 'The picture's missing.'

Rodriquez raised an eyebrow.

'Good catch, Kyle,' he said. 'Trophy killer. You think the husband did it?'

Sears was about to answer when his cellphone rang. He slipped it out of his pocket as he watched the forensics team swarm over the photograph.

'Sears,' he answered.

A soft, unassuming voice replied.

'*Captain, have you found the picture frame yet?*'

2

Sears almost combusted on the spot as he pointed frantically at his cellphone. Rodriquez instantly got the message and dashed from the lounge to get a trace on the caller.

Sears took a deep breath.

'Yes, we've found the picture frame. You've taken the photograph.'

The voice was eerily calm.

'*Yes I have, Captain, and for good reason. I need you to look out of the lounge window.*'

'Who is this?'

'*My name is Charles Purcell.*'

Sears managed to keep his voice calm.

'How did you get my number, Charles?'

'*From the Miami-Dade Police Department website.*'

Sears frowned. 'But how did you know that I would be the officer attending, or even on duty?'

'*Please, Captain, all will be revealed. The window, if you will.*'

Sears turned on the spot to see several officers rush across the lawn outside.

'I'm looking.'

'The third officer on the right will jaywalk and get hit by the white Lexus.'

Kyle Sears' train of thought slammed to a halt as he tried to understand what Purcell was telling him. All at once he turned his head and saw a white Lexus moving out of the corner of his eye. His officers scattering to make calls and get equipment up and running. Sears realized that Purcell, the crazy bastard, must be in the car.

Sears whirled and sprinted from the lounge, down the hall and onto the lawn outside to see the car rolling by. Bobby LeMark, one of the newer guys, dashed out from behind the forensics van toward his squad car. *Jesus, no.* Sears couldn't help himself and yelled out.

'Bobby!'

LeMark turned as he ran, floundered and lost his balance. In a terrible instant, Sears saw the Lexus swerve to avoid him and then the terrible crunch of a fender as it slammed into LeMark's legs. The officer crashed down onto the asphalt with a dull thump. Tires screeched as Sears stared in horror.

'Arrest the driver!' he bellowed as he staggered down the lawn toward the sidewalk.

A swarm of officers drew their weapons and aimed at the white Lexus as they rushed forward. Sears heard Purcell's voice in his ear.

'I'm not in the car, Captain. It will be an old lady of at least sixty. Don't worry, your man will be fine, nothing more than

a twisted ankle. I'd have warned you earlier if it was going to be anything worse.'

Sears stared in confusion as an elderly and transparently terrified lady was hauled from the Lexus by heavily armed cops. Sears waved them down, watching as LeMark was lifted to his feet by his comrades, his face pinched with pain as he hobbled awkwardly on his left foot.

'*It's his right ankle, isn't it, Kyle?'*

Sears stared at LeMark for a moment and then shouted down the phone.

'Where the goddamned hell are you, Purcell?!'

'*Your partner will work that out in precisely one minute and seventeen seconds. Right now, I need you to listen to me while there is still time.'*

Rodriquez rushed to Sears' side and held up his fingers as he mouthed words silently. *One minute, fifteen seconds.*

Confusion whirled through Kyle Sears' mind as he struggled to comprehend what was happening. Charles Purcell's voice sounded again in his ear, calm and controlled.

'*Captain, I need you to listen very carefully to what I am going to tell you. It will not make sense but I swear to you that if you do as I say, you'll understand why it is so important.'*

Fourteen years of training and experience pulled Sears back from the brink of disbelief. He took another deep breath and controlled his thoughts. Keep him talking. *Just keep the bastard talking.*

'Charles, did you kill your wife and child?'

A long pause followed, and when Purcell spoke again his voice crackled as though his vocal cords were being torn from his throat.

'*No sir, I did not.*'

'You were seen leaving the scene of the murders, Charles.'

'*By Madeleine, our neighbor,*' Purcell confirmed. '*She's with you guys now, holding her dog, right?*'

Sears felt a chill lance down his spine as he pivoted on one foot to see Madeleine still watching the forensics team. Slowly he turned full circle, his eyes searching parked cars and the windows of nearby houses.

'There's no sense in hiding, Charles,' he said. 'If you're not guilty, then handing yourself in right now is the best course of action.'

'*I wish that were true, Captain, but my life is already over. Sir, I need you to visit an apartment in Hallandale that you've never been to before, and I need you to contact a man you've never met.*'

'What the hell are you talking about? I know you can see me, Charles.'

'*I can't see you, Captain. But I have watched you.*' Before Sears could respond, Purcell continued, his words charged with a strange timbre, as though he were saying goodbye to an old friend for the last time. '*In less than twenty-four hours I will be murdered and I know the man who will kill me. My murderer does not yet know that he will commit the act.*'

Sears' mind buzzed with disbelief. 'Then how can you know that he will do it?'

'*You will find that out soon enough,*' Purcell replied, '*and it cannot be prevented.*'

'Hand yourself in and let us protect you.'

'*If I was to do that, Captain, then the man who murdered*'

my family will never see justice. It has to be this way.' Purcell paused. '*The ambulance is coming now, correct?*'

Sears looked up and saw an ambulance turn onto Sistina Avenue, its lights flashing but its sirens silent.

'Where are you, Charles?'

'*You'll know in fifteen seconds, Captain. For now, please listen to me. The bullets that killed my family are still in the house. Find them and have them analyzed for a compound known as Rubidium-82. Then, go to one-one-seven on Sixty-Fourth, Hallandale. When you're there, you'll need to contact a man named Ethan Warner.*'

'What the hell for?'

'*Please, Captain. If you want to bring my family's killer to justice, do as I say. Time is literally everything. Your colleague will tell you where I am, right about now.*'

The line went dead in Sears' ear just as Rodriquez dashed to his side.

'We've got him,' he announced. 'He's at one-one-seven on Sixty-Fourth, Hallandale.'

Sears stared at Rodriquez. 'You're sure?'

'Absolutely. We've got units on their way already.'

Hallandale was several miles away. Purcell might have installed a camera somewhere close by, but even then, how the hell could he have predicted the accident that twisted LeMark's ankle?

Rodriquez gestured to Sears' cellphone. 'What did he want?'

Sears looked blankly at his cell and shook his head. He glanced up at the nearby news crew standing around their vehicle setting up to broadcast a report. Whatever the hell was going on here, Sears wasn't about to take any chances that Purcell could see what they were doing.

'We need to get to Hallandale, right now, and get that camera crew out of here. I want the media kept out of the loop until we can figure out what the hell's going on.'

3

SOUTH BIMINI ISLAND, BAHAMAS

June 27, 19:24

'*Bimini this is November two-seven-six-four-charlie, airborne and turning two-seven-zero in the climb.*'

Captain James MacDonald clicked off the transmit button on his control column as he pulled back on the Grumman Mallard's controls. The foamy white spray blasting past the windshield and the rumble of water thundering beneath the fuselage gave way to smooth and subtle gyrations as the aircraft lifted off from the sparkling azure waters of the Florida Straits.

MacDonald turned and looked out of the cockpit windshield at the distant horizon, where the sun was sinking between soaring cumulonimbus clouds that glowed like the wings of giant angels.

'Always looks good, doesn't it?'

The voice of MacDonald's First Officer, Sarah Gleeson, was followed by a bright smile as she gestured with a nod to the sunset as the Grumman climbed upward, its turboprop engines hauling the vintage airframe ever higher.

'Sure does,' MacDonald agreed. He scanned the horizon for other aircraft, then checked his instruments and turned onto a new heading, locking his VOR radio-navigation frequency onto Miami International Airport. 'You'll never get tired of this job.'

Sarah Gleeson had joined Bimini Wings just six months before, fresh out of getting her Commercial Pilot's License and her water-plane qualification on the Grumman Mallard. MacDonald had been tasked with seeing her through her first year of flying with the company, a task that he had undertaken happily. After thirty-four years of service he enjoyed seeing the next generation of pilots coming up through the ranks.

He settled back into his seat, placed his flight notes in his lap and let Sarah handle the climb out and cruise. Miami was just sixty nautical miles away across the Florida Straits on their westerly heading. Sitting behind them in the passenger cabin were a dozen scientists returning home after some kind of fieldwork exercise out on the coral reefs near Bimini, probably conservationists or some such.

'Last chartered trip of the afternoon,' Sarah said. 'You got anything planned?'

MacDonald shook his head. 'Back home and a long shower.'

Sarah leveled the Grumman Mallard off at six thousand feet, MacDonald taking quiet pride in the fact that she ignored the autopilot and flew the aircraft by hand. A real pilot, not some overpaid geek trained to press buttons. He ensured that she trimmed the aircraft perfectly, then looked out over the ocean to watch the scattered clouds floating serenely past below, casting blue shadows on the crystalline ocean. Even after so many years flying in the Bahamas he still reveled in the unparalleled purity of the environment, especially on a day like today, with perfect conditions: CAVU, as they called it. Clear Air, Visibility Unlimited. Damn, even the thermal currents rising off the warm water were gentle, just swaying the wings in a—

The aircraft lurched to the right with a violent shudder as though something had slammed into the tail. Sarah instinctively kicked hard at the left rudder as MacDonald grabbed the throttles in anticipation of a sudden updraft or downdraft.

'The hell was that?' Sarah uttered as the aircraft settled again.

MacDonald scanned the instruments with practiced eyes, but saw nothing amiss.

'Damned if I know.'

They both looked instinctively out of the windows. With Bimini far behind and Miami just over the horizon in the glowing golden haze ahead, they may as well have been a thousand miles from anywhere.

MacDonald held the controls with a light touch and felt the tension slip from his body as he relaxed again.

'Probably just a hole in the air, happens from time to time.'

MacDonald knew that aircraft had been known to plummet hundreds or even thousands of feet without warning when the lift beneath their wings was snatched away by invisible pockets of low pressure. Even the giant Boeing 747s weren't immune to such volatile events . . .

MacDonald's train of thought slowed as he glanced at the magnetic compass on the instrument panel before him. Moments before it had been pointing rock steady at two-seven-zero degrees, dead west. Now, it was swinging gently between two-five-zero and three-zero-zero, as though unsure of itself.

'You got a heading?' he asked Sarah.

She glanced at her own instruments and shook her head. 'Damn, no. Gyro's out.'

'Mine too.'

MacDonald glanced at the GPS screen used by pilots as a backup to traditional compasses, useful when dealing with multiple issues and in need of a quick position fix. But this time there was nothing to see. The screen was blank but for the No Signal message blinking urgently at them.

'The hell's going on?' Sarah muttered, tapping the screen and pressing the reset button. The screen remained blank.

MacDonald keyed his radio-transmit button.

'*Bimini, November two-seven-six-four-charlie, radio check.*'

A dull hiss of static hummed in their earphones as they exchanged a glance.

'Switch to Miami Approach,' MacDonald instructed Sarah, who dialed in the international airport's radio frequency.

MacDonald tried again, twice, but heard only static in response.

'This isn't good,' Sarah murmured, looking at her instruments.

'We're not in trouble yet,' MacDonald soothed her. He gestured ahead out of the windscreen toward the sun hovering low over the horizon. 'Keep the sun on the nose. That way we'll still be heading due west and should pick up the coast soon enough.'

Sarah offered him an embarrassed smile.

'Good idea,' she said. 'I should have thought of that.'

MacDonald didn't reply, instead watching as his magnetic compass began spinning ever more wildly. The secondary instruments were also beginning to lose cohesion as though tugged by unseen forces. A dread began to settle on his shoulders.

'What was our last known position fix?' he asked.

Sarah thought for a moment. MacDonald waited for her to figure the math in her head, and tried to be patient.

'Twenty-six nautical miles due east of Bimini South.'

MacDonald was making rapid mental calculations when Sarah spoke again. 'Oh hell, we're headed into cloud.'

MacDonald looked up out of the windshield to see a mass of cloud ahead of them, materializing as though out of thin air. His brain struggled to resolve what he was seeing, and he realized that the towering cumulonimbus clouds on the horizon must have concealed the cloud bank directly in their flight path.

'Altitude!' he snapped as he reached down to slam the throttles wide open. 'Get above the clouds and keep the sun in sight!'

Sarah eased back on the control column and the Grumman Mallard climbed upward again. MacDonald looked back at his instruments and saw that the artificial horizon was now spinning crazily. The most vital of all instruments. Without it they would be doomed if they flew into the cloud.

He stared out of the windshield as a swirling vortex of dense cloud raced past the aircraft, the sunlight that had beamed into the cockpit beginning to flicker and fade.

'Keep climbing!' he shouted at Sarah. 'Keep the sun in front of us!'

'Maybe we should turn back!'

MacDonald hesitated for a brief moment before shaking his head.

'We're more likely to find the Florida coast than Bimini, even though the island's closer. Keep climbing!'

MacDonald peered forward to search for the orb of the sun and felt his bowels clench as he realized that he could no longer see it. He searched desperately for the horizon as the cloud thickened around them, tinged with a weird green glow like nothing he'd ever seen before. A blue haze enveloped the wingtips and the nose of the aircraft, shimmering like an electrified sparkler. *St Elmo's Fire.* He recognized the bizarre effect once feared by sailors in storms − electromagnetic fields hovering around the aircraft − and a sickening fear lurched through his guts as he realized that he had absolutely no idea what was happening.

A surge of G-force crushed him into his seat and he heard Sarah cry out as the Mallard plunged from the sky as though being dragged by a giant fist down through the clouds. MacDonald grabbed the control column and struggled to pull the nose of the aircraft up again.

Then, all at once, he saw the flight notes in his lap shoot upward past his face to land on the cockpit ceiling above his head. For a moment his brain could not understand what he had witnessed, and then it hit him in a moment of pure terror. They were inverted and already out of control.

'Altitude! Altitude!' he shouted to Sarah.

He heard shouts of alarm from their passengers as people and equipment were hurled around the fuselage as the aircraft spiraled down through the sky.

'I've got nothing!' Sarah screamed back, holding the throttles to the firewall. 'All primary instruments have failed!'

The turboprop engines wailed as the Grumman Mallard plummeted out of control, the instruments whirling uselessly and the horizon lost in a thick swirling fog that enveloped the entire aircraft in an electrically charged halo.

MacDonald reached out, his arm fighting against G-forces far greater than the aged aircraft was designed to take, and flipped an intercom switch to hear his own voice trembling in his earphones as he cried out.

'*This is your captain speaking! Brace for impact! Brace for imp—*'

A flare of golden sunlight burst through the cockpit as it reflected off a perfect blue sea, and for a brief instant James MacDonald believed that they had a chance. Then he saw that they were barely a hundred feet above the rolling waves. The glittering surface of the ocean raced toward his screen at two hundred miles per hour and then smashed through the thick glass to greet him.

4

CHICAGO, ILLINOIS

June 28, 07:15

'*I'm right behind him, stand by.*'

Ethan Warner sat back casually and watched the nearby freeway from his vantage point in a service alley between a Taco Bell and a hardware store. The breeze from the passing traffic ruffled his light brown hair as his gray eyes squinted into the early morning sunlight. The disembodied voice of his partner, Nicola Lopez, sounded in the earpiece and microphone he wore.

'*Turning right onto South Lake Shore, southbound.*'

'Copy that,' he replied. 'Remember not to get too close. You know what happened last time.'

'*It was just your fender, let it go asshole.*'

Ethan smiled quietly to himself as he spotted Lopez's sports car, a bright yellow convertible Lotus Seven, zip into view a quarter mile away as it joined the freeway. Ethan glanced ahead of it and saw a large silver GMC Yukon suddenly swerve out of a line of traffic and accelerate away from her.

'*He's made me!*'

Ethan sighed. Nicola Lopez was a 29-year-old Latino with long black hair who looked hot no matter what she was doing. She caught attention from most all guys, and unfortunately the driver of the GMC knew them both well enough to have recognized her the moment she let her enthusiasm and desire for money get in the way of her professionalism.

'I can see you. I'm on my way.'

Ethan reached out and flicked a switch. An engine growled into life beneath him as he kicked the Erik Buell 1190RS superbike into gear, the twin-cylinder symphony echoing down the narrow alley like rolling drums. The Yukon and the Lotus raced past in front of him as Ethan slipped the clutch and the superbike surged out of the alleyway and turned in pursuit. Frantic acceleration yanked on Ethan's arms as he twisted the throttle and the motorcycle raced up through sixty, seventy, eighty, the front wheel leaving the ground.

Ethan eased the bike around Lopez's accelerating Lotus, just able to hear the roar of her car's engine above his own as he raced past and crossed the lane in front of her.

He focused on the Yukon ahead as it swerved past traffic in an effort to escape the yellow car behind. The driver's attention was all on Lopez as she whipped the Lotus left and right in an effort to pass.

Ethan aimed for a gap between the Yukon and the central reservation and wound the superbike's throttle open as he screamed through the narrow space, the howl of the engine vibrating through his chest. He glanced left as he came alongside the Yukon and saw the bulky shaven head of Hayden Decker glaring at him from the driver's seat. Two-time bail jumper, $18,000 bond, manslaughter charges. Decker was worth a lot of cash to Lopez and Ethan.

Decker, one side of his face smeared with a huge purple spider-web tattoo, shot Ethan a savage grin. His mouth sparkled with gold as he span the Yukon's wheel toward the motorbike.

Ethan twisted the Buell's throttle and thundered clear as the Yukon narrowly missed his rear wheel and slammed into the central reservation to spray a blossoming fireball of sparks into the air. Ethan peered into his rear-view mirror and saw Decker wrestle the vehicle back under control. Lopez's voice chortled in his ear.

'*Very James Bond, but I can't get by him and if you brake he'll plough straight through you.*'

Ethan scanned the traffic around him, judged the distance to the next vehicle as 100 yards, and made his decision. He stamped the Buell down a gear and reveled in the wail of the engine as he raced away from the Yukon until the big vehicle was a small black spot in the center of his mirror.

'*Where the hell are you going?*' Lopez asked in confusion.

Ethan grinned as the wind howled like a banshee past his face. The past few years of his life had been almost entirely loathsome, the months and years grinding past beneath a crushing burden of repressed grief. The disappearance of his journalist fiancée Joanna Defoe from the Gaza Strip years before had left in its wake a chilling vacuum in his soul, devoid of passion, scoured of hope. Learning that she had not died in Gaza had somehow been both a blessing and a curse, for the mystery of her disappearance had only deepened further. It had been whilst hunting for her that he had encountered former Washington Police Detective Nicola Lopez, and if nothing else had happened since, his work with her had brought him back from the abyss. He hadn't felt so alive since he'd rappelled out of a US Marines CH-47 over Afghanistan, straight into a Taliban ambush.

Ethan closed the throttle and squeezed the brakes hard. The Buell's forks dove toward the ground as the rear wheel soared into the air behind him. Ethan leaned back to keep the weight central as the superbike shuddered to a halt in the center of the freeway. He kicked the side-stand down and climbed from the saddle, then turned and faced the Yukon bearing down on him from sixty yards away.

Ethan strolled forward, the sound of the big engine roaring closer with Lopez's Lotus just behind it. He stood in the center of the freeway and watched Hayden Decker's craggy features rush toward him behind the screen.

'*Ethan?*'

Ethan grinned as he saw Decker's face screw up in confusion.

'Drop your anchor, Nicola, now!'

The Lotus's wheels locked up in a cloud of blue smoke as Lopez stamped on the brakes. Ethan reached beneath his leather jacket and whipped out a Beretta M9 9mm pistol. The weapon had been the standard-issue sidearm of the Marine Corps in Ethan's day, and he had liked the weapon despite concerns about its stopping power.

Compact, light and easy to use, he kept one for what he liked to call 'special occasions'. Ethan dropped onto one knee and aimed double-handed. He squeezed once and a single shot recoiled the pistol with a sharp crack.

The Yukon's front nearside tire folded upon itself as the big truck swerved violently to one side and slammed again into the reservation, grinding metal against metal in a screeching cacophony. Ethan stood his ground as the Yukon shuddered along the reservation and came to rest ten yards away, Decker's door pinned against the metal railings. Ethan saw him scramble across to the passenger door and kick it open before tumbling from the vehicle as Lopez screeched to a halt somewhere behind the Yukon.

Ethan dashed forward and aimed the pistol at Decker.

'Get down, stay still!'

Decker ignored him and stood upright, over six feet tall and 250 pounds of muscle bursting from a white vest. He glared at Ethan without concern.

'What, you goin' down for homicide too? You can shoot a tire, Warner, but you can't shoot me.'

Ethan lowered the pistol.

'Got that right,' he agreed. Decker squinted at him and then turned to run.

He made a single pace before Lopez's elbow ploughed into his solar plexus with a dull thump that made Ethan wince. Decker doubled over with a strangled gasp as Lopez span gracefully on one heel, ducked down and stabbed a boot across the inside of the big man's knee. Decker quivered and toppled like a fallen tree before slamming down onto the asphalt. Lopez whipped her cuffs out and thrust one knee deep into Decker's back as she forced the restraints around his thick wrists. She looked up at Ethan's Beretta.

'We're not supposed to be carrying.'

The state of Illinois had a strict No-Issue policy over concealed weapons, meaning that no permit could be obtained from the courts or local law enforcement. Only Illinois and the District of Columbia had such policies in place. Ethan shrugged as he slipped the weapon into a shoulder holster beneath his jacket.

'I got tired of chasing dudes like Decker here with nothing more than pepper spray.'

Lopez hauled Decker to his feet. The shaven-headed, tattooed criminal towered over her.

'I got my rights!' he shouted at Ethan. 'You're carrying and you shot at me!'

Ethan was about to answer when the sound of roaring engines cut him off. He turned to see a pair of Police Interceptors screech alongside them, blocking off the lane as four officers tumbled out of the vehicles with their weapons drawn.

'Drop the piece!'

Ethan winced in disbelief as he raised one hand while carefully laying his pistol down on the asphalt at his feet. From the corner of his eye he saw Decker flash a spiteful grin. Ethan reached to the badge dangling from his neck and showed it to the officers as they advanced, their weapons aiming unwaveringly at his chest.

'Bail Bondsmen, custody's ours, guys.'

The larger of the two officers reached out and grabbed the badge with thick fingers before ripping it from

Ethan's neck. As his partner covered him he grabbed Ethan's shoulders and span him around before ramming him up against the Yukon's crumbled hood.

'You *had* custody, right up to illegally discharging a weapon on a public highway.'

'Give us a break, guys,' Lopez called, holding Decker by his cuffs like a dog on a leash. 'We spent over a week chasing this walking trash down.'

The second pair of officers yanked Decker away from her and prodded him toward their patrol vehicle.

'You'll be more careful next time then, won't you,' one of them shot back at her.

Ethan felt the cold steel of handcuffs wrap around his wrists, and then he was hauled upright and twisted around to face his arresting officer. The podgy man's pallid face shone with the satisfaction of mindless spite.

'You ever been to Cook County Jail before?' he uttered.

Ethan was about to answer when a black Dodge Durango SUV pulled in alongside the reservation. Ethan watched as two men in gray suits and sunglasses climbed out, moving to flank an elderly man in a dark blue suit who hurried toward them.

Ethan watched as the old man surveyed the crashed Yukon, the cops, Ethan's cuffs and the blown-out tire.

'Release him immediately,' he ordered the cops and pointed at Ethan. 'He's on government time.'

'Who the hell are you?' the podgy officer uttered, his face now twisted with indignation.

'Douglas Jarvis,' the old man replied. 'Defense Intelligence Agency.'

'He's under arrest for illegal discharge of a firearm,' the cop protested. 'He's going nowhere but jail.'

Jarvis reached into his jacket and produced a cellphone that he brandished like a weapon.

'One phone call and your career will be over. Finished. I'm here on government business and you're an obstruction. There was no gun, no discharge and you were never here. Either remove yourself from this scene or I'll remove you from your job. Your call, son.'

'You've got no jurisdiction,' the cop snapped back, but his resolve was weakening before Jarvis's uncompromising glare.

'The Pentagon is my jurisdiction,' Jarvis replied. 'You feel lucky?'

The cop's jowls trembled with suppressed rage for a long beat as he glanced at the identity tag hanging from the lapel of the old man's jacket. His brain slowly digested the gravity of the threat, and then he cursed and unlocked Ethan's cuffs before marching back toward his vehicle. Jarvis wasted no time as he directed his men.

'Get this mess cleared up. We've got to move, right now.'

Ethan stared at Jarvis in surprise. 'Where's the fire?'

'Still haven't got the hang of abiding by the law, Ethan?' Jarvis asked, gesturing to the wrecked Yukon and the Beretta pistol at his feet.

'The job gets done,' he replied. 'I take it this isn't a social call?'

'It's a clean-up operation now,' Jarvis said moodily, and gestured to one of his men. 'Find the bullet in that Yukon's tire and lose it.' He looked at the cops now holding Decker. 'You guys dump that moron back at Cook County Jail where he belongs.'

'I got my rights!' Decker shouted as he was shoved toward one of the squad cars, and pointed at Ethan. 'I want him arrested for shooting at me!'

Jarvis glanced at the fugitive with an expression of mild disgust.

'Son, you lost your rights the moment you broke the law. You're not out of here in the next sixty seconds I'll arrange life without parole in Pelican Bay for you. Agreed?'

Lopez shook her head and started toward Jarvis. 'No way, we need that bond money.'

'Too late, you've lost it,' Jarvis shot back. 'We don't have time to argue. I need you in Florida, right now.'

'The hell you do!' Lopez snapped and jabbed a finger at him. 'You can't just come out here, click your fingers and take us off the street! That bond will pay the bills for two months.'

'There *was* no bond after what Ethan did,' Jarvis replied. 'Are you ready to go to work for some real money, or shall I just leave and let Ethan get himself arrested?'

Lopez simmered in fury but did not reply. Ethan, suddenly ashamed for having wrecked their latest mark, looked across at the old man.

'We got time to pick up some stuff before we leave?' he asked.

'Ten minutes,' the old man nodded. 'Believe me, there's no time to lose.'

5

RIVER FOREST,
ILLINOIS

June 28, 07:22

Ethan Warner pulled off his leather biker jacket and
tossed it onto a couch in the office that he and Lopez had
rented since founding Warner & Lopez Inc. Lopez and
Jarvis followed him inside. The office contained little
more than two desks, some filing cabinets, a safe, a cooler
and a small television. Posters on the walls portrayed
numerous bail-jumpers in the Chicago area, right out as
far as the Michigan border. Being bail bondsmen wasn't
a glamorous part of their work, and nor was being hired
as private detectives, but both jobs paid the bills.

Since losing everything years before in the aftermath of
his fiancée's disappearance, Ethan had been prudent with
the money that Warner & Lopez Inc. brought in, but Lopez
was another story. Impulsive to the point of recklessness,
she had bought her Lotus despite having only managed to
furnish half of her tiny apartment. Forced to send a third of
her salary home to her impoverished family south of the
border, she seemed to have given up on her once responsible attitude and thrown caution entirely to the wind.

Lopez shot Jarvis a dirty look as she tore an image of Hayden Decker from the wall and tossed it into a wastebasket with a flourish.

'Eighteen thousand bucks down the drain,' she said to him. 'Thanks.'

Jarvis said nothing as Ethan and Lopez gathered cameras, notepads, cans of pepper spray and, from the safe, two sports bags that contained a change of clothes for each of them. Jarvis surveyed them from one side of the office, checking his watch every few moments.

The old man had once been Captain of a United States Marines rifle platoon, and Ethan's senior officer from his time in the Corps in Iraq and Afghanistan. Their friendship, cemented first during Operation Iraqi Freedom, and later when Ethan had resigned his commission and been embedded with Jarvis's men as a journalist, had led to Warner & Lopez Inc.'s unusual and discreet accord with the Defense Intelligence Agency, where Jarvis continued to serve his country. So far, Ethan and Lopez had been involved in two major investigations for the DIA, both of which concerned what the agency liked to discreetly term *anomalous discoveries.*

'So what's the story?' Ethan asked as he hefted his pistol thoughtfully in his hand. Then he stuffed it into his kit bag. Better safe than sorry.

Jarvis frowned at the weapon but did not protest.

'Homicide, way down in Miami. County Sheriff sends in officers to investigate a witness report of a man fleeing his home under suspicious circumstances. The cops arrive, gain entry and find a dead woman and child, both executed with a single shot to the head.'

Ethan grimaced.

'Any idea on the perpetrator? Could be family if the kid was shot too.'

'The man who fled the scene is one Charles Purcell, the husband and father of the victims. He hasn't been seen since, but he has contacted the police.'

Both Ethan and Lopez stopped what they were doing.

'Why'd he do that?' Lopez asked.

'That,' Jarvis replied, 'is why you're heading down there right now. He made a call to the officer heading up the investigation and told him to contact you, Ethan.'

Ethan stared at Jarvis for a long moment. 'I don't know anybody down in Miami.'

'We've already run checks,' Jarvis agreed. 'There's nothing to show that the two of you have ever met.'

Ethan felt a wave of foreboding sweep over him. Visions of a psychopathic serial killer with twisted plans of vengeance for some unknown or long-forgotten offense flickered darkly through his mind. Most all victims of the truly insane had no real understanding of why they were targeted, often because the reasons made sense only within the tortured crucible of their killer's mind.

'Then how does this guy Purcell know who I am?' Ethan asked. 'And what the hell's a suspected murderer want with me?'

'That's what's bothering us,' Jarvis admitted. 'This guy must have gone to some lengths in order to locate you.'

Ethan almost laughed at the absurdity of it all, but he glanced out of the office windows as though he were being watched. 'How would he know where to find me if he doesn't know me? It doesn't make any sense.'

'Believe me,' Jarvis replied, 'not much about this case makes any sense right now. You two ready?'

Ethan, his thoughts fogged with confusion, zipped up his bag as Lopez slung hers over her shoulder and they walked out of the office onto the street outside. Ethan had just locked the door when a UPS truck pulled up alongside and the driver stepped out with a board-back envelope in his hand.

'Ethan Warner?' the driver asked him.

Ethan stepped forward and signed the driver's palmtop, then took the envelope and looked at it.

'You can open it when you get back,' Jarvis said as he snatched the envelope away and slipped it through the mailbox. 'We've got to move, okay?'

Ethan shrugged and followed Lopez and Jarvis into the Durango, which immediately pulled out and sped toward the nearest freeway heading south. Ethan experienced a mild sense of self-importance as he glanced around the hushed interior of the SUV and saw several other Durangos join them on the on-ramp and form an honor-guard around them as they sped through morning traffic. Silent hazard lights flashed on the roofs. Working for the DIA had often proved dangerous, but it had its advantages too.

'Where are we going?' Lopez asked.

'Scott Air Force Base, Belleville,' Jarvis replied. 'I'll explain when we get there.'

'What's the rush?' Ethan asked. 'Fugitive's on the run. The first forty-eight hours are crucial, but isn't local law enforcement on the case already?'

'We've shut them down for now. Only the senior investigating officer is still in the loop. As far as we know we have about twelve hours to solve this case. Time is everything.'

'Fill us in then,' Lopez suggested, as the SUV careered through the rush-hour traffic. 'What's so special about this guy Purcell?'

Jarvis opened a glossy black folder emblazoned with the DIA's logo, handing Ethan and Lopez each an identical file as he read.

'Charles Purcell is a physicist who worked for fifteen years at NASA, down at Cape Canaveral. He was a major player in many of the scientific experiments that were carried into space aboard the Shuttle, not to mention his contribution to the Hubble space telescope. Apparently, however, the central focus of his work within the agency was the study of time.'

Ethan felt a faint glimmer of relief. As psychopaths went, a diligent scientist was somewhat less threatening than a coked-up Hell's Angel. He raised an eyebrow. 'So he was a clock-watcher then?'

'I'll do the jokes,' Jarvis replied, without looking up from his file. 'Purcell made some astounding theoretical breakthroughs during his career, but they were considered so radical that NASA routinely denied him funds to conduct experiments to confirm his equations, preferring to support more conventional work instead.'

'So what happened to him?' Lopez asked as she leafed through her copy of the file without interest and twirled a loop of her long black hair through her fingers.

Jarvis turned a page in his file.

'Purcell resigned his post at NASA and began working

freelance for various private organizations, many of them charities.'

'That's a major change of pace for a physicist,' Ethan observed. 'You think that he just got tired of doing equations?'

'Quite the opposite, or so we suspect,' Jarvis replied. 'You see, Charles Purcell had followed in his father's footsteps for most of his life. Montgomery Purcell had worked with the US Government on the Manhattan Project, which led to the dropping of the atomic bombs on Japan and the end of the Second World War. From what we can gather, Purcell Senior continued working in the government's weapons programs until his death.'

'What happened to him?' Ethan asked. 'He can't have been very old when he died, if Charles Purcell is his son.'

'That's the interesting bit,' Jarvis replied. 'Montgomery Purcell disappeared without trace whilst flying a light aircraft in 1968. No wreckage was ever found, nor were there any witnesses to the crash. Essentially, he vanished.'

After the trauma of recent years, Ethan considered himself something of an authority on vanished people. Even before Joanna had disappeared they had worked together on government corruption scandals in various countries that had involved enforced abductions of wealthy citizens: ransom to order. Many of the unfortunate victims had been located and liberated due to their investigations in countries like Mexico and Colombia.

'Where exactly was he when he vanished?' Lopez asked Jarvis.

The old man looked up at them. 'The Bermuda Triangle.'

6

During his military years Ethan had spent a fair amount of time training out in the Florida Straits, so the area was familiar, but he had never before even considered the fact that he'd probably spent much of that time in the legendary Triangle.

'You're kidding,' Lopez uttered, flipping the file in her lap shut. 'You want us to go down there because you think this guy's dad disappeared in a puff of smoke in the Bermuda Triangle?'

'There may be some kind of connection,' Jarvis replied. 'We're keeping an open mind about it.'

'I'll say,' Lopez replied.

'Some kind of connection how?' Ethan asked. 'The father disappearing into the Bermuda Triangle is one thing, but the murder of Charles Purcell's family is another entirely. They don't share anything in common.'

Jarvis tapped the file in his lap with his finger.

'There's nothing to suggest that Montgomery Purcell was murdered, but then there's nothing to say that he wasn't either. However Charles Purcell's wife and daughter were most definitely the victims of homicide.'

'You think that this has something to do with a death that occurred over forty years ago?' Ethan asked.

'Wow, Doug, this just gets better and better,' Lopez murmured and glanced across at Ethan. 'Doesn't want us to grab bail-running criminals down the road in Chicago, but he's happy to send us all the way to Florida to look for rotting corpses.'

'Montgomery Purcell was a big enough name during the Cold War that the agency feels there's justification to send you two down there,' Jarvis pointed out. 'By all accounts what Purcell didn't know about nuclear weapons wasn't worth knowing. Not only that, but there may have even been sensitive documents or similar on his person when he disappeared.'

'They'd have rotten to nothing by now,' Ethan said. 'If he went down in the water there's not much that would have survived the best part of fifty years.'

'The risk warrants the effort,' Jarvis replied and gestured out of the window. 'Terrorist organizations would kill, literally, for the chance to obtain details of nuclear weapons, even those from half a century ago.'

Lopez looked at Ethan with interest as she spoke.

'So why send us down there and not official DIA agents? Because of what the police said, that Purcell was asking for Ethan?'

Jarvis smiled as he closed his folder.

'It's not so much what he asked as the *way* that he asked it.'

Ethan blinked. 'What does that mean?'

'You'll have to see that for yourself,' Jarvis said. 'Right now, we need to get down to Miami as fast as possible, and for that we'll need a ride.'

'We?' Lopez echoed.

Jarvis's jaw twisted into a tight grin.

'The Defense Intelligence Agency has some concerns about the way the operations that involve Warner & Lopez Inc. have been conducted. You'll remember Washington DC, and of course Santa Fe.'

Ethan sighed and leaned back in his seat. Years after they had gone their separate ways from the Marine Corps, Jarvis had approached Ethan in Chicago and begged him to search for his granddaughter, who had gone missing in Israel. At the time, Ethan had been grieving for the loss of Joanna. Tempted by the possibility of resurrecting the search for his missing fiancée in Gaza, Ethan had agreed. The chase had brought them back to Washington DC, where he had met Nicola Lopez and founded Warner & Lopez Inc. Much later, he and Lopez had travelled to New Mexico as partners on another mission for the DIA. The resulting carnage out in the lonely deserts had proved difficult for Jarvis's department both to justify and to cover up.

'We did what we could under extremely difficult circumstances.' Ethan glanced at Lopez. 'Sometimes you just can't keep these things entirely under the radar.'

'Indeed,' Jarvis murmured. 'Abraham Mitchell has insisted that in this case I accompany you on your investigation and provide a full report on your methods.'

Ethan knew Abraham Mitchell, Director of the DIA, as a towering pillar of patriotism and not a man he would cross lightly. But placing Jarvis in the line of fire was an uncharacteristically reckless gesture. Christ, he was in his sixties. Ethan stared at the old man. 'No offense, but that could slow us down, Doug.'

'Wasn't my decision,' Jarvis said with a shrug. 'I'm too damned old to be charging about, but I can oversee and hopefully justify your work to Command.' He leaned forward in his seat. 'Fact is, I gave up a great deal in order to get this department of the DIA sanctioned and provided with both a budget and trust. After what happened in New Mexico, there's concern that you're unable to maintain a discreet profile.'

'We get results,' Lopez challenged.

'You do,' Jarvis conceded. 'But if the cost is too high then this whole thing will be over and I'll be looking at retirement, so let's just play the game the way the high and mighty want to, and see what comes up. Right now, our priority is getting down to Miami the fastest way possible.'

A shadow of concern fell across Lopez's features. 'Just how fast are you thinking?'

7

LOIZA,
PUERTO RICO

June 28, 07:31

'I've never seen anything like it.'

Joaquin Abell stood on a roof on the outskirts of what was one of the poorest towns, in one of the poorest nations, in the western world, and surveyed the scene of utter devastation lining the shores of the Rio Grande de Loiza river. He smoothed down his glossy black hair and straightened his tie. His expensive suit, a blue so dark it almost seemed black, contrasted sharply with the dust-coated piles of shattered rubble beneath him.

A handful of television crews from international networks focused their lenses on him as he slowly turned on the spot and took in the entire panorama.

The magnitude-7 earthquake had hit just twelve hours previously, the mysterious depths of the Puerto Rico Trench that surrounded the island shuddering with a force equivalent to innumerable nuclear explosions as the strain on tectonic plates far beneath the earth's surface had been released in a spasm of seismic energy. Joaquin knew that the Puerto Rico Trench was a unique geological formation due to plate subduction, and one that geologists had for decades been predicting would produce a major quake. Warnings of increased seismic activity in the Caribbean had gone largely unheeded by the population and the world at large, and now the consequences were writ bare upon the landscape.

The roof on which he stood was only four feet off the ground, the building having collapsed in a cloud of fractured masonry. Seventy school children and their teachers had been entombed in the debris, none had survived. Beyond, the roads were churned like the desiccated plates of a dry river bed, immense chunks of asphalt split and upturned to expose the raw soil deep beneath them. The palm trees lining the roads had been torn from their roots to block what little access to the town remained. Across the landscape, dotted amongst the handful of standing trees, was a barren wasteland of collapsed houses and apartment blocks, drifting clouds of cement dust churned by countless desperate hands clawing to locate family members suffocating in their macabre tombs.

But worse even than the collapsed buildings were the now-silent rivers of mud encrusted with lethal shards of splintered wood and debris, and upturned and half-buried vehicles lodged like discarded toys, filled with unmoving bodies that were already beginning to rot in the sweltering heat. The sullen gray sky above seemed to reflect the somber mood in the town, which had been destroyed overnight by the savage power of the tsunami that had engulfed it minutes after the quake.

Joaquin turned to face the cameras. A silent, motionless throng of local citizens and emergency-response teams, their faces and clothes caked in grime and blood, stared up at him, their faces rigid with the paralysis of shock.

'This, ladies and gentlemen, is what happens when people fail to act in the defense and support of their neighbors,' Joaquin said, his voice sounding muted in the listless, muggy heat. 'This is what happens when lack of investment, lack of infrastructure and lack of political will strands a population in poverty and exposes them to nature's wrath. These people could have been helped: instead they were abandoned by our government, by their government, by us all.'

Abell, his flawlessly tanned skin sheened by the heat, gestured to a brilliant white helicopter that had landed nearby on what had once been the school playground. The craft was emblazoned with a bright blue logo: IRIS.

'It is for just this reason that International Rescue and Infrastructure Support was founded, the legacy of my father's success, to go where our hallowed leaders fear to tread, to provide the kind of support that politicians have proven themselves too conservative, too greedy, to give. It will take the United Nations weeks to even begin to organize the humanitarian effort necessary to lift the people of this island nation out of their tragedy.' Joaquin directed a stern gaze at the cameras and pointed down at the churned earth beneath their feet. 'I'll put four hundred trained experts on the ground here and ten million dollars into the rebuilding of this country before the sun goes down tonight!'

From behind the camera crews a meager crowd of locals gave a muted cheer, their ragged clothes and weary faces blossoming with new hope as translators gave them Joaquin Abell's good news.

'There are some thirty-five million people living here in Puerto Rico and the surrounding islands,' Abell went on, 'all low-lying territories vulnerable to both earthquakes and tsunamis. Despite all of the natural disasters that have occurred around the world in recent years, from Aceh to Haiti, despite all of the warnings, *still* world governments wait until tens of thousands of people are maimed and killed before they even begin to act. Already there are reports that this disaster alone, when disease and starvation from lack of resources are taken into account, will result in the loss of up to one hundred thousand lives.'

A voice called out from among the reporters.

'What makes you think that you can make a difference? IRIS is a powerful company, but you can't change the world in one stroke.'

A lance of irritation pierced Abell's studied calm. It was followed by a vision of the late, great Isaac Abell: upstanding, proud, his jacket buttoned tight along with his collar, a pipe jutting from beneath his neatly trimmed moustache. His words echoed through Joaquin's mind. *No man can do everything son, but all men can make a difference.*

Isaac Abell had been a product of a generation more noble than that which had inherited the earth, a man of rigid principles and immaculate morals. Born just early enough to witness the unspeakable horror of the rise of the Kaiser and the First World War, when millions of young lives had been lost in senseless slaughter amidst trenches of freezing French mud, Isaac Abell had returned home from those bitter killing fields aged just twenty-one. As he had related to his son a thousand times, he had sworn that he would devote his life to the task of learning, not killing. Within a few years he had become a physicist and a brilliant star in the dawning of the atomic age.

And then his worst fears had been realized, as once again Europe was torn apart in the wake of the Third Reich's rise to power. When the United States dropped the world's first atomic weapon on Hiroshima, Isaac Abell was transformed from a valiant champion of scientific endeavor into an embittered recluse consumed by the conviction that mankind was incapable of saving itself from an endless abyss of self-destruction.

'You're not the Pope,' another reporter pointed out, breaking Joaquin's somber reverie.

Abell smiled as the images of his father vanished, whipped away by an uncaring wind sweeping in from the nearby ocean.

'Thankfully, no, I am not,' Joaquin replied. 'Because I deal in reality, not fantasy. The difference that IRIS can make is to show the world, to show those who *govern* our world, that it is beneficial to help our fellow human beings without reserve, without thought to the consequences, because if we help each other then we become greater than the sum of our parts. Why wait? Why debate whether or not we can *afford* to help? Why debate anything at all when people are dying, right now, right here? Would you prefer that we delay, sir?'

The reporter said nothing in reply and Joaquin Abell surveyed the watching, growing crowds.

'It's just as my rocket-scientist father once said: it's not rocket science,' Joaquin continued, and was rewarded with faint chuckles from the news crews. 'Either we move without hesitation, without compromise, without condition, to the aid of our fellow human beings, or we leave these people to rot whilst we in the wealthiest countries worry ourselves over which restaurant we're going to dine in tonight. I'm going to provide the funds that these people need to save themselves, so if you'll excuse me ladies and gentlemen . . .'

A ripple of applause clattered amongst the Puerto Ricans, many of whom crowded around Joaquin as his last words were translated, their skeletal hands patting his back and clouding his suit in dust as he climbed carefully down off the collapsed roof of the school.

Joaquin reached up and brushed the dust from his shoulders as a swarm of his personal staff huddled protectively around him. One, a striking red-haired woman called Sandra, who had been his personal assistant for the past ten years, strode to his side and held out a thick wad of papers.

'Court orders from Mexico, blocking our donations to the rebuilding of wells in the southern territories. They're citing unspecified health-and-safety concerns.'

'Build them anyway,' Abell replied briskly as they walked. 'What can they do, sue us?'

Sandra flipped the page over and selected another.

'We're also getting obstruction from landowners in Aceh, who want to build hotels on the land destroyed by the tsunami in 2004. What should we do?'

'Tell them that if they don't back off, I'll buy the controlling share of their hotel chains and then raze them to the ground. They don't own the land, the people do. Get our people in Singapore onto it – they know the legal terrain out there.'

Sandra produced another file.

'And New Orleans? We're still bogged down by the new wave of building regulations being enforced by the mayor. If we're pushed out, you know that they'll build malls rather than replace the homes destroyed by the hurricane.'

Joaquin considered for a moment.

'Get the people to rally, in their thousands. Organize something really visual and let IRIS pick up the bill for it. If the mayor doesn't fold he'll probably lose office over it. People-power, Sandra, is sometimes more effective than lobbying Congress.'

Sandra was about to answer when her cell trilled. She picked it up immediately, and Joaquin turned away as two noisy children bounded toward him, delight on their faces. Joaquin knelt down on the debris-strewn road as Jacob and Merriel leapt into his arms. At four and six years respectively, they seemed oblivious to the tragedy around them.

'How are my two firecrackers?' Joaquin asked, holding them tightly.

Behind them, Joaquin saw his wife glide up the road, dressed in a smart charcoal suit and with her long auburn hair flowing like liquid velvet across her shoulders. Katherine smiled at him as she picked her way through the debris, and as he picked up the two children she leaned in and kissed him on his cheek.

'How did it go?' she asked.

'As well as can be expected,' Joaquin replied. 'Let's hope that when the government sees the news tonight, they'll be provoked to get off their asses and start doing something about what's happened down here. We need investment, not debate.'

Katherine smiled.

'I know you'll get it.'

Before he could reply Sandra tapped him on the shoulder, a phone to her ear and a concerned expression on her face. Joaquin set his children down beside their mother and joined Sandra as she beckoned him discreetly to one side.

'What's wrong?' Joaquin asked.

'There's been an accident,' Sandra whispered. 'One of our planes crashed in the Bahamas yesterday evening. I'm afraid there were no survivors.'

8

SCOTT AIR FORCE BASE, ST CLAIRE COUNTY, ILLINOIS

June 28, 07:48

'You're not serious.'

Lopez stared at the drab olive overalls as she pulled them on, along with the heavy black boots and the over-suit festooned with tubes and cables.

Ethan yanked on his flight suit and was handed a helmet with a glossy black mirrored visor, oxygen mask and a pair of fire-retardant gloves. He watched as Lopez struggled into her own flight suit and then followed as an ensign directed them out of the building in which they stood and into the bright sunshine. The sound of count-less jet engines whined, and Ethan saw a giant KC–135 re-fuelling tanker slip off the runway and soar into the clear blue sky. But it was not the big aircraft lining the servicing area that caught his attention.

Two sleek, angular fighter jets sat on the tarmac await-ing them, technicians swarming around the craft as they approached. Jarvis gestured to them.

'F–15E Eagles from the 85th Test and Evaluation Squadron at Eglin Air Force Base in Florida,' he said.

'Requisitioned by me to ensure a swift arrival on site. I'll follow you down on an Air Force transport and brief you when you're airborne on a secure channel.'

Ethan stared at the fearsome-looking aircraft and then at the two female pilots awaiting them. Ethan raised a surprised eyebrow.

'You got a problem with women drivers?' Lopez challenged. 'Man up.'

A woman almost a foot shorter than Ethan, who looked no more than twenty-five, her blonde hair tied in a neat ponytail, extended a hand to him.

'Captain Emma Rawlings,' she said, smiling brightly. 'I'll be your pilot for today. If you'd like to get aboard?'

Ethan nodded, lost for words as he climbed the ladder beside the cockpit and clambered in. A bewildering array of dials, switches, television screens and lights faced him on the control panel as a crewman strapped him into the ejection seat. He looked across at Lopez, who was being strapped into the other aircraft, and saw her make the sign of a crucifix across her chest as her pilot closed the canopy and began starting the Eagle's engines.

Ethan wasn't afraid of flying. Throughout his time with the Marines, both in training and on deployment in Afghanistan and Iraq, he had flown in various types of aircraft – CH-47 Chinooks, Black Hawks, Hercules and Super Stallions, to name but a few. But they were all helicopters. This was a fighter jet, the real deal, the kind he'd seen screaming overhead in battle zones, dropping ordnance powerful enough to vaporize small villages.

The canopy on Ethan's F-15 closed and he heard a distant whining sound as the turbofan engines started.

Captain Rawlings fired off a quick broadside of radio commands to the control tower, and within minutes they were priority taxiing to the active runway right behind Lopez's aircraft. The two jets lined up on the runway in a tight formation and then, with another barked command, Captain Rawlings eased the throttles forward. A distant roar erupted from somewhere behind Ethan and he saw bright jets of flame blast from the nearby Eagle's exhausts as it thundered down the runway, its wingtip mere feet from that of his own aircraft. A terrific acceleration pinned Ethan into his ejection seat as the jets roared along the dark asphalt, and then suddenly both aircraft lifted off the runway, undercarriages rolling up as they climbed steeply away from the airfield in close formation. A scattering of cumulus cloud shot past them as Ethan saw the altimeter spin through five thousand feet.

'Jesus,' he uttered, his voice distorted by both the aircraft's intercom system and his tightly fitting oxygen mask, 'that would have taken two hours in an airliner.'

Captain Rawlings' voice chortled back to him over the radio.

'*We were being gentle,*' she replied. '*We only use minimum afterburner when we take off in formation.*'

Ethan watched as Lopez's aircraft led them up through the cloud layers to twenty thousand feet, the long teardrop canopy of the F-15 affording him a vertiginous view of the world below, hazy fields and glittering towns beneath a scattered patchwork of small clouds trailing shadows. The other F-15 was so close he felt as though he could reach out and touch it as it bobbed and weaved on the wind currents as the east coast passed by beneath them.

Ethan saw Lopez's F-15 drift away out of formation until it was a silvery speck on the hazy band of the horizon.

'Where are they going?' he asked.

'*We're moving to battle flight,*' Captain Rawlings explained, '*to avoid the shockwaves.*'

'What shockwaves?'

Captain Rawlings didn't reply to Ethan, instead broadcasting to her fellow pilot in the other jet.

'*Scorcher flight, buster-buster!*'

A moment later Ethan felt the F-15 surge forward as the throttles hit the firewall. Full afterburner launched the aircraft toward the horizon as though it had been fired from a cannon, and suddenly he realized what she had meant. They were going supersonic. The airspeed indicator shot through Mach 1 as Captain Rawlings hauled the F-15 up into a steep climb. G-force slammed Ethan down into his seat, straining his neck as the aircraft soared up into the atmosphere. Rawlings slowly rolled the F-15 upside down, and the sun flashed through the sky around Ethan before the cockpit was plunged into shadow. The straps from his harnesses dangled before his eyes, the upside-down world and the curve of the earth easily visible some fifty thousand feet beneath them.

Ethan's senses reconnected themselves as the colossal G-force eased, and he saw the coast of Virginia passing by beneath rippled blankets of cloud as Rawlings rolled the F-15 right-side up. The sky above was almost black, the sleek fighter flirting with the edge of space.

'How fast are we going?' he enquired, as a vague sense of nausea poisoned his innards.

The reply came back as casually as though Emma Rawlings were driving a car.

'*Just over Mach 2, faster than a rifle bullet. We'll have you in Florida in an hour. I'm opening a three-way data-link channel with your boss, stand-by.*'

Ethan heard a hiss and a squawk across the airwaves, and then Jarvis's voice crackled in his ear as one of the screens in the cockpit showed the old man's face as he spoke from the cavernous interior of a transport aircraft. A second screen showed most of Lopez's face obscured by her oxygen mask and helmet, only her exotic almond eyes visible.

'*Ethan, Nicola, pay attention. If the situation in Miami is not resolved within twelve hours, then we feel certain that the answers we seek at the Defense Intelligence Agency will be lost forever.*'

Ethan frowned beneath his oxygen mask.

'Why the time limit?' he asked Jarvis.

'*I told you that Charles Purcell was involved in research into the nature of time at NASA,*' Jarvis explained. '*It would appear that after leaving the space agency he continued his work. When he contacted the police at the scene of his family's murder, Charles Purcell accurately predicted future events as they unfolded.*'

Lopez's voice crackled over the radio.

'*No way! I've read about things like that. You can't see into the future, it's impossible. Physics won't allow it. You're saying you pulled us off eighteen thousand dollars of bond money for pure fantasy?*'

'*That may be so,*' Jarvis responded. '*But fact is fact and this guy got it right several times during a single conversation.*'

He also claimed that he wasn't responsible for the murder of his family, and would himself be murdered sometime today.'

'He knows that this will happen?' Ethan asked in surprise.

'Apparently so,' Jarvis replied. *'He even stated that his killer does not yet know he will commit the act.'*

'Which is why we're being rushed down there,' Ethan said. 'To try to stop it before it happens.'

'Correct,' Jarvis replied. *'Whatever this guy's been up to, he's either an exceedingly clever psychopath or exceedingly desperate to prove his innocence. The FBI has written the case off as nothing more than the ramblings of a madman, sheer coincidence. I only saw the paperwork myself four hours ago, and managed to get control of the case.'*

'It sounds like Purcell's smart enough to fool people into thinking he's seen the future,' Lopez suggested. *'If he's lost his mind he could be presenting like a classic psychopath – severe narcissism combined with a god complex.'*

'Where do we start?' Ethan asked Jarvis.

'Captain Kyle Sears of the Miami-Dade Police will meet you at Homestead Joint Air Reserve Base. He'll be your liaison. I'll meet you when we arrive. For now, you'd best be on your way.'

A thought crossed Ethan's mind.

'How do you know that we've only got twelve hours left to solve this case?'

Jarvis's voice sounded ominous over the radio as he replied.

'You'll have to see that to believe it. Jarvis out.'

9

HOMESTEAD JOINT AIR RESERVE BASE, MIAMI, FLORIDA

June 28, 09:18

Warner sat in the front seat of a Crown Victoria Interceptor as it sped away from the airbase at Homestead toward Miami, lights blazing and sirens wailing as it joined the freeway and accelerated past lanes of traffic lumbering north. He felt mildly disorientated after the fearsome speed and maneuverability of the F-15, as though he'd awoken in a different time zone.

'We'll be in Hallandale shortly.'

Captain Kyle Sears, his eyes concealed behind a pair of Aviators, looked in his rear-view mirror at Lopez sitting in the rear seat. Ethan guessed from the weary creases lining Sears' face that he was a career officer, probably in his late forties, highly experienced and most likely allergic to bullshit. That he'd experienced first-hand somebody predicting the future probably hadn't gone down too well.

'You guys got here in a real hurry,' Sears observed.

'Priority case,' Lopez said.

'That so?' Sears replied. 'Well, we sure could use the

help, because I don't have a damned clue what the hell's going on down here.'

Ethan concealed a smile as he replied.

'Tell us what you know.'

'We walk into a crime scene, two victims shot in the head. I get a call from the husband and father of the victims, Charles Purcell, who then predicts what's happening around me, doesn't miss a damned thing. I figure maybe he has cameras set up or something, but the area is clean. He predicted an automobile accident, the ambulance turning up, when my partner would trace the call, everything. Turns out that Purcell was calling from an apartment in Hallandale several miles away, no chance he could have observed what he saw as it happened.'

Lopez frowned, her long dark hair rippling in the breeze funneling through the Interceptor's open window.

'I take it he took off before you got there,' she said.

Sears nodded as he took the next exit off the freeway.

'His prints were all over the apartment; he'd made no attempt to conceal his presence, but he was long gone. We checked local cameras for his movements but the guy had cut the cables before calling us. That's what's so weird. He claimed that he didn't kill his family, but this whole thing must have been set up in advance, else how could he have predicted the phonecall, the accident, everything?'

Ethan watched palm trees flashing past against the blue sky outside. Most all people associated palms with vacations, but he'd only ever seen them against the war-scarred deserts of Iraq or in the sweltering alleys of

Colombia. He and Joanna had rarely had any downtime, travelling from one warzone to another in pursuit of the next big story. He briefly regretted that they had not taken the chance to spend time together doing something else.

Now, here he was again beneath a burning sun and swaying palms, yet in the middle of an investigation.

'Anything else odd that you noticed?' he asked Sears, shaking off his reverie.

'You mean apart from this guy predicting the future? Well, he asked us to pick up the ammunition used in the homicides and analyze them for traces of something called Rubidium-82.' Sears leaned forward, grabbed a sheet of paper from the dash and handed it to Ethan. 'We sent the rounds to the labs and sure enough, the compound turns up. Some kind of mildly radioactive dye used by scientists and medical teams. Again, how could he have not committed the murders and yet know that the bullets were dipped in that dye? It doesn't make any sense.'

Ethan looked down at the sheet of paper. Rubidium-82 was a form of rubidium chloride that contained a radioactive isotope and was used in a technique called PET perfusion imaging. Easily absorbed by heart muscle cells, its presence helped identify regions of poor blood flow in heart muscle. A graph recorded its radioactive signature on each of the two bullet casings found at the scene of the murders. While Ethan had heard of some killers going to extraordinary lengths to tease officers in their pursuit, leaving hints and clues behind as to their identity, he could see no sense in leaving traces of such a material on the bullets and then blatantly informing the police of its presence. Surely doing so only risked confirming Purcell's guilt, or at least some kind of involvement in the crime?

'What about the apartment?' Lopez asked. 'Anything there that could help us?'

Sears chuckled. 'Oh yeah. You're going to have to see it to believe it.'

'People keep saying things like that,' Ethan replied uneasily.

'You're sure that you've never met this guy Charles Purcell, right?'

'As far as I know,' Ethan replied. 'The DIA checked him out and we've got no apparent history. Only time I ever visited Miami was on a family holiday when I was ten years old.'

Sears nodded but said no more, guiding the Interceptor between lanes of traffic that parted before his blazing sirens and lights. A few minutes later and they pulled in alongside a cheap-looking motel, the kind with tired, flickering neon lights over thin and unkempt lawns.

'Not the usual haunt of a NASA scientist,' Lopez said as she got out of the car.

One of the first-floor apartments was sealed off with ribbons of crime-scene tape that fluttered listlessly, and two uniforms guarded the entrance.

'Crime scene and forensics been through yet?' Ethan asked Sears as they walked across the half-empty lot toward the apartment.

'Yeah, like I said, they found his prints everywhere but no evidence of a weapon or other residues from the homicide. If Purcell hadn't called us we'd probably never have known he stayed here.'

Sears waved his badge at the uniforms and they opened the apartment door for him. He gestured for Ethan to take the lead, and Ethan stepped through the doorway.

The apartment was tiny, a narrow hall leading to a functional kitchen at one end that backed on to a shower stall and latrine. To the left and right of the hall were doorways to the lounge and bedroom.

'It's the lounge you'll want to see,' Sears directed him.

Ethan turned right and walked in to see a tired-looking but clean room adorned with a coffee table and couch, a wall-mounted television and a tall mirror on the wall at the rear. As he walked in and turned to survey the room, he froze in place and stared at the back wall.

'See what I mean?' Sears asked.

Across the wall was scrawled a message, written with a thick black marker.

PLEASE HURRY ETHAN WARNER!
TIME IS RUNNING OUT!!!
20:48, June 28

'Jesus.'

Lopez stared at the message as she joined them in the room.

'Charles Purcell told me to come here immediately,' Sears explained to Ethan as they stood looking at the message. 'He told me that I must contact you. He kept insisting that time was of the essence and that if I didn't do what he was asking, the killers of his family would never be brought to justice.'

Ethan found himself still transfixed by the scrawled message on the wall.

'Today is June 28,' he said.

'Yup,' Sears confirmed. 'Whatever that time means, it's referring to something that hasn't happened yet. Given what Charles Purcell has managed to do so far, my guess is that he's completely lost his mind and that this is all some kind of goddamn freak show that he's arranged, all based around him. Most killers are severely narcissistic and display exactly this kind of behavior.'

'Like I said,' Lopez nodded, 'this is the start of his game and it's all about him. He's the star, we're the audience, and he'll continue to crave more and more attention right up to the moment he's captured or gets himself killed.'

Ethan looked at Sears.

'Except for the fact that he did accurately predict the future, right?'

'He did,' Sears conceded. 'That part, I got no explanation for.'

'Anything else?' Ethan asked.

'The opposite wall,' Sears said, and gestured behind them. 'We haven't got a clue what the hell it means.'

Ethan turned and strode across to the window, pulling aside threadbare net curtains to reveal another message written on the wall just above the window pane in small, precise strokes.

N2764C

'Looks like some kind of equation written backwards,' Lopez said as she moved alongside Ethan and peered at the strange symbols. 'Same person wrote both messages?'

'Purcell was a physicist,' Ethan suggested. 'He'd have spent much of his life using math. It fits his history, if nothing else.'

'You actually know what it means?' Sears asked.

'Not in the slightest,' Ethan admitted. 'And how did he know I would come here at all?'

Sears smiled but it was tinged with anxiety.

'I got a letter this morning, sent by UPS, from Charles

Purcell. It had a picture of you, taken off a website from your old high school in Illinois. It helped us track you down, and that's how your man at the Defense Intelligence Agency got involved. We called the FBI when we realized that we were getting out of our depth. They wrote us off, but the DIA picked up the case.'

Sears slipped a print from his pocket and showed it to Ethan. The image showed a young man in his late teens, his light-brown hair still scruffy despite having been combed for the shot, his gray eyes clear and sharp. Ethan's jaw looked slightly leaner than it did now, and the creases etched into his skin by years of physical and mental hardship were missing, but there was no mistaking the defiant set of his shoulders and the crooked grin on his face.

'You were actually almost cute once,' Lopez said, with a smirk. 'The hell happened?'

'Life,' Ethan replied. 'This code must mean something. Why did he write a huge message for me on that wall, but then conceal a tiny one over here?'

'Either the guy's crazy or he's just trying to buy himself time to get away,' Lopez replied. 'By the time we're finished decoding this, even if that's possible, Purcell could be clean out of the state.'

Ethan shook his head.

'He could have been clean out of the state without doing *any* of this. He's leaving us messages, leaving us a trail.'

'Why leave anything?' Lopez asked. 'And why us? Why you? You've never met this guy. Surely if he'd wanted private detectives on his case he'd have contacted someone in Florida instead, somebody nearby?'

Ethan nodded in agreement but could find nothing to say that could explain Charles Purcell's bizarre actions.

'My guess,' Sears said, 'is that he's suffered some kind of mental breakdown and all of this is the result of his illness. Until I'm convinced otherwise, I'm putting out an APB for this guy as a wanted murderer. We need him off the streets and in custody because we can't risk the chance that he won't hit some other family just like he's iced his own. Believe me, once these freaks really lose the plot, anyone and anything is fair game.'

Sears headed out of the lounge to leave the apartment. As Ethan turned to follow, his gaze settled on the mirror hanging on the wall opposite the window. He focused on the reflection of the room around them and then a smile curled from the corner of his mouth.

'Maybe Charles Purcell knows *exactly* what he's doing.'

11

LOIZA,
PUERTO RICO

June 28, 09:24

'Do we know what happened to our aircraft.'

Joaquin Abell kept his voice down, not wanting his children to hear the news that Sandra had related to him.

'We chartered a Grumman Mallard from Bimini Wings to bring home our staff from their work on the coral-conservation project in the Florida Straits. It went down late yesterday afternoon. No mayday call from the pilots, radar contact was lost by Miami at seven twenty. Search and Rescue haven't found a thing.'

'Why didn't you tell me sooner?' Joaquin stared at her.

'I was waiting for confirmation from the coastguard before I broke the news,' Sandra said. 'I didn't want to bring this to you until I was sure.'

Joaquin massaged his temples, his eyes closed. 'How many people were aboard?'

'Nineteen, including the two pilots.'

'Jesus,' Joaquin whispered, 'the poor families. Get in touch with all of them, I'll want to speak to them in person and reassure them that we'll stand by them. IRIS is a family, Sandra, and I want them to know that they're members too.' Sandra nodded and jotted down notes as Joaquin spoke. 'Then contact the families' litigation teams and let them know that appropriate compensation will be provided, regardless of whether IRIS is considered legally responsible for the loss of life, understood?'

Sandra finished scribbling and looked up at him, a flourish of admiration on her features.

'Absolutely, sir. I'll get on it right away. At least it seems there may be a survivor from the conservation project, that's something that we can take away from this tragedy.'

Joaquin's eyes fixed on hers. 'Who?'

'Charles Purcell, one of our lead scientists. His name was absent from the aircraft's departure roster at South Bimini. He can't have been aboard.'

'Excellent news, Sandra. See if you can find Charles and let me know the moment that you do.'

Joaquin watched as Sandra dashed away, and then walked across to his wife. Katherine was now accompanied by a short, pale-looking man with baleful eyes that peered out from behind thin glasses. Dennis Aubrey was a lifelong friend of Katherine, a physicist who had attended the University of Florida as she had. Just as she had grown to become a powerful lawyer, so Aubrey had grown alongside her from a shy, plump little boy into a physics genius, sought after by some of the most prestigious laboratories and universities in the continental United States. Joaquin had recently hired Aubrey, always preferring to appoint family friends to his organization rather than cast his net and take on potentially unreliable employees. People tended to work better for their friends than for anonymous corporations, and despite its size he had worked hard to make IRIS a family and not just an employer.

'Mr. Abell,' Aubrey said in greeting. 'Katherine tells me that the news broadcast went well.'

Joaquin nodded with a brief but weary smile. 'Let's hope it garners support in Congress and the funding we'll need out here.'

Katherine reacted to the shadows of restrained grief that drifted behind his eyes, and immediately moved to his side. 'What is it?'

Joaquin whispered so that Jacob and Merriel would not hear.

'There's been an accident and I need to deal with it personally,' he said. 'Why not take the children back to the airport? I'll meet you in Miami after we've surveyed the island.'

'You sure?' she asked, concerned but not alarmed.

'It'll be fine,' Joaquin assured her, and gestured to Dennis Aubrey, who was chatting amiably to the children. 'You sure he's able to lip-read?'

Katherine chuckled. 'Of course, his brother is deaf so he learned sign-language and lip-reading as a child. I still don't understand why you need a scientist working for you who can lip-read?'

'Communications,' Joaquin replied. 'Sometimes we have issues with equipment on the conservation projects and we only have visual and not audio.' He waved for Aubrey to join them. 'Dennis, something's come up. You okay to accompany me before we head back to Miami?'

'Not a problem,' Aubrey agreed, clearly eager to please.

Katherine kissed his cheek. 'Talk to me,' she said quickly. 'Whatever this is about, don't keep trying to save the world on your own, okay?'

She turned and led their children away from the shattered remains of the school and down to the white jeep waiting for them. Joaquin watched as they were driven away down a hill littered with debris that wound its way to a distant, broad bay.

'This way, Dennis,' he said to Aubrey.

Joaquin turned and walked further up the hill with the physicist to where the helicopter waited. Standing alongside it with his arms folded was a tall, powerfully built man in an expensive suit that did little to conceal the ranks of muscles bulging through the fabric. Olaf Jorgenson, Joaquin's personal bodyguard, watched them approach and then turned and rapped on the cockpit window. The pilot inside immediately started the helicopter's engines.

'What's happened?' Aubrey asked Joaquin as they walked. 'Something urgent?'

'Yes, I'm afraid so,' Joaquin replied. 'You've just been promoted to head scientist at the IRIS Deep Blue facility on the Miami Terrace reef.'

Dennis Aubrey's round face broke into a bright smile as his pasty skin glowed with a brief flourish of color.

'That's fantastic news.' His expression sagged slightly. 'You don't seem very happy about it.'

'I'm afraid that your promotion is due to a tragedy, Dennis. There was an airplane crash yesterday afternoon. I lost my entire Deep Blue staff.'

Aubrey's skin dulled again to its familiar wan tones.

'My God, I'm sorry. Do we know what happened?' Joaquin shook his head.

'I'm sorry that this promotion hasn't occurred under better circumstances, Dennis,' he said. 'But I need your help. It will take some time to find replacement staff, and between now and then I need somebody reliable to man the Deep Blue facility. It might entail you being on the site for a few days, until I can get everything sorted.'

Aubrey grabbed the helicopter's door handle and opened it for Joaquin.

'Consider it done,' he promised. 'When do we leave for the facility?'

'We're headed for Miami right now,' Joaquin said. 'You'll join me at the facility as soon as I've tied up some loose ends in the city.'

Olaf Jorgenson joined them inside the helicopter, as did Sandra, her red hair flying in the downwash from the spinning blades, until Olaf's giant arm slammed the fuse-lage door shut. The four of them donned headphones, and Aubrey's voice cut through the static.

'What about Katherine and the children? Will they be joining us?'

'Katherine is due to lead the defense for IRIS at the opening of a court case in Miami this morning,' Joaquin explained, 'and won't be able to join us until later. We'll have to make do until then. The children will be in school for the week.'

The helicopter lifted off, the downwash from the blades shuddering through the palm trees below as it flew low over the battered shanty towns. Joaquin looked out across the crippled island as it swept past beneath the helicopter, a barren and mud-strewn wasteland of misery and despair. Tiny figures stared up at him, their bare legs ankle-deep in cold mud, their clothes smeared with filth and their eyes wide with shock and disbelief, haunted by the loss of their families and homes.

Joaquin felt a burden of responsibility weigh down on him, strong enough that it seemed it could send the helicopter in which he sat plunging back down to earth. One man, one company, one chance to make a difference. Most people lived under a comfortable illusion that the whole world was now connected, that all people had some idea of what technology was, had access to medicine, had a chance in life. The truth was that only one fifth of the world's population lived in the developed world. Half of all the people on earth had never made or received a telephone call. The vast majority of mankind had little or no access to clean water. Several hundred million children died every decade from easily preventable diseases or starvation. And all the while politicians in designer suits, chauffeured in cars that cost more than many people would earn in several lifetimes, attended huge conferences and told the world how much better it all would soon be. How much they were doing to help. How much brighter the future was.

Joaquin looked down at the devastation and considered once again how nothing changed. Not ever. Governments would never be able to save their own people, not unless there was a chance of generating a profit at the same time, anyway. Too much corporate interference now. As one government gave millions to dig wells in one impoverished country, another would sell arms to its rival. The whole charade continued, decade after decade, century after century, propping up the wealthy and keeping the poor incarcerated in poverty for all time. A line from Homer's *Iliad* drifted through his mind: *We men are wretched things*.

Sandra's voice cut through his glum reverie.

'There's no word from the Miami–Dade police about Charles Purcell,' she said, looking at an e-mail on her tablet. 'He's not been reported as missing and there's nothing from South Bimini about him either. He must have missed the flight, but I can't locate him.'

Joaquin nodded and glanced at Jorgenson. The huge man's angular, expressionless face and pale-blue eyes returned his gaze as though he were hewn from solid granite, but his square head gave a barely perceptible nod.

'What will I be doing at the reef?' Dennis Aubrey asked Joaquin, his features vibrant with enthusiasm.

'Manning our sub-aquatic research station,' Joaquin replied, turning away from Olaf's gaze. 'It's on the edge of an underwater terrace shelf about twenty miles offshore of Miami beach. You'll be responsible for some of the technological assets we have built there.'

Aubrey frowned in confusion.

'I thought that it was some kind of wildlife preserve? What have we got down there that would need a physicist?'

Joaquin grinned conspiratorially and patted Aubrey on the shoulder.

'The future, Dennis, or at least that's what I hope – something that will benefit mankind for all time to come. You'll see soon enough. Right now, we have to get back to the city. I have some very important guests to meet for breakfast, and I need you to be there with me to get to know them. I'm sure that you'd like to meet the Florida governor?'

'The governor?' Aubrey almost choked. 'Is he involved in the conservation effort?'

Joaquin chuckled.

'Not yet, Dennis, but it's time to make government work for the people and bring some balance back into their lives. By the time I'm done with him, he'll be up to his neck in it.'

Olaf's broad jaw fractured like a glacier into a broad grin.

12

HALLANDALE, MIAMI

June 28, 9:34

Ethan stared at the mirror on the wall of the motel room, captivated by the reflection.

'What are you talking about?' Lopez asked. 'You see something?'

Ethan nodded, tilting his head to one side and looking at the strange symbols written on the wall above the window, and then looking again at the reflection in the mirror.

'It's not an equation,' he said finally. 'I need a piece of paper.'

Sears reached into his pocket and provided Ethan with a small notepad and a pen. Ethan leaned on a table and copied down what he saw in the mirror before showing it to Lopez.

N2764C

She scanned the figures and frowned.

'It doesn't mean anything,' she said. 'It's just junk.'

Ethan grinned and reached out to tap her head with his knuckles.

'Don't tell me you can't see it. What do we know about Charles Purcell's father?'

Kyle Sears stared at the symbols.

'Looks familiar somehow,' he said.

'Purcell's father was a physicist too, but he died in a plane crash in the Bermuda Triangle, right?' Lopez said. 'Still doesn't add up to much.'

'Yes it does,' Sears replied as he suddenly recognized the configuration. 'Tail code? I drive past O'Hare airport virtually every day and I'm sure I've seen codes like that on small aircraft.'

'November two-seven-six-four-charlie,' Ethan confirmed. 'It's a standard tail code for a civilian-operated aircraft in the United States. My sister got her pilot's license a few years ago, and she flies a light aircraft with a similar number.'

'I'll be damned,' Kyle Sears said.

'So will I,' Lopez murmured as she looked at Ethan. 'You never told me you have a sister.'

Ethan didn't respond to her and turned instead to Captain Sears.

'Whatever the reason, it seems that Charles Purcell wants us to follow the clues he's leaving. You think you could check out that aircraft and find out where it is? My guess is that it belonged to his father.'

'I'll get right on it.'

Sears left the room as Ethan stared up at the code on the wall.

'Okay,' Lopez said, 'you've done good, but let's not

dwell on it. What's your sister's name?'

'Natalie,' he replied, still staring vacantly at the symbols on the wall.

'How come you never mentioned her before?'

Ethan stared up at the wall and the code, but for a moment his thoughts switched to his family. His folks were both retired, his father from the Marine Corps and his mother from banking, living out their lives in peaceful seclusion in the Chicago suburbs. Truth was, he saw them rarely and had only recently begun speaking to his father again, long after he'd resigned his commission in the marines and ended his father's dreams of a high-ranking son. Natalie was studying politics at college in New York City, shooting for a job at the White House last he'd heard. There wasn't much he could tell Lopez about any of them.

'It never came up,' he replied, dodging her question as deftly as he could.

'That's crap,' Lopez scolded him. 'You don't talk about them, but I know that you'd have bugged out of the Windy City a long time ago if they weren't important to you.'

Ethan blinked. What *did* keep him in Illinois? He shrugged it off as he looked up at the odd symbols and rubbed them with his finger.

'Will you cut it out?' Lopez laughed. 'Your work here is done, Einstein.'

'Why'd you think Purcell would do this?' Ethan asked her. 'Leave messages like these for us to find?'

Lopez shrugged. 'He's a scientist – they get their rocks off on stuff like this.'

Ethan shook his head.

'He's just lost his wife and child in a brutal murder that he says he did not commit. I don't reckon he'd be interested in playing mind games if he's trying to prove his innocence. Surely he'd just write the tail code in big letters like he did the other message, or he'd just call the police again and tell them to search for the aircraft in question, not conceal them in a tiny scribble up here.'

Lopez fell silent for a few moments as she considered this.

'Unless maybe there's somebody else looking for him too,' she suggested. 'Somebody who he knows might not search as thoroughly as the police have. But then why leave the blatant message for you on the other wall? Why not hide *everything*?'

Ethan spoke without breaking his gaze.

'Maybe the *real* message is the coded one, the rest just enough to satisfy whoever he thinks is pursuing him. So he hides the coded message here behind the curtain, maybe figuring that the police will search more thoroughly and have more resources to figure out what he's trying to tell them, before whoever else he's hiding from finds him.'

Lopez looked across the room at the scrawled message.

'He'd still have to know in advance that we'd definitely be here.'

Ethan turned on his heel and looked at her. 'And how might he know that? Sure, he called Sears and told him to contact me, but how could he be absolutely sure that I'd turn up?'

'I don't know,' Lopez admitted, 'but why else would

he have written your name up here and then left a code for you to find?'

Ethan was about to respond when another voice answered for him.

'Because Nicola is right, and he knew that you would be here.'

Ethan turned and saw Jarvis standing in the doorway of the room. The military transport he'd travelled down on was not even half as fast as the F-15s, but Ethan knew they'd have been given priority status as they raced south. The old man sauntered in with his hands in his pockets and looked up at the walls where the scrawled messages taunted them.

'That's crazy,' Ethan pointed out. 'You saying this guy really can see into the future?'

'We're not sure,' Jarvis admitted. 'But he's leaving you clues and he must have a reason for doing so. I was just listening to what you said, and there's no point in Charles Purcell concealing selected information in codes unless he's hiding something from one person whilst trying to inform another.'

'Sure,' Lopez agreed, 'but who's to say that it's us Purcell wants to figure all this out? Maybe this is all a double bluff to throw us off the scent, and he really did murder his family.'

Jarvis shook his head.

'Given what we know about him I'd say it's unlikely. He has no history of mental instability and was by all accounts extremely happy in his work at NASA.'

'But he works for somebody else now, right?' Lopez pointed out. 'Maybe something happened?'

Sears re-appeared in the apartment.

'I'll say,' he said, as he waved a piece of paper at them. 'I had that aircraft checked out for you.'

'Did you find it?' Ethan asked.

'Kind of.'

Lopez looked at the captain with an uncomfortable expression. 'The hell does that mean?'

Sears looked somewhat pale as he replied.

'It didn't belong to Charles Purcell's father. November two-seven-six-four-charlie was a Grumman Mallard that went down yesterday afternoon off the coast of South Bimini island in the Bahamas. There were no survivors.'

Ethan stared at Sears for a moment and then looked at the code that Charles Purcell had scrawled across the wall.

'When was Purcell booked into this apartment?' he asked.

'Checked in yesterday at five thirty in the evening, and according to the hotelier he left in his car two hours later and did not return . . .' Sears broke off as he realized what Ethan was getting at.

'When did the aircraft go down?' Jarvis prompted the captain.

'Radio contact was lost just before seven thirty in the evening,' Sears replied. 'The aircraft was reported missing at just after eight, after it failed to land at Miami International at the allotted time.'

Ethan looked at Jarvis. 'Purcell wrote that coded message before the aircraft had gone down.'

'He knew it was going to crash,' Lopez said. 'You

think he somehow saw the crash in advance, like the scene at his home yesterday evening?'

Kyle Sears shook his head. 'It's more likely that Purcell had something to do with the plane going down than that he's able to see the future. We could be dealing with a mass murderer.'

'Has any wreckage been found?' Ethan asked.

'That's part of the problem,' Sears replied. 'The aircraft vanished without trace. The Miami Coastguard conducted a search at the aircraft's last known position but nothing was found. The airplane was travelling through the Bermuda Triangle when it disappeared from radar screens.'

'The Bermuda Triangle,' Ethan echoed.

'This is getting weirder by the minute,' Lopez said.

Ethan turned to Jarvis.

'Purcell used to work at NASA. We need to go and talk to some of his colleagues and find out what he was doing there.'

Jarvis nodded as he slipped a cellphone out of his pocket.

'I'll get us a ride. We'll be in Cape Canaveral within the hour.'

Ethan stared at the wall and its cryptic message.

'What's up?' Lopez asked him.

Ethan sighed.

'I want to know,' he replied, 'what happens at 20:48 on June 28. I've got a feeling that, whatever it is, it's not going to be good.'

13

MANDARIN ORIENTAL HOTEL, MIAMI, FLORIDA

June 28, 10:02

Joaquin Abell stood at the ceiling-to-floor windows of his penthouse suite and looked across the water to the Miami skyline, where the British Consulate dominated the scenery. The channel between the hotel and Bricknell Key, a wedge-shaped island just off the shore, glittered in the morning sunshine as it flowed south in deep eddies before trailing away to be lost into the endless ocean, like time irretrievably passing him by. Lost, but still there.

And at what price? The late, great Isaac Abell watched him from history and gave a deep and disapproving shake of his head. Joaquin swallowed thickly.

'This is worth it, Father.'

The words spilled from Joaquin's lips without conscious effort, as though even now he was compelled to justify himself. Once, he had been intimidated and dwarfed by the incorruptible morals of his father, which seemed too pristine and too perfect to follow. And then the towering monolith, the indestructible center of Joaquin's entire universe, had toppled and fallen, his father's life extinguished not by disease or years but by the insufferable disgrace of suicide.

'What's worth it?'

Joaquin bit his lip and cursed his melancholic reverie as he turned to see Katherine walk over to join him. She had changed into a smart, knee-length suit with a crisp white shirt, and as usual looked stunning.

'Everything that IRIS is doing,' he replied with a smile, as she slipped her arm round his waist.

'And what is IRIS doing?'

'Right now?' he asked rhetorically. 'Right now it is on the verge of being able to not just come to the aid of those suffering natural disasters around the world, but to prevent those disasters from happening in the first place.'

Katherine looked at her husband for a few moments and smiled brightly, but a veil of confusion shadowed her green eyes.

'You can't save the entire world, Joaquin,' she said. 'It's too big, even for you.'

Joaquin chuckled. 'Never say that. Nothing is impossible.'

'The government wouldn't let you do it, even if you could,' she replied. 'You know that.'

Joaquin sighed.

'They're far too busy looking after themselves to be concerned with the needs of so many anonymous lives.'

It was that same truth that had so embittered Isaac Abell and sent him into alternating paroxysms of fury and despair over the callousness of humanity and the self-interest of those charged with representing and protecting their fellow human beings.

There were approximately seven billion people on earth, yet their lives were governed by just a few thousand politicians, many of whom struggled to serve honorably under the crippling demands of corporate capitalism, the twisting arm of the media and the machinations of countless narrow-minded pressure groups concerned only with their own personal or religious views of the world. Such idiocy enraged Joaquin as much as it had infuriated his father. No president, no matter how adept, could reach the White House without asserting their belief in God, despite the fact that nobody on earth even knew if any such deity existed. The media and major corporations funded the very campaigns that launched the careers of presidents, safe in the knowledge that their investments would result in policies carefully tailored to ensure their profits. The whole charade was a circus of self-serving, profiteering bullshit, democracy lost at the expense of civil liberties and justice.

And so Joaquin had infiltrated the halls of power and set his organization to work rebuilding lands devastated by natural disasters, ravaged by disease and scoured of life by the horrors of man's endless conflicts. Contracts were awarded by Congress, often after months of lobbying by IRIS, to reconstruct entire cities shattered by war, while at the same time IRIS was fighting off the equally determined lobbying of corporate giants which sought those same contracts purely for profit. Those contracts that IRIS won were used to bring peace where once chaos had reigned. Over, and over, and over again. It was becoming harder and harder to secure funding for charitable ventures, forcing Joaquin to entertain ever more radical ideas to force the hands of the politicians.

'Your mind's wandering,' Katherine interrupted his thoughts with a gentle jab to his shoulder, 'and the look on your face suggests weighty concerns that you can't solve alone.'

Joaquin sighed again.

'You're right,' he said, 'as ever. Maybe soon this will all come to an end, but for now I must try to convince the governor of Florida to lobby Congress to provide us with the funds we need to get supplies and medical equipment on the ground in Puerto Rico.'

Katherine's features sagged.

'I thought we were staying here for a few weeks,' she complained. 'I only have to defend IRIS against a civil action, for which there is no evidence, and then I'm done. The kids have barely seen you these last two months and school's out in a couple of weeks. You promised them.'

Joaquin nodded and rubbed his temples.

'I know, it just can't wait. I'll have to spend some time out on the reef at Deep Blue. It should only take a day or so at the most – in fact I know it will, and then we'll be free.'

Katherine sighed. Joaquin could see in her eyes that, despite her disappointment, she understood that the work he did took precedence over their own needs. One more day was often the difference between life and death for those in need. A delay in funding, or one of the infuriating legal barriers that often blocked IRIS's access to disaster areas, could result in the loss of thousands of lives.

'What's so important, Joaquin?' she asked him. 'What did Sandra say to you this morning? And why do you need to be out on the coral reefs?'

'I'm not going there for the coral,' Joaquin explained patiently. 'One of our aircraft was lost yesterday in the Florida Straits. I want to find and retrieve it before the damned media start swimming around like hyenas looking for corpses.'

Katherine's face fell again as one hand flew to her lips.

'Oh, I'm sorry. I didn't know. Were there any survivors?'

Joaquin shook his head.

'The situation's under control but I want to oversee this personally, identify the victims, and then hand the aircraft over to the National Transportation Safety Board so they can figure out what the hell went wrong out there.'

Katherine nodded, and he felt her arm slip from around his waist.

'I'll tell the children we'll be away for a few days,' she said. 'They'll be in school anyway.'

'Okay,' Joaquin replied. 'The helicopter will meet you later today and will take you to the yacht when the court case is over. All I need you to do is keep the damned litigation wolves at bay for a little longer and then we can walk away from all of this and spend some time together, just like we used to.'

Katherine nodded and smiled. Joaquin remembered the days before IRIS had taken on its mission to change the world, when he and Katherine had lived high on the company's immense profits. They had met during a fund-raiser in New York for victims of the attacks that had so irrevocably changed the world in 2001. Katherine had been the legal representation for many of those victims, Joaquin a beneficiary and contributor to the fledgling plans to build the Freedom Tower. One night dedicated to the lives of others less fortunate had brought them together and neither of them had ever looked back. A whirlwind of travel followed, official appearances as a couple and then marriage and children, all of it featuring in glossy magazines on newsstands across the globe. And yet, despite all of that, they shared the same yearning for those early years that seemed so far away now – years of excitement and new love familiar to every couple, wealthy or not.

'The prosecution doesn't have a leg to stand on,' she reported. 'My guess is that the court will rule that there's no case to answer. Damn it, the family wouldn't even be living in the United States if it wasn't for what you and IRIS did for them.'

Joaquin smiled and kissed his wife on the cheek.

'Give 'em hell,' he said finally.

Katherine picked up her bag as she left, and Joaquin turned to look out across the bay once more. The clouds across the immense sky above were being torn to shreds by high-altitude winds gusting through the atmosphere, invisible yet deadly. The oncoming storm.

The door to the suite opened and Olaf Jorgenson walked in before closing the door behind him. Joaquin turned as the huge man lumbered across to his side, his eyes cold points of ice, as though still reflecting the bitter glaciers of his Nordic home.

'What would you have me do?'

Olaf's thick, stilted accent only served to accentuate his appearance, that of a ruthless terminator unhindered by such pitiful emotions as remorse or guilt. Utterly reliable, the big man was nonetheless several lifetimes short of genius, and Joaquin chose his missions with care.

'Watch after Katherine,' he said finally. 'She's likely to be targeted by activists or maybe enemies of the state: we don't know who might try to prevent her from doing her job. Do what is needed to ensure the outcome we require.'

14

KENNEDY SPACE CENTER, MERRITT ISLAND, FLORIDA

June 28, 10:12

Warner stared in awe out of the window as the Gulfstream C-20D settled onto the runway of Cape Canaveral Air Force Station's skid strip. As the aircraft slowed he could see rows of immense launch pads dominating the horizon, epic constructions of welded steel forged into history at the dawn of the space race. The names of missions that carried the weight of legend flashed through his mind, memories of what he'd witnessed in his childhood, as America's most valiant heroes soared into the final frontier: *Voyager*; *Mercury*; *Gemini*; *Pioneer*; *Apollo*. *Eagle*.

Launch Complex 39 stood out from the rest, the home of the entire history of the space shuttle, and where the Apollo program's moon-shots had thundered into the Florida skies aboard the mighty *Saturn-V* rockets, still the largest and most powerful launch vehicles in history.

'We'll disembark and drive to the operations center,' Jarvis informed them as they unbuckled from their seats. 'I've called ahead and gathered a couple of Charles Purcell's former colleagues to see what they can tell us.'

Ethan, Lopez and Jarvis were picked up by an Air Force crew transport and driven across a causeway that linked the base to Merritt Island and the Kennedy Space Center. Ethan watched as the headquarters building came into view, a long white three-story affair lined with palm trees, which shone in the bright sunlight as the truck pulled in. Jarvis led them out and a young Air Force ensign guided them into the building, hurrying through the administrative areas and into a large briefing room guarded by a pair of security personnel.

The guards recognized Jarvis on sight and opened the doors to the briefing room.

'Judging by the guards they've got everybody in on this,' Lopez whispered to him as they walked through the doors. 'At least we're not on our own this time.'

Ethan frowned.

'That's what makes me nervous,' he replied. 'I'm wondering what's gotten them so worked up.'

Two men were waiting for them within the room as Jarvis closed the door behind Ethan.

'This is astrophysicist Thomas Ryker,' Jarvis introduced the younger of the two men, a scrawny guy with a narrow beard, big round glasses and a T-shirt bearing a picture of *Star Trek*'s Seven of Nine, 'and this is astronaut Mitch Hannah. They both worked with Charles Purcell on the Hubble Space Telescope program.'

Mitch Hannah was a grizzled-looking older guy who wore a jacket emblazoned with the legend 'VF-84' and a skull-and-crossbones motif. Ethan recognized it immediately.

'Fighting 84th,' he said, identifying the legend. 'You're Navy, right?'

Hannah nodded with a proud grin.

'Twenty-two years,' he replied, 'Phantoms and Tomcats, Nimitz and Enterprise. With the astronaut program now. You a Navy pilot?'

'Fifteenth Marines,' Ethan replied by way of an explanation. 'You been up in the shuttle?'

'STS-117,' Hannah nodded.

'Goddamn,' Ethan smiled in awe, 'I'd have given my right arm for a ride on that thing and—'

'Good to see you two are on the same page,' Jarvis cut him off. 'You can catch up on old times later. Right now, we need to talk about Charles Purcell. Thomas Ryker worked with him for years.'

Ethan and Lopez looked at Ryker. The astrophysicist, for his part, stared wide-eyed at Lopez, as though captivated by a work of art.

'You can put your tongue back in,' Ethan said. 'We're here on business.'

Ryker shifted his gaze away from Lopez with some considerable effort and blushed.

'What's up with Charles?' he asked, in an effort to distract the visitors from his flushing cheeks.

'When was the last time you saw him?' Lopez asked.

'Couple of weeks ago, I guess,' Ryker replied. 'Visited his family down Coral Gables way – his wife's a great cook. But since he started working freelance we haven't met up as often as we'd like. Are they all okay?'

Ethan decided not to hold back any further.

'He's on the run and his family have been shot and

killed. We're trying to figure out if he's responsible for the murders.'

All of the emotion dropped out of Ryker's features. 'Michelle and Amy are dead?'

'Yesterday evening,' Lopez confirmed gently. 'Both were shot in the head. Purcell was seen fleeing the scene.'

Ethan watched the kid closely. He was staring at Lopez again but this time the adolescent lust was replaced by cold disbelief.

'He wouldn't have, he couldn't,' Ryker uttered. 'There's just no way.'

'That's not how it looks right now,' Ethan pointed out. 'And if Purcell is innocent we've only got a few hours to prove it.'

'How come?' Mitch Hannah asked.

Ethan glanced at Jarvis, who nodded, and Ethan explained what he and Lopez had seen in Purcell's rented apartment in Miami: the code and the scrawled warning. Ryker and Hannah exchanged a glance with each other and the older man looked at Jarvis.

'I've got less time with Purcell than Tom here, but I'd vouch for him as being a straight up kind of guy. If he'd had marital problems he'd have shared them, not gone home and shot his family.'

'Right on,' Ryker chimed in. 'Charlie loved his family, never stopped going on about them. Whatever happened, he didn't kill them.'

Ethan sat down on the edge of a desk.

'Point is, Purcell appears to have been able to predict things happening before they actually did.'

Ryker leaned forward. 'How far in advance?'

The direct question left Ethan momentarily stumped, and he realized that he'd expected Ryker to say that what he'd suggested was impossible, like most everybody else.

'At least twenty-four hours,' Ethan replied. 'You think that he could actually do that?'

Ryker sat back again and pushed his spectacles up on his nose as he considered the question.

'It's not impossible, let's put it that way.'

'Yes it is,' Mitch Hannah scoffed. 'Time travel is the stuff of science fiction. It just can't be done.'

Ryker nodded.

'That's absolutely right,' the kid agreed. 'Time travel is indeed impossible as far as we know. But I didn't say anything about *travelling* through time, did I?'

'Then what did you mean?' Lopez asked, confused.

Mitch Hannah rolled his eyes.

'Tom, these guys are investigating a homicide. We don't have time for *Star Trek* fantasies. They need answers, and if there's one thing I'm damned sure of it's that Charles Purcell can't see into the future.'

Ryker blinked, suddenly unsure of himself. Ethan was about to interject when the door to the room opened and a member of the center's staff poked their head inside.

'There an Ethan Warner in here?'

Ethan turned to face him. 'Sure, that's me.'

The staffer walked in with a package and handed it to Ethan. He took it in surprise, seeing his name on the parcel and the address of the Kennedy Space Center.

'What's this?' he asked.

'Arrived a moment ago,' the staffer said.

Ethan looked at the postmark on the parcel and felt a shiver run down his spine.

'It was posted yesterday,' he uttered in disbelief.

Mitch Hannah stood up from the desk and stared at the parcel as though it were a ticking bomb.

'Tell me that somebody knew you were going to be here.'

Ethan shook his head.

'I've never been in this building in my life and didn't know I was coming here until an hour ago.'

Lopez looked at Ethan. 'Who sent the parcel?'

Ethan looked at the bar-coded UPS sticker on the parcel.

'It's from Hallandale, Florida,' he murmured. 'Where Purcell was hiding out.'

The parcel contained something slim and hard, like a CD case but larger. Gambling that there was nothing sinister within, Ethan tore off the edge of the parcel and slid the contents out.

'It's a diary,' Lopez said, looking at the black book in Ethan's hand.

Ethan set the packaging down on the table beside him and opened the diary's first page.

The words that he read there chilled him to the core.

'Oh my God.'

15

KENNEDY SPACE CENTER

'What does it say?'

Lopez tried to look at the diary that Ethan held in his hands, and he turned it to face her.

'Holy crap,' she muttered.

By now Ryker, Hannah and Jarvis were all craning their heads to see the diary. Ethan turned it to them and Mitch Hannah read the message scrawled on the open page.

> *You've cracked the first code by now, Ethan. Crack this one and you'll understand why my family were killed. Ivy Mike has the answers. Time is running out and more will die before this is over. Make sure you're not one of them.*
>
> *CP*

'Who the hell is Ivy Mike? And how the hell could Purcell have known that we would be here?' Lopez asked.

It was Thomas Ryker who replied.

'Because he has seen the future.'

Mitch Hannah ran a hand through his hair in disbelief. Ethan looked at Ryker.

'How? You said yourself that time travel is impossible.'

Ryker searched the air above his head and stroked his feeble beard, as though hoping a suitable response would fall from the ceiling.

'We don't have enough time for a physics lesson here, Mr. Warner, so this is going to have to be brief. Have you ever looked into the past?'

Ethan shook his head. 'No, of course not.'

Ryker grinned.

'Yes, you have. We all have. Every human being on earth has looked into the past, back in time. We do it every minute of every day.'

'What are you talking about?' Lopez snapped impatiently.

Ryker gestured to one of the windows, through which shafts of sunlight passed from outside.

'Light, is what I'm talking about,' he replied. 'The speed of light in a vacuum is a constant across our universe – its velocity never changes. What's important here is that the speed of light's velocity can be measured: it doesn't cross vast distances instantaneously, but over periods of time.'

Jarvis, standing with his hands in his pockets, frowned at the young physicist.

'How fast does it go?'

'Three hundred thousand kilometers per second. 'Fast

enough,' Ryker said, 'for a photon of light to zip around our planet's equator seven times in one second. Fast enough that the human eye cannot detect the movement of light.' The kid jumped up and walked across to a blackboard, picking up a piece of chalk and drawing three circles: a big one on the left, a little one in the middle, and then a large oval disc on the right side of the board.

'What's important, though,' Ryker continued, as he pointed at the nearby window, 'is that it's still a measurable velocity. The photons of light coming in through that window have to bounce off me and reach your eyes before you can see me. Even though I'm only a couple of yards away, you're still looking into the past.'

Ethan blinked in surprise.

'So wherever we look, we're looking into the past.'

'Exactly,' Ryker smiled. 'What I meant when I said that Purcell could see the future wasn't that he'd travelled in time, only that he'd perhaps found a way to *see* through time.'

Lopez glanced at the window.

'But if it takes light to be reflected off something in order to see it, then how can he have seen events that haven't happened yet? The light won't have been able to reach him.'

Ryker raised an eyebrow in surprise.

'That's incredibly astute of you, Miss Lopez,' he said, as he gestured to the diagram he'd drawn on the blackboard, 'and entirely correct. But we're getting ahead of ourselves a bit. Look at these circles: the one on the left is the sun, the one in the middle is the earth, and the egg-shaped one on the right is our nearest galactic neighbor, the Andromeda galaxy.'

Ryker turned to face them.

'It takes light from the sun eight minutes to reach us, so we see the sun as it was eight minutes ago. If the sun vanished from the center of our solar system right now, we wouldn't know about it for eight minutes. In comparison, the light from the Andromeda galaxy takes about two million years to get here, so we see that galaxy as it was two million years ago.'

Jarvis nodded as he got the message. 'The further away you're looking, the further back in time you can see.'

'That's right,' Ryker agreed. 'And if someone in the Andromeda galaxy had a big enough telescope and they zoomed in to this very spot here, what do you think they would see?'

'Not this office,' Lopez guessed.

'They'd probably see saber-toothed tigers and woolly mammoths,' Ryker confirmed. 'Whatever was living on this spot two million years ago.'

'Okay,' Ethan said, 'I've got that much, but how does all of it translate into Charles Purcell being able to see into the future?'

Ryker stepped away from the blackboard.

'Well, the simplest way to put it is that time and space are effectively the same thing. You need space in order for light to be able to travel from one place to another, and how long it takes light to cross that space gives you the definition of time. Each needs the other in order to exist, and what affects one will affect the other. This relationship is known as the space-time continuum.'

Lopez nodded.

'I've heard of that before,' she said. 'You reckon that Purcell has somehow worked out how to alter the continuum?'

Ryker shook his head.

'I'm not sure. What I do know for sure is that time does not always run at the same speed across the universe, or even here on earth.'

Ethan frowned. 'How can that be true, if the speed of light's velocity is fixed?'

Mitch Hannah spoke up.

'It's a fact of physics,' he explained. 'It's not the velocity of light that changes. If an object starts moving at high velocity, then time begins to run more slowly compared to another object that remains stationary. The discrepancy was predicted by Einstein in his Theory of General Relativity. The Air Force ran tests using a Boeing 747 with an atomic clock on board, and another synchronized atomic clock that stayed on the ground. The aircraft flew around the world, and when it landed again the clocks were compared: the clock from the aircraft showed a slightly different time as a result of its sustained velocity.'

'So the clock on the airplane had travelled through time?' Lopez asked.

'Not exactly,' Hannah corrected her. 'Time had flowed at a *different rate* for the travelling clock than the one that stayed on the ground. The same effect occurs for satellites orbiting our planet at seventeen thousand miles per hour, especially the ones that provide Global Positioning data. If the different rates in the flow of time for the satellites compared to us on the ground were not accounted for, then GPS systems would be wildly inaccurate.'

'That's not all,' Ryker said. 'It's not just velocity that affects the flow of time. If you're close to an object of great mass, like a planet or a star, then time slows down for you compared to another observer out in space, well away from any gravitational fields.'

'How can mass make a difference?' Jarvis asked.

'Because a large object like a star warps the field of space-time around it,' Ryker explained. 'This results in the effect we know as gravity. Light follows this gravitational curve, as do other objects around the star or whatever object is warping space-time. That's why planets like the earth orbit the sun: they follow this bend in the field of space-time like a ball rolling around a casino wheel. Point is, when the planet or star warps space it's also warping time along with it.'

Mitch Hannah spoke up again.

'This was also predicted by Einstein, and was proven in the last century when his equations were used to explain why Sir Isaac Newton's laws of gravity perfectly predicted the orbits of all the planets around the sun, except Mercury. Mercury orbits very close to the sun and always seemed to appear slightly out of place. It turned out that the sun's mass curved the light reflected from Mercury's surface when seen from the earth, making it appear in a different place to where it actually was. Newton's laws were correct – Mercury just *looked* like it was in a different place.'

Ryker nodded, picking up from Mitch.

'The bottom line is that time is relative to the observer, and can flow at different rates depending on how fast we're moving and how close we are to planets and stars. The effect of these phenomena on time is known as *time dilation*.' Ryker gestured up to the sky outside the window. 'The world record for what some people might call time travel is held by cosmonaut Sergei Avdeyev, who orbited the earth almost twelve thousand times over 750 days whilst aboard the Mir space station. At such velocity, and farther from the mass of the earth than those of us on the ground, the time dilation he experienced sent him 0.02 seconds into the future, because time passed slower for him than for the rest of us.'

Ethan thought about this for a moment.

'So I take it that unless Charles Purcell has spent the last two years sprinting faster than the space shuttle, he must have found some other way of achieving time dilation.'

Hannah shrugged.

'So you'd suppose, but I'm not aware of a single way that he could have done that.'

Ethan looked at Ryker. 'Can you?'

Ryker held Ethan's gaze for a few moments. 'There's a great deal of evidence suggesting that we can see into the future, albeit in a basic and somewhat nebulous way,' Ryker said. 'Virtually all the great scientific formulae which explain how the world works allow information to flow both backwards *and* forward through time. For many years the CIA funded a secretive project called "Stargate", which investigated everything from psychics to remote viewing in an attempt to turn such skills into defense initiatives for the military. More recent experiments have repeatedly shown that people have the ability to respond emotionally to images shown them on television screens some three seconds before they occur, with those results confirmed by replication in laboratories as far afield as Edinburgh University and Cornell, and that this ability shows parallels in real-life events. Trains and aircraft that crash are consistently found to be unusually empty, suggesting that people due to travel on them decide not to at the last minute for reasons they cannot define and probably aren't even aware of.'

'That's not enough for Purcell to have predicted what he saw in such detail,' Lopez pointed out. 'He can't have done so much on the basis of a psychic vision.'

'I guess,' Ryker replied. 'What else is in the book?'

Ethan looked down, having almost forgotten he was holding Charles Purcell's diary. He opened the pages and flicked through them. There were contact details for almost a hundred people: names, addresses and telephone numbers. Ethan shook his head.

'Looks like a normal address book,' he said with a shrug.

'There's nothing normal about Purcell,' Lopez said, as she tapped the pages of the book with a finger. 'You cracked his last code. Ten bucks says this one beats you.'

Ethan flipped through the diary one page at a time, as Jarvis moved to stand alongside him.

. . . *Barker. Carson, Devereux, Elliot, Forbes, Griffiths* . . .

'I could send this to the DIA, have them call the numbers and find out who's on the other end,' Jarvis suggested. 'But there might not be an actual code in there that can be deciphered by computers.'

'Not enough time then,' Lopez pointed out. 'We need to figure this out, right now.'

Ethan frowned as he scanned through the alphabetically arranged list of surnames, none showing any sign of hidden codes.

. . . Hillier, Innes, Jackson, Kellerman, Lamont, Marchant, Nancy, Osborne, Peterson . . .

Ryker stared down at the pages as Ethan flipped them.

'See anything?' Ethan asked, flipping the pages as he went.

. . . Thompson, Ustanov, Vernoux, William, Wilkinson . . .

Ryker shook his head.

'Looks normal enough to me.'

Ethan scanned down the pages and shook his head.

'Maybe you're not quite the sleuth you thought you were,' Lopez said, as she leaned back on the table and folded her arms. 'Ten bucks it is.'

Ethan stopped reading and flicked back a few pages. All at once, it leapt out at him as clear as the sunlight streaming into the room.

'The code's not *in* the names,' he said. 'It *is* the names.'

16

MANDARIN ORIENTAL HOTEL, MIAMI

June 28, 10:40

'Gentlemen, welcome.'

Dennis Aubrey stood unobtrusively to one side of the private breakfast room that Joaquin Abell had hired, and watched as he spoke to the men of substance before them. Behind Joaquin was a suspended silver screen, and behind his guests, a projector. To Aubrey's surprise, four heavy-set men in suits stood like guards around the edge of the room. Aubrey was unused to being in such company, and equally uncomfortable being under armed guard, something that Joaquin had neglected to mention before they had entered the hotel.

All of the seven seated dignitaries before them looked entirely at home in their opulent surroundings. Champagne bottles worth more than some cars lay in buckets of sparkling ice, and the bright sunlight from outside was shielded by glowing opaque blinds.

'Thank you all for taking the time to come here,' Joaquin said. 'You may wonder why I've asked for this breakfast meeting so urgently, but I know that within just a few minutes you will all understand, as well as appreciating the need for absolute security.'

Joaquin paced up and down slowly as he spoke, his movements giving rhythm to his words.

'All of you wield immense control over the lives of the people that you govern,' he said, and selected a member of his audience with receding red hair. 'Congressman Ryan Goldberg, you've served Congress for over twenty years and your word is considered your bond. Mr. Murtaugh,' he went on, indicating an elderly man, 'you own and operate one of the largest news networks in the continental United States, providing 24-hour coverage to millions of homes.' Joaquin turned to another, middle-aged man who wore a Stetson and sunglasses. 'Mr. Reed, you are the Executive Officer of one of our largest oil companies, providing fuel for our modern world.' One of the men watching was a widely respected statesman, a face known to millions of Floridians. 'Governor MacKenzie, the people of Florida look to you to represent them, and follow you respectfully.'

Joaquin paused, as though thinking. Aubrey knew it was a theatrical flourish. Joaquin Abell was never lost for words.

'Yet despite your combined wealth and influence there is one thing that none of you can control. Time. Like the rest of the world you are held captive by what you know in the here and now.' Joaquin smiled at them. 'I, however, am liberated by the knowledge of tomorrow. And it is this that I wish to share with you this morning.'

Aubrey frowned as he watched, caught unaware by Joaquin's astonishing claim.

Joaquin glanced across at him and, as previously instructed, Aubrey pressed a button on the remote control he held in his hand. The projector flickered into life and the screen behind Joaquin lit up. Almost immediately, Aubrey recognized the face of news anchor Juliette Parker as she appeared on the screen – the iconic face of one of Robert Murtaugh's best-known employees. But there was no sound to the image and it flickered strangely, as though Parker's studio had been filmed through a rippling heat haze. Brief flares of static leapt across the image as Parker silently mouthed her lines. Aubrey caught a few words from her lips: *earthquake*; *sudden*; *casualties*.

Suddenly, the image changed to one of a devastated shoreline, upturned boats and vehicles scattered across roads buckled by the immense seismic might of a churning tectonic plate. Aubrey watched the silently flickering images of stricken survivors afloat amidst vast swathes of floodwater filled with the detritus of smashed buildings. A tsunami, he realized, sweeping vulnerable human life before its wrath across a land devastated beyond all recognition.

'This,' Joaquin said as the images played, 'is a sadly common event on our planet, and one which we have never been able to predict. Until now.'

Reed stood from his chair, removing his Stetson and rubbing his head in confusion.

'What are you jabbering about, Joaquin? That quake happened yesterday in Puerto Rico. Either get to the point or I'm outta here, goddamn your hide.'

Joaquin grinned and gestured to the screen.

'This news report *is* the point,' he replied, and looked at Murtaugh. 'Isn't it, Robert?'

The old man squinted at the screen as though confused, and then slowly his rheumy eyes began to widen as his jaw fell. The scrolling text on the bottom of the screen pinpointed the scenes of destruction at the town of Puerto Plata, on the coast of the Dominican Republic.

Congressman Goldberg stood up out of his chair. 'There hasn't been an earthquake in the Dominican Republic,' he uttered. 'I haven't seen anything on the news about it.'

'The anchor, Juliette, is on vacation at the moment,' Murtaugh murmured.

Joaquin let the realization of what the men were seeing begin to dawn upon them, and as though on perfect cue, after the appalling scenes of destruction and loss, the news anchor smiled brightly and the image changed to the weather forecast. At the bottom of the screen, clearly displayed, was the date. June 28.

'That's not possible,' Reed stammered as he whipped his sunglasses off to reveal surprisingly bright blue eyes. 'That's this afternoon!' He whirled to point at Robert Murtaugh. 'This is some kind of set-up. You must have pre-recorded the broadcast.'

Murtaugh, with some effort, struggled up out of his seat to face the Texan.

'I can assure you, Harry, that I have done no such thing.' The media tycoon turned his gaze upon Joaquin Abell. 'But I also believe this to be some kind of pointless joke. I have better things to do, the first of which will be to fire Juliette when I get back to New York.'

Joaquin shook his head.

'I wouldn't do that, if I were you,' he said. 'She'll be the face of the disaster when it hits, seen more than any other anchor on television throughout the world. That's exposure you cannot afford to lose.'

'Bullshit!' Murtaugh spat. 'You can no more look into the future than I can look up my own ass.' His wrinkled features twisted into a grin. 'Perhaps, Joaquin, this is the result of you spending too much time looking up yours.'

Laughter rippled across the guests as they began standing and gathering their jackets. Dennis Aubrey looked across at Joaquin in surprise, but the younger man grinned happily for a moment before speaking.

'Perhaps, Robert, you should pay more attention to what I have to show you. It would be such a shame if your wife were to find out just how many times you've fucked her sister over the years.'

Aubrey flinched at Joaquin's sudden and unexpected profanity. Every one of the guests fell motionless, as though frozen in time. Slowly, Murtaugh broke his chains of disbelief and turned to face Joaquin.

'What in the name of God are you talking about?'

Aubrey felt a pinch of concern as Joaquin's smile twisted cruelly. He produced a remote control of his own and aimed it at the projector. The news image behind him flickered to another broadcast, another anchor for a rival station speaking silently. Behind her were images of Robert Murtaugh, and the scrolling text revealed his lover's admission of an affair with the tycoon. Aubrey picked up more words from her silent lips: *affair*; *sordid*; *decades-long*; *divorce*.

Joaquin watched as the rest of the guests stared in fascination at the screen, and all at once Aubrey realized that he had them right where he wanted them. Despite himself, he felt a quiver of excitement.

'What I'm talking about,' Joaquin snapped, 'is tomorrow's news. It would appear that your lover will soon have an attack of regret and spill everything to the entire world. Just imagine, Robert, how much that will hurt your family. And if that's not enough, just imagine how much your soon-to-be ex-wife is going to hurt your wallet when she drags you through the courts. I'm no fortune-teller but my guess is that she'll take you to the cleaners, and there's not a goddamned thing you can do about it unless you sit your ass back in that chair and listen to what I have to say.'

The guests exchanged wary glances. Robert Murtaugh eased himself back down into his chair. Joaquin watched as the rest of the guests followed the old man's lead, and he waited until they were all watching him attentively before he spoke again.

'I know about all of you,' he said. 'I know that all of you have something to hide, and that's why you are here today – because I have seen the future and I know that all of you are about to see your worlds collapse around you. You're about to be on the news for all the wrong reasons, gentlemen.'

Governor MacKenzie remained standing.

'This is a set-up,' he murmured, eyeing Joaquin. 'He

could have found out about the affair any number of ways and paid for that video to be shot. It could even be an innocent report with the scroll altered to say anything he wants it to.'

Twenty pairs of eyes looked expectantly at Joaquin, who raised an eyebrow.

'Is that a chance you're willing to take, Governor?' Joaquin asked rhetorically. 'If so, then you risk losing both your office and the respect of the people, something that has taken you years to achieve.'

'Something,' the governor replied, 'that wouldn't crumble overnight because of your bizarre little experiment here.'

'Unless,' Joaquin countered, 'it were revealed, as it will be, that you too have dipped your fingers in the dirty little pie of corruption. You lost the vote for the governorship of Florida, didn't you James, but it was so much easier to bribe officials into altering the new digital voting machines to guarantee your victory than it was to force a recount of ticker tapes.'

The governor's expression collapsed, the brutal simplicity of Joaquin's accusation catching him unawares.

'That's ridiculous!' he uttered. 'I have never done any such thing!'

'Yes you have,' Joaquin assured him, 'and a whistle-blower within the company that builds and maintains the voting machines will reveal all to the media in just a few days' time.'

Congressman Goldberg, his face trembling with indignation, jabbed a finger to point at Joaquin.

'You have no right to do this! No matter how you've achieved it, this is an invasion of privacy!'

'No it's not,' Joaquin replied, 'because it hasn't happened yet. I take it, Congressman, that after years of voting for laws that stigmatize gay and lesbian marriages, you'll be concerned that the world will soon learn of your own homosexual encounters with escort agencies in Washington DC?'

Goldberg almost gagged as his skin flushed a pallid red, but he said nothing. Joaquin looked across the faces of the men seated before him, before settling on Reed, who was now hiding once again beneath his hat.

'Or you, Harry.'

'Don't you even think about it, you sniveling little shit,' Reed hissed.

'I've already thought about it,' Joaquin smiled, 'and I have seen it, and believe me, it's not going to turn out pretty for you. Remember that famous story of how you started your empire by building a single pump in Texan soil with your own hands? Trust me, it'll take a lot less than the thirty years you then spent building up your company to lose it all when it's revealed that you didn't build the pump after all, preferring instead to unload a shotgun into the owner's face after a bar-room brawl and take over his operation.'

Reed lurched out of his seat toward Joaquin, but instantly the four bodyguards materialized from their discreet positions around the room, weapons drawn. Reed glared at them.

'Sit down, Harry,' Joaquin said. 'You of all people know what a terrible mess it makes when somebody's head gets blown off, right?'

Reed sank back into his chair, his gaze still fixed on

the guards. Robert Murtaugh spoke up when the rest of the men remained silent.

'What do you want from us?'

Joaquin theatrically searched the ceiling above them as though for inspiration, before replying. He's enjoying this, thought Aubrey.

'By now, it's obvious to you all that I have asked you here because I know what will happen to you all in the near future. I selected you based on your imminent vulnerability, to allow me a certain amount of leverage, lest your dirty little secrets get out to the wider public. However, I also have the means to allow all of you to avert disaster. Just as I know what will happen, I also know something of *how* it will happen, and I am willing to share with you the means to prevent disaster from shattering your privileged little lives.'

Harry Reed's eyes narrowed. 'In return for what, exactly?'

Joaquin smiled again.

'Your undivided support. It is my intention to change the face of our world and I shall do it first by generosity and then by guile. Our world is a dangerous place, and we must ensure that American superiority over both our enemies and our allies remains secure.'

'I thought you were all for *charity*,' Murtaugh sneered. 'Didn't you want to save Africa last year?'

'I did, and I still do,' Joaquin said, 'but not at the expense of our own country. Charity starts at home, my mother used to say. I see no sense in shoring up another nation only for it to become more powerful than our own. We help them, but on our own terms by ensuring that they remain subservient to the United States.'

'And how, exactly, are you intending to go about this little scheme of yours?'

Aubrey felt a shiver of concern at the speed of Joaquin's apparent mood swings, and the audacity of his claims. Joaquin was all charm again, now that he had gained the complete attention he so obviously craved.

'Simple. At the next presidential primary we will all be backing Governor James MacKenzie, who will run for the office of the president of the United States.'

The men looked at each other quizzically before MacKenzie stood up.

'If it's power that you want, why don't *you* become the president?'

Joaquin laughed and waved the governor off with one hand. 'Do you have any idea how many hours the president has to work? The paperwork they have to deal with? The stress? Most of them age by a decade in their first term. The hell with that. You can do the donkey work, James.' Joaquin's cheery smile turned cold. 'But you'll be working for me, as will your entire administration. From my position as a *silent partner*, shall we say, I will be able to shape this great nation using a force no man on earth has ever wielded before: the power of presentiment, the ability to look into the future and act upon what I see.' Joaquin looked down at his guests and smiled with supreme confidence. 'I, alone, will be invincible.'

The guests exchanged looks of incredulity before Murtaugh spoke again.

'I don't know whether to believe you or not, Abell, so before we go any further I want to know that you can prevent any of us from falling. You say you can see into the future and that you want our help? Prove it.'

Joaquin surveyed the guests with a serious expression, and then nodded.

'That, gentlemen, has been my intention all along. I will show you this afternoon, aboard my yacht, the *Event Horizon*. I take it that all of you will be able to make space in your diaries?'

One of the gathered men, a property developer named Benjamin Tyler, stood up from the group.

'No, I won't,' he muttered. 'I don't care what you've got on these guys, there's nothing for me to fear from you, Joaquin. I haven't slept with anyone other than my wife, I haven't cheated anybody, lied to people or swindled anyone out of money. So what the hell am I doing here?'

Joaquin sighed and his face fell as he looked at Tyler.

'You're not here because you've muddied your reputation, Benjamin. You're here because you have only months to live, and I'm hoping that I can help you.' Tyler's anger dissipated as he stared at Joaquin, who spoke softly. 'I will show you at the yacht. Be there at three o'clock, please.'

17

CAPE CANAVERAL

June 28, 10:42

'What do you mean the code *is* the names?'

Lopez moved to stand beside Ethan and looked at the list.

'They're all recorded as surnames,' Ethan said, 'except these two.'

He flipped between the pages and pointed to two of the names.

'Nancy . . . and William,' Lopez read.

Ryker peered over the top of the diary, then grabbed his cellphone and began typing in the phone number alongside the name Nancy.

'Let's see who's home,' he suggested, and held his cell to his ear.

After a few moments he lowered the phone again and shook his head.

'Number doesn't exist,' he said.

'Try the other one,' Ethan said, gesturing to the name William and reading the number out. Moments later, Ryker shook his head again.

Ethan thought for a moment. Charles Purcell had gone to great lengths to leave codes behind at his apartment, but then had left a blatant message for Ethan scrawled in big letters across his wall. As Lopez had said, it seemed as though he were both leaving a trail for Ethan and at the same time attempting to conceal what his intentions were from other as-yet-unnamed individuals, presumably those who he said intended to murder him.

'You guys got a notepad?' he asked Ryker, who handed him a pad and a pen.

Ethan wrote down the two numbers and stared at them for a few moments.

Nancy: 25 443 592. William: 79 510 890.

'Those codes don't match any region in the United States,' Doug Jarvis said as he looked down at the numbers. 'Could be international.'

'I doubt it,' Ethan replied. 'I think they denote something else.' He looked up at Ryker. 'You said that you might have some idea of how Charles Purcell could see into the future. This would be a good time to share it.'

'It's really radical stuff,' Ryker muttered, 'things that Charlie's father, Montgomery Purcell, was working on back in the day.'

'How far back?' Lopez asked.

'The Manhattan Project,' Ryker said.

'The building of the first atomic bombs,' Ethan said, recognizing the name of the project that resulted in America dropping the bombs on Hiroshima and Nagasaki in Japan and ending the Second World War.

'Charlie's father was one of the scientists who helped build the weapons,' Ryker confirmed. 'They were using the results of theoretical physics based upon Albert Einstein's field equations, his work on Special and General Relativity. These equations predicted that the energy contained in atoms, if released, would be more powerful than any other kind of bomb in existence at the time. Turned out he was proven right, yet again.'

'So Charles Purcell's father was working on something else at the same time?' Jarvis hazarded.

'Just after the war,' Ryker replied. 'Montgomery Purcell took the field equations much further than anybody else had dared. Using theoretical physics that, frankly, we still don't quite understand today, he began a thought experiment that devised a means of using gravity to affect the flow of time.'

'How?' Ethan asked, intrigued.

'Well,' Ryker said, 'his idea was to place some kind of camera aboard a spaceship and send it into orbit around the sun for long periods of time at a very high velocity. The camera, which would require a very high resolution, would be pointed back at earth. The ship would then return to earth, and the record of its cameras would be analyzed: the idea was that the high velocities and close presence of the sun's immense mass would allow the cameras to peek into earth's future, just by a few minutes.'

Ethan digested the idea slowly.

'Would it have worked?'

'No,' Mitch Hannah cut in. 'The distance from earth to the orbiting camera would have negated any advantage in time because there was no way of getting the information instantaneously back to earth. That's something that Einstein also predicted correctly – that information, which is what light effectively carries, cannot breach the laws of causality.'

Lopez frowned in confusion.

'Which laws are they?'

'Simply put,' Ryker explained, 'it means that, in our universe, *cause* cannot precede *effect*, otherwise our lives would be filled with paradoxes, so therefore time travel is not possible. So the old example goes, if I were to travel back in time and kill my grandparents before they could meet and give birth to my parents, then I myself could not exist and therefore could not have travelled into the past in the first place.'

Lopez blinked. 'Sure, but what kind of idiot would go back in time and erase themselves? The paradox is pointless.'

Mitch Hannah smiled ruefully.

'Cause cannot precede effect, that much is true, but it's also true that although the speed of light cannot be exceeded, if one were to travel at *close* to its velocity, on a big journey around the galaxy, for instance, then upon your return to earth far more time would have passed for people here than on your spaceship. If you travelled for one week in your own time at that velocity, when you returned to earth one hundred years would have passed by. You would have genuinely travelled into the future. The speeds required are far beyond our technology now, but the physics is well understood and the potential effects solidly proven.'

Ethan looked thoughtfully down at the diary in his hand.

'Charles Purcell wouldn't have had to go that far,' he pointed out. 'Judging from what he's done so far, he might only have had to see twenty-four hours into the future.'

'But if he could see that far into the future, why didn't he prevent the murder of his family?' Lopez asked. 'Surely that would have been his priority?'

'It would have been,' Ryker confirmed. 'He loved his family, just like I said. Something, somehow, must have prevented him from reaching them in time. He somehow saw what was going to happen, then tried to prevent it but failed.'

Jarvis walked up and down with his hands in his pockets as he tried to fathom what Charles Purcell had done.

'And the diary proves that, however he's managed to see the future, it's real. Otherwise he can't possibly have known that you'd come here, not when he posted the diary before he wrote the messages on the wall of that apartment. Even then, he can't have known which path you might take in this investigation. Coming here was only one of many different options.'

Ethan looked at the diary in his hand and then at the numbers he'd written on the pad.

'Which brings us back to the telephone numbers,' he said. 'They must mean something.'

Sears rubbed his temples with one hand.

'Most of this stuff is frying my brain. God only knows what Purcell is thinking or where the hell he was when he posted that diary.'

A moment of silence passed, and then Lopez stared at the numbers again as a little light of realization flickered within the darkness of her eyes.

'*Where* he was,' she said.

'What?' Ethan asked, excited that she might have made a breakthrough before him.

'They're not telephone codes,' Lopez replied, and reached up to tap her knuckles on Ethan's head. 'Don't tell me you can't see it.'

Ethan counted the number of digits in each telephone number, and the answer instantly leapt out at him. 'Damn, it's right in front of us.'

'Care to share?' Mitch Hannah uttered, looking at each of them in turn.

'Nancy,' Lopez said to Mitch, 'William. Don't you get it? Why he'd mark those names out? To identify which numbers were the codes, it's the only reason.'

Lopez grabbed Ethan's pen and rewrote the numbers beneath the originals on the pad, but this time she spaced the digits differently and changed the names.

North: 25 44 35 .92 West: 79 51 08 .90

'Coordinates,' Mitch Hannah said, before offering them both a wry smile. 'You two should do this sort of thing for a living.'

'Do we have a map?' Ethan asked.

'I'll find one,' Jarvis replied and hurried out of the room.

Ethan turned to Ryker.

'Charles had a glimpse into the future and he's used it

to try to prove his innocence. One way or the other we need to find out how he did it.'

Jarvis came back into the room and handed Ethan a map of Florida. Ethan spread the map out across a nearby table and with Mitch Hannah traced the coordinates out until they found the exact spot. He stood up and frowned, his finger hovering over open water.

'It's out in the Florida Straits,' he said in confusion.

Jarvis moved to stand alongside Ethan.

'On the edge of the Bermuda Triangle,' the old man pointed out. 'Between South Bimini and Florida.'

'Didn't Purcell's father vanish into the Bermuda Triangle?' Ryker asked.

Ethan nodded and looked at Lopez. 'And he's not the only one.'

Lopez saw the connection instantly.

'The downed aircraft, N-2764C. It's gotta be. That's why Purcell left us the airplane's tailcodes in his apartment – for us to be able to identify it and its location.'

'We need to get out there and take a look,' Ethan said, then turned to Jarvis. 'You got anybody able to sail us out there today?'

'I can find someone,' Jarvis promised. 'There's a lot of ex-navy guys running fishing boats down in Miami, people who can keep this discreet.'

'We've got to follow this trail,' Lopez said. 'We need to find out whatever it is that Charles Purcell wants us to see.'

Ethan looked again at the message in the diary.

'And we need to find out who Ivy Mike is and locate him,' he said.

Mitch Hannah chuckled as Ethan looked quizzically up at him.

'*Ivy Mike* is not a person,' Mitch said. 'It's the code name for an event, the first ever detonation of a thermo-nuclear fusion bomb by the United States, back in the Cold War.'

'Just like the first atomic bombs of the Manhattan Project,' Lopez said. 'But why would an event from that era have any bearing on what Charles Purcell is doing?'

Ryker leaned back against the edge of the table as he tugged at his beard.

'It's not about Charles,' he replied. 'Charlie wasn't involved in the Ivy program, he's too young. But he inherited his mathematical genius from his father, Montgomery Purcell.'

'Who was a NASA scientist too,' Ethan recalled.

'He was one of the chief scientists who worked on *Ivy Mike* and the United States' entire thermonuclear program during the fifties,' Ryker confirmed. 'He was a pioneer, one of the greatest physicists to have come out of the Manhattan Project.' Ryker looked up at them. 'Charlie's telling us that if we want to find out what's going on here, we need to find out exactly what his father was doing during the Cold War.'

'Get on it,' Jarvis ordered him. 'Find out everything you can on Montgomery Purcell. Ethan, Nicola, with me. We're going to find that downed aeroplane.'

18

MIAMI TERRACE REEF, FLORIDA STRAITS

June 28, 10:51

'I want to know exactly what's going on here.'

Dennis Aubrey joined Joaquin Abell on the quarter-deck of the *Event Horizon* as the engines churned the crystalline waters of the Florida Straits and rotated the yacht gracefully into the current, her captain skillfully programming the engines to maintain precise position in waters too deep for an anchor. Large enough for a heli-copter pad to be located near the stern, the vessel shone a brilliant white beneath the sun. Aubrey watched as dozens of crewmen in identical, dark-blue IRIS jump-suits swarmed down from the bridge to where a pair of large, bulbous-looking craft sat on the open deck.

'All in good time, Dennis,' Joaquin replied as he surveyed the yacht.

The deep-sea submersibles – named *Intrepid*, and *Isaac*, after Joaquin's father – were painted a bright orange and consisted of three large oval chambers, each tightly connected to the other and festooned with a complex assembly of robotic arms, multi-directional propellers, lights and small portholes of 6-inch-thick glass. The bow sphere was dominated by a single, larger acrylic dome, within which Dennis could see the cockpit. The craft had the appearance of giant, brightly colored insects.

'I've never done this before,' Aubrey pointed out.

'Don't fret, Dennis. It's perfectly safe, although at a depth of two thousand feet it only takes a crack two microns thick to collapse the hull and kill everybody inside.'

Dennis shot Joaquin a glance of concern. Joaquin burst out laughing and clapped his hand on Dennis's back with enough force to dislodge his spectacles.

'Relax, Dennis. The *Isaac* and the *Intrepid* are as safe as can be. Come on, let's go, shall we?'

Aubrey straightened his glasses and followed as Joaquin strode across to the *Isaac* and climbed a ladder set alongside the hull toward an open hatch above the central oval. Aubrey reluctantly followed the younger man down into the cramped interior, which was filled with a dazzling array of equipment and instruments. Joaquin made his way forward into the cockpit and settled down behind the control console as Aubrey joined him in the cockpit and strapped himself into a spare seat.

Behind Aubrey, more men dropped down into the submersible. They wore the same blue jumpsuits as their comrades aboard the yacht, but in addition they carried shoulder-slung M-16 rifles and belt-kits containing spare ammunition clips and grenades. The men buckled themselves into their seats with practiced efficiency. Aubrey stared at them and then at Joaquin, who pretended not to notice his anxiety. Moments later, Joaquin started the submersible's batteries and disconnected the power lines from the yacht as the top hatch was sealed and a large crane hoisted the *Isaac* off the deck and down into the churning ocean.

Joaquin keyed his microphone.

'*Isaac* is clear, batteries operational. Release the harness.'

A dull thump reverberated around the *Isaac*'s hull, and then the submersible sank slowly beneath the waves as Joaquin blew the air tanks. The light from the sky shimmered through the rippling waves above, and shafts of sunlight flickered down past the submersible as it descended into the deep water of the Florida Straits. Aubrey's stomach felt as though it too were plunging into unknown depths, and he felt a slight sweat on his forehead.

Joaquin leaned forward and peered up through the acrylic dome toward the surface to see the *Event Horizon* already underway again.

'We're based near the edge of the Miami Terrace reef,' he explained calmly, 'a large aquatic feature that drops a thousand feet, perfectly concealed from any vessels passing above us.'

'Does coral grow that far down?' Aubrey asked, unable to prevent his voice from twisting an octave higher.

Joaquin smiled. 'It does, but you know by now that we're not here to see coral, Dennis. I just know that you're desperate to find out what IRIS is doing here.'

'You're giving Benjamin Tyler false hope,' Dennis insisted. 'Seeing into the future is not possible.'

'Yes it is,' Joaquin countered. 'As a physicist, you

know that it is possible, provided the right conditions exist.'

'Perhaps, but we just don't have the technology to create those conditions.'

'Don't we?'

Aubrey did not reply, his prodigious intellect distracted as he calculated depth values, speeds and the crushing pressure of the water that would be pressing down upon them in the abyss. At the same time he rifled through the vaults of his mind for some way in which an ordinary man like Joaquin Abell could see into the future.

Outside the bulbous portal the water turned a deep blue and the shimmering curtains of light faded as the *Isaac* plunged into the depths. Joaquin flipped a series of switches above his head, illuminating the interior of the submersible as the ocean outside darkened until it became as black as ink. A lone manta ray glided past, glowing in the *Isaac*'s lights as though illuminated by a full moon on a dark night, only to fade into the darkness as it swam effortlessly away.

Aubrey could see that Joaquin was guiding the *Isaac* toward the edge of the reef shelf, following a magnetic compass and a GPS locator screen to find his way in the absolute blackness. As they reached a depth of two thousand feet, Joaquin fired the external thrusters and advanced slowly through the impenetrable darkness until, ahead, a dim galaxy of lights appeared, glistening like stars in an immense night and illuminating the sides of a geometrical object that loomed before them. Aubrey leaned forward to peer through the acrylic bubble, and then his jaw began to fall open as he whipped his spectacles off and stared wide eyed.

'Oh my God, what is that?'

Joaquin guided the *Isaac* toward a bright rectangle of light beaming from beneath the nearest structure to them, perched on the edge of the abyss.

'That, Dennis, is IRIS's Deep Blue research station.'

The vast construction before them resolved itself in the *Isaac*'s glaring lights. A huge interconnecting web of surge-resistant domes, each standing on multiple legs elevating them some twenty feet above the seabed. They glowed with a dull metallic sheen, small lights shining within like the windows of a spaceship that had just set down on the moon. The largest two domes lay close to each other in the center, towering spheres of hexagonal steel panels painted to prevent them becoming fouled with sea growth. Connected to each other by a single steel-reinforced cylinder passage running along the seabed, each of the two main domes was connected by shorter passages on the opposite sides to two smaller domes that formed the four corners of the complex.

Aubrey turned in his seat to look at Joaquin. 'Did IRIS build all of this?'

'Not all of it,' Joaquin replied.

'What have you got in there?'

Joaquin did not reply, piloting *Isaac* low along the surface of the seabed and beneath one of the smaller domes, where a rectangular shaft of light beamed down onto the seabed. The *Isaac* was maneuvered carefully into place, and then Joaquin reached out and flipped a series of switches that released compressed air into the submersible's auxiliary tanks. Slowly, the *Isaac* rose up, and Aubrey watched in fascination as the submersible broke the surface of the water into the center of the dome.

Bright light filtered into the submersible as Joaquin began powering the vessel down. Inside the dome, which looked to Aubrey like a purpose-built dock, IRIS personnel threw lines to secure the *Isaac* before Joaquin shut off the thrusters and the main power.

'Welcome to the safest research base on the planet,' he grinned, climbing out of the captain's chair as his armed security force clambered out of the hull and onto the dock outside.

Aubrey followed Joaquin and stretched his legs as he took in the new and unfamiliar surroundings. The dock was filled with neatly stored fuel lines, oxygen tanks, diving suits and all manner of nautical equipment that fascinated and intimidated Aubrey at the same time. He looked at Joaquin.

'What's this base for?'

Joaquin turned silently and beckoned with a finger for him to follow. Aubrey obeyed and followed Joaquin to a bulkhead that led into an enclosed passage heading toward the larger central domes. Small oval portals peered out into the immense blackness beyond the reinforced walls of the passage, causing Aubrey to shiver as he walked.

'Don't worry, Dennis,' Joaquin said. 'The cylindrical shape of these passages makes them stronger: they are easily robust enough to withstand the pressure.'

'The funds for a complex this size are not present in

IRIS accounts,' Aubrey said accusingly. 'Where on earth did you get the finances to build this place, if not through the company itself? Is this why that family is trying to sue IRIS?'

'All in good time,' Joaquin said. 'Right now, your main concern is providing technical support.'

'For what?' Aubrey asked.

'This way.' Joaquin directed him toward another bulkhead, which opened onto a long curving corridor that seemed to circumvent the first of the larger, central domes.

'What's in there?' Aubrey asked, gesturing to their left as they walked around the perimeter.

'Storage,' Joaquin replied dismissively. 'Some artifacts.'

Joaquin led him around to the passageway that connected the mysterious first central dome to the second, and they hurried through to the entrance hatch of the second main dome.

Aubrey climbed through the hatch, and as he stood up his heart seemed to skip a beat.

Before him was a huge steel sphere that sat in the center of the dome. On Aubrey's left was a curved control panel and walkway that hugged the wall across one half of the dome's circumference, whilst on the opposite side was a row of supercomputers.

An array of ten huge plasma screens dominated the upper circumference of the dome's walls, all staring down toward the sphere in the center. On each screen Aubrey could see news reports beamed from around the world, the anchors reading off autocues and reporters detailing tales of woe from far-flung corners of the world.

The massed voices of the news teams filled the command center with a murmur of commingled words.

Huge electrical cables that ran from the walls of the dome snaked their way toward the center, along with countless wires looped over railings above to descend into the giant sphere.

Aubrey began walking toward the twenty-foot-wide sphere, aware now of a dull humming sound that seemed to reverberate through his chest as he walked. He noticed that the sphere itself was plated with metal devices that he identified as immensely powerful electro-magnets. Aubrey recognized what he was looking at almost instantly.

'A spherical tokamak,' he murmured in fascination. 'Used to control plasma in nuclear fusion experiments.'

A row of small, rectangular observation windows that ringed the circumference of the sphere flickered with eerie bursts of light, as though a thunderstorm was raging within.

'What's inside the tokamak chamber?' Aubrey asked, his gaze fixed on the sphere.

'Don't get too close,' Joaquin warned. 'It's not easy to look inside.'

Aubrey hesitated, but then his curiosity got the better of him and he approached the steps that led up to one of the windows in the surface of the sphere. He noticed as he approached that each of the windows looked out toward one of the plasma screens mounted on the interior of the dome walls.

Slowly, his enraptured gaze fixed upon the flickering lights, Aubrey peered inside the huge sphere, and as he did so he felt his bowels clench and his breath catch in his throat. The tokamak chamber consisted of a vacuum tube surrounded by a series of magnets, normally designed to contain the immensely hot plasma created by nuclear fusion reactions. One set of magnets was wired in a series of rings around the outside of the tube, but unlike normal tokamaks that Aubrey had seen in experimental reactors, the magnets were not physically connected through a common conductor in the center, which normally formed a toroidal chamber through which the plasma flowed. Instead, the central column that usually housed the solenoids was absent, forming a perfectly spherical interior.

The interior of the sphere flickered as jagged sparks of electrical energy leapt and twisted like writhing luminous snakes from the sides of the chamber toward the center. They danced in blue halos around ten video cameras that were mounted on heavily braced metal stands to stare out through the windows toward the plasma screens beyond. Aubrey's face was reflected in the unblinking lens of the nearest camera facing him.

But it was the object in the center of the chamber beyond that captured and held his fascination.

Suspended within hovered a sphere of absolute blackness, a darkness so deep that as Aubrey gazed upon it he felt as though he were plunging into an endless abyss. He realized that the magnetic field generated within the chamber was suspending the sphere in mid-air, unimaginable forces chained and bound by immense electromagnetic fields. Although the sphere was featureless, reflecting nothing, it seemed to pulse with a terrifying energy, as though alive.

Aubrey stared for a moment into that infernal blackness and felt his guts turn to slime. He forced his gaze away, and noticed that up on the inside wall of the sphere was a large analogue clock that looked ordinary in every way except one.

The second hand was ticking far too slowly.

Aubrey turned away from the sphere and felt sweat on his forehead. He knew precisely what the object inside the sphere was, and it terrified him. He turned to Joaquin, his voice constricted.

'My God, what on earth have you done?'

19

SOUTH BEACH, MIAMI

June 28, 10:58

'You sure about this guy?'

Ethan glanced across at Jarvis as he drove the Yukon off North Ocean Boulevard and onto Alton Road. Brilliant sunshine glittered off the manmade harbor that enclosed Palm Island, a haven of multimillion-dollar homes as well as a thriving tourist center. Rows of quays provided moorings to both enormous private yachts and smaller vessels.

Jarvis shrugged.

'He was solid enough back in the day. He's a former United States Navy SEAL who was attached to my rifle platoon in Iraq back in 1991. He left the service a few years back and now runs a fishing business for tourists.'

'You don't sound like you're sure,' Ethan persisted.

'He likes liquor,' Jarvis explained, 'and he never was much one for authority.'

'Sounds like my kind of guy.'

Jarvis turned the Yukon right into Miami Beach Marina and drove slowly to the end, where barricades prevented vehicle entry to the marina. He parked and got out as Lopez shielded her eyes against the glare of the sun.

'That's the one,' she said, pointing at a boat and reading the name on the stern. '*Free Spirit*.'

Ethan led the way as they walked toward the vessel. The little ship looked to Ethan's eye to be a 43-footer sports fisherman, but judging by the stained hull and tired-looking rigging that sagged from her main mast, she'd been plying the Straits since the time of Blackbeard. Chrome fittings were dulled by both age and neglect, and the painted lettering on the stern was flaking away. There were racks of oxygen tanks and diving suits, which would save them having to hire extra gear, and he could see an atmospheric diving suit strapped to a rack near the bridge house. It was over six feet in height and constructed of glass-reinforced plastic; he had seen them from time to time in the US Marines, used by Navy SEALs and depth-rated for around 2,000 feet.

He walked to the boarding ramp and looked at Jarvis.

'You wanna call him out?' he suggested.

Jarvis strode up the ramp onto the vessel's stern. 'Scott? You in there?'

Ethan watched as Jarvis waited for a response, but the only sound remained the lapping of the water against the jetty and the boat's hull. The old man tried again.

'Scott Bryson? It's Doug Jarvis.'

The silence continued. Ethan was about to step forward when a hatch on the *Free Spirit*'s deck suddenly crashed open and a tousled head with a thickly forested jaw popped up to squint at the unexpected visitors. The first thing that Ethan noticed was the black patch covering Bryson's left eye.

'Who?'

'Doug Jarvis, 15th Expeditionary Marines, Iraq. We worked together.'

Ethan watched as Scott Bryson's brow furrowed as though he were trying to remember his own name, and then the eyebrow above his patch arched comically.

'*Captain* Doug Jarvis?'

'The very same,' Jarvis replied. 'Been looking for you, Scott.'

Bryson levered himself up out of the hatch on thickly muscled arms, his chest bare and tanned a deep brown by countless equatorial suns. Ethan guessed him to be at least six-two and 250 pounds, and there didn't look to be any spare fat hanging from his frame. A Navy SEAL tattoo adorned his right shoulder, and despite his unkempt appearance and piratical eye-patch he looked no older than Ethan.

From beside him, he heard Lopez whisper under her breath.

'*Hello*, Captain.'

'Keep it professional,' Ethan uttered from the corner of his mouth. 'We don't know if we can trust this guy yet.'

'Jealous?' she peered up at him, and then pushed past and followed Jarvis up onto the boat's quarterdeck.

Jarvis was already shaking hands with Bryson as Ethan followed Lopez and joined them on the boat. Jarvis introduced them and then gestured to the vessel itself.

'Nice piece, Scott. You been running her long?'

Scott Bryson opened his arms to encompass the vessel, his barrel chest looking to Ethan like the forested slopes of the Rockies in summer, as he launched automatically into a sales pitch.

'The *Free Spirit*'s a day-boat design built for hardcore light-tackle fishing,' he announced. 'Twin diesels at the stern, modern navigational equipment and fish-finding electronics, four fighting chairs and a four-rod rocket launcher. Four live wells and a thirty-foot tower. The head's on board, there's a stereo and comfortable seating. You guys will have a great time. When do you want to book her?'

Jarvis took a pace closer to him. 'Today.'

Bryson laughed out loud.

'I haven't even had breakfast yet, but okay. When do you want to leave harbor?'

'Right about now.'

Bryson's laugh faded away as he leveled Jarvis with a cool stare.

'What are you looking to catch? My tackle ranges from hundred-thirty-pound conventional to six-pound spinning. I can handle live-bait kite fishing, sailfish, shark, golden amberjack, almaco, grouper, and snapper. I've even got electric reels for tilefish, black belly rose-fish, sea bass and barracuda.'

Ethan stepped in.

'We're not hunting fish, we're hunting for a criminal,' he said, 'or more probably the victims of a crime.'

Bryson squinted at Jarvis, who produced a card from his jacket pocket and handed it to Bryson. The big man stared at it, winced and shook his head.

'Defense Intelligence Agency, huh?' he said. 'Sorry, I'm not for hire.'

Bryson turned his broad back on them and strode toward the open deck hatch.

'You got a problem with the DIA?' Jarvis asked after him.

'I got a problem with the government,' Bryson shot back over his shoulder. 'Pack of wolves, all of them. I don't deal with officials. Now get off my boat.'

Ethan stepped up onto the mid-ship deck and moved to stand in Bryson's way. The big man looked down at him as though he were examining a small insect.

'You'd best move,' he rumbled wearily, 'or I'll snap you like a twig.'

Ethan did not reply. Instead, he slipped an envelope from the pocket of his jeans, letting a wad of photographs face out toward Bryson. The image of a young girl with half of her head blasted away was face up. Behind it was the mother's body beside a blood-splattered wall. Bryson squinted at the images and then his cold blue eye fixed onto Ethan's gaze.

'Not my business,' he uttered.

Lopez moved alongside Bryson and gestured to the photographs.

'Nine years old,' she said. 'Last thing she saw was her killer. The father is top of the suspect list but it seems he may be innocent. If we don't prove it and find the real killer, then they'll never be caught. We've got less than nine hours to do that and nobody to help us.'

Bryson looked down at her for a moment.

'Why the time limit?'

'It's a long story,' Ethan said. 'We can tell you all about it on the way but we've got to move fast. You don't want to help us, we'll find somebody who will. But we'd prefer somebody who we know.'

'Yeah,' Bryson said and glanced at Jarvis. 'I bet you would. Easier to control, right?'

'What's your problem, Bryson?' Ethan asked.

Bryson turned and loomed over Ethan. He tapped his eye-patch with one finger.

'Afghanistan,' he growled. 'Lost my eye to shrapnel and damned near lost my life. And what did I get for my troubles? Forcibly retired from my unit and a lousy payoff. This boat was all I could afford to make a living from. And you wonder why I don't want to work for the goddamned DIA?'

'You signed up,' Ethan challenged him. 'What did you expect, a nice cozy desk job in DC? You knew what you were getting yourself into when you joined the SEALs. Standing here crying out of your remaining eye won't change anything. You aren't the only soldier who served out there and you weren't the last.'

'We went in first,' Bryson snapped back.

'Sure you did,' Ethan rolled his eyes. 'You guys did all the hard work and we all came in behind you clapping our hands and singing happy songs.' Ethan's features hardened. 'Wake up.'

'Take a walk,' Bryson snarled as he turned his back on Ethan, his fists clenched.

'What's up?' Ethan uttered. 'Want another medal? Not getting enough sympathy?'

'It ain't sympathy I'm looking for,' Bryson snapped back.

'Then what?' Lopez chimed in as she leaned on the deck railing nearby.

Bryson scowled at them both but said nothing. Ethan guessed that Bryson's physical size and history with Special Forces meant that he wasn't used to people standing up to him, much less challenging him. The injuries he'd sustained in Afghanistan had laden his broad shoulders with a gigantic chip and he felt the world owed him a favor. Like hell.

'I get it,' Ethan said. 'You don't like authority. So what? Do this for the kid who got shot in cold blood.'

Bryson glowered at Ethan for a moment, then turned his good eye on Jarvis. 'What's in it for me?'

Jarvis pulled his cellphone from his pocket.

'I'll call it in, but I'm sure that the agency will compensate you for your services.'

'Ten thousand dollars,' Bryson snapped.

'Ten thousand?' Ethan's jaw dropped open. 'Jesus Christ, we could hire an aircraft carrier for less!'

'Then go ahead,' Bryson smiled without warmth.

Lopez leveled Bryson with an appealing gaze.

'This is about finding a cold-blooded murderer, Scott,' she said. 'A child killer.'

Bryson nodded.

'That's why my fee is ten thousand. You want me to risk my neck looking for somebody who's psychotic enough to kill entire families then don't expect me to do it for goddamn charity. Take it or leave it.'

Jarvis, his cell to his ear, mouthed across at Bryson. 'Five thousand.'

'Eight.'

'Six.'

Bryson shook his head. 'Seven, not a cent less and up front.'

Jarvis sighed and relayed the price down the line. Moments later, he tossed the cellphone to Bryson who caught it in one giant, calloused palm.

'Done, seven thousand, but half now and half when we return to port,' Jarvis said. 'Give them your account details then get this boat out to sea.'

Bryson gave his details across the line and tossed the cell back to Jarvis. As the old man caught the phone, Bryson jabbed a finger in his direction.

'Just so we get one thing straight, that's the last time you tell me what to do on my boat. I'm the captain and I'll give the goddamned orders until . . .'

In perfect unison, Ethan and Lopez moved to stand between Bryson and Jarvis, cutting the big man off in mid-sentence. Ethan spoke quietly.

'Since you just got paid, this is *our* boat. You do what *we* say, right up until we're done here.' Bryson opened his mouth to argue but Ethan cut him off again. 'And you forgot to ask how long this would take. As far as I'm concerned this boat's ours for at least seven thousand dollars' worth of our time, whether you like it or not, understood?'

Bryson's thick arm moved to grab Ethan's throat, but Lopez stepped in and caught his wrist with just enough force to stop it as she folded her hand over his fingers and pinned Bryson's thumb back. She held it just on the threshold of real pain and looked up at him.

'I wouldn't do that if I were you. You'll get hurt.'

Bryson sneered at Ethan. 'He's nothing.'

'I wasn't talking about him.'

Bryson looked down at Lopez for a long moment and then a broad smile broke across his face and he laughed out loud.

'Don't tease me, honey.'

Jarvis stepped up to join them.

'Let him go Nicola,' he said, 'you don't know where he's been.'

Lopez stepped back and released Bryson's huge fist, the captain still grinning down at her. Ethan, feeling strangely excluded, jabbed a thumb at the mooring lines as he turned to Bryson.

'Jump to it, Captain Sparrow, we've got work to do.'

Bryson pretended not to hear, keeping his gaze on Lopez.

'So where are we sailing to, sweetheart?'

Lopez pulled out the scrawled notes Ethan had made back at Cape Canaveral and handed them to Bryson. He looked down at the coordinates.

'Barely an hour away,' he said. 'Any idea on the catch, exactly?'

Ethan unwound a mooring line from the jetty and replied over his shoulder.

'An aircraft.'

20

IRIS, DEEP BLUE RESEARCH STATION, FLORIDA STRAITS

June 28, 11:01

Joaquin Abell strode up the steps to the metal chamber and rested his hand on Aubrey's shoulder. The smaller man turned to look up at Joaquin, his features frozen with horror.

'It can't be,' he uttered.

Joaquin smiled. 'It is.'

Aubrey looked again into the chamber, at the terrible black sphere and the clock with the slowly ticking second hand.

'It's producing time-dilation,' he whispered.

'Congratulations Aubrey,' Joaquin said, 'you are one of only a handful of human beings to have ever gazed with their own eyes into the past.'

Aubrey turned from the window.

'It's impossible,' he uttered. 'You can't possibly have achieved such energies. It would take a particle accelerator the size of our solar system to generate enough pressure to produce this. Human technology doesn't even come close to what would be required to . . .'

'I have not used a particle accelerator,' Joaquin assured him. 'There are other ways to create a device like this, if you know where to look.'

'But you're not a scientist,' Aubrey protested, 'so how could you have . . . ?'

'I have people,' Joaquin cut him off again. 'People who know how to achieve the impossible.' He gestured to the chamber before them. 'Have you even thought about where we are, right now?'

Aubrey stared around him at the huge dome. As he focused on his surroundings and took in the immense superstructure around them, he began to realize that it looked old.

'We're in the Florida Straits,' he replied, 'maybe half-way between the coast of Florida and South Bimini.'

Joaquin nodded, his hands behind his back as he spoke.

'We are in a facility that has been here for a very long time, that was once responsible for the disappearance of dozens of vessels and aircraft from the region.'

Aubrey gasped as he realized the connection between Joaquin's immense undersea facility and the sinister device hidden there.

'The Bermuda Triangle,' he said finally. 'We're on the southern tip of it.'

'On the contrary, this *is* the Bermuda Triangle,' Joaquin corrected him. 'This dome is the source of the modern legend, Dennis.'

'Who built this place?' Aubrey asked.

Joaquin looked up at the dome around them.

'My father was responsible for building this central

dome to conduct experiments designed to harness the power of nuclear fusion to build power plants. His official plan was to search for neutrinos, so called *ghost particles* emitted by supernovas. He felt that if he could detect them then he could use what he learned to search for new physics, and acquire the ability to produce nuclear fusion – to generate a star on earth and use the resulting immense power to fuel our civilizations for a near-zero cost. He was shut down in 1964 because he couldn't generate enough energy to start fusion.' Joaquin stared into the distance. 'He never got over that. He took his own life a few years later.'

Aubrey looked up at the girders supporting the dome, marked with military-style lettering and US Army motifs. Faded radiation-warning signs plastered the walls, and many of the heavy cables and ventilation ducts were dusty with age.

'You added to his central dome,' Aubrey surmised. 'The military must have left it down here still pressurized.'

'It was used as a storage facility for highly classified military and intelligence materials and artifacts until the 1980s,' Joaquin explained, 'when private enterprise began building submersibles capable of reaching these depths. With the advantage of total security lost, the military mothballed the site. I bought it seventeen years ago and made damned sure that all Pentagon files came with the sale.' He smiled. 'Very few people who worked at this facility are still alive, and those who are have no idea that it's once again occupied and active. I opened the conservation project on the coral reefs nearby in order to place an exclusion zone around the site under the pretence of protecting the rare reefs.'

Aubrey shook his head in wonder.

'You're far enough off the coral reefs that nobody would come out here on the abyssal plain – there's nothing to see at this depth. My God, the Coastguard probably doesn't even know that it's inadvertently protecting this site from discovery.'

Joaquin nodded but did not respond, lost in his thoughts.

Aubrey guessed that it would have taken at least fifteen years to build the underwater facility, under the guise of an IRIS charter to create a wildlife refuge and deep-sea coral-research outpost. The original central dome in which they stood was dominated by the revolutionary spherical tokamak chamber built by Joaquin's father during the Cold War, a device used to contain immense plasma energy and generate intense pressures and temperatures.

Aubrey turned on his heel and looked out at the huge television screens mounted on the interior walls of the dome. The news feeds showed anchors from a dozen different networks revealing the latest events from around the world.

'This is how you did it,' he realized, and turned to the metallic sphere behind him, wherein the slow-running clock ticked. 'This is how you look into the future. Your father built this facility to generate nuclear fusion, but you've taken his work far further than he ever intended. You realize that what you have in there is not a star, Joaquin, and it is not of this earth?'

'This is the only place on earth where the present and the future coexist in perfect harmony,' Joaquin confirmed. 'This single device is worth more than all of the money on earth, and were it known that I possessed such a machine, every government on the planet would send its armies here to take it away from me.'

Aubrey looked at Joaquin and saw the radical glitter back in his eyes. The younger man was not a scientist, and would almost certainly be unaware of the immense power caged just a few yards from where they stood. Like a wayward god idly toying with lightning bolts, Joaquin was unwittingly treading a fine line between power and oblivion. All at once Aubrey realized that the tycoon was telling him something more than just the monetary value of his elaborate contraption.

'What are you going to do?' he asked.

'Ensure that no government, and nobody else, ever dares challenge me,' Joaquin replied.

Aubrey glanced at the nearby sphere and shook his head.

'This is dangerous, Joaquin. Do you know what you've actually got in there, the kind of power you're trying to wield? Nobody can control that kind of—'

'It's under control, Dennis,' Joaquin growled. 'Everything, and everyone, is under control. Do you understand?'

Aubrey stood his ground. 'If you detonated all of the weapons in the United States nuclear arsenal, it would not generate as much energy as you have contained in that one single chamber. You need help with this, Joaquin.'

'Indeed I do,' Joaquin replied. 'And you are my help. Agreed?'

Aubrey's features sagged as he realized that he no longer had any choice.

'Why have you done this?' he asked.

'Because, my friend, if you know the future then you can command the present. This is the key to my success, to our success. Trust me, Dennis, there's no news like tomorrow's news, and we're going to know all of it.'

Aubrey's face grew a shade paler.

'Do you have any idea just how much power that device can generate?'

'I do indeed,' Joaquin replied. 'And we're going to unleash some of that power into the world around us.'

Aubrey suddenly felt cold as he digested what Joaquin was suggesting.

'You're going to use it as a weapon,' he uttered, his throat dry.

'Soon,' Joaquin replied. 'But right now, we're going to take a look into the future.'

21

RICHARD E. GERSTEIN JUSTICE BUILDING, MIAMI, FLORIDA

June 28, 11:03

The cameras started flashing the moment Katherine Abell stepped from the chauffeur-driven car, surrounded by four heavyweight minders and her husband's security chief, Olaf Jorgenson. The towering court building was opposite the Dade County Pretrial Detention Center, both of them large and imposing buildings connected by an overhead walkway that spanned the entire street and was used to transport inmates from the cells to the courthouse. Hordes of television cameras jostled for position around Katherine as a barrage of questions washed over her.

'Mrs Abell, is it true that IRIS is being investigated by the United Nations for alleged atrocities by its security forces during charitable operations in Somalia?'

'Mrs Abell, do you have any comment on the discrepancies between government-funded IRIS programs in Africa and the Middle East and the reports from people on the ground that the money never gets through?'

'Mrs Abell, do you represent a charity or a business?'

Before the hacks could get too close, the four IRIS

bodyguards formed a human cordon around her and strode unstoppably toward the court building. The crowds of reporters stumbled away as Katherine Abell and her human cordon climbed the steps toward the entrance, where they were ushered into the relative peace within the building.

She breathed a sigh of relief, feeling more comfortable once inside, despite the hustle and bustle of lawyers, police officers, inmates and members of the public shuffling to and fro. The Eleventh Judicial Circuit of Florida, serving Miami-Dade County, was the largest in the state and the fourth largest trial court in the nation, with over a hundred judges serving some two million citizens.

'Please wait here, Mrs Abell.'

An usher directed Katherine and her bodyguards to a wood-paneled waiting room, replete with worn leather seats. As her escorts silently took up positions inside and outside the room, Katherine moved to stand beside a window that looked out across the ocean of television cameras.

Melancholy weighed down on her shoulders as she saw protesters holding placards bearing angry messages. 'IRIS: PROVOKING POVERTY FOR PROFIT'; 'IRIS: THE BIG DECEPTION'; 'IRIS: CHARITY STARTS AT JOAQUIN ABELL'S HOME'.

The Justice Building was the location of the latest legal challenge to IRIS programs, brought by immigrants from East Africa who had obtained US citizenship through the company's free-transport-to-America initiative, and had then promptly sued IRIS for breaches of their human rights. Katherine's heart sank as she thought of Joaquin's efforts to bring comfort to thousands of otherwise-doomed people, to bring them out of a medieval darkness of suffering and starvation and into the light of a modern democratic nation, only for them to turn the might of that nation's laws against him. She could scarcely believe that these people, liberated from a life spent on their knees groveling for scraps on the dusty plains of failed states, could so easily turn against their savior.

A lawyer before she had met Joaquin, she had watched as the company faced more of these suits every year, brought by those who had once hovered on the brink of death and who now looked forward to hundreds of thousands of dollars of *compensation* for their affronted human rights. This time, she intended to defend IRIS, and Joaquin, herself.

'Mrs Abell?' Katherine turned to see Peter Hamill approaching her. 'The court is ready.'

Peter, her assistant, was in his forties, with wispy blond hair, pale skin and a soft, unassuming voice that made him seem more like a choirboy than a successful lawyer in his own right. His wan appearance belied a sharp and inquisitive mind.

'Let's go and see what they have to say then,' she said, and gestured for Peter to lead the way.

Katherine strode out of the waiting room and followed Peter into an elevator for the trip up to a court on the seventh floor.

The public gallery faced a broad mahogany-paneled bar, behind which was a leather seat that would be occupied by the judge. An ornate curtained door in the wall behind the bar allowed easy access for the judge, avoiding the public entrance to the court. The door was flanked by the Stars and Stripes on the left and the court's emblem on the right.

Katherine strode confidently into the court and immediately heard a torrent of whispers from the gallery as the public recognized her. She sat down, and moments later the court rose as the judge glided in through the curtained door and took her seat behind the bar. She wasted no time in beginning as the court settled back down.

'The court is to hear opening arguments for Uhungu versus IRIS. Will the prosecution stand?'

Katherine watched as the chief prosecutor, Macy Lieberman, took the stand. Macy was an African American and a bleeding-heart liberal from California, who built many of her cases on her supposed *personal* understanding of immigration issues: her ancestors had been shipped to America in 1854 aboard a slaver from the Ivory Coast. Only four out of seventeen had survived, a story she never stopped telling anybody who hadn't already heard it. The fact that virtually every African American living in the continental United States could trace their ancestry back to slaves seemed to have escaped her, along with the fact that the Union they both now served had risen from the ashen battlefields of a Civil War fought to liberate those same slaves.

Macy Lieberman knew how to swing a jury, or a judge, with her sob stories. Katherine steeled herself as Macy addressed the court.

'Ladies and gentlemen, your honor,' she began in her sweet voice, flashing a bright smile. 'This case is being brought by a family who have been deeply wronged by a government-funded charity that serves not the people it purports to protect, but the people who own it. My clients, the Uhungu family, did not wish to bring this case to the courts, preferring instead to deal directly with IRIS itself. However, after two years of having their questions and concerns rebuffed, they feel that they have no choice but to bring their case into the judicial system.'

Macy Lieberman let the court digest this information before she continued.

'This is not the first time such a case has been brought against a major company. It has, in recent years, emerged that there is a trend within modern Western government to devise means by which to prevent the development of Third-World nations, in order that the military and economic superiority of the aforementioned Western nations is maintained.'

Katherine's eyes widened and before she could stop herself she was on her feet.

'Conjecture, your honor. Unspecified accusations beyond the scope of this case.'

'Upheld,' the chief justice agreed.

Macy Lieberman shot a sideways glance of irritation at Katherine, but she composed herself and went on.

'Then allow me to rephrase the point in hand,' she purred. 'In recent years, almost all government programs used to rebuild foreign countries such as Iraq, Afghanistan and so on have been placed in the hands of private companies which use funds provided by the taxpayer to help those in greater need. The problem is that they withhold the vast majority of those funds, usually blaming terrorist or insurgent activity for the lack of progress. Rebuilding comes to a halt, troop numbers are reduced after years of fighting and the companies then cite security concerns before pulling out, taking the majority of the rebuilding funds with them. It is a fact that before the US military went into Iraq it required little rebuilding at all. Billions of dollars were provided to restructure the country, but only a fraction of that funding reached the populace.'

Macy gestured behind her.

'This family was rescued from certain death by IRIS from the streets of Mogadishu. They have absolutely nothing but the utmost respect for what the company did for them.' She looked across at Katherine. 'What they cannot believe is that they are almost entirely alone: that their friends and families have known no such support from IRIS, a fact deliberately avoided in IRIS press releases which give the impression that hundreds have been liberated from squalor and conflict around the world. In fact, as far as we are aware, the Uhungu family is the only family *ever* to have been liberated by IRIS from East Africa in the last five years, to great media applause and propaganda generated by IRIS itself. It is our contention that IRIS has misappropriated taxpayers' funds in the same manner as so many other corporations over the last decade, in a never-ending cycle of palm-greasing and corruption.'

Katherine's eyes narrowed. There was no telling where Lieberman might have gotten such an idea: it might even be true, as IRIS's main focus was on provid-ing the resources for the *survival* of native populations, not spiriting individual families overseas to new lives. Most Africans did not want to live in another country, but rather wanted their own countries to have the same quality of life as those in the West.

'The court was persuaded to hear this case,' Macy went on, 'based on documents collected by the Uhungu family proving that IRIS claims of liberating countless lives in Somalia were falsified: that the monies provided by the taxpayer to IRIS has instead apparently vanished into thin air, and that IRIS has steadfastly refused to provide accounts that they claim show where the money was spent.'

With that, Macy Lieberman sat down.

The chief justice glanced across at Katherine.

'Will the defense stand?'

Katherine stood up and opened her casebook. Although she knew the case inside out, it was always good practice to have everything to hand. In the past some litigators she had faced had taken this as a sign of weakness. They had soon regretted it.

She cleared her throat, and began.

'Uhungu versus IRIS is a case built around the charge that the aforementioned company has failed in principle to uphold its duty of care to the extended family of the Uhungus, who were transported from East Africa to the United States. It is the position of my client, and the position that I intend to defend, that without the intervention of IRIS in the first place, these individuals would have no case to bring, as they would have neither the means nor the legal structure to do so.' Katherine let her gaze fall on the families in the gallery who had brought the case. 'In short, your honor, the complainants are lucky to be alive at all, and can only bring this case to the courts because of IRIS's generosity in saving their lives in the first place.'

'That's bullcrap!' A flabby, gray-haired old lady leapt up out of her seat and pointed a finger at Katherine. 'We din' wanna bring no case at all, but you forced us into it!'

The judge slammed a hammer down and glared up at the old lady, who Katherine recognized as Jala Uhungu, the matriarch of the family.

'Ma'am, may I remind you that this is a court. If I hear any further interruptions I will have the session dissolved and continue this case in private, is that clear?'

Jala Uhungu trembled with suppressed rage and tears quivered in her eyes, but she obeyed the judge and sat back down. Katherine watched as she dabbed at her eyes with a tissue and wondered at her audacity: that she could act so enraged and deprived when just years before she had been found by IRIS's representatives delirious with fever on a dusty street in Mogadishu, surrounded by her starving grandchildren.

'You may continue,' the Chief Justice said.

Katherine changed tack and turned the outburst to her advantage.

'It is not beyond our capacity as human beings to realize that, whilst one family has been saved, many others still suffer, and that this supposed injustice can create considerable outrage amongst those with a voice and a means to make themselves heard. But IRIS is just one company, and even were it to donate its entire assets it would be unable to make any noticeable difference to the sheer weight of suffering in the world. Contrary to the prosecution's claims, IRIS's charter is not designed to bring impoverished families from foreign countries back into the United States — such acts only occur spontaneously when it is clear that the suffering of those families is such that they cannot possibly survive their predicament. Such was the case with the Uhungu family.'

Katherine paused, glancing down at her notes.

'IRIS's chief objective, as laid out in its charter, is to use government funds to enable the people of foreign countries to help *themselves*, to give them the tools and the resources to build their own future. In this, IRIS has been spectacularly successful. In ten years of operations, IRIS has committed over one hundred million dollars to rebuilding programs across Africa, the Middle and Far East and the Malay Archipelago. Hundreds of thousands of lives have been saved by vaccination programs, freshwater wells, family-planning and contraception initiatives and grain supplies organized and delivered by IRIS.' Katherine looked directly at the Uhungu family. 'I apologize, on behalf of the company, if you somehow feel as though your extended family have been cheated in life by our work, or even if the burden of regret you feel for having been liberated in preference to others who still suffer seems too heavy. But IRIS is not to blame for the ills of countless countries across the world. It is a force for good, and I say again, with the deepest respect, that without it, none of you would be sitting here today.'

Katherine stood back from the bar and walked quietly across to her seat. She had barely sat down when Macy Lieberman's petite voice tinkled across the court.

'An emotive performance, Mrs Abell,' she said, 'delivered with all the conviction of a woman married to the owner of IRIS himself.'

A ripple of laughs fluttered across the public gallery.

Katherine did not react and simply read through her notes. Macy Lieberman's voice might dance lightly through the court but her words stung like a hornet.

'However, we have proof that of the 117 million dollars provided by government in approved contracts over the last five years, just twelve million dollars have reached the people who needed it most. The rest, it would appear, has simply vanished.'

Katherine sat bolt upright and looked directly at Macy.

'Where on earth did you drag that rubbish from?'

Macy Lieberman smiled and held up a slim blue folder.

'It would appear, Mrs Abell, that somebody in your company does not want Joaquin Abell's little operation to continue unchallenged any longer. Our prosecution has in the past been repeatedly blocked and hindered by IRIS's determination to prevent public access to its accounts despite considerable evidence on the ground in foreign countries of its failure to use those taxpayer funds for their assigned purpose. These extremely detailed files were received yesterday morning at my office, sent by UPS. They reveal the *true* extent of IRIS's fraudulent use of state money and provide the evidence we need to bring the company down.'

Katherine leapt from her seat, a weakness trembling in her knees as she stared at the blue file.

'Veracity?!' she demanded.

'They were provided, and signed, by a former employee of IRIS,' Macy smiled. 'A man you may even know. His name is Charles Purcell.'

22

IRIS, DEEP BLUE RESEARCH STATION, FLORIDA STRAITS

June 28, 11:12

Dennis Aubrey stood beside the control panel and watched as two security guards, their assault rifles strapped to their backs, opened the door to a chamber adjoined to the containment sphere. Joaquin stood to one side and directed their movements. One of the guards turned and picked up a robust-looking remote-control arm from the floor beside him and attached it to two rails secured to the floor of the chamber. The robotic arm carried a video camera attached just below a grappling claw at its head. The security guards closed the chamber's outer door and sealed it.

'Stand back, gentlemen.' The two guards backed away, and Joaquin looked up at Aubrey on the control platform.

'Over to you, Dennis.'

Aubrey took a deep breath and turned to his control panel. There, a television screen showed the view from the front of the remote-control arm. Aubrey checked the instruments and then pressed a button on the console before him. Instantly, the chamber's inner door whined open. Aubrey saw the air rush through the hatch in a whorl of vapor, ice crystals glistening in mid-air as they were whipped away into the main chamber, and then the plunging sphere of blackness within appeared on the screen, its attendant writhing coils of electrical energy snapping between the walls of the chamber.

'Chamber's open,' Aubrey announced. 'Advancing inside.'

He pressed forward on a simple joystick, and the robotic arm travelled along on the rails that prevented it from being hauled into the terrifying heart of the chamber. Slowly, the arm trundled along around the edge of the chamber, passing in front of the mounted cameras within.

'Camera number five,' Joaquin reminded him.

Aubrey considered reminding Joaquin that he could count for himself, but for some reason he feared any reprisal his new employer might concoct. Instead, Aubrey obediently guided the robotic arm to stand in front of camera five.

This camera, Aubrey had learned from Joaquin, was different from the others, in that it did not look at a televised newsfeed. Instead it watched a screen that showed the view from a small buoy bobbing on the surface of the ocean. There was no land visible nearby, nothing to betray where the camera was located.

Carefully, Aubrey used the arm's specially shaped grapple to dismount the camera from its base, and then placed the camera in a storage box on the arm's platform. Then, he picked up the spare camera and secured it to the mount within the chamber before turning it on.

'Well done,' Joaquin clapped. 'Now, let's bring it out shall we?'

Patiently, Aubrey guided the robotic arm along the rails and out of the chamber, making sure to wait for the automatic seal on the inner hatch to activate. As the camera waited in the entrance chamber, jets of steam hissed and enveloped the entire device in thick water vapor that poured onto the floor and drained away into narrow grilles. A precautionary measure, to wash away any particles irradiated by the immense energy within the chamber.

'Clear!' called one of the guards, who was monitoring a Geiger counter.

'Open the chamber!' Joaquin ordered.

The outer doors were opened and Aubrey guided the arm out. Immediately the camera was grabbed by Joaquin, who hurried up to the control panel alongside Aubrey and opened the device, handing him the USB hard drive within.

'Play it,' he ordered.

Aubrey slipped the drive into a player on the console before him, and watched as a pixilated image of the ocean far above appeared on the screen. Flares of white noise from the bursts of electrical energy within the chamber distorted the serene image of rolling waves beneath a cloud-specked blue sky.

'Fast forward,' Joaquin snapped. 'One hundred and twenty times faster.'

Aubrey obeyed, a swift mental calculation informing him that an hour on the camera's accelerated timeline would now pass every fifteen seconds. The rolling sea wobbled and bobbed crazily and the clouds above raced past as the sun arced through the sky. Day turned to night and then the sun returned again. Several minutes had passed before suddenly a white boat zipped into view and quivered on the waves in the center of the viewfinder.

Joaquin hit the 'Play' button. Aubrey watched as a small fishing vessel, maybe forty feet long, sat on the surface of the ocean with its anchor chain taut. He realized that the images were still moving at double speed, the same rate at which the camera recorded time passing outside of the chamber. Several figures milled rapidly about on the deck, and then quite suddenly two of them dropped overboard into the rolling blue waves.

They were wearing diving gear, Aubrey realized.

'Damn!'

Joaquin slammed a fist against the console and whirled to look at Aubrey.

'When will this happen?' he demanded.

Aubrey blinked, caught completely off guard by Joaquin's sudden agitation. 'When was the camera inserted into the chamber?'

'Twenty-four hours ago!' Joaquin raged. 'You're the physicist, do the math! Shall I fetch you a fucking abacus?'

Aubrey flushed red, as a sickening mixture of fear and anger swilled through his guts. His earlier ominous instinct about Joaquin's intentions now flared grotesquely. Joaquin had brought him down here along with ten armed guards. There was no escape except via the submersible. He was trapped. Aubrey's sense of self-preservation barged its way into his thoughts. *Humor the guy, keep yourself out of trouble, and then get the hell out of here as soon as you can.*

He looked at the camera image, his mind racing with numbers. The camera had been installed twenty-four hours earlier. The Schwarschild Radius of the object in the chamber and its attendant time dilation of one hour for every hour that passed meant that the camera had therefore seen a total of twenty-four hours into the future. They had then sped forward the first few hours before seeing the boat appear on the screen.

'It'll happen within an hour,' Aubrey said, before looking at Joaquin. 'Where is the camera that took this film?'

Joaquin did not respond. Instead, he turned to his security team.

'Get out there. I want those people gone before they can find anything, understood?'

The security guards dashed away, un–slinging their rifles as they ran. Aubrey watched them go and then turned to Joaquin. He mastered his revulsion and fear, his vocal cords tight as he spoke.

'Joaquin, if you want me to control this device of yours and do an effective job, then you need to tell me what the hell's going on here.'

'You're on a need-to-know basis,' Joaquin retorted as he walked away.

'You're looking into the future but you don't know what you're seeing!' Aubrey shot back, and for a brief instant was surprised at the force of his own outburst.

Joaquin turned slowly back to face Aubrey. 'What do you mean?'

For a moment, Aubrey wondered whether he should tell Joaquin anything. The arrogant fool was playing a dangerous game that could have far greater consequences than his narcissistic little mind could ever imagine. But then an image of Katherine and the two children popped into Aubrey's mind and he realized that he had no choice. Somehow, he had to get word out about what was happening.

'Time,' he said slowly, 'is not fixed. It can change.'

Joaquin's face twisted into a scowl of outrage and he leapt forward, grabbed Aubrey by the throat and pinned him against the console. Aubrey smelled a waft of expensive cologne as Joaquin's soft hands squeezed tightly around his throat and he leaned in close, a madman cloaked in the finery of a king.

'You think I have time for this? I know that time isn't fixed! Purcell explained it all to me!'

Aubrey, his skin sheened with sweat, decided not to tell Joaquin what Charles Purcell had clearly omitted. Instead, a plan began to form in his mind as he struggled to speak.

'I need more access to what these cameras are seeing!' he gargled. 'One image of the future means nothing. What if those people on that screen are just holidaymakers? You send your people in there with guns they'll do nothing but expose your operation!'

Joaquin, his grip still fixed on Aubrey's neck, peered sideways at the screen showing the boat on the ocean.

'They're not day-trippers,' he uttered. 'They're diving on a barren sandbar miles out to sea. There's nothing there.'

Aubrey managed to speak.

'Yes there is, and whatever it is you don't want it found, do you?'

Joaquin's gaze moved back to Aubrey. The anger in his eyes mutated into something new, a look of bemusement. Aubrey felt the vice around his neck slacken and he coughed to clear his throat. He heard Joaquin's voice above his own labored breathing.

'You surprise me, Dennis. For a while I believed that you were *entirely* spineless.'

Aubrey slid off the console onto his feet and staggered as he put one hand out to balance himself. With the other, he massaged his neck. Joaquin's grip had been tight, but not *that* tight. Aubrey faked another cough and stared at the deck as he considered what was on the screen. Joaquin's mention of Charles Purcell had sparked a flood of revelations in Aubrey's mind, none of them good. Purcell had been the previous chief scientist at IRIS's supposed coral-reef conservation project, and as a former NASA physicist with a history of studies into time itself, it didn't take much application of Aubrey's prodigious intellect for him to realize that Purcell had in fact been stationed here at Deep Blue. The fact that Purcell had recently vanished and that his family were dead suggested that his fate was less to do with a tragic mental breakdown and more to do with Joaquin Abell.

Aubrey recalled the loss of the chartered Bimini Wings aircraft, along with IRIS's entire scientific team, and a chill ran down his spine and sat, icy and cold, in the pit of his belly. That was probably what was below the water in the camera footage: Joaquin was planning to hide the wreckage. Joaquin Abell took a pace closer to him and pressed a finger hard into his chest.

'If you reveal anything, to anybody, ever, of what you've seen here, I'll make sure that you get a far closer look at that chamber than you'll be comfortable with.'

Aubrey nodded, finally getting his breath back, and glanced down at the control panel. If Joaquin Abell was responsible for multiple murders, then Aubrey had to get word to the outside world. He thought of Katherine, defending IRIS at trial in court, and of the costs associated with building something like Deep Blue. *It's all a lie. IRIS is guilty, and my new employer is a mass murderer.*

Aubrey looked again at the boat bobbing on the ocean. The stern of the little fishing vessel was pointing toward the camera, and he could read her name clearly.

Free Spirit.

23

FLORIDA STRAITS, 14 MILES WEST OF SOUTH BIMINI

June 28, 11:14

'Now we're moving!'

Scott Bryson hauled on a loose rigging line and secured it before ducking back into the wheelhouse. His voice was snatched away by the wind as the *Free Spirit* crashed through the rolling waves, thick clouds of white spray bursting over the bows to sparkle in the bright sunshine.

Ethan reveled in the fresh air as the little ship chugged her way busily out into deep water, her two diesel engines humming below decks. Most all people assumed that he and Lopez spent their time chasing down fugitives and bail runners on foot or in Lopez's Lotus, in the manner of *Miami Vice* or similar. In fact, most of Ethan's days were spent hunkered down behind a computer screen in their cramped office, or with a phone pressed to his ear as he called the fifteenth family member of a vanished convict, hoping for a break in the case.

When they did get out, it was most often to apprehend violent and dangerous criminals, many of whom had nothing to look forward to but decades of incarceration if caught. Needless to say they didn't go quietly. By comparison this was a vacation.

'What's our speed?' he called out to Bryson.

'Fifteen knots!' Bryson yelled back. 'Fastest you've been over water for a while, country boy!'

'We came down here at fifteen *hundred* knots,' Ethan replied. 'But hey, who's counting?'

Bryson shot him an uncertain look and turned his back as he guided the ship toward their destination. Ethan turned and watched as Lopez leaned over the port rail, her black hair rippling in the wind.

'How you feeling?' Jarvis asked her as he swayed unsteadily across the rolling deck and placed a hand on her back.

Lopez peered round at the old man, her face puffy and her eyes narrow.

'You telling me you couldn't have got us out to Bimini any other way?'

'Sorry,' Jarvis shrugged. 'Besides, how the hell was I supposed to know you get seasick?'

Lopez glared across at Ethan. 'He knew.'

Ethan shrugged as Jarvis shot him a dirty look.

'We chased a bail runner out across Lake Michigan a couple of months ago,' he said. 'Lopez got sick – I just figured it was nerves as our mark was armed.'

Lopez winced.

'I got sick *before* the shooting started.'

Bryson vaulted down onto the quarterdeck alongside them, and in one swift move gathered Lopez up in his arms and carried her toward the center of the deck beside the entrance to the wheelhouse. He set her down gently beside the scuba-tank racks, then squatted down in front of her and handed her a bottle of chilled water as he looked at her with one twinkling blue eye.

'Seasickness is just your inner ear playing up because it can't detect the roll and swell of the boat. Sit here, keep yourself hydrated and keep your eye on the horizon. The longer you do it, the quicker your brain will figure out the movement and the quicker the nausea will pass. Got it?'

Lopez managed a weak smile and nodded as she opened the bottle of water. Ethan hurried over.

'How long until we reach the spot?' he asked.

'Twenty minutes or so,' Bryson replied. 'You good to dive?'

Ethan nodded as he glanced at the scuba gear. 'What's the depth?'

'You're lucky,' Bryson informed him. 'The location is just off the Bimini coast on a sandbar near Gun Cay, so you'll be in no more than forty feet with good visibility.'

'I'm coming down too,' Lopez said between sips of water.

'Like hell,' Ethan said. 'You stay up on deck with Long John Silver here until you're back in shape.'

Lopez shook her head.

'It'll give me a break from feeling like crap,' she pointed out. 'Best thing for me right now is to stay busy, right, Scott?'

Bryson shrugged.

'I'd rather have you in sight because I like to look at you, honey,' he murmured. 'But if you want to dive it won't hurt you.'

'Fine,' Ethan said, having decided he'd rather have Lopez where he could see her. 'Let's get suited up. At this supposedly breakneck speed, we'll be there soon.'

Bryson turned to the scuba racks and unhooked the diving suits as he spoke.

'You're quite the comedian, Warner. Guess you must have been the joker in the pack in the Marine Corps. Could have done with a wit like yours in the SEALs, but I guess you were never gonna get that far . . .'

Ethan checked his diving equipment.

'I had my hands full,' he replied. 'I was a platoon officer during Iraqi Freedom and didn't get the chance to join Special Forces. We let the grunts do that.'

'That's what they all say.'

'No, it's not,' Ethan said. 'They all say they got an injury or some crap and were medically discharged from the course. Those that do get through the training develop an inability to stop talking about it, until they no longer need to shoot their enemies. They just bore them the hell to death.'

Bryson burst out laughing, a deep roar from his chest that made Lopez flinch as she was putting on her gear. He settled back down as he checked the oxygen cylinders, looking at Lopez as he worked.

'How'd you end up with this loser?' he asked her.

Lopez zipped up her suit. 'Met him in DC, hasn't left me alone since.'

'Can't blame him.'

Ethan saw that Lopez smiled back, her debilitating sickness apparently now forgotten. He grabbed a set of goggles and tossed them to her before turning to Bryson.

'I take it we're in the Bermuda Triangle here?' he said.

'Just inside it,' Bryson confirmed. 'The generally accepted borders of the Triangle run from Miami to the island of Bermuda and down to San Juan in Puerto Rico.'

'You don't honestly believe in all that crap, do you?' Jarvis asked the captain. 'I've read that this area is one of the busiest shipping and commercial air-traffic lanes in the world.'

'It is,' Bryson replied. 'Statistically there's nothing unusual about the number of aircraft and ships lost in this region. It's considered entirely safe by insurers and such-like, and most of the supposedly mysterious disappearances over the years were not mysterious at all. Various authors simply omitted facts in order to maintain the legend and sell their books.'

'Such as?' Ethan asked.

'Well, they'd tell of ships that had genuinely been reported missing, but not the fact that they turned up in port later. Or they'd write that a vessel vanished in clear weather when in fact it was caught in a storm. Some ships were reported as having been swallowed by the Bermuda Triangle when in fact they'd accidentally slipped their moorings in harbor and drifted out to sea.'

'There must be more to it than that,' Ethan argued. 'You've been sailing out here for a few years – you must have heard or seen things. I can't believe that the whole legend is just a charade.'

Bryson leaned against the bulwarks and squinted out across the ocean.

'You sail around these waters long enough, you see a lot of things you can't explain, but that doesn't mean that what's happening *can't* be explained. The Gulf Stream runs through here and its currents can quickly remove debris from accidents; the weather is unpredictable, with storms arriving and vanishing so quickly that they don't show up on satellite images, and the islands and ocean floor have both shallows and deep marine trenches that produce strong reef currents and a constant flux of moving water, producing regular navigation hazards to all shipping.' Bryson grinned. 'These waters might look pretty, but they're dangerous and unpredictable. It's no wonder that people go missing out here.'

'But . . . ?' Lopez teased him, and Bryson shrugged.

'Fact is, the Bermuda Triangle is one of only two places on earth where a magnetic compass actually points toward true north. If you don't compensate for this lack of magnetic variation, you can end up going off course. The other place where this happens, a region called the Devil's Triangle in the Pacific, is also a place where vessels and aircraft have gone missing, so there's definitely something odd going on out here, even if it's just navigational error.'

Ethan narrowed his eyes.

'But . . . there's something you're not telling, right?'

The captain sighed as he fiddled with an oxygen cylinder.

'There's weird shit happening out here, okay?' he muttered. 'People say that the Triangle's a recent phenomenon, but Columbus himself recorded problems with magnetic readings in his logs back in 1493. There may not be a statistically large number of vanishings out here, but some of those that do occur are real weird.'

'Do tell,' Lopez said, intrigued, as she sipped her water.

'There's a few,' Bryson said. 'A Tudor IV airplane vanished in 1948 with thirty-one people aboard; the freighter SS *Sandra* disappeared without trace in 1952; an English York plane vanished with thirty-three people in 1952; the Navy lost a Lockheed Constellation in 1954 and a seaplane in 1956; that's over fifty people vanished without trace, plus several large freighters from various countries.'

'It's odd that both ships and aircraft disappear,' Ethan said thoughtfully.

'And big ones, too,' Bryson noted. 'A DC-3 with twenty-seven passengers in 1948 and a C-124 Globemaster with fifty-three passengers in 1951. No apparent catastrophes, no radio warnings or distress beacons. They just disappear.'

'What about that Flight 19?' Jarvis asked. 'The Navy bombers that went down back in World War Two?'

'They were supposedly lost due to the formation leader's faulty compass and a storm that prevented them from navigating by eye over the islands,' Bryson explained. 'But the thing is, even if the leader's compass did fail, there were a lot of other airplanes in the flight and they all were in radio contact with Fort Lauderdale until they disappeared without trace. So either a whole bunch of military pilots let their leader fly them into oblivion in a faulty airplane, or something else got them all turned around.'

'Well, whatever happened to this airplane it's now a lot closer to Bimini Island than when it must have gone into the water, probably due to the currents,' Ethan said. 'The pilots would have been able to see land from here.' He looked at Lopez. 'Charles Purcell's coordinates must have taken that into account, which means . . .'

'He saw the future,' Jarvis replied. 'He can't have known how far and in what direction it would have moved without having seen it do so. But that still leaves us with the small question of *how?*'

'Nobody can predict currents in the Straits,' Bryson murmured, 'it's why the search-and-rescue teams never found your missing plane. Who knows how many other ships have disappeared from history out here?'

Ethan looked at Bryson, who was still standing by the bulwarks and staring out to sea.

'Okay, Blackbeard, we must be nearly there by now. Why don't you head up to the wheelhouse and guide us in before the four of us vanish out here, too – unless you're reading the waves or using the Force or something.'

Bryson stood up straight and jabbed his thumb over his shoulder.

'It's over there,' he said without looking. 'Less than two nautical miles.'

'Good.' Ethan clapped his hands together. 'Chop-chop, then.'

Bryson shot him a dirty look as he turned away and jogged up into the wheelhouse. Lopez looked at Ethan as she hauled on her oxygen tanks.

'You should take it easy,' she said. 'He's a big guy.'

'The bigger they are . . .' Ethan murmured.

'The harder they hit you.'

The *Free Spirit*'s chattering engines wound down to a soft chugging as Bryson guided them to the exact coordinates that Charles Purcell had left encoded in his diary. Ethan led Lopez across to the boarding platform at the stern of the boat, Jarvis joining them there. Moments later Bryson shut the engines down to idle and leapt to the bow, hurling an anchor that crashed down into the crystalline water.

Bryson made his way to the stern as the *Free Spirit* turned in the water to face into the current.

'Okay, she's all set. Sonar reads a depth of about six fathoms, and there's definitely something large and metallic down there.'

Lopez gave Bryson a thumbs-up and a wink as she closed her facemask and then rolled over the stern backwards to splash into the water. Ethan cleared his mouthpiece and flipped Bryson a lop-sided salute.

'Keep your eye on things,' he said.

Before Bryson could respond, Ethan flipped himself off the side of the boat and plunged into the waves.

24

FLORIDA STRAITS, 14 MILES WEST OF SOUTH BIMINI

The water of the Florida Straits was filled with shimmering beams of sunlight that pierced the rippling surface above to drift across the seabed below. Ethan watched the beams of light dance like golden snakes on the sand far below as he descended.

Lopez swam alongside him as they leveled out ten feet above the seabed. A flight of manta rays glided past nearby through the immense blue wilderness, and a swarm of brightly colored butterfly reef-fish flitted in a rippling kaleidoscopic cloud through a maze of driftwood trapped by the sandbar.

Ethan glanced up at the surface and saw the *Free Spirit*'s hull above them. Her anchor chain was at a steep angle, the swift current of the straits pulling on her. The solution to the disappearance of wrecked ships and airplanes in the Bermuda Triangle was often painfully simple: people were looking in the wrong place. They could hardly hope to find the plane, even if it had moved just a few hundred meters: even in clear waters, the blue eventually concealed anything more than twenty to thirty meters away, and a grid-pattern search of the seabed would take them months.

Ethan was about to curse himself for not organizing an aerial search first when Lopez signaled to him and pointed into the shadowy blue distance to their right.

Ethan squinted through his face mask and saw a feature barely visible through the gloom, a ghostly object made up of sharp angles that did not exist in nature. It had been a common theme of survival training in the US Marines to maintain a lookout for such features in the wilderness as signs of human occupation. Nature did not build in straight lines but instead used curves, coils and sweeping arcs, the elegant freehand strokes of creation.

Ethan turned toward the object and swam over the rugged driftwood debris and the attendant fish that scattered in shimmering shoals as he passed by. He saw the object resolve itself as the vertical tail-fin of an aircraft, the tail code on the damaged metal easy to read: N2764C.

Lopez gave him a thumbs-up as they approached the aircraft and ascended to glide over the wreckage. Ethan could see that the aircraft had hit the water hard, the aluminum nose crumpled like paper. The windscreen had imploded with incredible force, tearing the cockpit apart, and the wings had been sheared off to lie fifty feet either side of the crumpled fuselage. Both the fore and aft exit doors had been ripped away and also lay crumpled nearby on the seabed. Ethan realized that it was sheer chance that what remained of the aircraft had drifted so far from the point of impact and yet had come to lie upright in its watery grave.

Ethan descended until he was level with the exit and then slowly eased his way inside, careful not to hit his oxygen cylinder on the fuselage wall.

A pair of yellow eyes raced into his face and slammed him backwards as giant fangs scraped like scalpels against his mask, searching for his flesh. Ethan shot a panicked swipe at the creature's head and the barracuda snapped past him and raced away into the deep blue distance. Ethan's heart slammed against his chest as he struggled to get his breathing back under control. Idiot. It had been a long time since he'd dived, and he'd forgotten one of the cardinal rules: never, ever panic underwater.

He checked his watch as a diversion. Lopez watched him with concern and then reached out and squeezed his shoulder. Ethan gave her a thumbs-up and turned again toward the exit hatch to ease his way inside.

The fuselage was filled with fragments of floating debris that gently swayed from side to side as the currents outside heaved and churned. Ethan turned, and as he moved forward he saw rows of bodies still strapped into their seats. Mortified mouths gaped open, bare eye sockets stared sightlessly into oblivion, picked clean by countless fish, and clouds of hair rippled upright from scalps as though still alive.

Ethan saw the crushed cockpit ahead, the bodies of the pilots pinned against the bulkheads by the weight of the instrument panel that had smashed inward upon them. Ethan saw a wavy mass of long blonde hair drifting in the current and felt a surge of anger. Aircraft didn't drop out of the sky for no reason, and he felt certain that Purcell was trying to tell them that this crash was no accident. What Ethan could not tell was *how* the airplane had been brought down.

He turned and headed back out of the fuselage toward the tail, determined now to recover the one thing that could tell the authorities what had brought down the aircraft: the flight-data recorder.

Ethan knew that the device was usually located at the very rear of the aircraft. In this position, the entire front of the aircraft acted as a 'crush zone' to reduce the effects of shock in an impact. Double-wrapped in corrosion-resistant stainless steel or titanium, with high-temperature insulation inside, flight-data recorders were invariably colored bright orange; they were more than capable of withstanding immersion in water at such a depth.

Ethan swam to the rear of the aircraft, alongside the tail section, and looked down.

An open compartment stared back. The flight-data recorder had already been removed. Ethan's conviction that Charles Purcell was an innocent man on a mission for justice – and that this aircraft was a major key to the puzzle – swelled within him. Whatever else happened, he knew that he needed to get to the surface and inform the National Transport Safety Board of the wreck's location, and then get the Coastguard to prevent any further tampering with the evidence at the crash site.

As he looked at the tail, he noticed a thin cable tied to it. His eyes traced the cable upward toward the surface, where it vanished into the blue, but against the rippling sunlight hitting the surface of the ocean far above he could just make out a small buoy.

Ethan turned to indicate the buoy to Lopez, who was

hovering above him in the water. As he did so something zipped past his head at terrific speed, leaving a thin trail of bubbles in the water before burying itself in the aircraft's fuselage, behind where his head had been a moment before.

Ethan whirled in the water as four divers rushed down toward them, each wearing a ducted fan attached to their dive tanks that propelled them effortlessly through the water. Each held a weapon in one hand, and Ethan instantly recognized them as Heckler & Koch P11 underwater firearms. The pistols fired four-inch steel darts from the five barrels that gave the weapon its squat appearance.

Lopez's hand flicked to a knife in a sheath attached to her thigh as she darted away from Ethan, drawing two of the divers and some of the fire with her as she headed toward the front of the aircraft. Ethan turned and grabbed the metal flight-data recorder panel from the seabed before swimming directly at the nearest of their attackers, closing the distance in seconds as the diver plunged down toward him. The diver aimed at Ethan's face and pulled the trigger on his pistol from barely six feet away.

Ethan raised the panel as he saw the steel dart race toward him. The dart hit the panel hard, snapping the metal from Ethan's grip and spinning it away toward the seabed. Ethan caught the spent steel dart and grabbed the diver's pistol arm as he sailed past, yanked along by the power of the fan on his back. Ethan pushed the pistol away and then swung the steel dart over-arm and plunged it into the back of the man's shoulder.

A rush of bubbles exploded from the diver's mask as

he writhed in agony, a cloud of thick blood puffing like red smoke to trail behind them through the clear blue water. Ethan ground the dart around inside the man's shoulder as they rolled upside down, the diver squirming desperately to get away as they plunged down toward the seabed. As the diver looked round and exposed his face, Ethan yanked the dart out of his shoulder and smashed it into his facemask.

The steel dart plunged straight into the man's left eyeball in a cloud of blood and travelled upward to lodge deep into his brain. The diver relinquished his pistol as his hands flew to his face, and then began quivering and jerking as his damaged brain began to shut down.

A steel dart whipped past Ethan's shoulder and smacked into the dying man's chest with a dull thud.

Ethan whirled as a second diver rushed in with his pistol aimed directly at him. Ethan span in a grim pirouette to keep the shuddering corpse between himself and his new assailant. He reached down and grabbed the pistol now dangling from a cord attached to the dead man's utility belt, aiming it even as the second diver realized the danger and struggled to turn away in time to flee. Ethan jerked the dead diver's body around and let the still-running fan propel them in pursuit as he aimed and fired.

The first dart deflected off the fleeing diver's oxygen tank, and Ethan corrected and fired again. This time the dart struck the diver in his side, the metal sinking between his ribs. The man flinched in pain and turned, aiming himself back at Ethan on a collision course.

Ethan released the corpse and let the grisly projectile

plough onward through the water as he swam behind it. The onrushing diver struggled to get out of the way but the corpse plunged into his chest and hurled him out of control as Ethan rushed in and fired the last two remaining steel darts. Both quivered as they sank into the man's flesh, one almost vanishing into his stomach as the other lodged in his thigh.

The diver coiled up into a fetal ball, one hand searching desperately to remove the darts as the other aimed his pistol frantically at Ethan. Ethan yanked his knife from its sheath and smashed the pistol to one side before ramming his blade into the man's skull, just behind his ear. The blade splintered the thin bone and sank hilt-deep into the brain with a muted crunch like a boot on gravel.

Ethan wrestled the pistol from the dead man's hand, yanked the cord free from his belt and turned as he dove once more toward the aircraft wreckage, where he could see Lopez crouched in the buckled remains of the cockpit, using a twisted piece of the nose cone as a shield against the lethal darts being fired at her.

Ethan plunged downward and aimed at the nearest diver, firing a single shot from barely two meters away.

The cruel metal dart zipped across the distance between them and buried itself in the back of the man's head. The diver's body twitched and then froze as he began to sink toward the seabed below, his arms floating uselessly beside his head.

The second diver charged up toward Ethan without a moment's hesitation and plunged into him before he could fire. The impact knocked the wind from Ethan's chest and he choked briefly on his respirator as he struggled to hold the diver's pistol away from his body. They tumbled awkwardly, spinning upside down in a frenzied cloud of bubbles as with one hand the diver tried to rip Ethan's mask from his face. Cold seawater flooded Ethan's vision as he felt himself propelled head-first in a vertical dive toward the seabed.

The sandy surface of the bed slammed into the top of his skull and his attacker landed on top of him and pinned him down, the force of the fan on his back driving Ethan through a choking cloud of sand that swirled in a golden vortex around them. Ethan felt his grip on the pistol fail and then suddenly the weapon slipped from his grasp. He saw the diver jerk upright and aim the pistol at Ethan's heart, the man's eyes shining with hatred behind his mask.

In an instant one of those eyes burst like a water balloon as a steel dart punctured his mask and shattered the plastic. Ethan stared in shock as the mask filled instantly with blood. The man's expression sagged and, with his remaining eye, he stared unseeing into Ethan's eyes as the pistol slipped from his hand. Ethan rolled out from beneath the corpse and saw Lopez aiming one of the fat pistols double-handed as she hovered above him.

Ethan was about to give her a thumbs-up, but as his vision cleared he saw the hull of the *Free Spirit* above them and another boat circling at a distance. Even from the seabed, he could see bullets shooting into the water.

25

RICHARD E. GERSTEIN JUSTICE BUILDING, MIAMI

June 28, 11:23

Olaf Jorgenson had not expected any problems during his assignment. Katherine Abell was one of the finest lawyers in Florida, and though she rarely spoke to him he held her in the highest regard. He could not have predicted that he would hear the name that Macy Lieberman had spoken, as she airily waved a thick wad of files in her hand.

Charles Purcell.

Olaf watched from the public gallery as Katherine stared in disbelief at Macy Lieberman. The very fact that she was as stunned as he had been suggested that the defense of IRIS might not go according to plan, and the knowledge bothered him immensely.

'Charles Purcell is your whistleblower?' Katherine stammered. 'That's ridiculous! You couldn't have found a less reliable witness!'

Macy smirked across at Katherine.

'Would you like to share with the court your reasoning?'

Katherine turned to the judge as Olaf watched, willing her on.

'Charles Purcell is currently the subject of a manhunt,' she reported confidently. 'He is wanted for the murder of his wife and child, and any testimony from him can be considered null and void.'

The judge raised an eyebrow and looked across at Macy Lieberman. Olaf's muscles tensed beneath his shirt as he waited for the prosecutor's response. She did not look at all bothered by the revelations regarding Charles Purcell's murderous tendencies, and in fact the smile did not fall from her face as she responded.

'That is absolutely correct, your honor,' she agreed. 'However, these documents were received this morning and were posted yesterday afternoon, long before an arrest warrant was issued for the arrest of Charles Purcell.'

Katherine Abell laughed out loud.

'Are you serious?' she stammered. 'The man's a wanted killer. His word means nothing, no matter when this supposed evidence was sent or delivered.'

Macy turned to face Katherine across the court.

'I should hardly have to remind you, Ms Abell, that the law in this country clearly states that an accused citizen is innocent of any crime until proven guilty. Charles Purcell is *wanted* for the murder of his own family, but that does not mean that he is *responsible* for the crime.' Macy Lieberman raised the file in her hands. 'This, however, is most definitely the work of Charles Purcell, and regardless of what he may or may not have done elsewhere since, this file proves beyond reasonable doubt that the case being presented by my client has its basis in solid financial facts and constitutes a viable cause for this case to go to trial.'

Olaf watched as Katherine Abell turned to face the judge once again.

'And I say again, your honor, that this case is based upon a combination of one family's desire to profit from the generosity of IRIS and one prosecutor's determination to gain professional satisfaction from a high-profile case that has no substance in the eyes of any unbiased observer. This case is reliant upon legal-precedent cases involving military and industrial firms working in warzones, not the work of a charity on home soil with a long record of philanthropic success.'

The judge leaned back in her chair and looked out across the faces of the Uhungu family for a long moment before finally speaking.

'The court will adjourn until this afternoon,' she said. 'All rise.'

Olaf stood with the rest of the court and watched as the judge filed out of sight before looking down at Macy Lieberman and the blue file that she slipped into her bag. Olaf turned and strode out of the gallery. Joaquin's orders had been clear. Despite Katherine Abell's confidence, Olaf knew that the papers stolen by Charles Purcell would almost certainly be enough to bring Joaquin Abell to the stand, and that was the one thing that Olaf did not want to see happen.

Joaquin Abell was like a brother, a father even, and he owed him his life.

Olaf stepped out of the court into the muggy Florida

sunshine, watching the traffic flow by as he lit a ciga-rette. Pedestrians cast disapproving glances in his direction but his huge physique and stony expression stalled any complaint. It had been many years since anyone had dared threaten Olaf, a far cry from his childhood.

As he turned and walked along the sidewalk he reflected not for the first time how fortunate he had been to have encountered Joaquin Abell when he did, as a skinny, nervous 15-year-old. An orphan, he had been sent to a small school in Loen, nestled deep in the fjords of western Norway, where his companions had proved themselves every bit as cruel as the bitter winters that enshrouded his homeland in their icy embrace. After years of torment Olaf had become a virtual recluse within an already isolated community, taking any opportunity to avoid school and the torment of his peers.

He had been fifteen when tragedy struck the little village, a particularly severe snow storm producing an avalanche that killed almost half of his class. As others cried, Olaf struggled to contain his joy at seeing half a dozen of his hated tormentors hacked from the compacted ice, their purple faces twisted in the rigor mortis of death.

Days later, a ship had arrived bearing a large blue IRIS logo, and Joaquin Abell had promised money to rebuild the damaged school. Awed by the giant yacht and its charismatic owner, Olaf had seen his chance to escape the miserable little town in which he had been entrapped for so long. He had begged Joaquin personally for a job aboard the *Event Horizon*, only to be dismissed out of hand. Stricken with grief, for the first time in his life Olaf had taken matters into his own hands and stowed away aboard the giant yacht.

Years of evading his tormentors had given Olaf a primal instinct for survival, and it was almost three weeks before he was discovered by engineers and dragged before Joaquin Abell once more. To his surprise, Joaquin had agreed not to have him returned home. Maybe he had seen something in Olaf's desperate eyes or had simply taken pity on him, but by that evening Olaf Jorgenson was in his own quarters and sailing away from his homeland forever, into a world he had never seen before.

Over the years that had passed since, Olaf had grown closer to Joaquin. As a wiry little boy, working on the yacht had toughened his muscles and seen him grow stronger. His increasing size and confidence had led him to take up body-building, and that in turn had led him into the use of steroids. His habit financed by his employer, who always seemed to know precisely what he needed and wanted, Olaf grew into a giant. Now, at six foot four and 260 pounds, Olaf was an unstoppable force of nature who knew nothing of the meaning of the word compromise.

Olaf turned and followed the sidewalk around the edge of the court's parking lot, his cold blue eyes seeking his target. It was clear to Olaf that, win, lose or draw, Katherine Abell was not going to be able to prevent the court from hearing the details on the files held by Macy Lieberman. Therefore, he would ensure that the files simply disappeared.

The parking lot was overlooked on four corners by

CCTV cameras. Olaf looked across the lot and saw several cars parked beneath a clump of palm trees that hung listlessly on the humid air. The trees were mature, the fronds hanging six or seven feet long and obscuring the area under the tree from the view of the cameras.

Several cars had parked there, the owners evidently seeking the shade offered by the trees. Olaf worked his way around the edge of the lot, careful to walk nonchalantly and not draw any more attention to himself other than that caused by his impressive physique.

He spotted an old man in a cheap suit shuffling toward a battered old Dodge Polara, its red paint faded by years spent sweltering beneath the Florida sun. Olaf guessed the man's age as about sixty-five. The car, the threadbare clothes and the nicotine-stained teeth all told Olaf the same story: old, alone, and won't be missed.

Olaf moved around to the sidewalk in front of the Polara, the palm trees shielding him from the view of the cameras as the old man limped around to the driver's door and reached out for the handle. As he opened the door, Olaf leapt over the parking lot fence and was directly behind the old man in two giant strides. Even as the old-timer turned his head to squint up at Olaf with rheumy eyes, Olaf reached out with one huge hand that encircled the old man's jaw like a glove around a base-ball. He felt a thick wedge of his greasy, lank hair squeeze against his other hand as it folded around the back of the man's neck. The old man, his jaw clamped shut and his head pinned, gagged as he tried to cry out. Olaf turned him with unstoppable force and then drove his shoulders downward as he dropped violently at the knees.

The old man's forehead smacked with a sickening crunch across the top of the open driver's door. Olaf felt the brittle bones of the neck snap like dry twigs as he caught the old man's corpse and lifted him bodily into the car and shoved him into the passenger seat. Carefully, Olaf placed the seatbelt across him to keep the body upright as though he were caring for an elderly friend, and then climbed into the driver's seat. Olaf closed the door and reached into the old man's pockets, fumbling around until he found the keys to the Polara.

He started the engine and reversed out of the parking slot.

Now, all he had to do was wait for Macy Lieberman to leave the courthouse.

26

[FLORIDA STRAITS]

June 28, 11:27

Ethan broke the surface of the water alongside the *Free Spirit*'s hull, just in time to see a ragged line of bullet holes burst through it and spray fiberglass chips into the water around him. Lopez came up beside Ethan.

'What the hell's going on?!' she shouted as she pulled her respirator out.

Ethan saw a sleek speedboat roar past nearby, its powerful wake tossing him about on the waves.

'Get aboard!' Ethan hollered back, shoving her toward the *Free Spirit*'s stern ramp.

Lopez swam to the ramp just as Doug Jarvis appeared and reached out for her hand. He hauled her aboard with surprising strength before reaching out for Ethan. Ethan dragged himself up out of the water just as a deafening rattle of gunfire crackled out from the bridge.

Scott Bryson was on one knee against the port rail beside the wheelhouse, an automatic rifle pulled tightly into his right shoulder as he fired short, controlled bursts at the speedboat circling back toward them. As Ethan yanked off his diving equipment he saw the shots fall close around the speedboat's hull, keeping it at bay.

'Who the hell are they?' Lopez shouted.

Jarvis hauled the heavy oxygen cylinders off her back.

'More to the point, who do they think we are, and how did they know that we'd be here?'

From the bridge, Scott Bryson bellowed down at them.

'How about we have this goddamned chat later and concentrate on staying alive?' The captain turned and tossed the rifle toward Ethan. 'Keep them off our ass!'

Ethan caught the rifle as Bryson leapt up into the wheelhouse and threw the boat's throttles open. The *Free Spirit* surged forward and sent Ethan reeling as he struggled to keep his balance.

'Incoming!'

Ethan heard Lopez's cry of alarm and saw the speed-boat rushing toward their port hull at full throttle, two men with rifles aiming in his direction.

'Get down!'

Ethan hurled himself flat onto the deck, his fingers instinctively finding the safety catch and trigger with the same fluidity he had once possessed as a marine fighting in Afghanistan's Tora Bora caves. The weapon came up into his shoulder even as he saw the first burst of muzzle flash from their attackers' weapons and a lethal hail of auto-matic fire sprayed across the boat's deck. Ethan, enveloped in a bubble of adrenaline-fuelled silence, ignored the bullets that zipped and tore into the deck around him as he breathed slowly and took aim. A marine instructor's words drifted unbidden through his mind.

All the automatic fire in the world is useless against one well-placed round. Shoot slow, son, and you'll shoot sure.

The shooter raked the *Free Spirit* as the speedboat turned away at the last moment amid crashing surf and shining metal. Ethan's breathing stopped for a single second as he squeezed the trigger once.

The round hit the shooter low in his belly as the speedboat raced past and bounced on the churning waves. Ethan saw the man's mouth gape open in shock as he folded over at the waist, his legs crumpled beneath him, and he tumbled back into the speedboat.

Ethan looked over the barrel of the rifle and saw at least four other men in the rear of the vessel. He turned to Jarvis.

'We're going to need help!'

The old man already had a cellphone in his hand and was shouting into it as he sheltered close to the wheelhouse.

Scott Bryson shouted down at Ethan from the bridge.

'Nice shooting, boy scout! Now they'll be really pissed!'

Ethan stood up and rushed to the bridge, keeping one eye on the speedboat as it circled out for another pass. The adrenaline was now pumping through his veins like a freight train powering through the night as he leapt up the steps two at a time and pointed at their attackers.

'Turn the boat around,' he ordered Bryson. 'Head straight for them.'

'Like hell, son, this boat's my livelihood.'

'We sure as hell can't outrun them,' Ethan snapped back. 'And your livelihood's no good to you if you're dead.'

'We can't outshoot them, either,' Bryson pointed out. 'And you're not Jack goddamned Bauer, so what's the point of going down in a blaze of glory?!'

Ethan glanced out of the bridge windows to see the speedboat racing toward them again.

'You of all people should remember what you were taught in the SEALs,' he said. 'Defense and offense. When attacked by a superior force, you do the last thing that they expect.'

Scott Bryson looked down at him for a long moment, and then for the first time he smiled at Ethan.

'You advance on their position.'

With a flourish, Bryson span the wheel and the *Free Spirit* heeled gamely over, turning to face the speedboat until they were on a head-on collision course.

'Take them down the left side!' Ethan shouted as he jumped back down to the deck.

Ethan ran low to the stern of the boat, sliding onto his belly and aiming across the port stern. A crackle of gunfire snapped across the wind as he slowed his breathing. The speedboat soared past, two men firing their weapons from the hip with aimless abandon in the hopes of catching a lucky hit. A salvo of bullets splintered the hull close to Ethan's shoulder and showered him with debris.

As the boat thundered by, Ethan aimed at one of the shooters, taking advantage of the low-aspect movement now that the speedboat was moving almost directly away from him. Despite the pitching of the boats across the waves, the target was easier to track. Ethan held his breath and fired two rounds, double-tapping the trigger as he aimed for the man's torso.

The first round missed, hitting the deck low and to the man's left, but the second round hit him straight through the neck, a fine mist of blood spraying into the wind as the man was hurled backwards to sprawl on the deck in a tangle of writhing limbs and spilling blood.

Ethan rolled over and shouted to Bryson above the wind.

'Turn her around!'

Bryson responded without argument this time, the *Free Spirit* wheeling around on the churning surface of the ocean as she chugged her way toward their attackers.

Lopez struggled across the heaving deck and hurled herself down alongside Ethan.

'We can't keep this up forever,' she said. 'Sooner or later one of us is going to get hit.'

Ethan nodded and looked at Jarvis, who was huddled down behind a bulwark alongside the pressure suit, as he held a hand to one ear and his cellphone to the other.

'We've got to hang on until he gets the cavalry here.'

Lopez nodded and then clapped Ethan's shoulder.

'I've got an idea, be ready to shoot again.'

Lopez staggered across the heaving deck as a wall of spray hissed over the boat's bows. Bryson had aimed directly for the speedboat this time, and the psychological effect of their actions was already forcing their enemy to hang back and circle beyond weapons range.

'They're coming back!' Bryson shouted, as the speedboat suddenly turned hard into them and rushed head-on once again.

'Bring them down the starboard side!' Ethan heard Lopez shout to the captain.

Ethan shifted his position slightly as he heard the speedboat's powerful engines growling and the familiar rattle of gunfire as the men aboard opened up once again. Ethan risked a glance over his shoulder, and saw Lopez hefting an oxygen cylinder onto her shoulder as she balanced against the pitch and roll of the deck.

The speedboat thundered by and hurled a wall of spray up against the *Free Spirit* as Lopez took two paces forward and threw the oxygen cylinder in a graceful arc across the open water. She crouched down on the deck with her hands over her head as bullets hammered the deck around her.

The silvery cylinder slammed into the back of the speedboat, crashing through the legs of one of the shooters and flipping him over onto his back. As the speedboat turned away Ethan aimed once again and fired three shots at the cylinder. The second shot hit it even as he pulled the trigger and let fly the third round, and the cylinder wall ruptured. A blast of high-pressure oxygen burst out with the force of a jet engine's exhaust and the heavy cylinder flew across the speedboat's deck and smashed into the back of the pilot's legs, shattering them with a metallic clang that Ethan could hear even above the *Free Spirit*'s laboring engines. The cylinder spiraled crazily across the speedboat's deck as the pilot collapsed in agony, trailing a cloud of vapor as it crashed into the engines before shooting into the air and spiraling into the ocean thirty yards away.

Ethan saw a thick cloud of black smoke billow from both of the speedboat's engines as a limp body toppled over the taff-rail into the ocean in a tangle of flailing limbs. The speedboat began turning lazily in circles, its idling engines spitting flames that began to burn their way along the hull.

'That'll do,' Ethan smiled grimly as he stood up.

'We're not out of trouble yet,' Bryson called out.

Ethan saw the big man pointing out toward the horizon, where two more speedboats raced toward them on an intercept course.

27

FLORIDA STRAITS, 14 MILES WEST OF SOUTH BIMINI

'How much more ammunition do we have?' Ethan shouted.

Bryson yelled over his shoulder as he turned the *Free Spirit* toward the distant Florida coast.

'None! I only carry the rifle to finish off big catches like sharks and marlin!'

Ethan checked the weapon and saw only a single round remaining.

The two speedboats turned in unison alongside the *Free Spirit*, and Ethan saw four men aboard each vessel, all aiming their weapons directly at him. He looked across at Jarvis, who had lowered his cellphone from his ear and was watching their attackers with an expression of disbelief.

'Who the hell are these people?' he called out.

'I don't suppose the Coastguard's on its way?' Lopez asked.

'Not exactly,' Jarvis shouted back.

Ethan stared at the speedboats and felt a lance of fear

pierce his guts as he watched one of the gunmen lift what looked like a grenade in one hand, pulling the pin with the other and swinging his arm back to lob the weapon toward the *Free Spirit*.

'Hard to starboard!' Ethan yelled to Bryson.

The captain span the wheel to the right, and as he did so a thunderous blast of noise blazed overhead. For a terrifying instant Ethan flinched against the expected shrapnel as the unseen grenade exploded around them, but then he saw a flash of metal above them in the sky and a sound like that of a playing card caught in the spinning spokes of a bicycle.

An enormous fountain of white water erupted around the speedboats, a curtain of churned foam that zipped across the ocean at tremendous speed. Ethan saw both of the speedboats shudder as clouds of debris blasted into the air to spill onto the surface of the ocean, the gunmen and pilots torn apart like rag dolls. The grenade fell from the gunman's hand to land alongside him in the speedboat.

'Get down!'

Ethan, Lopez and Jarvis dropped down as the grenade detonated and the speedboat lurched as its engines failed and its rudder was torn off in the blast. The stricken vessel collided instantly with the other speedboat, smashing through the hull and splitting the second vessel in half. The two boats flipped up into the air and crashed back down onto the surface of the ocean amid a churning cloud of foam.

Ethan craned his head up and spotted a pair of F-15E Eagles turning sharply across the blue sky, bright white

vortices trailing from their wingtips. He looked across at
Jarvis, who shrugged as he brushed himself down.

'Why call the Coastguard when you've got the Air
Force on the line?'

Ethan got to his feet, steadying himself on the deck
as Bryson eased back on the throttles. Across the water,
Ethan could see the two speedboats and the bodies of
their attackers sinking rapidly beneath the waves, leaving only debris and an oily slick of spilled fuel floating
on the surface.

'Who were they?' Lopez asked him, shaking chips of
fiberglass from her hair.

'I don't know, but I'd like to find out. How deep is
the water here?' he asked Bryson.

'Hundreds of fathoms now we're off the sandbar,'
came the reply. 'You'll need the Navy to recover the
boats. The bodies might float up after a few hours,
provided they're not eaten beforehand.'

Ethan shook his head. Even if the bodies did survive
scavengers, they'd likely be carried for miles by the
currents and be lost far out to sea. He turned away and
looked at the damaged deck of the *Free Spirit*. Bullets had
hammered almost every spare inch of her. Ethan
crouched down and ran his hand across the scarred
surfaces until he found what he was looking for.

'You got any sealable bags aboard?' he asked the
captain.

Bryson turned to one of the deck lockers and lifted
out a small polythene bag used to hold live bait in water.
He handed the bag over, and Ethan grabbed his knife
from its sheath on his diving suit. He probed into one of

the jagged tears in the deck and prized from its depths the crumpled remains of a bullet. Jarvis watched as Ethan dropped the bullet into the bag.

'What are you thinking?' the old man asked.

Ethan stood up and looked at the rolling ocean around them. There wasn't a single other boat to be seen, nothing but endless sea and blue sky flecked with puffy white clouds. Lopez guessed his thoughts before he voiced them.

'Something to do with Purcell?' she suggested. 'He wanted us to be here after all.'

'What, to get us killed?' Jarvis uttered.

Ethan looked at the bullet in the bag.

'I don't know, but one thing's for sure: we didn't advertise our presence and Captain Ahab's boat here is just one among thousands moored in Miami.'

Bryson ignored Ethan's flippancy. 'Did you find the aircraft?'

'Yeah,' Lopez nodded, 'along with all of the occupants. And that's what doesn't figure. There were divers down there. They tried to ambush whilst we had our noses stuck into that airplane.'

Bryson squinted at the flotsam now drifting on the ocean nearby.

'We didn't see any divers leave those speedboats.'

'That's because they were already there,' Ethan said. 'It was an ambush.'

'But they couldn't have known we would be here,' Jarvis protested. 'Unless somebody on Kyle Sears' team is acting as an informer.'

'The police?' Lopez replied. 'I thought Kyle's team were kept out of the loop?'

'They were,' Jarvis agreed, 'but we can't guarantee that somebody with inside knowledge wouldn't be keeping an eye on us.'

'It's possible,' Ethan said. 'There was a buoy tethered to the tail of the aircraft wreckage, very small, but it could have held a camera.'

'We need to find it,' Lopez said.

'You won't,' Bryson cautioned her. 'The sea's so choppy we could be right on top of it and not spot it. It would take hours.'

'Hours we don't have,' Jarvis agreed.

'Somebody must have been here before us.' Ethan looked down at the bullet in the bag in his hand. 'Purcell's family were killed by bullets that were dipped in something called Rubidium-82,' he said. 'I'm hoping that these bullets have traces of the same compound.'

Jarvis looked at the slug.

'You think that Purcell's being hunted by the same people who were shooting at us?'

'Maybe,' Ethan said. 'Chances are the two are connected, and that could mean that Purcell is waiting for us to make that connection before he comes out of hiding. Once any doubt can be thrown on his role in the killing of his wife and child, he'll be able to start fighting his own corner.'

Lopez shook her head.

'But he could have done that anyway, just gone straight to the police with all of this information instead of leading us on a chase and nearly getting us killed. What good will it do him if we, the only people who know about his possible innocence, get iced?'

Ethan shrugged.

'I don't know, but right now it's all we've got for his motive. Somebody is hunting Purcell and us at the same time.' A thought occurred to him and he turned to Jarvis. 'What if Purcell saw into the future using some-body else's equipment? We're assuming he did it himself somehow, but he's been working freelance since leaving NASA, right? Purcell might have only a limited amount of time to clear his name. He said he was going to be murdered, right? We got any idea who he was actually working for when all this started?'

Jarvis nodded.

'Some corporation called IRIS,' he said. 'He was privately contracted, so we don't have any real details of what he was doing for them.'

'I've heard of IRIS,' Lopez said. 'Big charity headed by that Joaquin Abell who's always on television scream-ing for donations.'

Bryson chimed in from where he was leaning against the wheelhouse.

'IRIS is whiter than white, totally non-profit.'

Jarvis's cellphone trilled, the musical tone sounding strangely feeble amidst the vastness of the open ocean. Jarvis flipped it open and answered, listening intently for a few moments before he raised an eyebrow.

'You're kidding?' The voice on the other end of the line warbled for a few moments more. 'Okay, we're on our way.' Jarvis snapped the phone shut and looked at Bryson. 'Head for shore, pronto. Something's come up.'

Bryson remained leaning against the wheelhouse.

'Once we're ashore that's it; we're done,' he replied.

'This trip's already cost me a lot more than I bargained for.'

Lopez turned to the captain.

'We hired you for this,' she pointed out, 'and for a lot of money.'

'Yeah, sure you did,' Bryson agreed as he turned toward the wheelhouse. 'And that money's what I'm going to need to rebuild my goddamned boat!'

Ethan saw Lopez's crestfallen expression as Bryson stormed off up into the wheelhouse and threw the throttles forward angrily.

'We're done with him anyway,' Ethan said to her before turning to Jarvis. 'Who called?'

'My office was left with the task of monitoring any evidence of Charles Purcell's whereabouts. His name's just turned up as a witness in a court case being held today in Miami.'

'Let me guess,' Lopez said. 'IRIS?'

'One and the same,' Jarvis confirmed. 'Looks like Purcell turned whistleblower on the company, sent documents to a prosecutor in the city. Could turn the case in the prosecution's favor and expose corporate fraud by IRIS executives.'

Ethan looked again at the bullet in his hand.

'What's the chances that we can get this bullet analyzed today?'

'I'll see what I can do,' Jarvis said. 'In the meantime we need to get to that courthouse as fast as we can. There's people there we need to speak to.'

'Who?' Lopez asked.

'The prosecutor, a Macy Lieberman, and the defense

lawyer. Turns out she's none other than the wife of IRIS's Chief Executive Officer, Joaquin Abell.'

Ethan looked about them at the empty ocean and thought for a moment.

'We get codes from Purcell hinting at future events,' he said. 'He's seeing things that haven't happened yet. Then people turn up here and try to kill us before we can figure out what happened to this downed aircraft. Even if they did have a camera out here on the ocean, they couldn't have gotten out here so fast without knowing in advance that we would be here.'

Jarvis balanced on the boat's rolling deck.

'Nobody on the police force could have placed a camera all the way out here without somebody knowing about it,' he added. 'That rules out a mole in Kyle Sears' department.'

Ethan was about to respond when he saw in the water a small, round object bobbing on the waves. He leaned over and saw a buoy half sunk in the water, its shape distorted by the impact of a bullet. The round, black eye of a camera lens looked out at him as the buoy slowly sank into the churning water.

'Which means one of two things,' Lopez surmised as Bryson turned the boat around to head back toward Miami. 'Either Charles Purcell wants us dead, or somebody else is able to see into the future.'

28

RICHARD E. GERSTEIN
JUSTICE BUILDING, MIAMI

June 28, 12:31

Katherine Abell stepped out of the courthouse and closed her eyes as the sunshine caressed her face. Most all the television cameras had already dispersed, and the few that remained kept a respectful distance between themselves and the four minders lingering behind her. Some of the tension she had built up in the courtroom bled away onto the warm air as she focused on breathing from the pit of her stomach. *In through the nose, out through the mouth.* Yoga helped, but ultimately Katherine Abell felt as though she were struggling alone against an unyielding tide of self-serving litigation that threatened to overwhelm not just her career but the entire legal system.

Fact was, half a lifetime spent defending victims of injustice had infected her with the corrosive frustration of being unable to shield her clients from the very laws that were supposedly designed to protect them. During her career she had seen the altar of American law defaced by those for whom greed held greater value than justice.

In the modern age, the proud heritage of defending

the innocent, prosecuting the guilty and maintaining the delicate balance between effective deterrent and appropriate punishment had been bastardized into a crude business of making money from the crimes of the guilty and the misfortune of their victims. Lawyers no longer defended the presumption of innocence until the proving of guilt: they merely sought the exoneration of their client, regardless of guilt, in return for their fee and the reputation of invincibility it gave them on the circuit.

Katherine opened her eyes and let the sunshine in but it carried no warmth or comfort, only the muggy weight of gathering storms. Since the Uhungu family had brought their case to the courts, Katherine had felt herself slowly sinking beneath the burden of a society that seemed to have collapsed into a paranoid maelstrom, where even acts of kindness were met with spite and malice.

'It's just not worth it,' she whispered, the words falling unbidden from her lips, as though somebody else were speaking for her.

'Yes it is.'

She turned to see Peter Hamill standing beside her. His reassuring smile carried some measure of comfort, but she shook her head slowly.

'Joaquin saved the lives of that family, and this is how they repay him.'

Peter sighed and slipped his hands into his pockets.

'That's the way it is. It's not justice, but that's why we're here, isn't it? To make sure that they don't get away with biting the hand that fed them.'

Katherine was about to reply when she saw Macy Lieberman approaching them. The prosecutor carried

herself with an arrogant sway of her hips and a laser-
bright Hollywood smile that seemed to dull the sunshine.
Fashionably oversized sunglasses shielded her eyes, glossy
black discs that reflected the buildings and the sky above.

'Not like you to take a break from the stand,' Macy
observed as she reached them, her own assistant, a young
man named Michael, by her side.

'I needed some air,' Katherine replied, with the
briefest ghost of a smile.

'Me too,' Macy replied as she fished a menthol cigarette from her Gucci bag. 'It just gets so *stuffy* in those
courtrooms sometimes.'

Katherine held the brittle grin on her features but she
didn't miss the jibe.

'Must be something to do with all the hot air.'

Macy squinted at Katherine over the cigarette as she
lit it, and puffed a thin cloud of smoke between them.

'That's cheap,' she replied.

'Like your case?'

'Oh come *on*,' Macy smiled, the effort almost cracking
her glossy lipstick. 'We're on the same side here really,
aren't we?'

'Are we?'

'We're both lawyers. We both represent people. We
can't help that they're often blood-sucking scum who
would take their own grandmother to court over a dime.'

Katherine turned to face Macy, her fists clenched painfully as her nails dug deep into the palms of her hands.

'Your clients are an impoverished family from south
Miami,' she growled. 'And mine is my husband, who
saved their lives. You don't give a damn about either of

them. All you're interested in is the media coverage of the case and making sure you win, regardless of who's guilty of what.'

Macy sucked down another lungful of smoke and raised an eyebrow.

'Oh dear, we have hit a nerve, haven't we?' she purred. 'Surely you must be confident enough of your husband's integrity to be sure that he's not guilty of defrauding the taxpayer?'

Peter stood forward and raised a hand at Macy.

'Maybe we should save this for the courtroom, okay? Nobody *here* is on trial.'

Katherine said nothing, but Macy took another pace closer and pushed past Peter's hand.

'*Everybody* is on trial,' she snapped back at him, before turning to Katherine. 'They just don't know it yet. I can't wait to see the newspaper reports tomorrow, after we've blown IRIS's dirty little game out of the water for all to see. You do realize, don't you, Katherine, that your defense of a man who is little more than a petty criminal will raise suspicions that you yourself are a part of his fraud.'

Katherine felt excess heat simmering beneath her skin.

'I wouldn't put it past you to concoct any story to suit your case, Macy,' she replied. 'You're like a tabloid, spouting bullshit from one day to the next and hoping that nobody will notice that you change your stories as fast as you invent them.'

'Like your husband?' Macy purred.

'You disgust me,' Katherine uttered, feeling suddenly nauseous.

'What is it, Katherine?' Macy probed. 'Is there perhaps

just a little part of you that suspects that your icon of the great and good, the much-worshipped Joaquin Abell, is in fact nothing more than a glorified fraudster? You picked your husband well, didn't you? A corporate monster *and* a corrupt lawyer. I bet your kids will turn out as rotten as—'

Katherine's hand whipped out in one reflexive action and slapped Macy across the cheek with enough force to send the cigarette spinning from her mouth. Macy staggered backwards, her hand clasped to her face as passers-by stopped and stared at them.

In a flash, the four minders were at Katherine's side and glowering down at Macy.

'You bitch,' Macy hissed, but she smiled savagely as she looked at her assistant. 'Did you see that, Michael?'

'I did see that,' Michael replied. 'It makes me wonder if Mrs Abell is fit to take the stand in her husband's defense.'

'Just what I was thinking,' Macy said. 'Maybe we should bring His High and Mightiness Joaquin Abell down here to the courtroom to stand trial himself?'

Katherine stepped toward Macy. 'You threaten him and I'll—'

'You'll *what*, Katherine? Are you threatening to assault me *again*?'

'You provoked her,' Peter intervened as he thrust himself between the two women and looked at Macy. 'Is this the best that you can do? Force a confrontation and then use it to try to prove that your case has any validity? If so, you're an even lousier lawyer than I gave you credit for.'

Macy's eyes shone with satisfaction.

'We've got everything we need,' she snarled back,

'everything we need to bring down IRIS and Joaquin Abell with it.' She looked at Katherine. 'You know the most ironic thing about all this, honey? Until twenty-four hours ago even *I* had no idea just how dirty your husband was. I was all for an amicable settlement outside court, but having read these papers from Charles Purcell I'll be damned if I'll stop until IRIS is no more. I'm going to make it my life's work.'

Katherine refused to be intimidated.

'Go for it. I'll make sure you go down trying.'

Macy turned and headed for her car, Michael in tow. Katherine watched them depart and then looked at Peter.

'What the hell is she talking about?' she uttered. 'Whatever those papers are they can't contain anything useful. Joaquin's accounts clearly show that IRIS makes no profit, it's not possible for him to gain financially in the way she's described. Where would the money go? All he takes is enough to support our family from the estate he inherited from his father – everything else belongs to IRIS itself.'

Peter sighed and rubbed his temples.

'I think we'd better assume that Macy isn't trying to just scare us into folding over the Uhungu case. That would be too aggressive, even for her. You heard what she said: she's going to devote her career to bringing IRIS down.'

Katherine watched as Macy's bright-red Pontiac turned out of the lot and joined the traffic flowing toward 13th Avenue.

'Only because she's taking as fact the word of a wanted murderer. It's as likely that the account details she has are faked. Maybe Purcell's got a beef with Joaquin and drew up the papers to try to derail our defense.'

'Or maybe, just maybe,' Peter said delicately, 'she's actually got something on IRIS.'

Katherine stared at him in shock, as though it were she who had been slapped. She was about to speak when she saw a tall man approaching her. He looked slightly rough around the edges, with scruffy, light-brown hair and gray eyes, and he was accompanied by an attractive, petite Latino woman who somehow managed to look friendly and dangerous at the same time.

'Katherine Abell?'

'Who are you?'

'My name is Ethan Warner,' the tall man said, 'and this is Nicola Lopez. We understand you're the defense lawyer for IRIS in a trial here at the courthouse.'

Katherine guessed who they were. Journalists poking their goddamned noses into business that did not concern them, and then reporting false stories back to their editors, all just to turn out what they euphemistically termed 'good copy'.

'The case is ongoing,' she replied, 'and I cannot comment on it.'

'We're not reporters,' the woman named Lopez said. 'Ma'am, we need to speak with you right now regarding a man named Charles Purcell.'

Katherine glanced at Peter, who raised an eyebrow.

'What would you know about Purcell?' Peter asked the two strangers. 'And if you're not reporters and you're not police, then who the hell are you?'

It was an older, shorter man in a dark-blue suit who

replied as he arrived behind Ethan Warner and flipped a
badge at Katherine. Katherine saw the name Jarvis and a
familiar-looking emblem.

'Defense Intelligence Agency,' he said. 'This is important, Mrs Abell. What we know could affect your
defense. We don't need to know anything about the
ongoing case: it's what we've got to tell *you* that's
important.'

'In what way could it affect my defense?' Katherine
demanded to know. 'The prosecution thinks they've got
us over a barrel and there's nothing we can do about it.'

Warner's eyes narrowed. 'What do they have that's
such a big deal?'

'Papers,' Katherine replied, 'accounts that supposedly
show that my husband's company IRIS has been fiddling
the taxpayer out of millions of dollars. She says they were
sent to her by a man named Purcell, who's wanted for
murder. I argued that the warrant for his arrest invali-
dated any evidence he might have, but the judge ruled
otherwise. They're going to reveal the contents of the
accounts when the court reconvenes.'

Ethan Warner looked across at the courtroom.

'Where's the prosecution now?'

Katherine pointed out to the street where Macy's
Pontiac had disappeared, and was about to speak when
there was a sudden howl of a car engine followed by the
rending screech of metal on metal. Screams erupted from
the street nearby and Katherine whirled to see Macy's
bright-red car being broadsided by an old convertible.
The Pontiac folded like an envelope under the impact as
shards of sparkling glass exploded across the street.

29

Ethan saw the red Pontiac spin across the street and smash into a fire hydrant. A towering column of white water exploded into the air as the Pontiac hit the sidewalk, scattering pedestrians as it ploughed into the metal fences surrounding the detention center's southeast corner.

As Ethan began running he saw a battered old convertible swerve onto the sidewalk and smash again into the Pontiac. A thick cloud of acrid white smoke burst from beneath the hood. Ethan glimpsed an old man slumped across the front seats before the smoke obscured the vehicle and flames licked at the edges of the Pontiac's crumpled bodywork. Transfixed witnesses began backing away from the two cars, some of them shouting warnings to get back.

Lopez raced up alongside Ethan.

'The impact must have ruptured the fuel tank!'

Ethan nodded and looked back over his shoulder as he ran.

'Get backup!' he yelled to Jarvis.

Through the fences and the swirling veil of choking smoke beyond he glimpsed the Pontiac's passenger door swing open and a large figure lean inside the car before sprinting away down 13th Avenue.

Ethan rounded the fences of the detention center and ran out between the traffic that was now stationary either side of the smoldering wrecks. He kept his eyes on the big man who was shouldering his way past stunned onlookers and glancing over his shoulder as he ran toward 14th Street.

Lopez ran alongside Ethan, then jumped up and slid across the hood of a sedan toward the Pontiac.

'The convertible's on fire!' she shouted.

Ethan cursed and broke off his pursuit of the big man, changing direction toward the Pontiac as the flames engulfed both the convertible and the Pontiac pinned against the twisted metal fence. Lopez dashed in through the oily clouds of black smoke spilling from both cars, ignoring the searing heat of the flames as she grabbed the Pontiac's door handle and pulled for all she was worth.

Ethan shielded his face from the flames as he fought his way to her side, and together they hauled the warped door open. A young man in a suit lay slumped with blood pouring from a head wound that matched a spider's web of shatter marks fogging the passenger window.

Ethan leaned into the smoke-filled car and dragged the kid out, even as snarling flames reached out for him. Together with Lopez Ethan dragged him away from the car, the heat scorching his skin and drying his eyes as a stranger's voice rang in his ears.

'Get away from there!'

Ethan was suddenly surrounded by dozens of helping hands, ordinary citizens flooding in to help them
as the two cars were engulfed in a broiling frenzy of
burning fuel. Ethan tumbled backwards, coughing as
he watched the cars consumed by the angry flames.
The sound of a fire truck's sirens wailed from somewhere down the street, but with the nearest hydrant
out of action he knew that the remaining victims in
the cars were long gone.

A hand tapped his shoulder. Ethan looked around and
saw a kid of no more than ten years holding a cellphone,
an image on the screen of a big man with short blond
hair running from the scene of the accident.

'He went that way,' the kid pointed, toward the
corner of the block.

Ethan grabbed the kid's shoulder and pointed toward
Jarvis and the courthouse.

'Take your phone to that man,' he said. 'They're with
me and the woman's a lawyer, okay?'

The kid nodded as Ethan leapt to his feet and broke
into a run toward the corner of 12th and 14th. His lungs
ached from the smoke he'd inhaled but he pushed on as
a rush of thoughts whipped through his mind. *The man
was big, easy to spot in the crowds. Don't rush it. He won't
have gotten far.*

Ethan turned the corner of the block and slowed to a
fast walk as he scanned the bobbing heads of pedestrians
crowding the sidewalks. Hundreds of people, turning
into and out of shops, jaywalking, talking. Ethan spotted
a streetlight and hurried across to it, clambering up until

he was three feet above the shoppers milling around him. Traffic hummed on the nearby Dolphin Expressway and he could hear a metro rattling past on its elevated rails, the clattering of wheels on rails reminding him briefly of Chicago. He wrapped one arm around the pillar and made the shape of a box with his fingers, peering through it and sweeping the street. An old trick he'd picked up in the Marines – the smaller image seen through the frame of his fingers allowed his brain to process what it was seeing more easily, helping him locate his quarry amongst the confusion.

A moment later he spotted the man with the blond hair walking swiftly away beneath palm trees on 12th and looking back down the street toward him. In an instant he spotted Ethan clinging to the post and broke into a run.

Ethan let go of the post and hit the ground just as he saw Lopez race past him, already dodging deftly through the crowds like a gazelle. Pedestrians scattered left and right as they ran.

'Is he armed?' Lopez shouted.

'Don't think so,' Ethan hollered. 'Probably doesn't need to be. You see the size of him?'

Ethan saw the big man turn left onto NW Thirteenth Court, Lopez in pursuit and rapidly closing the gap. Ethan pushed harder, reaching the street into which the man had vanished.

The street was narrow and quiet, lined with heavy steel fences on one side and rows of trees and a shabby chain-link fence on the other. Ethan slowed as he saw Lopez vault over the chain-link into an area of dead ground strewn with debris and wiry grass. Ethan leapt over the fence and came up short as he saw the big man facing them, his broad chest heaving.

A cruel smile split the man's heavy jaw as he waved Ethan and Lopez forward with a brief motion of one hand. His other was clenched into a fist the size of a football.

'Ladies first,' Ethan suggested.

'What was it you said?' she uttered back at him. 'The bigger they are . . . ?'

Ethan stepped forward and raised his fists, focusing all of his attention on the man's eyes. *Keep moving, keep out his grasp and make him keep swinging. He wasn't able to keep running, so he'll tire soon enough.*

The man raised both fists now, his biceps bulging, and without any warning shot a straight left directly toward Ethan's face. Ethan dodged right and blocked the blow with his left forearm. The huge fist ploughed through his guard like a cannonball through a window and hit his left temple with enough force to send him reeling back four paces.

Ethan's vision blurred as he shook his head and blinked to see the giant rushing at him with both arms outstretched.

Ethan dropped down low, twisting on his left heel and shooting his right boot out toward the man's groin. His size-10 hit the man squarely between his legs with a satisfying steel-toe-capped thump, and Ethan saw him gasp, his vivid blue eyes widening with shock as he folded over and staggered sideways to crash into a discarded trash can. Ethan leapt to his feet and kept his guard up as he circled the stricken giant. The man straightened, tears flooding his eyes, but he growled with fury as he charged Ethan again.

Ethan stepped left, locking his fists together and batting the huge arms aside with his own as he brought his knee up into the giant's stomach. The big man folded again but it wasn't enough to drop him. A pair of immense arms crushed Ethan's waist as he was lifted bodily off the ground and hurled sideways.

The breath blasted from his lungs as he hit the trunk of a tree, his head cracking against the unyielding bark. Ethan slumped onto the hard ground and struggled to get up as the giant towered over him and lifted one enormous boot. With a flourish of malice on his face he stamped it down toward Ethan's head.

A smaller boot flashed into view from Ethan's left as Lopez's sidekick slammed into the giant's torso with a dull thud. The big man toppled over sideways as his boot flailed past Ethan's head and into thin air.

Lopez danced past Ethan as the giant turned to face her and swung an enormous right arm like a battering ram toward her head. Ethan struggled upright as he saw Lopez duck down beneath the blow and step fearlessly in, one tiny right fist whipping up into the giant's eyes with a sharp crack. The man's enormous square head did not flinch, but the skin above his right eye split into a wet, red tear as Lopez leapt back out of range and began circling him again.

'Game's over,' Ethan rasped at him. 'You're outnumbered.'

The big man reached behind him and grabbed the

discarded trash can, lifted it into the air above his head
and hurled it at Lopez. Lopez leapt aside and hit the
ground as it crashed past her and bounced across the
dusty earth. The big man turned to Ethan and from his
jeans produced a long, broad knife that flashed in the
light as he whipped the blade toward Ethan's neck.

Ethan lurched back out of range of the blade as it
flashed past, just in time to catch the big man's other fist
square in the center of his chest. It felt like being hit by
a train. Ethan hurtled backwards and tripped over Lopez's
legs as he slammed down onto the ground and collapsed
them both into an ungainly tangle of limbs. Through his
hazy vision he saw the giant turn and vault back over the
rickety fence as a brown Lincoln raced alongside the
sidewalk and screeched to a halt. The giant threw himself
into the vehicle and it accelerated away out of sight.

Lopez looked over her shoulder at him, her thick
black hair plastered across her face.

'You wanna get the hell off me?'

Ethan rolled to one side, crawled to his knees and
then got to his feet as Lopez dragged herself upright and
swept her hair out of her face. 'I'd have had him if you
hadn't got in the way.'

Ethan managed a bitter chuckle as he rubbed his back
and coughed. 'Sure.'

'Told you we could have done with Bryson,' she
suggested.

Ethan, already somewhat deflated, felt a new and
unexpected hollowness form in the pit of his belly.

'Will you quit with the sailor worship? Captain Ahab's
not playing ball, so let's just get back to the courthouse.'

Together, they walked and limped back to the scene of the wreck. Fire trucks and police cars swamped the streets in a blaze of flashing lights. Smoke hung heavily on the air but Ethan could see that the fires were already out. To his dismay, the red Pontiac was now a mangled black cage scorched by the flames. The front end of the convertible was also charred to the color of ash, a hastily erected white canvas sheet hung over the corpse of the driver still slumped in his now burned seat.

At the far end of the street, two television crews were avidly filming the carnage and setting up for the lunch-time broadcasts.

Doug Jarvis spotted Ethan and Lopez and hurried across.

'How the hell do you manage to get involved in these things?' he asked Ethan in exasperation. 'We only came here for a quiet chat with a lawyer. Now half the street's on fire. You keep this up and you'll be the ones facing jail time.'

'This was a hit, Doug, pure and simple. I don't suppose the prosecutor survived?'

Jarvis shook his head.

'No, and get this. She had the incriminating documents on her person when the accident happened. I just asked her assistant if she'd made copies before they took him to the hospital. But the documents were sent direct to her at the courthouse, so none had been made.'

'Which means the case literally goes up in smoke,' Lopez said without a trace of humor.

'Along with the Uhungu family's chances of a success-ful conviction against IRIS,' Jarvis agreed. 'Without those documents it's unlikely any charges can be brought against the company.'

'Which is a little too coincidental,' Lopez murmured. 'If Purcell worked for IRIS and decided to turn whistle-blower then it's possible, however unlikely, that IRIS is responsible for the murder of both Purcell's family and the prosecuting lawyer.'

'Are you telling me that Charles Purcell never made copies of these incriminating documents?' Ethan asked. 'Surely, with what's at stake, he would have covered himself for something just like this?'

'We can't know one way or the other,' Jarvis replied, 'unless we ask Purcell himself.'

Ethan clenched his fists in frustration.

'Damn it, how could that man we chased have known where and when these documents would come to light? He had to be in exactly the right spot at exactly the right time to know that he could destroy everything and make a decent getaway. Jesus, look at this place, it's a court-house and crawling with cops.'

'I take it he did indeed get away,' Jarvis said, taking in their slightly bedraggled appearance.

'Not without a fight,' Ethan replied. 'But a kid with a cellphone got a shot of him at the scene which we can give to local law enforcement, see if they can't identify him. He got picked up in a brown Lincoln.'

'I've got the picture on my cellphone now,' Jarvis said. 'I'll have the local uniforms check out the geta-way vehicle, but it'll most likely turn out to be stolen.'

'What about Katherine Abell?' Lopez asked. 'This all

happened right around her. Maybe it's something that she might have arranged?'

Jarvis gestured over his shoulder to where a small knot of police detectives led by Captain Karl Sears were questioning Katherine and her assistant.

'The uniforms figured the same,' the old man said. 'I'm guessing that Katherine will be taken in for questioning, but I can't believe that she'd have any involvement in this.'

Ethan looked across at Katherine and made a decision.

'Supposedly, neither should Joaquin Abell,' he replied. 'But right now the only thing that connects all of this is IRIS itself. We need to talk to Katherine right now. Trouble is she's not going to just sing to us if her husband's involved in this.'

'I agree,' Lopez said. 'Let me handle it.'

30

June 28, 12:42

Katherine Abell sat at a table in a waiting room inside the courthouse, two police officers guarding the door as Ethan and Lopez leaned against the wall opposite her. A knock at the door preceded Captain Karl Sears and Doug Jarvis, who closed the door behind them. Sears walked up to the table and looked down at Katherine.

'Mrs Abell, I understand that the chief justice has asked you to remain in the courthouse for the time being?'

Ethan watched as Katherine Abell nodded without looking up at Sears, her small fists clenched around a tissue and her eyes darkened where the little make-up she wore had smeared. There seemed little doubt that she was innocent of any involvement in the murder of Macy Lieberman but then again, beauty was often the veil that concealed hideous evil, and Karl Sears clearly saw just that.

'We would like to understand,' the detective asked her, 'what you know about what happened.'

Katherine looked up at him, speaking from behind her lawyer's facade of calm.

'I told the police outside everything,' she said. 'Both my assistant, Peter, and I saw it all happen from the courtyard. Macy got into her car and left, and then another vehicle crashed into her . . .'

Jarvis moved forward and took a seat on the edge of the table.

'That's right,' he agreed. 'But is it not true that, before the accident, you and Macy were involved in some kind of argument?'

Katherine sighed and nodded.

'Macy came out at me, trying to suggest that I was involved in some kind of conspiracy at my husband's company. She wound me up and I snapped.'

'You hit her,' Sears pointed out, 'in front of almost a hundred witnesses, all of whom will be on the record once the uniforms finish taking statements.'

'Then I guess those of them that were close enough will have heard what Macy was saying, too, won't they?' Katherine shot back.

Jarvis raised an eyebrow and glanced briefly at Ethan, who pushed off the wall and approached Katherine.

'You were defending IRIS in a lawsuit case brought by the Uhungu family,' he said. 'You can see why the uniforms are suspicious when the prosecution's star lawyer is killed just hours before she was due to deliver incriminating documents and evidence that might have resulted in convictions at IRIS.'

Katherine leveled a steady, cold glare at him, clearly not intimidated.

'*Alleged* documents, *alleged* evidence,' she snapped, 'and all of it brought to her by a man wanted for the suspected murder of his own wife and daughter. It meant nothing to the case unless whatever was in those documents could be verified.'

'Which it now can't,' Lopez said from further back in the room.

'No,' Katherine acknowledged softly, as though recalling the horror of what had transpired.

'IRIS has been accused of hoarding government funds instead of using them for charitable acts,' Jarvis said. 'Macy Lieberman was attempting to prove that accusation when she died. Do you know of anyone at IRIS who might try to do something like this?'

Katherine shook her head.

'No. IRIS is a charity and its employees are paid to help others, people in need. Going around killing lawyers isn't exactly part of the company's charter.'

'Are you sure?' Ethan asked.

'What the hell do you mean?' Katherine shot up out of her chair. 'Do you think that my husband is involved in this?'

'We don't know,' Ethan replied curtly.

'That's right, you goddamned well don't know!' Lightning flashed behind Katherine's eyes as she rounded the table to confront him. 'I'm a lawyer. Do you think that you can just waltz in here and start tossing accusations around? My husband has done more for the needy out there in the last ten years than most people do in a lifetime. Why is it that some people seem so determined to drag others down to their own goddamned level? How much does IRIS have to do before people start realizing that it's there to help, not to destroy?'

Ethan stood his ground before Katherine's wrath, but it was Lopez who stepped forward and spoke.

'This isn't a witch hunt, it's a murder investigation,' she said. 'We couldn't give a damn if Joaquin Abell and IRIS have found a cure for cancer, taken man back to the moon and found the original copy of the Bible. Everyone is a suspect when there's a possible motive, no matter how trivial or unfair it may seem. As a lawyer, you of all people should understand that, or maybe you're just too close to the client to have an objective view of what's happened?'

Katherine Abell glared at Lopez, but then suddenly all of the anger went out of her and she slumped back down into her chair. She rubbed her temples with one hand.

'I know how it looks, but surely it was just an accident?'

Lopez looked at Karl Sears, who nodded once.

Lopez slipped her hand into her pocket and retrieved a printed image taken from the cellphone of the kid who had witnessed the car wreck. The pixilated photograph showed a huge blond man turning to flee the scene. She turned it around and laid it on the table beside Katherine.

'This image was taken on a cellphone by an eye-witness,' Lopez said. 'Do you recognize this man?'

Ethan watched carefully as Katherine looked down at the picture, and he saw her lips part and her hand clench tightly around the tissue in her hand. Lopez didn't miss her reaction.

'Who is he, Katherine?'

Katherine shook her head. 'I don't know who he is.'

'You're lying,' Lopez said.

Katherine looked up sharply and for a moment Ethan thought that bolts of lightning might blaze from her eyes and strike Lopez down.

'I said that I didn't know him,' Katherine hissed, her words laden with venom, 'not that I didn't recognize him.'

'Where have you seen him before?' Ethan asked.

'He was in the public gallery,' Katherine replied, 'watching the case.'

'Are there cameras in the courtroom?'

'Yes, but they're not routinely turned on,' Katherine replied. 'Besides, what difference does it make?'

'He was driving the car that killed Macy,' Lopez said. 'Believe me, he had something to do with it all right. My partner and I chased him for three whole blocks. He got away but uniforms are looking for him. The car he was in belonged to the man in the passenger seat, who is dead. We'll have to wait for autopsy results to find out whether he died in the wreck or was killed by this guy beforehand.'

Katherine looked down at the image of the fleeing man.

'But if it was done on purpose then who would have wanted Macy dead? No supporter of IRIS would have wanted it, as it would have jeopardized my defense, and our detractors would have keenly awaited Macy's prosecution evidence. It doesn't make any sense.'

'Unless the accusations have a basis in fact,' Lopez

pointed out, 'and somebody at IRIS needed the prose-cutor to be silenced.'

'Based on the evidence of a suspected murderer?' Katherine challenged. 'You really think that there was something in those documents?'

'We don't know,' Lopez admitted, 'but we're here to find a killer, not bring IRIS to trial.' Lopez took a deep breath and decided to go for broke. 'Were you aware that earlier today an aircraft with almost twenty IRIS employees crashed, out in the Florida Straits?'

Katherine nodded.

'Yes, I was. It was a terrible tragedy.' Her shoulders sagged. 'It's been a tragic day.'

'Can you think of any reason why IRIS might want to silence members of its own staff?' Lopez pressed.

'You people just don't quit, do you?' Katherine uttered incredulously. 'You think that those scientists were killed on purpose?'

Lopez leaned in toward Katherine.

'We dived on the wreck of the aircraft,' she said. 'The black box had been removed. Whatever happened to that airplane it wasn't an accident. We were then attacked and barely got away with our lives. It's highly suspicious that so many people who might have been in a position to possess incriminating evidence with respect to IRIS have died recently: Macy, the scientists on that plane and Charles Purcell's family. Purcell himself is on the run. Doesn't that concern you?'

Katherine rubbed her face with her hands in exasperation.

'Of course it does, but I don't understand what's

happening here! Two hours ago I was defending my husband in a court case. Now one person is dead and you're effectively implicating Joaquin in a homicide!'

Ethan thought for a moment. 'Where is Joaquin, right now?' he asked her.

'On his yacht, out in the Florida Straits,' Katherine replied.

Lopez stared down at Katherine.

'You need to think carefully about what's happening here, Katherine, because one way or the other we're going to get to the bottom of it all.'

Lopez let the statement hang in the air for a moment and then turned and made for the exit, leaving Katherine looking down at the image of the blond giant as the others left the room behind her.

Ethan turned to look at Lopez as soon as they were out of earshot. 'Nice work, but we really need to speak to Joaquin Abell himself.'

'Agreed,' Lopez replied, leaning on the wall outside the room with her arms folded. 'There's only so much we can do with Katherine if she's innocent of any involvement in this.'

'No,' Kyle Sears insisted, and jabbed his thumb at his own chest. '*We* need to speak to Joaquin Abell. This car wreck is a homicide and therefore a police matter.'

Jarvis shook his head.

'It's a DIA case for now, Karl, and that's the way it's staying. Either way, right now we've got no grounds to bring Joaquin Abell down here from his lofty perch.'

'I don't care how high and mighty this guy thinks is,' Ethan replied, joining Lopez against the wall of the corridor, as lawyers and cops bustled past them, the entire building now a crime scene and closed down. 'He's got something to do with all of this, something to hide. The sooner we can get in his face the sooner we'll figure out what that *something* is.'

'This is a civil case,' Sears insisted, jabbing a finger at Jarvis. 'Nothing directly to do with Charles Purcell. I want my people in the loop.'

Jarvis looked back thoughtfully at the closed door behind which Katherine Abell sat.

'Joaquin Abell's too well-connected,' he said finally. 'I don't see how we can get to him on evidence this thin – it's all circumstantial, and his wife seems as surprised by all of this as we are. I don't think she can help us, at least not yet.'

'Leave that to us,' Sears said confidently. 'Threaten a lawyer with a prison cell and they'll soon start squealing.'

'Katherine won't,' Ethan said. He'd seen enough of her to tell that she was fiercely protective of her family but equally dedicated to upholding the law. 'She's too principled a lawyer.'

'Not so principled that she'd betray her husband and family,' Lopez pointed out. 'Maybe we can turn that to our advantage. Let's have a word with the uniforms and see if we can take her back to Joaquin ourselves.'

'Like hell,' Sears snapped, pacing up and down in the corridor. 'She's potentially a suspect and I'm sure the Chief Justice will agree. There's no way I'm letting her out of the state.'

'How do you figure that will help?' Jarvis asked Lopez, ignoring the detective.

'She's innocent,' Lopez said. 'Sure, she might know more than she's letting on, but she didn't pull a trigger. Let's get the police off her case here, and in return maybe we can find out if our big blond friend is on Joaquin's yacht and if there's any ammunition aboard that's been dunked in Rubidium-82.'

Jarvis's phone trilled in his pocket and he slipped it out and held it to his ear. Ethan watched the line of the old man's jaw harden as he nodded, listening, and then ended the call.

'What's up?' Lopez asked.

'That was the Coastguard,' Jarvis replied. 'They turned up on the sandbar where N-2764C went down.'

'They find the black box?' Ethan asked.

'Nope,' Jarvis said, 'they didn't find a damned thing.'

'What do you mean?' Sears said.

'The wreck's gone.'

FLORIDA STRAITS

June 28, 13:37

The IRIS helicopter skimmed low over the waves, the crystalline blue rollers churning beneath it. Through the windows, Ethan could see the shadow of the helicopter racing across the surface of the ocean.

Ethan Warner sat next to Lopez in the rear of the helicopter, with Doug Jarvis sitting opposite them flanked by two armed DIA soldiers. Katherine Abell had chosen to sit in the cockpit alongside the pilot, which at least gave Ethan the chance to speak freely given the engine noise in the cabin. As a precaution, Jarvis leaned forward so that he could lower his voice as he spoke.

'You do realize that if Joaquin is involved in this, he may decide to keep us aboard his yacht or feed us to sharks or something. We've only got two guards as escorts.'

'This isn't a Bond movie, Doug,' Ethan pointed out. 'If Joaquin has killed a lawyer as well as twenty-or-so scientists, having all of us iced is going to be one coincidence too many.'

'Is it?' Jarvis challenged. 'Or is it possible that there is simply nothing that this man will not do to achieve his goals?'

'He could flee,' Lopez pointed out. 'He could make Mexico or even Brazil on his yacht before anybody would know.'

'Which would kind of defeat the object of being a famous humanitarian,' Ethan replied. 'He's carved himself a niche as the world's nicest guy and he's not going to want to lose that popularity. If it goes public, he won't go down without a fight.'

The helicopter descended and slowed as Ethan saw the wake of an enormous yacht cruising the Straits. The helicopter slowed until it hovered alongside the yacht's stern, and Ethan caught a glimpse of the yacht's name emblazoned there: *Event Horizon*. The helicopter drifted slowly across over a large helipad and then settled down onto the deck. Immediately, men in blue jumpsuits ran out to secure tether lines to the helicopter's fuselage and open the side doors. Ethan jumped out into the down-wash of the spinning blades and jogged to the edge of the platform with Lopez and Jarvis close behind.

The helicopter's engines whined down as Katherine Abell climbed out and walked toward them. As she did so a door opened in the yacht and Joaquin Abell strode out from the interior, his black suit stark against his white shirt and the clinically clean white decks. He jogged up the steps onto the helipad and held his arms out to his wife. Ethan watched as the pair embraced tightly and he felt something pinch his throat as an image of Joanna appeared unbidden in his mind's eye. He missed that; the intimacy of returning home to someone who'd actually missed you.

Joaquin reluctantly released Katherine and turned to look at Ethan.

'You didn't tell me you were bringing guests,' he said. 'Or armed guards.'

'I didn't know that I would be,' Katherine replied, casting a wary eye at Ethan and his companions. 'Joaquin, this is Ethan Warner.'

Joaquin shook Ethan's hand. The billionaire's skin was soft, unblemished by the scars of honest work. Ethan introduced him to Lopez and Jarvis, who gestured to the two soldiers.

'Mr. Abell, these men are charged with searching this vessel for evidence of weaponry that we suspect may be linked to crimes committed in Miami yesterday and today. They cannot legally enter your vessel without your permission, but I trust that won't be an issue.'

Ethan watched as Joaquin processed what Jarvis had said. He couldn't tell if the man was affronted or confused by the thinly veiled threat, so unconcerned did he appear.

'What crimes?' he asked finally.

'Homicides.'

'I have nothing to hide,' Joaquin said, 'and we have no weapons aboard. If you must search this vessel then at least do so without damaging anything.'

Jarvis nodded to the two soldiers, who immediately began scouring the yacht. Ethan turned and followed the others inside.

Ethan had never really known luxury in his life. Although his parents had raised himself and his sister in comfort, they were a working-class military family and lived as such. Coupon days, holidays out by the lakes rather than abroad, buying used instead of new. Ethan had learned to live with a certain austerity and had been happy to do so. Now, he found himself marveling at every aspect of the yacht. Sumptuous carpets adorned the floors of even minor passageways, the wooden doors to various cabins polished to a deep mahogany. Oil paintings the size of tables depicting naval battles lined a gallery in the center of the vessel, that itself faced an ornate staircase leading up toward the bridge. Deep carpets, the tasteful decor, the paintings and the fittings – everything was highly polished and in its place, even the chrome railings and handles buffed to a mirror finish. And this was just the guy's yacht, for Christ's sake. Ethan couldn't even begin to imagine what Joaquin Abell's house might look like.

'This way, please.'

A young man dressed in black pants, white shirt and a bowtie waved them into a large, oval-shaped room ringed with cream leather couches that faced a plasma screen bigger than Ethan's entire lounge. The room was overlooked by a broad bay window that revealed the panoramic ocean beyond the yacht's stern.

'I'm afraid that I do not have any refreshments prepared,' Joaquin said as they sat down. 'Had I known in advance of your arrival I would have alerted the galley.'

'Not a problem,' Jarvis replied, 'we're here on business, not for fine dining.'

'They think that you killed Macy Lieberman,' Katherine told her husband.

'Macy Lieberman?' Joaquin said. 'The lawyer?'

'She was killed in a hit-and-run wreck in Miami barely an hour ago,' Jarvis confirmed. 'A suspect is being hunted as we speak. Do you know this man?'

Jarvis handed Joaquin the image of the big blond man. Ethan watched as Joaquin studied the image intently for a moment before shaking his head.

'I'm sure I don't; he looks very distinctive.' Joaquin handed the image back to Jarvis. 'IRIS employs a lot of people, but I've never seen this man before.'

'Your wife said she saw him in the gallery during the hearing,' Lopez said.

Joaquin sighed and opened his hands palm-outward in a gesture of helplessness.

'I don't know what you want me to say. I've been aboard my yacht for the past day and I was in Puerto Rico yesterday. I've only seen what's happened on the news channels. Perhaps this man you suspect of the killing is some kind of neo-Nazi? He looks somewhat the type, and the court case has garnered a great deal of press attention. Perhaps he disliked the Uhungu family's lack of gratitude for what IRIS had done for them.'

Ethan smiled thinly.

'If that was the case, he'd have likely killed the Uhungu family and not their lawyer and an innocent bystander.'

Joaquin's features sagged.

'Another murder?' he said. 'My God. This is dreadful.'

'And that's not all,' Jarvis cut in. 'Your company lost some twenty employees yesterday in an aircraft crash in the Bermuda Triangle, is that correct?'

'An appalling tragedy,' Joaquin replied softly. 'We're

talking to the families of the victims of the accident right now to arrange compensation for their loss and to secure their futures.'

'How do you know that the crash was an accident?' Lopez asked.

'I don't,' Joaquin replied. 'But there was nothing to suggest that the aircraft was tampered with in any way. It simply disappeared over the ocean.'

'Not quite,' Ethan said.

Joaquin looked at him expectantly, but Ethan purposefully let the silence hang until it became too much for their host to bear.

'What do you mean?' Joaquin asked.

'The aircraft was found,' Ethan replied, 'and there are some major questions being asked by the NTSB.'

Ethan saw the faintest quiver in Joaquin's studied expression, a tremor of unease.

'What kind of questions?'

'The ones that get asked when an aircraft disappears *after* it crashed,' Lopez answered for Ethan.

'That happens naturally from time to time,' Joaquin countered. 'The currents here in the straits are extremely powerful – it's these currents that are responsible for many of the Bermuda Triangle's legendary "vanishings". Aircraft and ships are downed by natural causes but drift for miles across the ocean before settling.'

'That's entirely true,' Ethan conceded, 'but the aircraft *was* found, lying flat on its belly in less than fifty feet of water. The nose and cockpit were crushed, revealing that it went into the ocean almost vertically, at very high speed, before falling onto its belly.'

Before Joaquin could answer, Jarvis leaned forward in his seat.

'And underwater currents don't open fuselage panels and remove the black boxes,' he pointed out. 'What's more, Mr. Abell, when the authorities returned to the site, the aircraft had vanished entirely.'

Joaquin gaped at them for a long moment.

'As I just said, the currents in these waters are notoriously powerful. And why would anybody have removed the black boxes? I had no reason to tamper with the wreck, if I even knew where it was.'

'Didn't you?' Lopez challenged. 'The court case your wife was defending concerned revelations revealed by a former employee of yours, a Charles Purcell. He's a whistle-blower claiming to have evidence of corporate fraud by IRIS. He was on the passenger manifest of that aircraft and was supposed to have been aboard when it went down, Joaquin. You see a pattern developing here?'

Joaquin stood upright and looked down at Lopez.

'Yes, I do. I see a lot of accusations all going in one direction: that I, or somebody in my company, is responsible for all of this. I see a more likely possibility – that this is being orchestrated by the likes of Charles Purcell in order to bring disrepute to IRIS and to my name.'

'Murder,' Lopez pointed out, 'is an awful long way to go to achieve that. If what you're saying were true, Purcell could simply have walked into any police station with his evidence and handed it over.'

Joaquin shook his head.

'The man is wanted for the murder of his own damned family! Does that not count for anything? You're here questioning and accusing me, without jurisdiction, when a man suspected of a hideous crime remains free – and yet is able to submit evidence to a court and be taken *seriously*!'

Ethan leaned back on the couch.

'All avenues need to be explored, Joaquin,' he replied, using the man's first name purposely in order to annoy him. 'Everybody who has a connection to these events is a suspect, and right now we're running out of time to find the perpetrator or perpetrators.'

'Why?' Katherine Abell asked. 'What's the rush?'

Ethan shrugged.

'It's always after the first forty-eight hours that cases start going cold,' he replied, and then fixed his gaze again on her husband. 'And it's not like we can see into the future to figure out what's going on, is it, Joaquin?'

Joaquin's eyes briefly flared with surprise and Ethan saw him swallow thickly.

'If only we could.'

'If somebody *had*,' Lopez murmured, 'then we'd know a little more about this case than the perpetrator might think.'

Joaquin's studied calm withered as he stared at Lopez, attracting the attention of Katherine, who stood up.

'That's enough,' she said. 'This is getting us nowhere. If you have no more questions, Mr. Jarvis?'

At that moment, the two DIA soldiers appeared in the doorway to the room. One of them looked at Jarvis and shook his head.

'Not a thing. The whole ship's clean sir, no weapons aboard.'

Jarvis stood up and extended a hand to Joaquin.

'Thank you for your valuable time, Mr. Abell,' he said, as Joaquin shook his hand. 'I foresee that we'll speak again — in the future.'

Joaquin coughed and managed a weak smile in response.

'I'll arrange for the ship's helicopter to take you back to Miami.'

Ethan and Lopez followed Jarvis out of the room. As soon as the door was closed behind them and they were walking down the corridor, Ethan turned to Jarvis.

'He knows something.'

'Indeed he does,' Jarvis agreed, 'but what?'

As they walked out onto the helipad Ethan looked back across the yacht, and something that he hadn't seen before caught his eye.

'There's no evidence that he's hiding anything out here,' Jarvis was saying, 'either physically or financially. Unless we can prove otherwise we're chasing rainbows.'

'Oh, he's hiding something all right,' Ethan replied.

'How can you be sure?' Lopez asked. 'There's nothing aboard this ship.'

'I know,' Ethan replied and then pointed toward the yacht's bows. 'But maybe what we're looking for isn't actually aboard.'

Jarvis and Lopez looked in the direction Ethan was indicating, to where two large yellow submersibles emblazoned with the IRIS logo sat on their launches.

'I'll be damned,' Jarvis said. 'Those things could give him access to the seabed.'

'Listen, Doug,' Ethan said. 'Somebody, somewhere, knows what's happening before it happens, and we can't do anything about it unless we can get the jump on them. It might be Joaquin Abell but we've got nothing solid on him yet. We've got to find Purcell and learn everything that he knows or this is going to wind up a cold case that'll never get opened again.'

'But if the people responsible already know what we're going to do,' Lopez said, 'then anything we can think of has already been pre-empted. We can't fight what we can't see.'

'It doesn't matter,' Ethan said. 'The only person that we know for certain has that ability is Charles Purcell. Maybe if we can trace his steps from the point where his family were murdered, we can figure out how to get ahead of him.'

Jarvis fished his cellphone out of his pocket.

'I feared that it would come to this,' he said. 'I've got something that I need to show you, and it might help us catch up with Charles Purcell. But this is above-Top-Secret, Cosmic clearance. You'll have to sign non-disclosure agreements before we leave.'

'Where are we going?' Lopez asked.

'Back to Cape Canaveral. But not a part of it you'll have seen before.'

'I want to know exactly what's going on.'

Katherine Abell stood in the center of the room, blocking Joaquin's access to the corridor outside. Despite her transparent fury, in the light flaring through the windows she was a vision of loveliness, he thought, her long hair falling down across her shoulders and glowing like a halo in the sunlight, as her green eyes stared into his.

'Nothing's going on,' Joaquin promised her. 'I'm glad you're here now. Let's sit down and—'

'Don't patronize me,' she shot back. 'What the hell have you been doing with the company's funds, and what were you talking to the governor about this morning at the hotel?'

Joaquin raised his hands.

'I wanted to speak to him about our plans for the conservation area, and my concerns for the livelihood of people living on the edge of Costa Rica's fault lines.'

Katherine seemed to rear up even taller, much as a cobra might when provoked.

'For that, Joaquin, a telephone call would have sufficed.' She paced toward him and her eyes blazed into his like laser beams. 'Do you really think that I'm simply going to believe that everything that's happened over the last twenty-four hours is some kind of bizarre accident?'

Joaquin stood rooted to the spot, suddenly unable to breathe.

'What do you mean?'

Katherine was now inches from him.

'The case against IRIS collapses,' she said rhetorically. 'A man named Charles Purcell, who once worked for you, is now on the run after his family are murdered. He provided evidence against IRIS that is conveniently destroyed in the same accident that killed the lead prosecutor. IRIS employees disappear in an aircraft accident out in the Bermuda Triangle, and then the wreckage mysteriously vanishes. And then there are the claims of millions of dollars of government-provided IRIS money disappearing into thin air.'

Joaquin swallowed, his throat tight.

'Our accounts were independently audited by—'

'Stop *lying* to me!'

Katherine's fury, incarcerated for hours, suddenly burst free from its cell. Her hand whipped across Joaquin's cheek with a sharp crack. He flinched away and toppled back down onto the couch, clutching his face in shock.

'Jesus Christ, what's gotten into you?' he uttered.

Katherine glowered down at him for a long moment before speaking.

'How long have we been married?' she asked.

'Fourteen years.'

Most people assumed that she and Joaquin were about the same age, yet she was almost ten years his senior. The genes she had inherited from her mother, combined with careful living, ensured that she looked almost supernaturally young. Her years as a lawyer and her maturity meant that, to her, Joaquin Abell often appeared a selfish little child prone to delusions of grandeur that would make a Saudi prince blush.

'Fourteen years,' she echoed. 'And in all that time don't you think that I might have learned to spot the signs that you're lying to me, dear husband?'

The stinging in Joaquin's face subsided enough for him to lower his hand as he looked at her.

'What the hell do you mean?'

'You're lying to me, and it's not just about your meeting with the governor, is it?'

Joaquin chose his words carefully. 'I'm not lying to you.'

Katherine folded her arms as she stared down at him, and for the first time in fourteen years Joaquin realized that his wife's relentless and calculating mind was more than capable of penetrating the veil of secrecy he had erected around IRIS's activities.

'I have spent many hours representing your company in courts across the United States. My reputation has been built on defending clients the way they were supposed to be defended: honorably, in accordance with the law. I've prided myself on only taking cases where I knew for sure that my client was innocent.' She leaned forward slightly at the waist and her hair fell across one side of her face. 'In the last two hours I've learned that IRIS has been involved in fraud, and I demand to know everything.'

Joaquin shook his head.

'No, it's not like that, it's—'

'From the beginning, Joaquin,' she interrupted. 'Don't you dare hold even the tiniest detail back. I'm a fucking lawyer and I'll know you're lying five seconds before you've opened your pathetic, spoilt little mouth.'

Joaquin gaped at her, uncertain whether he should speak, and where to start if he did.

'It's—' he began, then fumbled. 'It's complicated.'

'So is law,' Katherine hissed. 'Give me some goddamned credit and assume I can navigate my way to understanding your juvenile little scam. According to Macy Lieberman's evidence, more than seventy million dollars of taxpayers' money has disappeared from IRIS bank accounts over the last eight to ten years. You're going to tell me where that money is right now and what's being done with it.'

Joaquin shook his head.

'It's not that simple.'

'It *is* that simple,' Katherine assured him and turned to her handbag, producing her cellphone. 'One call, and whatever you're up to will be over. All I have to do is call the courts and tell them that I suspect that you are complicit in the murder of Macy Lieberman, and before you've had time to think you'll be on your ass in a maximum-security prison awaiting a trial that, if you're lucky, won't see you spending the next two decades on Death Row.'

Joaquin's jaw dropped. 'You wouldn't do that. You wouldn't betray our family like that.'

Katherine leaned in close.

'Family? *Family?* How dare you bring our children or me into your dirty little scam? I'm your wife and you've been betraying me with this for years. I'll turn you in because I'm a lawyer and to protect our children, because there is nothing that I would not do for them. By God, if you don't start talking in the next thirty seconds I'll lead the fucking prosecution myself.'

Joaquin stared at his wife in shock.

'This is insane.'

'Yes it is,' she agreed, 'and just the kind of moronic, self-centered scheming I've come to suspect that you're capable of. Perhaps you need some help in deciding where to start your story? Tell me, why was that thug Olaf in the public gallery during the trial hearing?'

'I sent him to keep an eye on you and—'

Katherine's hand slapped across his face again.

'He killed Macy!'

Katherine saw in her husband's collapsing expression the depth of Olaf's mistakes. Katherine waved her phone in the air between them.

'Talk, Joaquin, or I swear that by sundown you'll be history.'

Joaquin hesitated for a moment longer and then the words began tumbling from his lips as though they had been waiting there all along. The long years of finding men who understood his father's work, then his hiring of Charles Purcell; the purchase and expansion of the underwater complex and the difficulties in keeping such a major construction secret enough that only a few dozen people knew of its existence. The final, unavoidable task of causing an accident that would take the lives of those same people, so that only Joaquin and a select few remained. The sad, tragic task of preventing Charles Purcell from destroying everything that Joaquin had sacrificed so much to achieve – his altar to his father's memory. And then Purcell's escape and betrayal, taking with him one of the cameras from the Deep Blue chamber, evidence of Joaquin's laboratory.

Katherine stood in silence for the first half of the story, and then paced silently up and down for the rest, much as he had seen her do when preparing case notes for a trial. Joaquin finally finished speaking and immediately hated the silence that followed. He realized, belatedly, that it was Katherine's wrath that he feared the most, as though, if he were to simply keep on speaking, he could somehow avoid it. Despite having little else to say, he couldn't help himself.

'I felt that it was the right thing to do,' he murmured. 'That the opportunity was just too great to pass up. Imagine, Katherine – governments forced to bend to our will, to help those in need instead of profiting from their suffering? There would be nothing that we could not do.' Katherine did not respond, pacing up and down, her eyes glazed over, lost deep in thought. Joaquin sighed. 'But I didn't think that things would happen like this. I didn't mean for any of this to happen.'

Katherine stopped pacing and hurled her cellphone at him. Joaquin flinched as the phone hit the side of his face, followed by Katherine's bunched fists that pummeled his head as she leapt at him.

'You meant for *all* of it to happen!' she screamed, and then suddenly scrambled away as though appalled to be in physical contact with him.

Joaquin uncovered his face and saw her glaring down at him.

'You're sick,' she spat.

'I'm sorry,' Joaquin muttered, a feeble noise even to his own ears. 'I'm so sorry.'

'Shut up,' Katherine uttered.

Joaquin fell silent as she paced for another moment or two before speaking.

'We're finished,' she said finally. 'You can't hide what you've done and you'll end up taking me down with you. Nobody will believe that I had nothing to do with this.'

'You weren't supposed to get involved and—'

'I said *shut up!*' Katherine screamed at him. She closed her eyes, massaging her temples with one hand and calming her breathing by force of will. 'This device of yours, it sees the future?'

'Yes,' Joaquin replied. 'Via news networks. Any major stories can be pre-empted by up to twenty-four hours.'

'Why the time limit?' Katherine asked.

'It's to do with 'something that Charles Purcell called the Schwarzschild Radius.'

'Where is Dennis?' she demanded. 'Is he in on this?'

Joaquin looked up at his wife and came to a rapid decision. 'Dennis has been involved from the very start,' he lied.

Katherine almost gagged as she realized the depth of

Joaquin's betrayal and of Dennis Aubrey's involvement. She overcame her horror and took a deep breath.

'You need to use Dennis's skills to find Charles Purcell,' she said. 'If Purcell takes what he knows to the courts this will all be over.'

'You're coming in on this?' he uttered as he got to his feet.

'I don't have a choice!' she raged. 'You've doomed us both because of your greed. You had everything, the admiration of an entire country, maybe even all of humanity, and you've wasted it because you're like all men: enough is never enough!'

Joaquin sat back down, unable to find anything else to say.

Katherine grabbed her cellphone and shoved it back into her handbag.

'Find Purcell. Then you'll use this device of yours to make sure that nobody finds out anything about what has happened here.'

'What are you going to do?' Joaquin asked.

Katherine shouldered her bag and looked at him in disgust.

'I'm going to the IRIS medical camp in the Dominican Republic,' she replied. '*I'm* going to do what IRIS is supposed to be doing, and help people. Going there will help rebuild what's left of my reputation, too. I don't want anything more to do with you until this is all over, understand? If you call me or come near me, I swear I'll kill you myself.'

'But you should be here with me,' Joaquin pleaded. 'We can work this out and—'

'You're finished!' Katherine shouted. '*We're* finished! How can you possibly imagine that any decent human being would even consider being in the same room as somebody like you?'

Joaquin stared at his wife for a long moment. 'So you're leaving me, then? You're leaving our kids? You want a divorce?'

Katherine's features were racked with repulsion and her jaw trembled as she spoke.

'There is nothing I won't do for my children,' she repeated, 'even if it means remaining married to a monster like you.'

'Then you will keep silent about all that's happened?'

A tear traced a line down Katherine's perfectly sculpted cheek. She turned her back on him as she headed for the door.

'Thank you,' Joaquin whispered.

Katherine whirled and stormed back to him, leaned down and grabbed his collar in her fist as she shoved her face in front of his.

'You'll do nothing without my say-so, and you'll answer to me from this moment on or I'll scream every single word of what you've done to the Supreme Court and blow what's left of your despicable life right out of the water!'

33

CAPE CANAVERAL, FLORIDA

June 28, 14:12

The giant rotor blades of the V–22 Osprey rotated as the aircraft descended toward a landing platform at the space complex, avoiding the huge runway. Ethan Warner looked down at a scattering of unmarked cars forming a defensive phalanx around an Air Force transport. Soldiers with guns surrounded the cavalcade, some of them accompanied by guard dogs.

'What's going on?' he asked Jarvis.

The old man shook his head at Ethan. *Don't ask, don't tell*, he guessed. Ethan unbuckled himself as the Osprey touched down and a crewman hurried up and guided them aft. The rear ramp of the Osprey had lowered, allowing them to jog down onto the asphalt landing pad amid clouds of dust and sand whipped up by the giant twin rotors.

Ethan was ushered with Lopez out across the asphalt and into the waiting Air Force transport. The vehicle pulled away quickly, armed soldiers sitting silently either side of Ethan and Lopez, their expressions hidden behind sunglasses. Jarvis remained silent as the escort travelled across the vast complex toward ranks of security gates far from the administrative buildings and visitor centers to the east. The escorting unmarked cars peeled away as the transport passed through the gates and eased to a stop alongside a heavily fortified building that looked to Ethan like some kind of bunker. The transport doors opened and the soldiers spilled out into the bright sunshine, weapons at the ready as Ethan and Lopez followed Jarvis out of the transport and through an eight-inch-thick steel door.

The interior of the bunker was cool, the heavy walls sealing it from the blazing sun outside. Bare white walls stared at Ethan and simple gray tiles lined the floor. The bunker was entirely empty but for the industrial elevator shaft in the center. Outside the elevator stood four extremely competent-looking soldiers, each carrying enough weapons and ammunition to start a small war.

'What is this place?' Lopez asked.

'Former observation bunker for watching rocket launches,' Jarvis explained as he gestured toward the elevator. 'Hasn't been used since the fifties.'

Ethan looked at the heavily armed soldiers. If ever a place had screamed 'secret facility', this was it. He glanced questioningly across at Jarvis.

'What's down there?'

A bearded man wearing a light shirt and casual shorts opened the elevator's shutter doors as he beckoned for Ethan, Lopez and Jarvis to follow him.

'Something so classified,' Jarvis explained, 'that there was no real way to protect it except by making it look so uninteresting that nobody would bother investigating it. It can only be accessed via direct clearance from the Chief of Staff of the Air Force, which I obtained earlier this morning when the nature of this case became clear.'

The four guards moved neatly aside as Ethan stepped into the elevator alongside Lopez and Jarvis. The man in the shorts pulled the shutters closed, and with a press of a button they were on their way.

'You knew what we were up against beforehand?' Lopez asked Jarvis.

Ethan replied before Jarvis could.

'Of course he did. It's becoming your modus operandi, Doug, telling us the minimum that we need to know.'

'Official secrets are exactly that,' Jarvis responded. 'Secret. I wouldn't have brought us down here unless it was absolutely necessary.'

Lopez snapped, 'How many deaths does it take before something becomes necessary to you?'

Jarvis sighed, keeping his voice low. The man in shorts remained discreetly silent, standing with his hands behind his back.

'It's not always my call to make, Nicola,' he said, clearly frustrated at the limitations of his influence at the DIA. 'Sometimes it takes a catastrophe to get the top brass to relinquish some of their paranoia and give permission for classified technology like this to be used in non-military investigations. You know the score, both of you. It takes a lot of effort to support you from behind the scenes, and there are plenty of pen-pushing bureaucrats at the Pentagon who would be only too happy to see us shut down.'

Ethan watched as walls of dark earth passed by, braced back by huge steel pillars. Lights set into the bare soil cast shifting shadows through the elevator as it descended into the depths.

'How far down does this go?' Lopez asked.

'Three hundred meters,' came the response from the man in shorts, speaking for the first time. 'Deep enough to prevent any electromagnetic signatures showing up on privately held orbiting cameras or foreign spy satellites.'

'This is Michael Ottaway,' Jarvis said. 'He's our lead scientist here.'

The elevator continued to sink, and then the sound of activity permeated the air as the temperature began to rise. Ethan belatedly realized why Ottaway was wearing shorts. The elevator slowed down and an exit appeared that opened out onto a long, well-lit corridor. Four more guards awaited them and opened the elevator's shutter doors before forming a phalanx and marching away down the corridor.

Ethan followed, flanked by Lopez and Jarvis as they were led to the doors at the far end. The soldiers stopped, and one of them entered a key-code into a pad. The doors hissed open and the soldiers stood aside, allowing Ethan to pass through.

The underground facility was about the size of a basketball court and half-filled with computer terminals manned by an odd assortment of uniformed military figures and scientists whose civilian clothes, almost without exception, included shorts.

Across one wall, a huge screen displayed a digital map

of the earth, laced with orange lines mapping the trajectories of what Ethan guessed were satellites or spacecraft.

'This way,' Jarvis said, walking past Ethan and heading toward a large raised platform edged with padded railings, like a giant boxing ring.

Within the platform, a pair of soldiers stood wearing strange dark-gray helmets with visors and blocky-looking gloves. Each stood upon a rolling platform like a running machine. The platforms themselves were supported by a gyroscopic frame that rotated to match the soldier's direction of travel.

'What are they doing?' Lopez asked, watching the two soldiers.

'Retracing the paths of their fallen comrades,' Jarvis explained.

Ethan said nothing as they walked to where a group of men wearing the obligatory shorts were watching a series of plasma screens next to a computer terminal. Ethan spotted a large steel casing descending from the ceiling on the opposite side of the underground facility, a thick bundle of wires and optical fibers spilling from within the casing and snaking their way to the rear of the facility. Across the entire back wall were ranks of what Ethan could tell were supercomputers, all humming as they ran trillions of calculations through immense databanks.

Ottaway gestured to the plasma screens as he turned to Jarvis.

'So, what can I do for you?'

Jarvis handed Ottaway the photograph of Charles Purcell.

'I need you to find this man and let us follow him up until the present day, right this moment, if possible.'

Ottaway took the photograph from Jarvis and glanced at it.

'Do we have a name, address, where we should be looking, all that kind of stuff?'

'You will,' Jarvis said. 'His name's Charles Purcell and he used to work upstairs at NASA. Start searching in Miami.'

'Okay, no problem. It'll take us about ten minutes to track him down.'

Ottaway turned and pressed a button on his computer before speaking into a microphone that he clipped around his ear.

'Okay, change of plan. We need you to perform a search-and-identify mission. Stand by.'

The two soldiers on the platform stopped moving and waited with their hands clasped before them as Ottaway began scanning the image of Charles Purcell into his computer. Lopez turned to Jarvis.

'Okay, why don't you quit the cloak-and-dagger and tell us what this place is?'

'This,' Jarvis replied, 'is Project Watchman.'

'What does it do?' Ethan asked.

Ottaway looked up from his computer.

'Watchman is a classified program handled by the Air Force and NASA. Put simply, we collaborate with the Air Force's spy satellite program, gathering visual intelligence from global sources, and crunch the data streams here at this facility to produce a three-dimensional representation of the entire planet.'

Ethan hesitated for a moment as his brain attempted to digest and process what he had just heard.

'You mean this is some kind of virtual-reality device?'

'In a sense,' Ottaway confirmed. 'But this is a bit more than just virtual reality.'

Jarvis grinned as he looked at Ethan.

'Charles Purcell seems somehow to be able to see into the future. It would also appear likely that Joaquin Abell, or somebody within IRIS, possesses that same ability. But here, we can do something that they cannot.'

Michael Ottaway tapped a button on his keyboard and an image of Charles Purcell appeared, along with a progress bar emblazoned with the word *SEARCHING*. He turned to look at Ethan.

'We can look into the past.'

34

IRIS, DEEP BLUE RESEARCH STATION, FLORIDA STRAITS

June 28, 14:18

Joaquin Abell stood alone in his private quarters, his hands behind his back as he looked out of a portal into a bleak, dark, underwater wilderness. Thick glass protected him from the freezing water and the immense pressure outside, but the movement of the occasional fish fascinated him. Small, almost insignificant creatures, and yet they were perfectly adapted to the world in which they lived, one in which humans required the benefits of technology to survive.

He felt strangely alone now that Katherine had gone. The darkness outside seemed a little closer than it once had, his world devoid of meaning. Joaquin closed his eyes and struggled with an unfamiliar emotional turmoil. He called out to it, reeled it in, and then recoiled from the sensations that surged deep through his core, emotions that were as alien to him as the ancient creatures scurrying across the seabed. He crushed the shame and regret, for they were the true obstacles to enlightenment, the Achilles' Heel of success. *Stay the course*, he told himself, *and all will be resolved. There is no gain without loss.*

He felt uniquely privileged, standing down here, immune to the dangers of the world, his wealth and the technology of mankind enveloping him securely. And now he possessed a gift like no other, the ability to predetermine his own future, to see literally what no man had ever seen before. Mankind had ceased long ago in his subservience to his environment, to be subject to the harsh judgment of Mother Nature over those of her children who failed to adapt and thus to survive. But never had mankind believed it possible that he need not be enslaved by the bonds of cause and effect.

Joaquin breathed deeply in the knowledge that he would never again fail in any endeavor, never again be defeated. For centuries, millennia even, mankind had dreamed of travelling through time, of witnessing events from the past and those yet to come in the future, yet for all of that time the scientists and the dreamers had been doomed to failure. Only Joaquin, by way of his father's unique vision, had been able to come to the realization that the notion of *travelling through* time was itself the flaw in mankind's thinking. Just as it was not physically possible, with current technology, to travel through time, it was, in fact, not even necessary.

One only had to *see* through time.

The past surrounded every species that possessed sight, even the glass of the window through which Joaquin watched was, ever so slightly, a part of history. The distance is the past. Space is the past. Warp that space enough, wrap it into a ball so tightly that not even light can escape, and then the path of time becomes so distorted that, for an observer close to its immense influence, time elsewhere runs faster.

'So simple,' Joaquin whispered.

'Sir?'

Joaquin blinked and turned to see one of his men holding a satellite phone. Joaquin strode across to him and took the phone in his hand.

'Abell.'

The monotone voice on the other end of the line sounded out of breath.

'*It is done.*'

Olaf Jorgenson had proven his loyalty to Joaquin a thousand times and, despite everything, Joaquin knew that without his friend, much of what he had achieved so far would never have occurred. However, what nature had blessed the mighty Nordic with in terms of physical prowess it had taken from him in intelligence. The fool had exposed himself, and therefore was now a liability.

'The authorities have a photo of you, Olaf,' he said. 'It is only a matter of time before they hunt you down.'

'*I can remain ashore for as long as you wish,*' Olaf replied. '*My failure is my own.*'

Joaquin felt a distant pinch of concern that felt like something from his childhood, a sense of abandonment and enforced solitude. He shook his head and cleared his thoughts.

Katherine was unlikely to be charged with any crime, but considering what had just happened it seemed almost certain that, before long, he himself would be subjected to investigation. The prosecution could hardly fail to suspect that IRIS had somehow arranged the murder of Macy Lieberman. That was fine with him, just as long as they had no evidence of the Deep Blue facility in which he stood. Charles Purcell had done his work well in trying to expose Joaquin's work, but his vision of the future clearly had not gone far enough to anticipate Joaquin's responses. With the incriminating documents destroyed, the only thing preventing Joaquin from completing his greatest triumph was the possibility, however slim, that Purcell might somehow convince the authorities that IRIS was responsible for the murder of his family.

'How did Purcell contact the prosecution?' he asked Olaf. 'He must have spoken to them.'

'*He did not,*' Olaf replied with conviction. '*He posted all of the documents, which have now been destroyed.*'

Joaquin felt a new fear creep through him as he glanced around at the underwater facility he had built. Purcell could have posted more than one copy of those incriminating documents. It was, of course, the greatest weakness he had. Over a hundred people had been involved in the construction of the lair, most of them employees devoted to the IRIS cause. A few, here and there, had come to question Joaquin's true motivations; but as with any complex construction program, tragic accidents occurred from time to time, and none of those individuals had been able to air their concerns. When Charles Purcell had fled the complex after breaching protocol and viewing the future – a future that included the death of his own family – Joaquin had been forced to act immediately and without hubris. Two hours later,

Purcell's family had been murdered and his colleagues killed in a tragic air crash. Now only Purcell remained, a victim of his own curiosity. Had he not succumbed to the temptation of viewing the future, he would not be on the run now.

'*It's a wonder he hasn't gone to the press and revealed the location of Deep Blue,*' Olaf suggested.

'There's nothing on the news reports in the next few hours that suggests he's gone to the media, and with his family terminated there is no danger of their exposing us,' Joaquin explained. 'And as long as our media-tycoon friend Robert Murtaugh plays ball, any attempt Purcell makes to expose his knowledge will be buried, and we'll end up possessing any testimony he might make to the press. Murtaugh's network dominance will overwhelm any other media access to the story. Unless proven innocent, Purcell has no credibility and nobody to look out for him.'

'*That may not be quite true.*'

'How so?'

'*I was pursued by two cops, a man and a woman. I got away, but they were good. Too good to be normal detectives. Somebody else may be involved in this, people who might know what Charles Purcell is trying to do.*'

Joaquin considered this for a moment, an image of Jarvis, Warner and Lopez hovering ominously in his mind. He made a decision.

'Stand by, Olaf. Soon we will know where Charles Purcell is hiding. I will call you back as soon as I can.'

Joaquin cut the line off and turned to the soldier next to him.

'Tell Dennis to extract the Florida camera, immediately.'

Dennis Aubrey watched as the robotic arm lifted Camera 7 from the black-hole chamber and set it gently down before replacing it with a new camera, set to record. From his vantage point at the control-center panel, Dennis could see that the camera had been watching a screen that was tuned to one of the major Florida news networks.

Despite himself, Dennis was fascinated by the machine and found himself eagerly willing the camera out of the chamber.

So far, he had been able to watch the contents of only three of the cameras extracted from the chamber, but each piece of footage had riveted him. The flickering, grainy and entirely silent images were nothing short of spectacular, and as Dennis had watched tomorrow's news unfold before him he had found himself captivated by the ticking clock at the bottom-right corner of the screen showing the time many hours in advance. There was no doubt about it: Joaquin had achieved something utterly unique, something that could change the balance of power in the world. Even as he thought about it, Dennis found himself enveloped by a fear that, wherever that power went, tragedy would follow it.

He looked across the control panel to a series of radio stacks that controlled communications between the Deep Blue facility and the *Event Horizon*, and the yacht's onboard satellite receivers that picked up the news channels. A buoy tethered to the facility floated just under the water's surface, some two thousand feet above. Its depth was controlled by an automatic flotation bladder that was itself connected to a communications room on the opposite side of the Deep Blue complex. A series of radio transmitters and aerials extended from the concealed buoy up and out of the water. Barely visible on the surface, the aerials enabled both radio and satellite phone communications in all but the wildest of weather. However, the radio was currently disabled, and could be reactivated only via an access code on the control panel – further evidence that Joaquin did not want Aubrey contacting anybody on the surface.

Aubrey reached into his pocket and retrieved his cellphone, scrolling through his contact list until he found the name he was looking for. Just one call and he could reveal everything. Fear warred with loyalty to Katherine in his mind, and he stared down at the number intently as he tried to figure out how to tell her. He wondered briefly if he could use the communications room directly in order to bypass the access code.

'What news, Dennis?'

Dennis flinched as Joaquin's voice crackled across the chamber. He slipped his cellphone discreetly back into his pocket and turned as he strode up toward him.

'Camera 7 is ready,' he reported. 'I was just about to play it.'

Aubrey busied himself with downloading the files from the camera into the control panel's database, watching as the information bars slowly filled and racking his brain for some way to convince Joaquin to give him access to the communications room.

'How do you know that the governor and his friends won't simply tell the government about this facility?' he asked. 'Any one of them could be overcome with moral righteousness, especially Benjamin Tyler.'

'They are greedy men,' Joaquin replied impatiently, 'obsessed with power and image. They won't be able to overcome their vanity.'

Aubrey wondered at the depths of Joaquin's delusion, that he could say such things and be oblivious to the fact that he was describing himself. Aubrey mastered his fear and pressed further.

'You're in danger of pushing them too far,' he cautioned. 'Resentment forces men of power to do stupid things. Perhaps you should ask Katherine down here. Her influence might calm them, convince them to follow you.'

Joaquin's jaw clenched beneath his tanned skin.

'Katherine has gone to work on one of our charity projects in the Dominican Republic,' he snapped. 'She won't be coming here.'

'But she might be able to help us—'

'Nobody will oppose us!' Joaquin shouted. 'By the time I've finished with them here, they'll do anything I say!' The tycoon's rage subsided as quickly as it had arrived. He smiled and clapped Aubrey on the back. 'But I thank you for your concern. Now, play the damned tape.'

Aubrey pressed play. Immediately the image of the Florida news station appeared, racing forward at double speed. Aubrey squinted as he tried to follow the rapidly changing screens and the silently jabbering anchors.

Images of the Florida coastline, a Coastguard rescue, and the words falling silently from the moving lips of the anchors: a train wreck down Tampa way; a fugitive chase down the interstate; a murder suspect charged with . . .

'There, that's it!' Joaquin pointed at the screen.

Aubrey paused the image, rewound it to the beginning of the piece, and then set it playing at half its normal speed. Now, the images and the anchor's motions and lips appeared to move at normal speed, only the occasional flare of energy flickering to disrupt the image.

As the anchor mouthed her silent words at the camera, an image of Charles Purcell appeared behind her, captured from a holiday snap with his wife and daughter. Dennis Aubrey felt a terrible pang of impotent despair as he saw the beautiful woman and their angelic child, now lying in a morgue somewhere in Florida.

'It's just a piece on the manhunt for him,' Aubrey said, reading the anchor's lips.

Joaquin shook his head and leaned closer to the screen.

'They did that already, or rather they *will* do. This is new.'

Suddenly the image changed. A police cordon, tape strung between the twisted branches of mangroves way out in what Aubrey guessed was the Everglades. Aubrey saw that there were no police cars, the scene attended by small hovercrafts, the only type of vehicle able to access the immense swamplands.

'They'll find a body,' Joaquin guessed.

Aubrey glanced at the clock on the lower portion of the screen. The news report was from less than two hours' time. The shot of the Everglades disappeared as the anchor reappeared in the frame, with the shot of Charles Purcell beside her. Now, the scrolling text beneath her ran with new information:

SUSPECTED MURDERER SHOT DEAD IN EVERGLADES

Joaquin stood up from the screen.

'Charles, your time is about to come to an end.'

Aubrey looked at Joaquin in confusion. 'You think that the police killed him?'

Joaquin shook his head as he reached for the satellite phone on the control panel, whilst retrieving his access card and opening a communication channel.

'It would have said so,' he decided.

'Then who did it?'

Joaquin smiled as he held the phone to his ear. 'We did, Dennis.'

Aubrey heard the line connect, and the distorted but familiar voice of Olaf Jorgenson on the other end of the line. Joaquin was still smiling as he spoke.

'We know where Purcell will be in two hours' time.'

35

PROJECT WATCHMAN HQ, KENNEDY SPACE CENTER

June 28, 14:27

'You can look into the past?'

Lopez sounded incredulous and Ethan wasn't surprised, but Doug Jarvis nodded as though it were common knowledge.

'Project Watchman has been running under various budgets and with differing degrees of success for over twenty years,' he explained. 'It requires only a small premises from which to operate and thus remains extremely covert. Even Congress does not know of its existence, mainly because the funding is supplied through the Pentagon's Black Budget, which is protected from Congressional oversight by presidential mandate, due to military-and-intelligence community requirements for secrecy. The intelligence signals we receive are likewise lost amongst NASA's standard radio traffic, further concealing its presence.'

Ethan looked at the giant digital display across the nearby wall, where one particular object was highlighted with the designation USA-224 as it orbited the planet.

'How does it work?'

Michael Ottaway gestured to the map.

'Beautifully,' he replied. 'When USA-224 was launched, its optical ability completely surpassed anything that had gone before, anything that even I could have dreamed of.'

'Is it a satellite, then?' Lopez asked.

'Yes,' Ottaway said. 'National Reconnaissance Office Launch 49 is a KH-11 "keyhole" optical-imaging satellite, the fifteenth of her type to be launched. She went up aboard a Delta IV Heavy rocket from Space Launch Complex 6 at the Vandenberg Air Force Base in California. Upon reaching orbit, she received the International Designator 2011-002A, but she's now known as USA-224.'

Ethan stepped in and looked more closely at Ottaway's bank of computer screens. The search he had initiated was flipping through locations in the Miami area at a tremendous rate, and facial images flickered past in a blur of motion, as though the program were searching for Purcell's face amongst millions of Floridians.

'What does it do, exactly?' Lopez asked.

'USA-224 is in a low-earth orbit at ninety-seven point nine degrees of inclination,' Ottaway explained. 'This places it at a typical keyhole-satellite operational orbit, and allows for maximum target exposure on the earth's surface. In short, it can look down upon the planet in real-time and to a degree of resolution so high that if you forgot to wash your hair this morning, USA-224 could spot your dandruff from orbit.'

Ethan turned to look at Ottaway.

'Sure, that's impressive, but it doesn't warrant this level of secrecy: people already know about these satellites, even if they don't know exactly how they work.'

'True,' Jarvis said, 'but the difference is that in the past they could only take photographs or short-duration video of moving targets. The satellites would move out of visual range as they orbited the planet, making identifying targets within narrow timescales difficult, if not impossible.'

'So what's different now?' Lopez asked.

'The fact that we have four of them,' Ottaway grinned. 'Between them, 220 to 224 provide total coverage. Their lenses are of such high quality that they can operate together to not just image anywhere on earth, but to do so in three dimensions. By compiling the data from each satellite on a given target area and recording as we go, we can use supercomputers to crunch the data-streams to produce a three-dimensional world through which investigators can move, examining classified enemy installations or airbases, or replaying events from the past and witnessing them directly.'

Ethan turned and looked at the two soldiers waiting on the nearby platform as a sudden and overpowering realization swelled in his mind.

'How long have you been recording data?' Ethan asked.

'From the continental United States? Almost ten years, with varying degrees of detail, and with the supercomputers we keep every moment of it on record.'

Ethan forced himself to remain calm. Ten years of visual information from every last corner of the globe, the last few years in ultra-high resolution, three-dimensional full color. A single moment in time lodged in his thoughts like a splinter in his mind's eye: the December of four years previously, the Gaza Strip, Palestine. His fiancée, Joanna, abducted by persons unknown.

'You could solve any crime,' Lopez gasped in amazement, 'prove any event happened or didn't happen, just by stepping into the virtual world and viewing it.'

Ethan turned to look at Jarvis, who raised a hand.

'It's not quite that simple,' he said, focusing on Ethan. 'The cameras can only record in detail what happened in the open, not within buildings. True, Watchman also records in the near infrared, so we have some ability to look into interiors, and occasionally the angle of the satellite camera across the earth's horizon allows us to see a small distance inside buildings, but for the most part we're limited to exterior activities. We only have full coverage in daylight.'

The computer terminal pinged and Ethan turned to see Purcell's image and the word MATCH flashing in a red box in front of it.

'You've found him?' Jarvis asked.

Ottaway consulted the screen for a moment and then nodded.

'The face-recognition software has located him leaving a ferry in Miami, approximately twenty-two hours ago.'

'That's *before* his family was killed,' Ethan noted.

Ottaway looked up at the two soldiers on the platform and keyed his microphone.

'Okay, guys, I'm sending the information over right now.'

Ethan stepped forward. 'Wait a second. Why don't we go up there and do this ourselves?'

Ottaway chuckled and shook his head.

'I'm afraid that won't be possible. The equipment is highly specialized, not to mention classified, and if you damaged it or—'

'They're security-cleared *Cosmic*,' Jarvis interrupted the scientist. 'Right now, we have more than one suspect in this case. To brief your men on all of the details would take far too long and we're running out of time as it is.'

Ottaway glanced at Lopez and Ethan, then sighed.

'I want your name on the paperwork for this, Doug,' he said as he keyed his microphone again. 'Come on down, guys, change of plan.'

Ethan watched as the two soldiers carefully removed their headsets, gloves and boots and stepped off their platforms. They clambered down from the maneuvering area and looked at Ottaway questioningly before standing aside.

'Go on up,' Ottaway said, 'and put the gear on. Let me know when you're ready.'

Ethan and Lopez climbed up onto the maneuvering area, then each stepped onto a platform. Ethan pulled on the boots, then slipped the helmet over his head, strapping it securely under his chin before pulling on the blocky gloves laced with wires that ran to a miniature antenna on the right wrist. Ottaway's voice called out to them.

'When I say so, close the helmet visors and hold on to the rails either side of you for balance. It will take you a moment or two to adjust to the device.'

Ethan rested his hands on the railings and waited. Moments later, Ottaway gave him a thumbs-up. Ethan reached up and slid the helmet visor down, just catching a glimpse of Lopez doing the same, and then in absolute blackness he waited with his hands resting on the railings beside him.

'*Can you both hear me?*'

Ottaway's voice came through the earphones loud and clear and he heard Lopez reply.

'*Loud and clear.*'

'Roger that,' Ethan said.

'*Stand by, patching you in.*'

The blackness flickered in front of Ethan's eyes and then suddenly bright sunlight flared. Ethan squinted as his eyes adjusted to the brightness, and he gasped and almost lost his balance as the world appeared before him with absolute clarity. A brilliant ocean glittered, hundreds of sailing boats moored on the blue water, the sky above clear blue. People walked everywhere, cars rolled past nearby and a seagull arced through the sky above him. Ethan looked about and saw a stylized figure nearby, dressed in a strange silver suit with the virtual-reality helmet on. He realized that Lopez's image was deliberately designed to stand out, to make recognition easier.

The only thing missing was the sound, for the virtual world around them was entirely silent. As Ethan looked more carefully he saw patches of pixilated ground, shadows that shifted erratically, and deep black holes within shop windows and inside cars. The virtual world moved with incredible fluidity and yet looked stark and unnatural, like a highly realistic computer game that had not quite been finished.

'*Ethan, Nicola, we can see him. Can you confirm you have visual on the target? He is in the queue by the dock.*'

'Stand by,' Ethan replied.

A line of people were walking away from a ferry that was docked beside the quay. Ethan scanned their faces, their clothes, and their shadows on the ground as they walked. A seagull wheeled above them and Ethan noticed that it was jet black on its underbelly, its edges blurred and pixilated. The orbiting satellites could not see beneath the gull, so there was no information to relay into the virtual-reality world.

'*I see him,*' Lopez said. '*Fifth from the front, white shirt.*'

Ethan stepped instinctively to one side for a better view and almost fell as the rolling platform shifted beneath him with a slight delay.

'*Step slowly and carefully,*' Ottaway advised over the microphone, '*it'll take time to get used to it.*'

Ethan moved slowly to his right and saw Purcell amongst the crowd. He looked flustered, sweaty and nervous as he pushed past the people in front of him and dashed away from the dock to flag down a taxi. Almost before Ethan could move, Purcell was aboard and the taxi pulled away. He started walking swiftly in pursuit.

'How do we keep up with him?'

'*Wave your hand in front of your face,*' Ottaway replied. Ethan complied, and a digital list appeared to hover in front of his vision. '*Now select Manual Guidance.*' Ethan's hand in front of his face had automatically become a cursor, and he selected the option before him. '*Good. There will now be two joysticks activated either side of the railings beside you on the plat-form. The one on the right controls speed and direction, the one on the left altitude. You can fly in our virtual world.'*

Ethan fumbled either side of him and then got hold of the two joysticks. He gasped again as he was elevated instantly into the air. A sense of vertigo plunged through his belly as his brain caused the very sensation it expected to feel as he lifted off. Ethan, his eyes fixed on the taxi, flew along behind it in pursuit.

'Lopez, are you with me?'

'Way ahead of you,' came the reply.

Ethan looked up to see Lopez's silvery form zipping past in pursuit of the taxi. Ethan followed as the cab weaved its way through Miami's late-afternoon traffic.

'He's heading west, probably directly home,' Ethan guessed. 'If he saw what was going to happen to his family, maybe he tried to prevent it.'

'Stand by, I'll move you to his house and accelerate time until his arrival.'

Ethan watched as the dense Miami cityscape beneath him blurred briefly and he was whipped across the surface of the earth to be deposited outside Coral Gables with Lopez alongside him.

As they waited, Ethan saw the time-accelerated clouds race by overhead, the scenery around him flickering with bright sunlight and cloud shadows and trees quivering rapidly in the breeze as the sun arced down toward the west. Airliners zipped across the broad sky and cars raced past at impossible speed. Suddenly a cream Chevrolet appeared like lightning outside Purcell's house and then vanished.

'Wait,' Ethan said. 'Rewind that by a few seconds.'

The world around them froze and then was whipped into reverse. The Chevrolet appeared again and raced away backwards from Purcell's house.

'There,' Ethan said, 'play from there.'

The world returned to normal speed and Ethan watched as the Chevrolet rolled casually past him and pulled up alongside the Purcell residence, the interior of the vehicle a pixilated miasma of darkness. Ethan moved in alongside the vehicle as the door opened and the driver climbed out.

Over six feet tall, hugely muscular and with short-cropped blond hair.

'*I think we just found the killer of Purcell's family,*' Lopez said.

36

'*Follow him.*'

Ethan obeyed without question, following the giant man as he walked toward the front door of Purcell's house. Ethan realized that the man's brazen approach was either reckless or brilliant: what assassin would hit their target in broad daylight?

Ethan looked about, but there were no other people on the street. No witnesses. The date stamp hovering on his menu list was the same as the estimated time of death of Purcell's wife and daughter.

The big man got to the front door and reached into his pocket. To Ethan's amazement he produced a key and slipped it into the lock, then turned it slowly before pushing the door inward. It opened, and Ethan looked instinctively inside.

'Damn!'

The interior of the house was jet black, devoid of any visual data.

'*Could we switch to infrared and get above the house?*'

Lopez asked. '*We might pick something up.*'

'*IR view is on your visual menu,*' Ottaway confirmed. '*Try it out.*'

Ethan waved his hand in front of his face again and selected the IR view. Instantly the world changed from near-perfect visual clarity to a shadowy mixture of cool blue tones and hot oranges and reds as the recorded data from the keyhole satellite's heat-sensing cameras took over. Ethan grabbed his joysticks and levitated up over the roof of Purcell's house alongside Lopez.

To his horror, he saw the assassin's orange-and-red image stride down the main hall of the house below them and into the lounge, where two more figures were stationary, one standing and the other lying down on what Ethan guessed was a couch. In one terrible moment, Ethan saw the two figures' heads turn sharply to face the intruder. Then, the big man pointed at the standing figure.

A fleeting, hair-thin thread like a laser beam zipped from the man's arm and hit the standing figure, who slammed into a nearby wall and collapsed. Ethan realized that the passage of a bullet heating the air around it had caused the line. He felt a grinding hatred seethe through his guts as the man turned and pointed at the small figure on the couch. The child barely had time to try to scramble away before another hot little line flashed and her head jerked violently sideways.

'*Bastard,*' he heard Lopez whisper.

The man lowered his arm and seemed to stand for a moment regarding his handiwork before he hurried away down the hall and out of the front door. Ethan turned off the IR view and flew down alongside the giant, watching as he climbed into his car and drove away.

'*We should follow him too and see where he goes,*' Lopez suggested, moments later.

Ethan was about to reply when a taxi appeared at the end of the street, and they saw Charles Purcell climb out and run toward his house. Ethan switched back to IR view and felt his rage turn to empathy for the man who now sprinted inside, down the corridor and then stopped in the lounge. Slowly, Purcell collapsed to his knees. Ethan watched in silence as Purcell held his head in his hands and began thumping the floor beside him and tearing at his hair. Lopez's voice murmured softly.

'*We need to get this information to Captain Kyle Sears, right now. They're hunting down an innocent man.*'

'Wait,' Ethan said.

He watched as Purcell slowly got to his feet. The scientist stood for several moments, wiping his sleeve across his eyes and then running a hand through his hair. Then he turned and walked across to the mantelpiece, close to where the body of his wife now lay. He picked up an object and shook it, then placed it back on the mantelpiece. Then Purcell turned and ran through the house and upstairs toward the bedrooms.

'*What's he doing?*' Lopez asked, mystified.

'Taking the picture that was missing from the mantel-piece when we visited,' Ethan guessed.

'*What for?*' Jarvis asked.

Ethan watched Purcell rush into the master bedroom and rifle through a drawer.

'He had a plan,' he replied. 'He already knew what he was going to do if he was too late to save his family.'

Purcell ran out of the bedroom with what looked like a folder or file and then hurried back downstairs into the kitchen. He grabbed a pen and a pad, and wrote several messages. Ethan squinted as he tried to pick out what Purcell was doing, then saw Lopez descend into the house below them, ignoring the walls as she passed through them like a ghost until she was almost alongside Purcell's shadowy orange avatar.

'*It's a folder,*' Lopez said, identifying the package Purcell had retrieved from his bedroom. '*Maybe the documents he sent to Macy Lieberman?*'

Ethan descended alongside Lopez and saw Purcell produce a smaller, blockier object from his pocket.

'The diary,' Ethan guessed, as he recognized its shape, 'the one he sent to me at Cape Canaveral.'

Purcell spent several minutes writing on the folder and the diary, and then he produced from a shirt pocket two smaller sheets of paper and scribbled something on the back of each before enclosing them all in separate envelopes and writing addresses on each.

'*One of those must be the college picture of you that he sent to Kyle Sears,*' Lopez guessed. '*Probably got it off the Internet or something. But what was the smaller one?*'

'I don't know,' Ethan replied, 'but I've got a feeling it'll show up soon enough.'

Purcell got up and dashed from the house, climbing into a red car as Ethan turned off the IR camera and watched as the scientist drove away. To Ethan's left, a woman holding a small white dog watched as the car accelerated away.

'We can't follow him all day like this,' Ethan said. 'Ottaway, what's the chances of speeding time forward and finding out where Purcell is right this minute?'

Ottaway's voice came back a moment later.

'*The most recent images I can give you will be about an hour old. It takes that long for the computers to process the data streams coming from the satellites.*'

'It'll do,' Ethan replied. 'We've got to get to Purcell before that assassin or the Miami police do.'

'*Stand by.*'

Ethan watched as Purcell's car vanished into the distance. Lopez appeared alongside him.

'*I don't get it,*' she said. '*Why did the assassin kill Purcell's family? They had nothing to do with this, as far as we know.*'

Ethan shook his head.

'I don't know. Best guess is that Purcell may have been compiling evidence against IRIS for a long time, and that folder he took from his bedroom contained what he knew. Maybe IRIS couldn't afford to take the chance that he had told his family about what was happening, in which case IRIS has them iced to prevent exposure after Purcell is killed.'

'*Then why not just steal the folder back instead of murdering them?*'

'Whatever IRIS is hiding must be worth a lot more than just money,' Ethan said, himself unsure of Joaquin Abell's true motivation. 'There's something big behind all of this, and whatever it is it's enough to have entire families killed.'

Ottaway's voice cut through their chatter.

'*The computer's found Purcell, transporting you there now.*'

Ethan held onto the railings beside him on his platform, and then the leafy suburb vanished in a flickering blur of color and light as he and Lopez raced across the Florida mainland. The maze of gray cityscape and angular streets and suburbs suddenly turned the green and blue of racing trees and flashing water. Ethan came to an abrupt halt above a spit of land in the center of a river flowing through a vast expanse of wilderness.

'*Jesus,*' Lopez uttered, '*what the hell's he doing out here?*'

Ethan looked around and keyed his microphone. 'Can you see him? How far away is he?'

'*One hundred meters southwest of you,*' Ottaway replied.

Ethan grabbed his joysticks and elevated himself a hundred feet above the dense foliage of the Florida Everglades, then turned and glided across the landscape. Almost immediately he saw the figure of a man standing alone on the tiny spit.

'I see him, closing in.'

Ethan flew until he was directly above the figure and then descended. As he did so, he saw that the figure was standing in front of hundreds of small stones that had been arranged to spell out a message on the sand before him.

'*Oh my God,*' Lopez murmured as they got close enough to read the words.

Charles Purcell stood with his head tilted back, staring up at the sky and, it seemed, straight into Ethan's eyes. Slowly, Purcell raised his arms as though he was imploring god for assistance as Ethan read the words on the sand.

I AM HERE, ETHAN WARNER,
AND I AM WAITING.

'Get a GPS fix on his position,' Ethan said.

'*Already on it,*' Jarvis responded.

Suddenly, Purcell's desperate and pleading face disappeared as the screen went blank. Ethan wavered on the spot and grabbed the railings for balance before he reached up and pulled the helmet from his head. Lopez yanked hers off, her hair falling in thick black whorls across her shoulders.

'We need to get out there fast,' she said.

Ethan jumped down off the platform and rushed to the railings.

'Ottaway, get your guys to use Watchman and find out where the assassin went after the hit on Macy Lieberman!'

Michael Ottaway nodded, and Ethan looked at Jarvis. 'We're going to need another ride.'

'Get Scott Bryson on the case,' Jarvis agreed. 'If his boat's not in danger, he'll be more pliable. I'll head upstairs and chase up Montgomery Purcell's history to see if I can find any links with what Charles was doing at IRIS.'

Jarvis was about to turn away when Ethan grabbed his arm and leaned in close.

'You knew about Project Watchman when Joanna went missing.'

'I didn't have this level of security clearance back then,' Jarvis said defensively. 'And the DIA would never have cleared you in here anyway, Ethan. You were a wreck, remember?'

'Times have changed,' Ethan snapped. 'I want in.'

Jarvis shook his head. 'I'm sorry Ethan, but it's not going to happen. There's just no way the DIA will let you have time here searching for Joanna.'

'We're right *here*,' Ethan hissed.

'No, we're leaving,' Jarvis replied. 'Get to the Everglades and find Purcell. We'll talk about this another time.'

Jarvis yanked his arm free of Ethan's grip and strode away toward the elevator. Ethan watched him depart as he tried to ignore the suppressed fury that burned like acid through his veins.

'What's up?' Lopez asked, her dark eyes filled with concern.

Ethan forced himself to unclench his jaw. The urge to tell Lopez that he may have a way of finding Joanna slammed to a halt within him, because he knew that if he found Joanna, he might well lose Lopez.

'Nothing. We'd better get moving.'

37

KENNEDY SPACE CENTER, MERRIT ISLAND, FLORIDA

June 28, 14:48

Doug Jarvis arrived at Thomas Ryker's office with Ethan's angry accusations still ringing in his ears. The fact that Jarvis had been aware that the Defense Intelligence Agency possessed the means to find out what had happened to Joanna Defoe years before did not mean that he had either the rank or the influence to make it happen. Ethan, Lopez and even Jarvis himself were merely tiny cogs in the vast machine that was the United States' intelligence community, and besides, there was always somebody watching.

Jarvis was reminded of that the moment he saw two armed guards outside Thomas Ryker's office. The men blocked his way, only parting when Jarvis showed them his identification. He pushed open the door to the office, and was surprised to see a tall man with long, drawn features turn to face him. Dressed in an immaculate suit but bearing no identification, Jarvis knew him only by his last name. Wilson. Central Intelligence Agency, attached to the Pentagon. Security clearance far beyond that which Jarvis possessed. The last time Jarvis had seen him he had just ensured Ethan Warner's silence over events in Israel years before.

'Jarvis,' Wilson said, with a cold and dispassionate gaze. 'I was just leaving.'

Thomas Ryker was sitting in a chair before Wilson, with his hands in his lap and concern etched into his features so deep it could have been carved there with a scalpel. Wilson buttoned his black jacket and turned for the door. As he passed, Jarvis deliberately blocked his way and whispered low enough for Ryker not to hear.

'What are you doing here? I thought the CIA would be busy with Pakistan right now?'

Wilson did not smile. His gaunt features belied the fact that he was probably twenty years Jarvis's junior. His smart suit hid a superbly honed physique and his calm demeanor a lengthy career in covert operations. He looked down at him with eyes that reminded Jarvis of a bird of prey scanning for its next victim.

'What you need to know about me, you already do,' he replied. 'Everything else, you never will. Don't make me move you.'

Jarvis backed off, and Wilson strode past. Jarvis let out a breath as he closed the door behind him.

'Who in hell was that?' Ryker uttered, standing up. 'I thought the grim reaper had come to visit.'

'He's a spook,' Jarvis replied. 'High-level CIA. What did he want?'

'What didn't he want?' Ryker said. 'Asked about everything that you're doing here. What's his problem? I thought you government guys were all on the same side?'

'You'd be surprised,' Jarvis replied, and looked at a nearby table scattered with files and photographs. 'What have you got for me?'

'There's a lot of information here,' Ryker said, pulling at his scrawny beard. 'But I'm not sure how it will help your case.'

Jarvis sat alongside him at the table. Some of the files before them were decades old, drawn from NASA's archives. Most of them bore the name Purcell and most were stamped 'Classified' or 'Top Secret'. The passing decades had seen many of the files being declassified by various administrations, a drip-feed of information leaking out into the world, until once-sensitive documents vital to national security became fodder for television documentaries and books by historians.

'Why don't you start at the beginning and help paint a picture of what went on?' Jarvis suggested. 'Your friend Charles seems to think that the answers are in America's nuclear program from the fifties, so why not start there?'

Ryker sat back in his chair and gestured to one of many photographs on the desk. Jarvis looked at the black-and-white image of an icon of destruction, the towering pillar of a mushroom cloud soaring over a desert.

'The Trinity Test,' Ryker said. 'America detonates the first atom bomb as part of the Manhattan Project, just southeast of Socorro, New Mexico, July 16, 1945. Its success resulted in the dropping of atomic weapons on the cities of Hiroshima and Nagasaki, ending the Pacific Campaign and the Second World War. What most people don't know is that, in the short time between those two bombs being dropped, the technology was already advancing at a terrific rate. The bomb that hit Hiroshima was a fission weapon using Uranium-238, whereas the Nagasaki weapon was a more advanced plutonium-based implosion weapon.'

'Keep it simple,' Jarvis cautioned.

'Essentially, a nuclear weapon is like making a small sun on earth,' Ryker said, 'that's why they're so powerful. But instead of the reactions being contained by gravity, like our sun, they radiate outward entirely in an explosive manner. However, all of the Trinity weapons used nuclear *fission*, the splitting of the atom, to produce their power by chain reaction. Our sun uses nuclear *fusion*, the fusing of atoms under immense gravitational pressure, to produce energy, and it's much more powerful. So Montgomery Purcell and his team began working on building a weapon based on fusion, using tritium or deuterium as a fuel.'

Jarvis scanned the documents before them. 'And that's where this Ivy Mike comes in, right?'

'Exactly,' Ryker enthused. 'Look, here's Montgomery Purcell's name on the Manhattan Project roster for work on uranium enrichment at Sylacauga, Alabama, and at Oak Ridge, Tennessee. This work led to the Trinity test and ultimately the end of the war. But the work does not stop. As the Cold War got into full swing and McCarthyism got everybody hysterical about Communism, so scientists like Montgomery Purcell found themselves the subject of immense demand. National laboratories were opening up everywhere as America raced to stay ahead of its nuclear rivals, and men like Purcell were offered resources they could only have dreamed about a decade earlier.'

Jarvis was well aware of the escalating nuclear arms race of the post-war years, and the associated paranoia and fear of atomic Armageddon that had overshadowed the lives of every human being on the planet. For almost half a century, governments had maintained secret bunkers designed to withstand the tremendous devastation that modern nuclear weapons could unleash. Ordinary families, meanwhile, had been sent leaflets detailing how best to survive the coming holocaust, and had built their own pitifully inadequate bunkers in their backyards stocked with dehydrated food and bottled water. None of them had realized that, with the world outside consumed by the nuclear fires and irradiated for decades, surviving the initial attacks only guaranteed them a later, much slower death amid the crumbling remnants of civilization.

'Where did Montgomery Purcell go?'

'The Pacific proving grounds,' Ryker informed him. 'He becomes one of the leading scientists on Operation Crossroads, testing and detonating atomic weapons on Bikini Atoll. Soon after, he's in Nevada on Operation Ranger, a further series of tests. Finally, he ends up back in the Pacific for the legendary Ivy Mike shot, part of Operation Ivy.'

'Early fifties?' Jarvis hazarded.

'Enewetak Atoll in the Pacific Ocean, November 1, 1952,' Ryker confirmed. 'It was the location of the first ever fusion-bomb detonation, a true thermonuclear device that let fly with a blast of over ten megatons, or the equivalent of ten thousand tons of TNT – four hundred-fifty times more powerful than the Nagasaki weapon. The Ivy Mike shot produced a fireball over three miles wide and a mushroom cloud that reached an altitude of twenty-five miles in less than five minutes. The shot entirely destroyed the island of Elugelab in the atoll, totally vaporized it. That was pretty much the start of the Cold War, right there.'

Jarvis rifled through the documents, searching for Purcell's name.

'How does this figure with what his son might have achieved, this ability to see into the future?'

Ryker leaned forward, stroking his beard. 'That's the really interesting bit,' he said, and picked up one of the documents as though he recognized it on sight. 'Montgomery Purcell was being provided with almost limitless funds to continue his research. Congress was willing to virtually write blank checks, so obsessed were they with maintaining their lead over the Russians. But there were other groups working on entirely different uses for nuclear detonations.'

'Such as?'

'Earth moving,' Ryker said. 'The Sedan test on July 6, 1962 yielded a blast of 104 kilotons, but it was detonated underground, demonstrating that weaponry was not the only product of the nuclear age. Such bombs could be used for industrial purposes, and of course for power generation via controlled nuclear fission. One of the scientists who had worked on the Manhattan Project had resigned from the military soon after the war, to continue his research using a private company he'd founded before the war, seeking government funding to research peaceful uses for nuclear power.'

'What was the company called?' Jarvis asked.

'Pacific Ignition,' Ryker said with a wry smile. 'Sounds ominous, until you realize that the word Pacific means *peaceful*.'

'What's the interesting bit?'

'The person who founded the company,' Ryker replied, and handed Jarvis a black-and-white photograph of a stern-looking man with a broad mustache. 'Isaac Abell.'

'Joaquin Abell's father,' Jarvis murmured.

'The very same,' Ryker confirmed. 'Charles and Joaquin's fathers were rivals for almost a quarter of a century after the end of the Second World War, each competing for government funding. Montgomery Purcell sought money for weapons research, while Isaac Abell focused on the holy grail of energy generation: controlled nuclear fusion. He'd begun experiments off the coast of South Bimini Island in 1941, experimenting with huge magnetic-field generators, but got sidetracked into the Manhattan Project.'

'The plot thickens,' Jarvis murmured. 'What happened after Ivy Mike?'

'The Eisenhower administration remained focused on the defense of America, so weaponry maintained the upper hand when it came to funding from Congress. The other problem for Isaac Abell was that nuclear fusion is so incredibly difficult to produce on earth: the pressures required are tens of thousands of atmospheres, the temperatures in the millions of degrees. It's only in the last few years that it's become a potential reality: our National Ignition Facility at the Lawrence Livermore Laboratory in California has reported that it may achieve ignition soon, and in Cadarache, southern France, they're building the ITER reactor, which may possibly become the first commercial nuclear-fusion reactor.'

'Sixty years later,' Jarvis said. 'So Isaac Abell failed.'

'It wasn't his fault,' Ryker explained. 'The man was a genius and a hero, a real philanthropist, who, like most scientists, was working to benefit all mankind. But he was trying to build a device using 1950s technology that could ignite and entrap a miniature star and keep it burning just like our sun. Isaac spent over a billion dollars of taxpayers' money on his work, with no positive results, and was rumored to have built some kind of underground test chamber before Congress cut his funding in 1964. Pacific Ignition continued with private funding, but at nowhere near the levels required to make progress.'

Jarvis nodded, and glanced at a picture of Montgomery Purcell.

'And Charles's father?'

'Montgomery Purcell continued working for the United States Army and Air Force after Ivy Mike, building ever more dangerous weapons, culminating in the most powerful detonation in American history: the Castle Bravo shot, off Bikini Atoll in the Pacific. He was at the height of his power and reputation when he is reported to have been invited by Isaac Abell into talks about how to combine their work. Abell was at that time struggling for funding, and Pacific Ignition could not continue its research without financing its operation by doing weapons work.'

Jarvis raised an eyebrow. 'They went into business together?'

'Monty Purcell attended the talks in the Bahamas, but apparently walked out after a blazing row with Isaac Abell. Purcell got into his plane, took off for Miami and was never seen again, the aircraft lost without trace in the Bermuda Triangle.'

Jarvis looked down at the photograph of Isaac Abell. 'What happened to Abell's company, Pacific Ignition?'

'With Monty Purcell dead, Isaac Abell found himself on the receiving end of new government grants, some for weapons research, some for nuclear-power projects. Looks like the government was forced to compromise in order to get him back on their books, to replace Monty Purcell. Isaac Abell worked for them for several years, but after his failure to achieve nuclear fusion, funding for Pacific Ignition's research was finally halted in 1968. Isaac Abell committed suicide in 1973. A trust was maintained by Isaac's wife until she died twelve years later. It seems that Isaac was smart enough to filter a large sum of money from government grants and royalties from patented inventions into a trust fund for their son to inherit on his eighteenth birthday.' Ryker smiled at Jarvis. 'Joaquin Abell did exactly that, and then changed the company name.'

'To International Rescue and Infrastructure Support,' Jarvis guessed. 'Joaquin inherits a fortune and his father's life's work.'

Ryker tapped the picture of Isaac Abell with his hand.

'Before their fathers became enemies they worked together and were the best of friends. It's unlikely that their sons were unaware of their connection. It's plausible that they might even have met from time to time, as young children. Either way, Joaquin certainly knew exactly who Charles Purcell was, long before he gained access to his father's fortune.'

Jarvis saw it all come together in his mind.

'Joaquin didn't inherit his father's mathematical mind, so he used Charles Purcell's skills to continue his father's work.' He thought for a moment. 'But it still doesn't explain how Joaquin can now see through time.'

'No,' Ryker agreed, 'but it gives us a clue. Isaac Abell built a facility using government funding, that much we know. But we don't know where he built it. There's mention here of the construction of large tokamaks, torus-shaped devices that are designed to produce magnetic fields to contain plasma in modern nuclear-fusion generators; and the purchase of vast amounts of graphite.'

'What does that tell you?' Jarvis asked.

'That Isaac Abell was on the right course for building an ignition chamber that could contain a nuclear-fusion reaction,' Ryker replied. 'But the only way that such a device could be used in order to twist the fabric of time is if the star created within it were crushed to such densities that the electron repulsion of the atoms within it were overcome. Mankind does not have the ability to do this, but if by some chance reaction it did occur, then a heavily modified tokamak chamber might just be able to contain it.'

'Contain what?' Jarvis asked. 'The star?'

'A different kind of star,' Ryker said. 'I can't believe I'm even considering it, but if such a collapse of ordinary matter were to occur, then there are only two possible outcomes: firstly a neutron star, a tiny ball of degenerate material where all of the space between the atoms has been squeezed out. An object of this matter the size of a grape would weigh as much as a mountain.'

'And secondly?'

Ryker shook his head.

'If the pressure was too great, the neutron star would continue to collapse, and would condense time and space down to a singularity: it would become a black hole.'

38

FLORIDA EVERGLADES

June 28, 15:17

The powerful V-8 engine propelled the airboat across the silky waters, more like an aircraft than a boat, as the huge eight-foot-diameter propeller roared behind Ethan. The simple, square hull contained two rows of seats, a raised pilot's chair and the engine at the stern. He reveled in the breeze as they soared between enormous sawgrass marshes and reed islands stranded in the endless expanses of cypress swamps, estuarine mangrove forests and pine rockland.

The subtropical wetlands of the Everglades comprised the southern half of a large watershed that was born in the Kissimmee River, which discharged into Lake Okeechobee. Essentially a slow-moving river sixty miles wide and more than a hundred miles long, the system represented the perfect hiding place for a lone fugitive: if they could survive

'The Native Americans that used to live here called it *Pahayokee,* the "grassy waters",' Lopez said above the roar of the engine. 'But it only looks pretty. Living here would have been hard at the best of times.'

Ethan scanned the broad waters filled with periphyton, a mossy golden-brown substance that floated on bodies of water throughout the Everglades, and the scattered islands of ubiquitous sawgrass, a sedge with serrated blades so sharp they could cut through clothing.

'The satellite's GPS coordinates fixed Charles Purcell's position five miles to the southwest!' Ethan shouted up to Scott Bryson, who nodded as he glanced down at a GPS screen next to the airboat's wheel.

'Was he alone?' Bryson called back.

'Yeah,' Ethan nodded, 'or at least he was a couple of hours ago.'

'How can you be sure?'

'Never mind.'

Ethan turned back around in his seat and looked straight at Lopez as she watched Bryson guiding the airboat. She had been able, with her considerable charm, to convince Bryson to continue helping them, with the proviso that no more of his property was exposed to bullets or blades. Considering what they were going up against, it was of considerable interest to Ethan that Bryson had agreed. Then he looked at Lopez again, and guessed that maybe it wasn't just the captain's sense of honor that had guided him.

Lopez's long black hair streamed behind her in the wind as she reached up and pinned it back. Ethan found himself watching her openly as she flicked her head to one side and tied her hair off into a ponytail. The speed of the airboat across the water and the thrill of the wind had touched her face with a bright smile that lit her features like the sunlight on the racing water beneath them. It was something that he saw less and less in her these days.

For a brief moment Ethan forgot where he was and realized that, despite everything, despite the fact that Joanna might yet still be alive somewhere out in the world, Nicola Lopez meant more to him than he was comfortable admitting to himself. Maybe it was a sign of just how big a stick he had up his ass that it had taken him this long to realize it. This realization in turn raised the ugly and unwelcome question of what he was going to do about it. An image of Joanna flickered like a phantom through the darkened vaults of his mind, her long blonde hair, green eyes and quiet confidence contrasting with Lopez's dark looks and fearsome temper. Somehow, though, as he pictured Joanna in his imagination, the differences weren't so great after all.

'You need a photograph?'

Ethan blinked. Joanna vanished and he found himself staring straight at a bemused Lopez. He stopped breathing.

'Just enjoying the view. You want to get out of the way?'

Lopez laughed out loud. 'You're an ass sometimes, Ethan.'

Before Ethan could answer, Bryson's voice bellowed down at them.

'I reckon he's swallowed a love bug, honey!'

Lopez's laughter turned to a curious smile as she stared at Ethan, who avoided her gaze whilst turning to look at Bryson.

'You need a wooden leg to go with that eye, skipper?'

Bryson let out a belly laugh but said nothing. Ethan turned back in his seat, not looking at Lopez, but he could see out of the corner of his eye that there was still a smile on her lips. He was trying to come up with something useful to say when the engine note changed as Bryson throttled down. Ethan glanced over his shoulder at the captain, who lowered his voice and gestured ahead of them.

'The island's just up there. We'll coast in the last hundred meters. Get tooled up.'

Ethan reached down behind his seat to where a canvas sack lay on the deck. He unzipped it and retrieved a pair of M-16s, both fully loaded and with two spare clips each. Ethan handed one to Lopez before picking up the other weapon.

'Jesus,' Lopez said as she checked her rifle.

'We're not getting caught out again. To hell with the goddamn rules.'

Lopez's almond eyes watched Ethan for a moment.

'You're starting to sound like me,' she said. 'I don't want to hear that.'

Ethan looked up at her, one hand on his M-16, and nodded. 'Just this once,' he promised. 'There's no back-up for us out here.'

'Heads up,' Bryson said, cutting the engine off as the airboat slid silently across the water toward the shore of a small island of rough sawgrass surrounded by dense tangles of mangroves. With the breeze gone, a heavy blanket of heat settled over them, clinging to Ethan's shirt as beads of sweat formed on his forehead.

Ethan eased his way toward the bow and crouched

down with his M-16 held at port-arms as the boat nudged gently up against the thick, twisted mangrove roots. A heron lifted off further down the shoreline, its wings flapping as it climbed away into the distance, but the Everglades remained silent as Ethan watched the waving sawgrass before him, dense thickets of cypress trees listless in the heat.

Bryson vaulted down off the wheel seat and crouched alongside Ethan and Lopez.

'The GPS coordinates place him about a hundred-fifty yards ahead,' he whispered. 'Plenty of cover in there: he could bed down like an Alabama tick and not be seen for weeks.'

Ethan shook his head.

'He's not a soldier. Whatever Charles Purcell is up to, this must be his endgame. He's not running.'

Bryson looked at Ethan. 'So what's your plan, boy scout?'

Ethan didn't take his eyes off the sawgrass.

'Well, Captain Silver, I'm going to head straight in. Lopez, you cover my left flank. The mangroves on our right aren't passable, so nobody's going to come at us from in there.'

Lopez thought for a moment.

'Maybe, but if they already know we're coming and where from, there's not much we can do to defend our position.'

'Best hope that we got here first, then.'

Without another word, Ethan hopped off the airboat's bow and moved in a low run through the grass and into the trees. He heard Lopez jump off the boat and head out through the undergrowth to his left.

Ethan was suddenly overwhelmed by the cloying humidity of the forest as he crept forward, clouds of mosquitoes tumbling on the hot air around him as he moved from cover to cover. He kept one eye open for alligators and pythons coiled in the dense undergrowth as he blinked sweat from his eyes.

A thought occurred to Ethan. Why would Purcell have come out here into an entirely unpopulated area beyond the reach of civilization? The 'glades were notoriously difficult to access, and dangerous for the uninitiated. Purcell was an academic who was likely most comfortable in a laboratory, not suffering the hardships of survival in the wilderness. Yet he had purposely placed himself in this particular spot, as though it were somehow his destiny, his endgame – in order to fulfill a prophecy of some kind.

The thought tied in closely with Purcell's supposed knowledge of the future, but the man himself had said that he would die soon. Why willingly fulfill that particular prophecy? Surely he would serve himself better by getting as far away from the Everglades as he could?

'Don't move.'

Ethan froze, and then realized that the whispered voice belonged to Lopez. He turned his head fractionally to his left and saw her crouched with her M-16 tucked into her shoulder and one eye staring like a hawk down the barrel.

'What have you got?' Ethan asked.

'Purcell,' she replied. 'I can see him. Dead ahead, thirty yards.'

Ethan squinted through the forest and slowly a human

shape resolved itself before him, standing on a narrow spit of land jutting out into the water. Ethan eased his rifle up to his shoulder and looked down the scope.

Charles Purcell stood beside the edge of the shore, the stones with their message beside him on the sand, and then looked at his watch. Slowly he turned to face the forest, and for a moment Ethan was looking straight into his eyes.

Then Purcell called out.

'Come forward, Mr. Warner. It is time.'

39

Ethan looked across at Lopez, who raised an eyebrow at him from over the barrel of her rifle and shrugged.

'Whoever else is looking for Purcell hasn't got here yet.'

Ethan got to his feet and, with Lopez following, picked his way through the dense foliage until they broke through onto a narrow beach of sand littered with rotting palm fronds. Before them, standing in dirty beige slacks and a torn white shirt, stood Charles Purcell. Even at first glance Ethan could see that the man was running on empty, his features gaunt and tired, his eyes sunken within darkened rings, and his hair in disarray.

'Charles,' Ethan greeted him cautiously.

'Mr. Warner,' Purcell said, his voice hoarse from dehydration and exhaustion, 'Miss Lopez. Glad you both made it.'

Ethan sensed that whatever Purcell had in mind he was in no state to threaten anybody physically. He lowered the M-16.

'Why are we here, Charles?' he asked.

'Because this is where the end begins,' Purcell replied. 'Everything that happens from this moment is dependent upon the two of you.'

'What do you mean?' Lopez asked. 'How can you know that? How can you see into the future?'

Purcell smiled, a bleak and heartbreaking smile that no one could ever possibly fake. Ethan realized with an unbearable certainty that he was bearing witness to something unique in history: a man who had crossed the boundary of causality and seen his own future. But Purcell's haunted eyes and terminal appearance suggested that his gift was also his curse.

'I have seen one possible future,' Purcell replied, 'and in doing so have condemned myself to follow its path.'

Ethan stepped toward Purcell but the physicist raised his hand to forestall him.

'Please don't come any closer,' he urged. 'Just stay precisely where you are and you will learn everything that you need to know.'

'We need to leave,' Ethan said. 'You're being hunted and it's possible that they know exactly where you are.'

'As did you,' Purcell replied, and glanced up into the sky above him. 'Can I ask how you actually discovered that I was here? I knew that you would come, of course, but I assumed you would arrive by aircraft.'

'Military spy satellite,' Lopez answered. 'They've adapted face-tracking software to search for fugitives and war criminals from space.'

Purcell smiled faintly. 'I'm honored.'

'We don't have time for this,' Ethan pointed out. 'We've got to get out of here.'

Purcell shook his head.

'No, Mr. Warner. *You* have to get out of here. I must remain.'

'Why?' Lopez asked. 'What difference does it make? You'll be safe if you come with us right now.'

Again the faint smile, as though Purcell were wistfully wishing that it were true.

'Yes, I would be safe. But then everything that I have achieved so far would have been for nothing.'

'The codes, and messages,' Ethan said. 'You left two trails.'

'One for you, designed to help you learn something of what has happened,' Purcell nodded, 'and another for the person who is hunting me down as we speak. He is a fool, albeit a dangerous one who will not stop until he finds me.'

'Why did you write that date and time on the wall of the apartment in Hallendale?' Lopez asked. 'What happens at 8:48?'

'This evening, at 8:48,' Purcell said, 'marks the end of everything and justice for my family.'

Ethan took a deep breath.

'Okay, you'd better lay down what you know for us in a real hurry.'

Charles Purcell reached down to the earth at his feet and picked up a small but chunky digital camera. He spoke slowly, his timbre conveying the gravity of his words.

'You must listen to me extremely carefully, for what

I'm going to tell you will often sound impossible or go against your common sense and intuition, but trust me, every word is true.' He waved the camera in his hand. 'In this camera is a drive that contains a digital record of a series of news feeds, and thereafter images captured through the camera's own lens that extend six months into the future.'

The silence permeating the Everglades seemed to deepen around Ethan as he processed what Charles Purcell was saying.

'That camera has seen *six months* into the future?' Lopez asked incredulously.

'Yes,' Purcell said. 'I have seen everything that has to happen to ensure that those responsible for the murder of my family, and for many other crimes, are brought to justice.'

Ethan took a pace forward.

'Copy the drive,' he said, 'then you won't have to—'

'Freeze!' Purcell shouted, his voice causing a small flock of storks a hundred yards away to take flight, their wings flapping into the distance. 'Don't move another inch.'

Ethan looked down at the ground for any sign of buried mines or explosives, but the sand was unmarked apart from Purcell's own footprints.

'Copying the drive will be ineffectual in altering the space-time continuum,' Purcell went on. 'You must listen to what I have to say whilst there is still time.'

Ethan took a pace back from Purcell, who continued.

'The people who have pursued me, and who appear

now to be hunting the two of you, work for a company called International Rescue and Infrastructure Support.'

'IRIS,' Ethan replied. 'We know all about them.'

'Not *all* about them,' Purcell assured him. 'Joaquin Abell has for years been filtering government and taxpayer charitable donations into the building of a complex beneath the Florida Straits. I was contracted to IRIS as a freelance consultant, working on what Joaquin claimed was a series of electromagnetic devices designed to produce an alternative source of fuel that could save humanity from the impending fossil-fuel crisis known as "peak oil".'

'What's that?' Lopez asked.

'The point where the consumption of fossil fuels totally outstrips supply,' Purcell replied. 'It will start with rising fuel costs, then economic shocks, rapid recessions, and end with the lights going out in all of the world's industrialized nations.'

'Jesus,' Lopez uttered. 'It's already happening.'

'Yes, but the project Joaquin has engineered has nothing to do with generating energy,' Purcell said.

'You had evidence,' Ethan said to Purcell, 'documents you stole from IRIS that contained proof of Joaquin's fraud. They were destroyed in an attack on a courthouse in Miami earlier today. Did you make a copy of them?'

Purcell's features hardened, a brief glimpse of the iron will that still resided within.

'I did,' he replied.

'Where is it?' Lopez asked quickly. 'If we can present it to a court as evidence, then we have a chance to bring Joaquin to trial for what he's done.'

Purcell glanced around him as though somebody was listening.

'That is a secret that I shall take to my grave,' he replied finally. 'Only time will tell.'

'That's not good enough!' Lopez snapped. 'You want this guy to go down for what he's done, then you need to start helping us!'

'Joaquin pretends that he's a philanthropist,' Ethan said, 'and right now the entire world believes that. You knew that wasn't true and you did something about it. Why? What started all of this?'

'Joaquin Abell is not a scientist and has no idea that, to me, his deception was obvious from the moment I started working for him,' Purcell explained. 'When I first visited his site I saw that the electromagnets he had built were enormous and the tokamak structure was clearly designed to contain something of immense power; but nothing that he was doing looked relevant to nuclear fusion. After a couple of years, Joaquin's lead scientist was killed in what was called a "tragic car accident" and I was offered a more permanent, on-site role.'

'What was he really building?' Ethan asked.

'Joaquin had justified his fiddling of the taxpayer's money by saying that a source of free, clean energy would repay humanity back a million times, and most of his employees were happy to believe that. But when I saw what he'd created, I knew that he had no such repayment in mind. What he was building was a device to see through time, and he'd built it purely so that he could see the future and profit from it, both financially and politically. What Joaquin has created is a black hole, here on earth, contained within a vacuum chamber surrounded by electromagnets that keep the black hole suspended in place.'

Lopez stared at Purcell for a long moment.

'I thought that black holes sucked things in and destroyed them?'

Purcell shook his head.

'No. Black holes do not *suck* anything in at all. They possess such enormous gravity that they wrap space, and with it time, around themselves so tightly that, once you're close enough, all paths lead to the black hole's center. Nothing, not even light, can escape. The point of no return is known as the "event horizon", and if you're stationary alongside the horizon, you would perceive time as being "twisted" along with space. Essentially, the closer you get to a black hole's event horizon, the slower time will run for you, while time beyond your perspective will appear to run faster. Joaquin's genius, if you could call it that, is to get these cameras to do the viewing for him.'

'So why doesn't he just use the thing to win the lottery?' Ethan asked.

'Because it would be too obvious,' Purcell said, 'and because Joaquin's ambitions don't stop at money. He has his eyes on changing the world, with him at its head.'

'How?' Lopez asked. 'Supposedly he's all about helping the needy.'

'That's his cover story,' Purcell replied, 'and one he intends to stick with. However, his plan is not to just wait for disasters to come along so that he can sail in and rescue the needy. His plan is to create the disasters himself, and become the savior of mankind.'

40

Olaf Jorgenson crouched low on the bow of his airboat as it drifted silently on the still water, ignoring the swarms of mosquitoes that hummed on the heavy air. Through the swaying reed beds that rose like islands from the water, he watched as the big man with the eye-patch sat idly on the deck of his airboat and smoked a cigarette.

Olaf scanned the island ahead and guessed that the man's two accomplices had gone ashore. He had recognized them both, the Americans who had chased him back in Miami. He could not understand how they had arrived here in the Everglades before he had, but that could not be changed. Now his only thought was to overcome this unexpected adversity and complete his mission. Luck had favored him and he had spotted their airboat several miles back as he searched the Everglades for Charles Purcell. The news feeds that Joaquin had accessed had not been accurate enough to pinpoint the scientist's location, but the images had been good enough to put Olaf within a few miles. Spotting the airboat with the two Americans aboard had been a shock initially, and then an opportunity.

But there was a problem.

They had guided their boat with unerring accuracy to this one tiny spit of land marooned amidst the wilderness. That could only mean one of two things: that they had already been in contact with Charles Purcell, or that somehow they had access to the same images as Joaquin Abell, visions of the future that had allowed them to find Purcell. Olaf could only assume that Joaquin's missing camera was what had enabled them to move one step ahead of him and find Purcell in the middle of nowhere.

Olaf would no longer be able to stay ahead of them. This had to be finished now, and then he would be forced to flee back to Joaquin's yacht. Olaf intended to ensure that he took the contentious camera with him before Purcell could hand it over to the authorities as evidence that would sink Joaquin, and with him, Olaf.

Olaf carefully used one of the emergency oars to push the airboat forward out of the dense reed bank, using his immense strength to shift the vessel and then letting the boat's momentum on the water do the work for him. The boat drifted silently across the lagoon, closing in on the big man in the boat.

It was rare for Olaf to encounter a man who was bigger than he was, and such an event required delicacy and planning. Much of Olaf's impressive physique had been forged by the steroids he had for years forced into his unwilling veins, and the gains he had made in musculature had been paid for by the weakening walls of his equally inflated heart. Olaf was incredibly strong, but was only able to sustain his exertions for a short duration. As he had found out to his cost years before, his labored heart's ability to pump oxygen into his grossly over-grown muscles failed him after a few minutes and his strength vanished as swiftly as it had arrived.

A quick glance at the man ahead suggested that he was born large but did not work out. That might have satis-fied Olaf, were it not for the large SEAL tattoo adorning the man's shoulder. Impressive physical fitness and an almost psychotic will to succeed meant that this oppo-nent would be incredibly dangerous. Worse, Olaf could not shoot him without alerting his companions.

Only one thing was in Olaf's favor. He was approach-ing from behind and to the man's right, the side obscured by the eye-patch he wore. The big man reached down into a cooler by his side and lifted out a bottle of liquor. Olaf smiled, waiting and watching as the man took a deep mouthful from the bottle and wiped his lips across the back of his forearm. A drinker. His reactions would be slowed, his judgment impaired.

Olaf looked down into the water around him. Although the surface was smooth and reflected the blue sky above, he knew that alligators and snakes swarmed in the murky depths below. To slip into the water now could be tantamount to suicide, and even if he were able to reach and board the boat ahead, doing so would quickly alert the former Navy SEAL to his presence.

His only chance was to let his own boat slip alongside and then leap across and kill the man before he could turn to defend himself. Olaf quietly slipped a huge hunt-ing knife from a sheath secured beneath the shirt on his back, holding the blade low against his thigh as the boat drifted silently closer. *Ten feet. Eight feet. Six.*

The man took another long pull on his bottle, scanning the forest ahead intently, and oblivious to Olaf's approach.

Four feet. Two feet.

Olaf crouched down, his legs coiled like giant springs beneath him.

The boats' hulls bumped together with a dull thump.

Olaf thrust himself forward, almost spread-eagled in midair as he hurled himself onto the other boat's deck. The big man responded instantly and whirled in his seat, with the bottle already swinging with impressive force and speed. The glass smashed into Olaf's wrist with a jarring pain that sent the blade spinning from his grasp to splash into the water alongside the boat.

Olaf slammed his head into the man's chest like a freight train and they smashed down onto the deck together, the big man's head cracking against the hard deck. Olaf saw his eyes roll up into his sockets and he raised a chunky fist ready to finish him off. To his surprise, the SEAL exhaled a foul blast of alcohol fumes and his head rolled to one side.

Olaf screwed up his face in disgust. The impact had knocked the man out cold – he was probably already halfway there from the liquor. Olaf considered retrieving his knife from the water, but there was no time.

Olaf made to roll the body off the boat and into the water, but then hesitated. The SEAL probably knew the Everglades well, enough so that he could be of use if any kind of law enforcement showed up.

Instead, Olaf tore off a length of his own shirt and used it to gag the man. Then he stood up and walked across to the boat's fuel tank, yanked the rubber feeder pipe out and strode back to the unconscious man. He heaved him onto his front and bound his wrists with the length of rubber hose, then vaulted back across to his own boat and pushed away from the shore, once again letting the momentum take him away downstream until he was sure nobody on the island would be able to hear the engine. Then he started it and turned the boat around, aiming for the far side of the island. He would come at them from there, and his first priority would be to silence Purcell.

He looked down into the hull of the boat, where a Dragunov SVU-A sniper rifle lay in its case alongside an M-16 assault rifle and a small pile of hand grenades.

41

'What's Joaquin's endgame?' Ethan asked Purcell, as they stood on the little spit of land. 'What's he going to do with this black hole of his?'

Charles Purcell sighed.

'Joaquin's great plan is to use the enormous energy contained within his black hole to create seismic events in the deep-water channel off the coast of Puerto Rico. It's a geologically volatile area, one that could easily be destabilized by the gravitational influence of Joaquin's device.'

Ethan and Lopez shared a confused glance.

'What's the point of that?' Ethan asked. 'He's going to wreck countries and hold them to ransom?'

'No,' Purcell shook his head. 'He'll appear to be the only private company willing to help developing countries hit by natural disasters because he'll have foreseen the disaster and will be on the scene first, which will continue to increase his international popularity. But even that's not why he's doing all of this.'

'What then?' Lopez asked.

'Have either of you ever heard of something called economic shock-therapy?'

'Economic enhancement, used to break communist state-controlled economies and replace them with capitalist free markets,' Ethan replied. 'It's been the way forward for decades.'

Purcell grinned tightly.

'*The way forward* is one way of putting it,' he replied, 'but it's also been the cause of the collapse of economies, the murders of millions of people and the transformation of governments into regimes as bad as anything communism had to offer.'

'How come, and what's this got to do with Joaquin's insane plan?' Lopez asked.

'Joaquin's plan is a natural extension of economic shock-therapy. It happened under Reagan here in America, under Thatcher in the UK, under Gorbachev in the former Soviet Union, Pinochet in Chile . . . the list is endless.'

'Wait,' Ethan said, 'you're talking about privatization, right?'

'At the expense of human rights,' Purcell replied, 'to the financial benefit of foreign governments and large corporations bent on securing the profits to be had. Essentially, economic shock-therapy is used to take over entire countries and bind them to debts that they cannot possibly repay.'

Lopez began putting the pieces together.

'You think that Joaquin is targeting countries hit by disasters, providing them with funds to rebuild, and then tying them into debts to IRIS.'

'Precisely,' Purcell nodded. 'This is what economic shock-therapy is designed to do – to convert a struggling country's economy to free-market capitalism, with loans provided by organizations like the International Monetary Fund and the World Bank. But in doing so the country in question is placed forever in thrall to world markets and its own debt. A country's natural resources are partitioned out to major corporations who have a stake in the funding, so the country loses its own natural wealth and the profits that it could have reaped from those resources. No self-respecting government would admit to being so heavily indebted to a private company, so IRIS would remain free from public criticism of his charitable status.'

'Iraq,' Ethan said, as images flashed in his mind of the destruction wrought there by the coalition forces. 'Huge sums of money were handed to private companies by our government to rebuild Iraq, but instead of hiring local people the big corporations went in with their own staff, did nothing, blamed their lack of activity on insurgent attacks and then left. Before we even got there the oil fields had been divided up between international petrochemical companies. Iraq never needed rebuilding at all until it had the crap bombed out of it, and we saw half of the population out of work, while foreign corporations kept their staff in luxury compounds. The supposed handing back of the oil fields to the Iraqi people is just a thin veneer, a corporate subterfuge – America owns Iraq's oil because we own their debt.'

'And Joaquin Abell intends to do something similar,' Lopez surmised, 'but this time *causing* the catastrophe that drives the economic change.'

'He intends to test the device off the coast of the Dominican Republic this afternoon,' Purcell confirmed, 'as a proof of concept to major figures in government and business. Once he has their support he can move forward and start lobbying Congress. The lawmakers will easily be won over by the colossal advantage the IRIS device will bring to American supremacy, both economically and militarily, and Joaquin will almost certainly engineer the nomination of a suitably obedient president. Anybody who opposes him will be branded in the same way that anybody who opposes unbridled capitalism: as *un-American* or *unpatriotic*. Joaquin needs to make a lot of money to fill the gaps in IRIS's accounts, to replace the money he has laundered over the years to build his device. Holding entire countries to debt is the perfect way of doing that. If he achieves his goal, there will be nothing to stop him, because the missing money will have been replaced, and IRIS will appear to be saving lives instead of destroying them.'

'We need to stop him,' Ethan said, 'and we need your help to do it.'

'You are already helping to stop it,' Purcell replied.

'By changing the future that you saw?' Lopez asked.

'No,' Purcell smiled, 'by fulfilling it. Joaquin Abell has the ability to see into the future, but just as he does not know the true scope of what he has achieved, so he does not know of its limitations.'

'What limitations?' Ethan asked, frustrated. Time was running out.

'His device can only capture light,' Purcell explained. 'There is no sound to accompany what he sees on these cameras. Therefore, the images can be taken out of context.'

Purcell explained how the cameras viewed the rolling news feeds capturing not only footage of future events but also the anchors as they narrated at their desks.

'He must rely on the scrolling text banners as much as the speaking anchors,' Lopez guessed.

'Exactly,' Purcell agreed. 'He always employs somebody on his team who can lip-read, which gets him some extra information from the reports; but often the image quality means he must rely purely on the pictures.'

'He still has the advantage,' Ethan said.

'Only to a certain extent,' Purcell replied. 'There's something else about light that Joaquin does not know, and it could tip the balance in your favor, if only for a while.'

'We're listening,' Lopez said impatiently.

'It's called the Observer Effect,' Purcell said, 'one of the deepest mysteries of quantum theory. Put in the simplest terms, the world around us reacts to the act of us looking upon it.'

'It does what?' Lopez uttered.

'It reacts to us observing it,' Purcell repeated. 'A stream of photons of light fired through a single opening onto a screen that are not observed produce multiple patterns on the screen instead of a single dot, as though they had passed through several openings and not one.'

'Does the stream spread or something?' Ethan asked. 'Like a shotgun cartridge?'

'In a sense,' Purcell agreed. 'It happens because the quantum duality of photons allows light to act as both a particle and a wave at the same time, just one of many bizarre properties found at quantum scales. But as soon as the photons are observed they act as you would expect through common sense – they form an orderly line and produce a single spot of light on the screen.'

Lopez blinked. 'I don't get it.'

'Nor do most people, but it is an aspect of quantum physics experimentally verified by a team at the Weizmann Institute of Science in Israel. Electrons perform in exactly the same manner, and the resulting pattern is known as *interference*. What it means is that particles can act as either particles or waves depending on whether or not they're being observed.'

'So reality literally reacts to us being here,' Lopez surmised.

'It reacts to any observation, not just human,' Purcell said. 'Even a camera observing the experiment will cause interference.'

Ethan made a connection.

'So the future that Joaquin Abell has seen may be affected by the fact that it has already been observed by that camera?'

'Yes,' Purcell said. 'Finding me is not Joaquin's priority. It's this camera that he wants. It alone has seen the electrons and photons of reality streamed into its lens for months to come, whereas Joaquin only has a small part of the picture. To put it simply, his limited view of the future through news broadcasts might allow him to win the battle, but this camera will tell him if he's going to win the war.'

'It's only fixed for him once he observes what happens

himself?' Ethan said, gradually piecing together the bizarre links that joined reality with what Joaquin Abell and Charles Purcell had witnessed.

Purcell nodded, apparently pleased with their progress.

'There is a similar phenomenon known as quantum entanglement. If particles are split into pairs and separated, then when one is observed and its wave function collapses, the same effect will occur in the other particle even if it is on the other side of the universe.'

Lopez's expression brightened.

'The future for any individual can only be fixed once it has been observed,' she said. 'Until then, it's just . . .'

'Just a wave,' Purcell finished the sentence for her. 'It's vague and unmeasured, nebulous and unclear, constantly being shaped by events in the present. Electrons behave in this way – it's called the uncertainty principle, because you can locate an electron but then you can't measure its energy state. Likewise, you can measure its energy state but then you can't precisely fix its position. Reality has a way of preventing us from knowing absolutely everything.'

Ethan looked at the camera that Purcell held, and he finally got it.

'Only you have seen the future that awaits you personally,' he said to Purcell. 'As long as Joaquin can't see what's on that camera, your future will be one that sees him pay for his crimes, because that's what *you* saw.'

'Precisely,' Purcell confirmed. 'When I realized what Joaquin intended to do I lied to him, telling him that the future could only be seen a certain distance ahead because of a property of black holes known as the Schwarzschild

Radius. I said that the cameras would be fried if left too close to the event horizon for too long, which is true, in some respects. Part of my job was to place and retrieve each of these cameras once every forty-eight hours or so. I altered this one by enclosing it in a Faraday cage to protect it from electrical forces within the black-hole chamber, and then left it in place for several weeks and used a spare camera instead to cover for it. Joaquin never knew what I'd done until I was forced to flee when I looked at the future as seen by this camera, and saw what would happen to me and my family.'

'Joaquin realized what you'd done,' Ethan put the pieces together, 'and sent his people to try to silence you. They headed for your family home first in case you were there . . .'

Purcell nodded, tears welling in his eyes as he struggled to keep his emotions in check.

'I couldn't get to them in time,' he uttered.

Lopez clenched her raised fist as she spoke.

'Well, now's your chance for payback. I'd say we've got IRIS by the balls. Let's get out of here and find out what happens.'

Ethan saw Purcell's smile fade.

'You've seen the camera's images, though,' he said to Purcell.

'I've seen everything right up to tonight. The future can never be seen in its entirety because it is always in motion, affected by events in the present. The only future we can see is the one viewed from our own perspective.'

'Tell us,' Lopez urged. 'We can help you.'

'No, you can't,' Purcell replied. 'I've already seen what will happen. I've caused the interference myself by viewing the future, and in doing so I've fixed it into place. My destiny cannot now be changed.'

'Yes it can,' Lopez insisted. 'You can get out of here right now and into protective custody. We know you didn't murder your family, Charles. You're innocent.'

'Yes I am,' Purcell said as tears formed at the corners of his eyes and his voice choked, 'and Joaquin Abell is guilty. But for him to be brought to justice . . .'

'You have to die,' Ethan said, 'because you saw it happen, didn't you? If you don't fulfill your own role within it, then you think that the future might change and Joaquin Abell might get away with what he did.'

Purcell's jaw quivered as he fought back indescribable fear, weighed down by the burden of a moral dilemma greater than anything Ethan could imagine.

'I saw my own death,' he whispered, as the tears now ran freely down his face. 'But I saw more than that, and I cannot tell you any of it. While it was alongside the event horizon of Joaquin's black hole this camera saw a future that included both my death and the fall of IRIS. It doesn't matter where it goes now, whether or not it's turned on or off or who possesses it. Its own future is recorded here, on its hard drive memory. And in order for it to be fulfilled, I must play my part. You must journey onward alone now, for my time has come to an end.'

'No way,' Lopez said, taking a step forward, 'you're out of here.'

Purcell raised a desperate hand and waved her back, swiping the tears from his face on the back of his sleeve.

'No! Please, do this for my wife, for my daughter. Let me go, because if you don't, then their killer will never be found.'

'What makes you so damned sure that they'll be found if you're dead?' Lopez snapped.

Purcell looked again at his watch, then turned and pointed to a large tree some twenty yards to his right. He spoke quickly, as though to hesitate any further would make him lose his resolve.

'The bullet that you'll find in that tree will lead you to my killer,' he said. 'Retrieve it and look for traces of Rubidium-82.'

'We found that compound on the bullets that killed your wife and daughter,' Ethan said.

'And you'll find it on all ammunition used by personnel at IRIS,' Purcell said. 'I took the liberty of dousing all of their weapons and ammunition in the armory before I fled.'

'What armory? And how do we find the black hole that IRIS is using?' Lopez asked.

'Wait for the earthquake,' Purcell said, 'at precisely sixteen-seventeen hundred hours and twelve seconds this afternoon, off the coast of the Dominican Republic. Search for electromagnetic anomalies in the Bermuda Triangle at the same time. You'll find IRIS there.'

'There must be another way,' Ethan pleaded. 'Some other path that will still ensure justice for your family.'

'That's not a chance I'm willing to take,' Purcell said. 'Katherine Abell is innocent of any crime. She may be able to help you bring him to justice, if you can prove to her that he is behind all that has happened, and that it is better to oppose him than stand with him.'

'She's devoted to him, it's no use,' Lopez replied. 'We need you, Charles.'

Purcell checked his watch again and then suddenly stood up straight and lifted his chin. He wiped the rest of the tears from his face. There was a terminal determination in his eyes.

'Good luck, both of you,' he said. 'Find the man who killed my family.'

Lopez shook her head and leapt forward. 'No!'

Ethan opened his mouth to speak but a sharp crack split the air around him.

Lopez slammed into Purcell, the pair of them spinning sideways in a gruesome pirouette. As if in slow motion, Purcell shuddered as a bullet slammed into his side and a fine mist of crimson spray exploded from his shirt as the projectile smashed through his chest cavity and exited from between his ribs. The scientist's body went limp as it fell, Lopez rolling with him through the air as they plunged down onto the soft sand.

Ethan saw the tree that Purcell had indicated shudder as a spray of bark fell from its trunk and the bullet buried itself in the wood. He leapt forward, hurling himself down on the sand alongside Purcell as Lopez grabbed his face in desperation, her other hand pressed against the exit wound spilling bright blood across his white shirt.

'Stay with me, Charles!' she shouted. 'Don't goddamn quit now! Where are those documents?'

Purcell looked at her as Ethan watched, his eyes hooded and his expression sagging as he whispered. 'My father took his secrets to the grave, as shall I,' he murmured. 'Time will tell, Nicola.'

Ethan felt his heart sink as Purcell gasped, and then the life in his eyes was extinguished like a distant dying star.

A burst of automatic fire raked the bushes around them, and Ethan grabbed Lopez by the arm.

'He's gone!' he shouted. 'Fall back!'

42

Ethan hit the ground and rolled into a dense thicket of reeds as a lethal hail of automatic fire blasted the edge of the forest. He saw Lopez hurl herself down behind a tree trunk, covering her face as chips of bark showered down across the foliage around her.

The shooting stopped, the Everglades silent in the heat again as leaves and bark chips dislodged by bullets drifted down around Ethan. He squinted through the reeds and saw Purcell lying on the sand, the side of his chest a bloody mess, and he felt a crushing melancholy for the man's tragic sacrifice. Then he saw the camera pinned beneath the scientist's body.

'We've got to get that camera!' Ethan whispered to Lopez.

'Where the hell's Bryson?' she asked in reply.

Ethan aimed his rifle through the reeds, searching for muzzle flash or signs of movement. He was expecting another broadside of gunfire, not the pair of grenades that thumped down onto the sand barely ten feet from where he lay.

'Grenades!'

Ethan leapt to his feet with Lopez and they both sprinted away from the spit of land as another hail of automatic fire swept the forest around them. Ethan hurled himself down into the bushes alongside Lopez and threw one arm over his head and the other over her as he waited for the grenades to explode.

Two feeble pops crackled on the hot air around them, and Ethan turned to see thick clouds of smoke billowing out through the dense undergrowth, as bullets whipped through the forest around them.

'They're coming ashore!' Lopez shouted.

Ethan cursed as he heard the sound of another airboat engine somewhere in front of them beyond the billowing wall of smoke. He could see no more than Lopez, and their attacker was so close that he could not shoot for fear of hitting the precious camera. More bullets flew past, mostly above their heads, and he realized that whoever had come ashore was firing only to keep their heads down.

'Damn it, we need to cut them off. Where the hell is Bryson?'

The choking smoke curled around them, stinging Ethan's eyes as he tried to see through the gloom. Another rattling volley of gunfire zipped and popped through the branches above their heads, and then Ethan heard the sound of the airboat's engine roar and glimpsed through the trees to his right the craft thunder past, the tall man with blond hair at the wheel.

Ethan leapt to his feet. 'Let's move!'

Lopez followed him at a run as they leapt fallen trees and pools of stagnant water until they burst out of the forest to see the airboat accelerating away. Ethan dropped down onto one knee and raised the M–16, selected single-shot and using the telescopic sight to aim not for the helmsman but for the much larger target of the engine. Ethan squeezed the trigger and the rifle jolted into his shoulder. Five shots cracked out as he fired one after the other and was rewarded with a puff of white smoke that spiraled from somewhere within the engine block.

A second airboat soared into view, swerving around the corner of the island and racing toward them. Ethan could see Bryson at the wheel as he guided the airboat in alongside the shore.

'The hell happened to you?' Lopez shouted at him.

Bryson's face was flushed with a mixture of anger and embarrassment as he looked at her.

'He snuck up on me, God knows how.'

Ethan scowled at Bryson. 'I thought you were a professional!'

'And I thought you told me Purcell was alone,' Bryson shot back.

Ethan cursed and looked over his shoulder at the spit of land where Charles Purcell had died. The camera had vanished.

'We can still get the bullet Purcell mentioned,' Lopez suggested.

Ethan leapt off the shore and onto the airboat as he looked back at her.

'We can come back for them!' He turned to Bryson and pointed down the river. 'Drive, damn it!'

Bryson gunned the engine as Lopez jumped aboard and the airboat span on the spot before accelerating out into open water in pursuit of the camera. As the deck heaved, Ethan saw a broken bottle of Jack Daniels rolling about near the stern. Lopez spotted the bottle and glared up at Bryson.

'You were supposed to be covering our backs!'

'I was. He got lucky.'

'What, lucky that you were drunk?' Ethan challenged. 'How the hell did you ever get into the SEALs?'

Bryson glared at Ethan but said nothing.

'He's out of sight,' Lopez complained. 'We won't catch him now.'

Ethan scanned the broad horizon of reed beds and water ahead. He raised his hands and used his fingers to make a box shape, focusing on one small area at a time just as he had in Miami. A few moments later he spotted a fine haze of translucent blue smoke hanging on the listless air a hundred yards ahead, the trail weaving between towering walls of reeds and sawgrass islands.

'There!' he shouted, pointing between the islands. 'He went through there.'

Bryson guided the airboat into a steep turn, white water spraying in glistening clouds from beneath the hull as they plunged into the narrow corridor. The smell of burning oil tainted the air, a tantalizing hint that Ethan's shot had fatally damaged the airboat's engine. The dense reed banks flashed past on either side of the airboat as it raced between them toward a gap that opened out onto a broader flood plain ahead.

Ethan pulled the M-16 into his shoulder and crouched down on one knee at the bow as he scanned the narrow horizon ahead for any sign of the other airboat. Lopez moved alongside him, her own rifle at the ready as the opening ahead loomed up on them.

They burst out onto the open water and Ethan looked left and right. A flash of gray metal caught his eye to his right, and he shouted a warning to Bryson as he saw the other airboat launch toward them from where it had been waiting in ambush. Bryson span the wheel and the airboat's hull shuddered as it turned hard, but he wasn't quick enough to prevent the bow of the second boat ramming into their stern.

Ethan was hurled sideways under the impact and tumbled across the deck as the airboat beside them accelerated away, trailing a thin plume of white smoke. A clatter of machine-gun fire rattled off the decks, showering Ethan in sparks as he ducked his head down low.

To his right, Lopez rolled alongside him and let her rifle fall onto his back, using his body as a rest. Ethan remained still as she took aim and opened fire on the fleeing airboat. Four rounds cracked out, and Ethan saw at least two of them send sparks flying from the airboat's propeller.

Bryson shoved the throttles fully forward and they surged in pursuit.

'He's lighter than us,' Lopez guessed. 'Only one man aboard! We can't pass him.'

Ethan was about to reply when the big blond man looked over his shoulder and tossed something up in the air. The small black object span as it climbed and then arced down toward their airboat.

'Grenade!'

Bryson yelled the warning as he swerved the airboat aside. The craft heaved and bounced across the wake of their quarry as the grenade hit the water nearby and exploded in a towering column of white water that splashed across the deck. Ethan and Lopez ducked as a hail of supersonic shrapnel sliced through the air around them, pinging off the hull and the propeller cage in a deafening metallic ricochet.

'Just get us as close to him as you can!' Ethan yelled at Bryson.

Bryson wrenched the airboat back under control and turned back toward their quarry as Ethan shouted at Lopez.

'Covering fire! Keep that bastard's head down!'

Lopez responded instantly and took up a prone position on her belly in the bow of the airboat. She took aim and fired three rounds in quick succession, the wind whipping the sound of the shots away. Through the spray Ethan saw the big blond man flinch and duck his head down.

Ethan crept forward onto the port bow, staying clear of Lopez's rifle as he prepared to make the jump.

'You can't take him on your own!' Lopez shouted. 'We already tried that. Just let me take out the engine!'

'No!' Ethan shouted as a plan formed in his mind. 'I've had an idea!'

Lopez looked up at him from behind the scope of her rifle but Ethan didn't elaborate. His idea wasn't without risk, and this wasn't the time for debate. The big blond man had realized that they were almost alongside him, and in an act of desperation he did the last thing that Ethan had expected him to.

He yanked the airboat across their path, the hull banking steeply in front of them until they could see deep inside as they rushed toward it on a collision course.

43

The airboat slid broadside amidst a wall of churning white water, its spinning propeller spraying a vortex of water vapor onto the hot air, and Ethan realized that there was no way that they could avoid smashing into it.

Bryson yelled out in alarm as he desperately tried to turn the airboat away from the impending collision. Ethan threw himself down again onto the deck as the bow of their airboat crashed into their opponent's hull in a whining crescendo of clashing metal. Ethan felt the airboat mount the bow of the boat below them, screech across it and crash down onto the water on the other side.

Ethan rolled over in time to see the big blond man kneeling in his violently rocking boat, his rifle pulled into his shoulder. A fearsome blast of automatic fire smashed into their engine, the huge propeller blades shattering to clatter against the inside of the cage as a dense pall of oily black smoke spilled from the engine block.

The blond man reached down and threw the throttles of his airboat forward, the craft surging forward past them. Two words passed unbidden through Ethan's mind.

Semper fi. The motto of the United States Marines. Always loyal.

Ethan scrambled to his feet and sprinted across the rocking deck of the airboat. He leapt into the air as the blond man's airboat thundered by, arms outstretched for the one place where the killer could not fire. The cage around his own engine.

Ethan hit the huge cage with a deep thump that reverberated through his chest as he landed. His fingers ached as they grasped the metal wires and the windblast from the blades pummeled his chest.

The airboat accelerated across the water, the vibrations from the engine shuddering through Ethan's bones as he struggled to maintain his grip on the cage. The blond man sitting in the pilot's seat could not fire through the blades at Ethan for fear of destroying his own craft, and the metal cage prevented him from reaching around it with his rifle to shoot Ethan off. The killer instead aimed his airboat at a dense bank of towering sawgrass.

Ethan braced himself as the blond man turned the vessel, sweeping along the edge of the reed banks. Thick blades slapped and sliced across the rear of the airboat, scraping painfully across Ethan's face and tearing at his shirt, but he held on grimly as the airboat soared back into open water.

Ethan reached up and hauled himself onto the top of the cage, the wind and spray stinging his eyes. As the blond man looked over his shoulder to see if he had dislodged him, Ethan hurled himself down onto the killer's broad shoulders.

The impact felt as though Ethan had hurled himself against a tree. The blond man roared as he was propelled forward to fall flat onto his face against the seats in the boat's hull. Ethan tumbled over him and rolled into the bow alongside the camera that he sought. He grabbed it with both hands and scrambled to his feet just as the killer rushed toward him with huge hands outstretched.

Ethan ducked down beneath the giant arms and barged his shoulder deep into the man's belly, spinning him aside to topple onto the deck as Ethan made a grab with his free hand for the M-16 propped alongside the driver's seat. He grabbed the butt and turned as he let the weapon slide down through his hand until his finger slipped onto the trigger. He took aim.

The blond man's fist smashed the barrel aside even as Ethan squeezed the trigger. The weapon stuttered as it fired and the barrel flew up into the air from the recoil. Another chunky fist flashed toward Ethan's face and he ducked his head down, letting the solid bone of his skull take the full impact of the blow. He heard the blond man howl in pain as his knuckles crunched across the top of Ethan's head, but the huge force of the punch sent Ethan reeling across the boat. He collided with the row of seats and sprawled onto the rolling deck. The camera was pinned beneath him and dug painfully into his ribs as the M-16 span from his grasp and clattered out of reach.

He crawled onto his hands and knees and reached out

for the weapon, only to see a heavy boot swing upwards to thump squarely across his chest. Ethan gasped as his lungs convulsed and he was flipped over onto his back, his hands wrapped around the camera. The killer reached down and picked up the M–16, looming over Ethan against the blue sky and aiming the rifle down at him. The blond man's angular features contorted into a malicious grin and his eyes shone with hatred.

One thick finger curled around the trigger and squeezed.

A flash of green reeds blasted into Ethan's field of view as a crash of rending metal screeched in his ears. The M–16 flew high in the killer's grasp, the shot smacking through the hull inches from Ethan's head as the man was hurled forward through the air over Ethan's body. Ethan curled up into a fetal ball as the airboat slammed into dense coils of mangroves and launched itself clear of the water. Ethan felt himself float briefly in mid-air before the airboat slammed bow-first into a thick bank of trees. Ethan hit the deck hard and cracked the back of his skull as he flew toward the bow and was hurled out of the boat.

He saw the world spin and then the ground rush up at him in a blur. On instinct he threw his hands out to break his fall and the camera span from his grasp. He hit the foliage with a tremendous impact that blasted the air from his lungs and sent spots of light spiraling across his vision. He rolled twice across the hard and unforgiving ground and slumped to a halt against the gnarled trunk of a tree.

For several moments he lay unable to move, his lungs

devoid of air, his limbs numb and his vision blurred into a haze of disconnected whorls of color. Somehow he managed to suck in a lungful of air, and his sight sparkled and returned. The sound of crackling flames entered the battered field of his consciousness, and he turned to see the buckled wreckage of the airboat crunched up against a thicket of trees, black smoke and flame spitting from its ruined engine.

Ethan struggled to focus and looked to his left just in time to see the big blond man run into the dense forests nearby with the camera tucked beneath his arm. Ethan reached out to haul himself up alongside the tree he had fallen against, but bolts of agony shot across his shoulder and he slumped back down again.

'Damn.'

Ethan lay on the bank for almost twenty minutes until he saw Bryson and Lopez paddling their crippled airboat up the creek toward him, homing in on the spiraling pillar of dirty smoke that stained the bright blue sky above.

Bryson guided the airboat in to the shore as Lopez hopped off the edge of the deck and rushed to Ethan's side.

'You didn't get the camera,' she observed.

Ethan struggled to his feet as he massaged his shoulder. 'I'm fine, thanks for asking.'

'Were you hit?' she asked, looking at his arm.

'Not by bullets,' Ethan replied, 'but just about every-thing else.'

Bryson called across to him. 'Speak for your goddamned self.'

Ethan saw a roughly applied tourniquet adorning Bryson's left forearm, where either a bullet or shrapnel had grazed him.

'Jarvis is on his way with the police,' Lopez said. 'I called him the moment you took off.'

Ethan nodded.

'Good work. We need to get back to Canaveral,' he pointed out as he turned to Bryson. 'And we need to search that spit of land where Charles Purcell died. He just sacrificed his life to find justice.'

44

FLORIDA EVERGLADES

June 28: 16.04

'Just what are we supposed to be looking for?'

Captain Kyle Sears looked expectantly at Doug Jarvis, who in turn looked at Ethan. Nearby, two uniforms guarded the spot where Charles Purcell had died, while other officers scoured the forest in pairs. A flotilla of police airboats were moored side by side on the surface of the water nearby.

'Bullet casings,' Ethan replied. 'Treat any that you find as forensic evidence. Have them bagged and sealed and sent to the nearest suitable lab for analysis. If I'm right, or rather if our victim was right, they'll have traces of Rubidium-82 on the surface.'

Kyle Sears squinted at Jarvis.

'Why the hell didn't you call us in to provide back-up?' he demanded.

'Same reasons as before,' Jarvis replied. 'This is too sensitive for local law enforcement.' Jarvis turned to Ethan. 'What happened?'

'We got jumped, same guy who killed Macy at the courthouse.'

'Any leads from Purcell before he died?' the old man asked.

Ethan explained what Purcell had related to them; the details held on the camera, the future that he had seen, and IRIS's implication in his family's murder. Jarvis remained silent for a long moment after Ethan had finished speaking.

'So he gave his life to keep the investigation on track,' Jarvis replied.

'He'd already lost everything,' Ethan replied pragmatically, then regretted it. 'But he was a hero, and we should ensure he's remembered that way. What I don't get is why he wouldn't tell us where the copies of the documents he stole from IRIS were.'

'He knew he was about to be killed,' Lopez said. 'My guess is that he couldn't tell us for fear of letting his assassin know. You saw the way he was looking around.'

'This camera,' Jarvis said, 'you say that its hard drive holds the record of six months' future events?'

'As seen through its own lens, starting at a secret complex supposedly built by IRIS,' Lopez nodded. 'Doesn't matter now where the camera goes or where it's pointed. It's already seen the future while in the black-hole chamber and recorded everything to the drive.'

Ethan could see the old man's eyes sparkling with intrigue, and realized that he was already entertaining the prospect of acquiring the camera and its uniquely valuable record for the Defense Intelligence Agency.

'We have to stop Joaquin Abell,' Lopez said, sensing the same as Ethan. 'He's got a game plan and this is only the beginning of what he intends to do. The camera can wait – it's only of secondary importance to shutting IRIS down.'

'That camera,' Jarvis replied, 'could save all of our butts. I'm down here trying to persuade the powers that be to continue funding our investigations, and not for the first time the two of you are at the epicenter of gunfights, accidents and general mayhem. I'll be lucky if I have a job when I get back to the district. But if this technology were to be acquired by us then the DIA would change their tune overnight.'

Ethan smiled, the pain in his shoulder momentarily forgotten.

'Then you'll be relieved that I let our attacker get away with the camera.'

Jarvis's eyes widened as he stared at Ethan. 'You *let* him get away?!'

'Bryson took a bullet so that you could let him get away,' Lopez snapped. 'What the hell were you thinking? Why chase him in the first place?'

Ethan raised a placating hand at her.

'Look, right up to this moment we've been one step behind, all the time. If Joaquin Abell really can see future news reports then he's had us by the balls ever since we got here. Everything we do is only a reaction to what he has already anticipated and acted upon.'

'So?' Jarvis asked.

'So, that all changed the moment we met Charles Purcell,' Ethan explained. 'He said it himself – only *he* has seen the future as it will unfold over the next twenty-four hours. Joaquin only sees news reports from the future, and uses what he sees for his own ends. But Charles Purcell took a camera *outside* of the IRIS facility, out into the world. It would have already seen our conversation with Purcell, and its being stolen by that assassin; it would have seen everything that occurs into the future for six months, with absolute clarity, with regard to this very case.'

'Effectively, the camera's hard drive carries a record of everything that the camera will see for the next few months,' Lopez explained. 'But because it was taken away from the facility, what it's seen is potentially different from what Joaquin's cameras may have witnessed.'

'Because of the observer effect,' Jarvis said. 'In principle, the events in the future that the camera saw are now fixed, but only for that camera.'

Kyle Sears furrowed his brow.

'So you're saying that one future vision trumps another, somehow?'

'No,' Ethan said. 'Only that I think Purcell was trying to tell us that viewing the future may fix certain events into place, but only for the viewer. Joaquin can only see the future through the narrow lens of the cameras he has watching the news channels, not the wider picture around those events. It's like being able to look into the future to see a boxer win a fight, but not being able to tell whether they'll win the title.'

Lopez raised an eyebrow.

'Yeah, until he gets that camera back. Then he'll be able to see everything that the camera has. If it goes back to this supposed IRIS facility you mentioned, then any attack we try to launch on it, he'll see coming.'

'Yes,' Ethan agreed, 'but we had to let the camera go in order to prove who's behind all of this. Considering the lengths that they've gone to, they obviously want that camera very badly indeed.'

'Then we need to move fast,' Jarvis said. 'Turns out that Joaquin Abell had both the motive and the know-how to both build his machine and kill Charles Purcell. Their fathers knew each other and they weren't best buddies. Not only that, but Isaac Abell built some kind of underground base meant for housing a nuclear-fusion plant, but it never got finished.' He looked at Ethan. 'So how do we find the assassin now?'

'Project Watchman,' Ethan said. 'By the time we get back to Canaveral, they could focus in down here on the Everglades and track the assassin's movements. If as we suspect he's working for IRIS, then Joaquin will no doubt have instructed his man to return immediately. We just follow him all the way home.'

Jarvis frowned.

'He may anticipate our attempts to track him,' the old man said. 'Even though they won't know about Watchman, they'll try to hide their movements, and our satellites have their limitations.'

Lopez smiled as she realized what Ethan had done. 'It won't matter, as we'll have another way of confirming IRIS's involvement.'

Ethan nodded.

'Charles Purcell made a prediction, probably based upon what he managed to view of the camera's memory. He said that there would be an earthquake at sixteen-seventeen hours and twelve seconds this afternoon, northwest of the Dominican Republic. He said to search for electromagnetic anomalies in the Bermuda Triangle and that we'd find IRIS there, at the epicenter.'

Jarvis blinked.

'The Bermuda Triangle? You think that the IRIS facility is *underwater?*'

'Charles Purcell told us that's where we'd find IRIS,' Lopez explained, 'and if this device of Joaquin's was being tested on a regular basis then the magnetic fields generated could be responsible for the disappearance of ships and airplanes in the Bermuda Triangle over the years.'

'If he's really got a black hole down there,' Ethan said, 'then going after him directly could be very dangerous. Joaquin's got a nuclear option if he wants it, and judging by how many people he's killed in such a short space of time I'd say he'll use it if his hand is forced.'

'Katherine Abell,' Lopez suggested. 'Purcell claimed that she was innocent of any crime. We could use her, if she can be convinced of her husband's guilt.'

'Do it,' Jarvis said, and glanced at his watch. 'That earthquake is due in a couple of hours, and if Charles Purcell's predictions are true, he's now aiming it at the very island his wife has fled to'.

'Katherine's in the Dominican Republic?' Ethan asked in amazement.

'Flew there from Miami International less than an hour ago,' Jarvis confirmed. 'Looks like Joaquin's own family might be a target too. He may have even planned deliberately to silence Katherine. Something must have happened between them – maybe she's started to suspect that Joaquin's not quite the philanthropist he's claimed to be, and we can use that to our advantage. Lopez, you go after Katherine and make sure Bryson helps you out. Ethan, you get back to Cape Canaveral and track down Joaquin via his assassin.'

'What are *you* going to do? We need all the help we can get,' Lopez asked.

'I'll go with Ethan for now.'

'And what about if we have to go underwater to find Joaquin's base?' she pressed.

'We don't have time for this,' Jarvis interjected.

'Well then *make* time,' Lopez insisted. 'You're asking us to go into an area that's due a major earthquake, then infiltrate a hidden underwater base against unknown and armed opposition. I wouldn't mind so much except that you and your cavalry only ever turn up after the shooting's done.'

Jarvis recoiled, and then his bright blue eyes turned hard and cold.

'I can't just whistle up military intervention whenever it suits the two of you by making a quick phone call or calling in a debt. Do you have any idea how much it costs to support you both, especially when you insist on tearing up the countryside wherever you go? Scrambling those two F-15s earlier, plus the ride down from Illinois, plus this team of police and their transports, has set our budget back by almost a hundred thousand dollars in just one day. Think about that for a moment: *a hundred thousand dollars* in a little over six hours, is what it's cost my department to keep the pair of you in goddamned work.'

Lopez exhaled and closed her eyes. 'And we appreci-ate it.'

Jarvis kept his gaze on her for a moment, then looked across at Ethan.

'Stopping IRIS is a priority, but so is convincing the DIA that their taxpayers' dollars are being wisely spent. Recovering that camera and what it contains might just ensure that the Defense Department has the upper hand against rogue nations for several months to come. The intelligence could be priceless and I intend that our department recovers it. Is that understood?'

Ethan nodded, and saw Lopez do the same. Jarvis gathered himself.

'Ethan, let's get back to Watchman and find out where that asshole who took the camera went. Lopez, when you return from the Dominican Republic we'll send the pair of you to shut him down. Any further questions?'

Ethan was about to turn for the nearby airboat when a police officer hurried up alongside them and raised an evidence bag to Jarvis.

'The bullet that killed Charles Purcell,' the officer said, then looked at Ethan. 'We found it right where you said it would be, lodged in that tree trunk.'

'How long will it take to have the casing analyzed?' Ethan asked.

'We can rush it through back at base, sir,' the officer replied. 'We already know the compound you're look-ing for, so it should only take a couple of hours or so to confirm its presence, if it's there.'

'Enough time for the assassin to make it back to Miami,' Ethan said to Jarvis.

'And enough for us to track him to wherever IRIS is hiding,' Jarvis agreed, and then looked at his watch. 'We'd better hurry – we've an earthquake to catch.'

Another police officer rushed up to them.

'Crime scene investigators are working on Purcell's body,' the cop said to Kyle Sears. 'You need to see this, captain.'

Ethan followed Sears as he was led to Purcell's body, Lopez and Jarvis behind him. As they reached the spit of sand, Ethan could see that the CSI team had removed the shirt from the scientist's corpse, to photograph more clearly the entrance and exit wounds. Now, Ethan could see what had not been visible beforehand.

'Oh my God,' Lopez uttered.

Across Purcell's chest was scrawled lines of letters.

'What the hell does that mean?' Sears asked.

frsbz racjotrl kbnq sf bpuzl
mibmo yuwtez jrrwe

Lopez stepped forward.

'Charles said that he would take the secret of where he had put the documents to the grave,' she said. 'If he already knew that he was to be killed, then he might also have known that we would find this on his body. It must be another code of some kind, maybe the location of the documents.'

'It looks like a cipher code,' Jarvis said. 'Not complex in itself, but the number of possible combinations runs into the tens of millions.'

'What do we need?' Lopez asked.

'It'll be a string of numbers, used to scramble the alphabet,' Jarvis said. 'Could be two numbers, could be ten, even a hundred. I could send this to the NSA and get them to work on it, but it could still take days, weeks even, and we only have a few hours.'

Lopez stared at Purcell's body.

'He wouldn't have made it that difficult,' she said. 'He was only covering his tracks. He must have left us a clue somewhere.'

'Well, right now we don't have the time to decode it, not here anyway,' Sears said, and turned to the nearest police officer. 'Have the remains flown out of here immediately. I want a lid kept on this: no media, no leaks, understood?'

The officer was about to carry out the order when Ethan stepped in.

'Wait. If this is Joaquin's work, then how did he know where to send his assassin?'

Sears stared blankly at Ethan for a moment. 'Maybe he followed the two of you?'

'Not a chance,' Lopez said. 'Ethan's right. He ran like hell to get away from us in Miami, remember? Tracking us since then, from Cape Canaveral and then out here on these airboats, would have been next to impossible.' She looked at Ethan. 'What are you thinking?'

'Well,' Ethan began, 'if Joaquin uses television reports to judge what's happening in the future, then maybe he saw one that showed Purcell's body being recovered.'

Sears rubbed his eyes wearily. 'Jesus, this is going to really start messing with my head.'

'Point is, Joaquin would have to have known about

what would happen out here in order to have sent his man in to try and recover that camera,' Lopez said.

'You think that we should let him see he's been successful?' Jarvis asked. 'Fulfill what Charles Purcell himself saw?'

'Damn right,' Ethan said. 'Put this on the news, tell everyone. Suspected murderer found dead in the Everglades.'

'That's a mighty big risk,' Jarvis said. 'And anyway, does any of it matter? Surely from Joaquin's perspective anything we do now has already been preordained. Whatever we choose to do with news reports he'll have already seen.'

'Yes,' Ethan nodded, 'but Purcell said that what Joaquin sees isn't necessarily precisely what happened. We can use that to our advantage. Joaquin will be searching for something like this to confirm that what he saw in the future has actually now happened. If he sees it, it will boost his confidence, and that might make him drop his guard. We shouldn't disappoint.'

Jarvis finally nodded in agreement and turned to the officer.

'Have the body recovered, then inform the local PD and the press. I want everybody else out of here within fifteen minutes, is that understood?'

'Yessir!'

The officer left and Ethan looked at the old man.

'Time to turn the tables and give Joaquin what he wants to see, right?'

'I'll handle the press release,' Jarvis said, looking at his watch. 'You concentrate on finding IRIS. We don't have much time.'

As Lopez and the cops turned away, Ethan grabbed Jarvis's arm and leaned in close.

'Work or no work, I'm not going up against IRIS alone without something in return.'

Jarvis shot him a look of concern, as though he knew exactly what he was suggesting, but Ethan released him before he could respond and strode away toward the waiting airboats.

45

IRIS, DEEP BLUE RESEARCH STATION, FLORIDA STRAITS

June 28, 16:12

Joaquin Abell stood at the control panel and watched ten armed guards led by Olaf Jorgenson escorting Governor MacKenzie, Harry Reed, Robert Murtaugh, Congressman Goldberg and property tycoon Benjamin Tyler into the hub. Dennis Aubrey stood behind the control panel and as far away from Joaquin as he could.

Aubrey had heard that Olaf had returned barely half an hour before, Joaquin meeting the giant aboard the yacht before travelling down to the facility aboard the *Isaac* as his guests followed aboard the *Intrepid*. On his arrival, Joaquin had handed Aubrey a camera identical to those in the black-hole chamber and ordered it to be locked away until further notice.

The five men were looking about them with uncomfortable expressions, set somewhere between curiosity and disgust. Men of power, Aubrey guessed, were not used to being kept in the dark and disliked being told what to do and when to do it. Effectively brought here against their wishes, and without their bodyguards and other familiar security measures, they probably felt precisely as Joaquin wanted them to feel: exposed and alone.

Joaquin spread his hands in a gesture of welcome.

'Gentlemen, thank you for coming.'

Robert Murtaugh scowled up at him.

'We're only here because you've forced our hands, so don't presume to believe that we're willing visitors.'

Governor MacKenzie nodded in agreement.

'I've had to put a major meeting on hold for this, Joaquin. It had better be worth it. You said we were meeting on your yacht. Why the hell are we down here? What is this place?'

The Texan, Harry Reed, pointed to the huge metallic sphere dominating the center of the hub.

'What in the name of darnation is that goddamn thing?'

Congressman Goldberg scanned the large plasma screens lining the walls of the hub, their coalesced news feeds taunting them with hundreds of voices.

'Why all the news channels?'

'All will be revealed,' Joaquin said as he stepped down off the control platform. 'For now, suffice to say that this hub is the center of my organization, the beating heart of what will, in time, become the most powerful company on earth.'

Robert Murtaugh coughed out a bitter laugh and shook his head, his jowls swinging beneath his chin.

'My ass, Joaquin. Your jumped-up little outfit isn't worth a tenth of what my broadcasting network turns over.'

'Not right now,' Joaquin agreed, refusing to be baited. 'But tomorrow . . .'

'Something else you've seen in your damned visions?' Governor MacKenzie uttered.

Joaquin smiled and extended one hand toward the metallic sphere nearby.

'You will observe, gentlemen, that the sphere in the center of the hub has windows, and that those windows look out toward the television screens around the walls of the hub.' The men glanced up at the various news-feeds. 'We see those feeds in the present, but from within the metal sphere, those newsfeeds are greatly accelerated by time dilation, allowing me to see tomorrow's news today.'

Robert Murtaugh glanced at the contraption. 'Caused by what, exactly?'

Joaquin did not reply, and Dennis Aubrey took his cue.

'A black hole,' he explained, his own voice sounding small in his own ears, 'large enough to cause sufficient time dilation to allow IRIS to see into the future, small enough to remain under our control.'

Robert Murtaugh spat his response.

'That's impossible,' he uttered. 'I studied physics at college. Black holes form from collapsed stars of tremendous mass. You can't possibly have achieved such energies. It would take a particle accelerator the size of our solar system to generate enough pressure to produce a black hole. Human technology doesn't even come close to what would be required to . . .'

'I haven't captured a star,' Joaquin replied.

'You're no scientist,' Reed sneered at Joaquin in his Texan drawl, 'so how could you have . . . ?'

'I have people,' Joaquin cut him off. 'People who know how to achieve the impossible.' He gestured to the chamber before them. 'Do you even know what a black hole is?'

When none of the gathered men responded and Murtaugh simply scowled, Joaquin looked across at Aubrey and raised an eyebrow. The scientist took a breath.

'Black holes are formed when giant stars exhaust their nuclear fuel and begin to collapse under their own gravity,' he explained, finding solace from his fears in the knowledge accumulated from a life's work. 'Stars ordinarily are a balancing act, with the force of gravity that formed the star in the first place trying to crush it ever further inward, balanced by the energy from nuclear fusion in the star's core blazing outward. But when the fuel is exhausted, the nuclear fusion ends. With the core of the star no longer burning, there is no force to prevent the star from being crushed by its own weight. Eventually, the core of the star collapses into itself with immense force, blasting the outer layers of the star away in what's called a supernova. The super-dense core usually remains as a smoldering remnant, but if the parent star was massive enough the core is crushed with such gravitational force that nothing can stop the collapse of its entire mass into an infinitely small space. A singularity is formed, the heart of a black hole. It is a place without dimension, yet of incredible mass, where time literally comes to a stop.'

Joaquin nodded.

'Absolutely correct,' he agreed, as he strolled off the platform and surveyed the control room. 'However, in the event that formed our universe, the Big Bang, there were such pressures and densities that much smaller, micro black holes were formed in their billions. More are produced daily by cosmic rays from the sun that collide at almost the speed of light with particles in our earth's atmosphere, creating micro black holes that pass through the earth at close to light-speed. All of these tiny black holes possess little more mass than a grapefruit and pass through the earth almost unnoticed.'

Benjamin Tyler frowned. *'Almost?'*

Joaquin turned and lithely leapt up to the control panel.

'Time-slips,' he said grandly. 'They produce tiny slips in time, their gravity distorting the flow of time around an observer just enough to cause them to experience events that some people refer to, rather naively, as *supernatural.'*

'Such as?' Governor MacKenzie asked.

'Déjà vu,' Joaquin replied. 'The feeling that you've been somewhere before. The reason for that is because you *have* been there before, moments before you actually arrived. The micro black hole causes a tiny loop in time, too small to detect with the senses but enough that the human subconscious *remembers* what's about to happen after one of these micro black holes flash through your brain.'

'That's pure speculation,' Murtaugh argued, leaning on a thin white cane. 'You have no evidence to support it.'

'What about ghosts?' Joaquin suggested. 'Albert Einstein himself stated that time can flip and loop over on itself, and it takes little imagination to picture the past replaying itself before the eyes of those in the present. It wouldn't take much for a small swarm of micro black holes passing through the earth to generate such a loop in time, the shadowy past temporarily revived.' Joaquin shrugged. 'But I digress – I take it that you can see the basic structure of the device, now that you know its purpose. It contains an object of tremendous power. Dennis, if you will?'

Aubrey gestured to the giant tokamak chamber and the huge magnetic-field generators.

'A magnetic field is generated around the central sphere to attract and capture passing micro black holes as they travel through the earth,' he said. 'Black holes can carry a charge depending on the particles they consume from matter around them. If any black holes captured are given a negative charge by firing electrons at them from a cathode-ray tube, they become entrapped within the negatively charged surface of the chamber's interior and forced into suspension in the center. They are repelled by the surrounding plates and thus combine.'

Joaquin clapped his hands in delight as he addressed the guests.

'The chamber contains a pure vacuum which stops the black hole from consuming any particles and getting bigger,' he explained. 'We couldn't create the pure vacuum on our own, of course: what particles remained within the chamber were consumed by the first micro black holes that we caught.'

'But how did you know where the micro black holes would be?' Murtaugh asked. 'It should have taken millions of years to have accumulated so many, even if solar cosmic rays were producing them in our atmosphere.'

Joaquin smiled, expanding his arms to encompass the entire underwater complex.

'Our planet has a number of what are known as magnetic anomalies,' he explained. 'They are regions where compasses fail, radio devices are cut off and all manner of atmospheric phenomena prevail. The two best known are the Devil's Triangle off the coast of Japan, a place so dangerous that it is actually a controlled area which is avoided by aircraft and vessels. The other, here in the Florida Straits, is the Bermuda Triangle.'

Aubrey took over, the eyes of the guests fixed upon him.

'The anomalies are caused by the micro black holes passing through the earth's magnetic field, which directs them toward these points on the earth's surface. This is why so many anomalies seem compacted into a small geographic area. It's why the facility was built here; Isaac Abell was trying to capture neutrinos, but instead the facility has been capturing black holes.'

Joaquin must have learned from reading countless popular science books that black holes coalesced when they came into contact, creating larger black holes and in doing so, greater time dilation. Out in deep space, Aubrey knew that truly gargantuan black holes dance in terminally declining orbits as they spiral in toward each other, causing tremendous warps in time and space so violent that they form temporal ripples that spread across the entire universe. The largest yet found possessed the mass of twenty *billion* suns. By contrast, Joaquin's black hole was a tiny speck, but a speck that nonetheless could produce truly dramatic results.

'How do you translate that into the ability to see into the future?' Congressman Goldberg demanded.

Joaquin looked up at the plasma screens surrounding them on the walls of the dome.

'That, gentlemen, is down to both the ubiquity of global news channels and something that you may have heard of before, a legend of science fiction, if you will, that was once considered the stuff of fantasy and yet is now known to be real. It is the barrier between existence and oblivion, and is called the *event horizon*.'

46

'What in the name of God is an event horizon?' Reed asked. 'And what the hell does it have to do with those news channels?'

Aubrey gestured to the plasma screens as he spoke. Joaquin clearly knew enough of the physics to understand that the black hole's mass governed how much space, and therefore time, would dilate around it. But the legendary event horizon was another matter.

'All objects reflect light under normal circumstances, but a black hole is different,' Aubrey said. 'When vessels like the space shuttle seek to reach orbit, they have to do so with tremendous force in order to reach a velocity of 17,500 miles per hour, the speed required to break free of earth's gravity. This velocity is known as the escape velocity. The more massive the planet, or star, the greater the velocity required to escape it.'

He turned, and gestured to the containment sphere.

'A black hole compresses enormous amounts of mass into an infinitesimally small space,' Aubrey said. 'So much so that the fabric of space-time becomes so tightly twisted that the escape velocity becomes greater than the speed of light and a darkened barrier forms between the black hole and the outside universe: the event horizon. Should an observer cross the event horizon there is no going back, for nothing can travel faster than light. It is for this reason that black holes neither reflect nor emit light, for anything they consume is, by the laws of the universe, forever trapped within. The bedtime stories of black holes "sucking" unwary travelers inside are a fallacy – the hole simply wraps time and space around itself so tightly that, once close enough, there is no path to follow but one that leads directly into the singularity itself.'

Joaquin's voice rang out in scarcely concealed delight: 'Dennis here has calculated the black hole's mass, and therefore its Schwarzschild Radius. This has given us the precise location of the event horizon, and the precise amount of time dilation the black hole can produce.'

Congressman Goldberg peered up at the plasma screens.

'So if you're close to this event horizon, time moves at a different rate?'

'Brilliant!' Joaquin clapped. 'That's precisely what happens.'

'The video cameras inside the chamber film the news channels . . .' Murtaugh said.

'Go on,' Joaquin encouraged.

Aubrey realized that Joaquin was getting more excited by the moment as the devious nature of his device was revealed. But Murtaugh's knowledge allowed him to go no further, so Aubrey picked up the explanation.

'But the cameras are close to the black hole's event horizon, and so time moves at a different rate for them because the black hole's immense mass twists both space and time around it so tightly. Therefore, time beyond the horizon appears to run more swiftly. We retrieve the cameras after they've been in the chamber for a certain amount of time and replay what they've seen.'

'They play the future,' Joaquin said. 'They tell me what's going to happen next via international news broadcasts.'

Governor MacKenzie looked up when Aubrey had finished speaking.

'And how far, exactly, can this thing of yours see into the future?'

'Approximately twenty-four hours,' Aubrey replied. 'The mass of the black hole limits how far we can see into the future. Currently, for every hour of time that passes, a further hour into the future is seen by the cameras.'

MacKenzie turned away.

'It's time for me to leave,' he said. 'This crap isn't worth the risk or the hassle.'

'The ability to look into the future does not interest you, Governor?'

'Of course it does,' MacKenzie growled over his shoulder at Joaquin, 'but twenty-four hours is not enough notice to swing voters or settle economic markets. This has no real use for my office, and what about events that don't make the news? All you've got here is major breaking stories, disasters and the like. Sure, big government might be all over you if you told them about this, but on a state scale it's just not enough for me to risk my tenure by doing whatever dirty little deals you've got in mind, Joaquin. I'm done here.'

MacKenzie took another two paces before Joaquin nodded at his guards. The soldiers moved in front of the governor and blocked his path.

'Oh, right,' MacKenzie uttered, turning back to face Joaquin. 'So now you're going to keep us here? You know you can be a real ass sometimes when you . . .'

'I haven't finished yet!' Joaquin bellowed, silencing the governor. Aubrey watched the tycoon struggle to gain control over his sudden rage. 'Seeing the future is only the beginning of what this device can achieve.'

Harry Reed peered up at Joaquin from beneath his broad-rimmed hat.

'An' just what might that be?'

Joaquin gestured to the black-hole chamber.

'The black hole is maintained in stasis, carefully balanced, by magnetic fields. But when we were building the device it was discovered that by temporarily destabilizing it we can direct its gravitational energy wherever we wish. Carefully manipulating the electro-magnetic field produces powerful pulses of energy.'

Benjamin Tyler glanced at the metallic sphere. 'How much energy?'

Joaquin shot Tyler a mischievous grin and whispered theatrically as though imparting a childish secret.

'You will recall the earthquake that I showed you yesterday.'

A shocked silence descended upon the five men before him as they digested what he had said.

'You're going to *cause* that earthquake?' Goldberg uttered.

'I am.'

A flutter of *Jesus Christ*s whispered amongst them as they looked at Joaquin.

'You'll kill millions,' Harry Reed pointed out.

'Only a few thousand, in the end,' Joaquin replied without emotion.

'You've lost your mind,' MacKenzie muttered. 'No matter how hard you try, this place will never remain totally secret forever. Sooner or later the military will uncover what you've done here and before you know what's happened you'll be locked up in Guantanamo for the rest of your miserable little life.'

Joaquin ignored the governor as he focused instead on the other men in the group.

'Electromagnetic weapons deliver heat, or mechanical or electrical energy, to a target. They can be used against electronic equipment, military targets and even humans. We adjust the fields within the tokamak chamber to act like a parabolic reflector, to direct the energy of the black hole wherever we wish, much like more conventional electromagnetic weapons.'

'Is there any defense against such an attack?' Congressman Goldberg asked.

Joaquin, caught off guard by the question, glanced up at Dennis Aubrey.

'A Faraday cage would provide protection from most directed and undirected electromagnetic pulses,' Aubrey said, 'but against gravitational forces there is absolutely no defense.'

The men remained silent, apparently unable to form a cohesive opposition to Joaquin's remarkable achievements. Aubrey watched as Joaquin took a deep breath, sucked in the moment and let it fill his lungs with the first scent of victory. Now, terrifyingly, everything that he had sought to achieve was at Joaquin's fingertips, the first steps on a final journey toward ultimate power.

'And what happens once you've installed us in the White House?' MacKenzie asked. 'What happens if any one of the many people you must have employed to build this facility decide that they will blow the whistle on you?'

'Yeah,' Reed joined in. 'What's to stop you getting some of your own goddamned medicine?'

Benjamin Tyler stepped forward.

'Speaking of medicine, why am I here? You told me that I will die, soon. I want to know how and I want to know how to stop it.'

Joaquin looked down at Tyler for a long moment.

'I can answer all of your questions at once by answering just one of them,' he said, before looking at Tyler. 'I cannot stop your illness, Benjamin,' he said. 'You have a malignant tumor deep within your brain stem that is the cause of the headaches you've been having over the past few weeks. It is inoperable. I can only make your suffering swifter and less painful.'

'What the hell are you talking about?' Tyler snapped, his fists clenched by his side.

Joaquin grinned mischievously. He turned to a DVD player laying on a table nearby, connected to a television screen. The screen lit up and a news article, distorted like the ones they had viewed in Miami, showed a news anchor, her voice silent but the scrolling text at the bottom of the screen as clear as day.

BENJAMIN TYLER COMMITS SUICIDE AFTER TERMINAL ILLNESS CONFIRMED

The group read the news bulletin and gasped as one. Aubrey watched in horror as they all turned to look at Tyler. Benjamin Tyler stared at the screen in confusion.

'What the hell is *that*?' he uttered.

Joaquin Abell smiled, his face contorted into a chilling chimera of pity and delight.

'Your obituary, Benjamin,' he replied. 'The results of a routine health check will arrive tomorrow, revealing the presence of your malignant tumor, but it will be assumed that you already knew you were a dead man and took your own life.' Joaquin looked at Governor MacKenzie. 'You asked about how I would deal with whistle-blowers?'

Joaquin raised one hand and clicked his fingers.

Before anybody could react, ten armed IRIS troops lunged into the crowd and grabbed Benjamin Tyler. They lifted him bodily off the ground and carried him toward the chamber.

47

'What the hell are you doing?!' Tyler bellowed in terror as he struggled. 'Put me down!'

Congressman Goldberg tried to grab one of the guards, who whirled and drove the lawman back, slamming him to the ground with a savage blow from the butt of his rifle.

'Stop them, Joaquin!' MacKenzie shouted. 'This is insane!'

'There was only one thing missing from my presentation to you,' Joaquin replied, his features hardening as he spoke. 'A demonstration of my determination to succeed.'

The guards carried Tyler to the black hole's outer chamber, opened the access door and roughly bundled the businessman into it before slamming the steel door shut. Tyler banged desperately on the thick glass, but like the news broadcast of his demise, no sound reached the horrified onlookers. Quickly, one of the soldiers carried a video camera on a tripod and stood it outside the chamber, this one looking in. Almost immediately, one of the giant plasma screens showed the black hole, flares of searing energy writhing in blue-white coils against the walls of the chamber.

Joaquin looked up at Dennis Aubrey, whose heart had begun to hammer against the walls of his chest. Prickly heat tingled across his collar as he stared back at Joaquin.

'Dennis, if you will, prepare to destabilize the black hole as soon as our unfortunate friend Mr. Tyler has been . . .' Joaquin searched for an appropriate word, 'cured.'

Aubrey, unable to believe what he was seeing and yet unable to intervene, flipped switches like an automaton on the console before him. Joaquin turned to face his guests, his expression cold.

'Gentlemen, should any of you be tempted to interfere with my campaign . . .'

He let the sentence hang in the air for a long moment and then nodded at one of the soldiers now standing beside a control panel at the black-hole chamber. The soldier flicked a switch before him and then yanked down on a large handle, tiger-striped with yellow and black chevrons.

Wailing sirens echoed around the hub and beacons span and flashed. From his vantage point Dennis Aubrey watched the screen, frozen immobile with horror, as the chamber's interior door opened agonizingly slowly.

Benjamin Tyler was hauled off of his feet by an incredible force, flying through the air toward the terrifying chamber beyond. His hands managed to grab the inside of the door as his body was held horizontally in the air as though in the grasp of a hurricane, but he wasn't able to hang on for more than a split second before the immense gravity of the black hole yanked him away.

A bright flare of electrical energy shone within the chamber, and Aubrey watched with morbid fascination as Benjamin Tyler's body shot toward the black hole. Aubrey glimpsed the tycoon's face, laced with a sheen of sparkling ice crystals as the latent heat of his body was vacuumed out, his flesh turning hard as stone and his horrified eyes turning to brittle balls of ice. Tyler's pain-racked face froze with fear as, in a millisecond, his body was unwound from its normal height to an infinite length, stretching him around the black hole's orbital axis at the speed of light as he was torn apart, atom by atom, in a flare of radiation that glowed in a brilliant disc around the black hole's circumference.

The last thing Aubrey saw was the image of Tyler's head turn a deep red as it vanished beyond the black hole's event horizon, the time dilation red-shifting the light to the extreme end of the spectrum until it could no longer emit radiation and Tyler disappeared altogether.

Aubrey realized that his breath was fluttering awkwardly in his throat, his caged heart now hammering like a convict trying to batter down the bars of a cell. He wiped his brow with the back of his hand and felt cold sweat on his skin. With everybody below him staring at the screen on which Tyler had vanished, Aubrey reached out and grabbed the satellite phone from the control panel and slipped it into his pocket. Joaquin spoke to his horrified guests below, his voice devoid of any emotion.

'Gentlemen, Benjamin Tyler no longer exists. Every atom that made up his body has been destroyed within the oblivion that is the black hole.'

Joaquin turned to Aubrey and pointed at the control panel.

'Begin the second part of the demonstration,' he snapped.

Aubrey took a breath. If ever he had needed confirmation that Joaquin Abell had lost his mind as well as his humanity, then this was it. He could hear Joaquin's words ringing in his ears. *Katherine has gone to work on one of our charity projects in the Dominican Republic. She won't be coming here.* Joaquin was not only demonstrating the power he wielded: he was attempting to murder the only person left ashore who knew what he had achieved. Dennis made a decision that he knew could threaten his own life, but which was unavoidable.

'I'll need all of the staff's door passes,' he replied, as he grasped for the most confusing scientific terms he could summon. 'The gravitational cavitation we'll experience is capable of scrambling the polarity of the magnetic access chips at this close range.'

Joaquin glared up at him. 'You did not tell me about this.'

'You didn't tell me you were about to cause an earthquake,' Aubrey shot back, finding his rhythm. 'So I wouldn't have been able to tell you about the effect that the ensuing gravitational waves will have on magnetically polarized circuitry, or on our communications hub. The frequencies will be so high that they could rupture antennas, reverse magnetic polarity and maybe even fry circuitry. I hope that nobody here has a pacemaker? Or cares about the life-support systems that keep the air breathable down here and the lights on?'

The gathered dignitaries gawped at Aubrey as he stepped down from behind the control panel holding a small box.

'I have a pacemaker,' Murtaugh said, and tapped his chest with one crooked finger.

'This is a Faraday cage,' Aubrey explained, holding up the box. 'It will protect the access cards. Once the experiment is over they can be retrieved and will be none the worse for wear. I'll go to the communications hub and shut down the antennas and re-route the power to life-support until the experiment is over. Mr. Murtaugh, I advise you to remain at least twenty feet away from the chamber, just as a precaution, when the experiment begins.'

Aubrey boldly reached up to Olaf Jorgenson's chest and unclipped his card. Without any further prompting, Joaquin Abell removed his own and dropped it into the box. His men automatically followed suit, and Aubrey sealed the box shut and turned for the exit.

'Olaf will take the box,' Joaquin said. 'You will go to the communications hub. Olaf?' The big man raised his chin questioningly. 'Shut off the comms from here.'

Aubrey reluctantly handed the box to Olaf, who smirked down at him. Aubrey walked up to the control panel and with a heavy heart pressed a single button. Immediately the chamber began emitting a humming sound, and on the screen above them the black hole began deforming into an oval.

'It's stretching,' Congressman Goldberg said, pointing at the screen.

'No,' Joaquin corrected him. 'We have reduced the magnetic field in the lower right quadrant of the chamber. The black hole is now cavitating within the chamber at immense velocity and releasing its energy. As you may recall from high school, for every action there is an equal and opposite reaction.'

Governor MacKenzie turned and stared at Joaquin in horror.

'My God,' he uttered. 'You're no philanthropist. You're nothing but a mass murderer.'

'A revolutionary,' Joaquin corrected him. 'There is no gain without loss, no enlightenment without sacrifice. Mankind only moves forward through catastrophe: better one that is controlled, than one that is entirely unpredictable, I say.'

Aubrey felt snakes of disgust slither through his belly as he considered the scope of Joaquin Abell's insanity. But at the center of his thoughts was Katherine Abell. As he caught Joaquin's eye, he saw a man committed to his cause and yet quite aware of the crimes he was committing.

'I'll head for the comms hub,' Aubrey said.

Joaquin flicked his head dismissively toward the exit hatch before turning away from Aubrey, who strode from the chamber toward the exit. He didn't see Joaquin glance across at Olaf before he left.

48

CAPE CANAVERAL

June 28, 16:17

Ethan leapt from the helicopter that deposited them near the bunker, with Jarvis close behind, running low as the wash from the blades flattened the grass around him with rippling waves of down-force.

The guards inside the bunker had once again been forewarned of their arrival and opened the elevator doors without fuss. Moments later they were descending in the elevator shaft.

'You really think that Joaquin can cause an earthquake?' Jarvis asked as he glanced at his watch.

'Given everything else we've seen so far today, I wouldn't put anything past him,' Ethan replied. 'What really maddens me is that he's doing all of this on the back of men he has killed, the scientists who built the device that he's been using. He's a small man standing on the shoulders of giants.'

'Including his father,' Jarvis pointed out. 'A man who had some kind of genuine desire to benefit humanity, but whose work Joaquin has twisted to gain power.'

'What's his motivation?' Ethan wondered out loud. 'There must be more to this than just gaining power, or money, or even creating disasters into which IRIS can heroically sail and save lives, increasing his popularity. He must have some purpose – political, maybe. Purcell said that Joaquin was flirting with high-level figures in government and congress.'

Jarvis nodded.

'It's an angle we haven't checked out. You think maybe he knows people, has friends on the inside who want to see him reach the senate, maybe even the White House?'

The elevator slowed as it reached the bottom and Ethan opened the gates.

'Men of power and influence – they're exactly the kind of people who move in his circle,' he said as they walked down the corridor and into the Project Watchman facility. They hurried toward the main control panels where scientists were already programming the virtual-reality feeds.

A man was wearing a virtual-reality suit and headgear up on the platform as Michael Ottaway turned to them.

'You got the coordinates?' Ethan asked.

Ottaway nodded and gestured to a large plasma screen.

'Yes. Our man's in position. You can view his perspective on this screen,' he said, and gestured to a nearby monitor.

Ethan and Jarvis looked at the screen and saw the feed from the VR headset. They watched as the viewer zoomed in on Bryson sitting on his airboat, swigging from a bottle. Behind him, a second airboat drifted silently toward him.

'Damn it, I told you Bryson was a waster,' Ethan said.

'Speed it forward,' Jarvis muttered to the scientist. 'About five minutes.'

The scientist obeyed and the scene changed to the two airboats racing away from the spit of land. The viewer changed his position, catching them up as the airboats raced between the reed banks. Ethan saw the assassin firing bullets from his rifle, saw himself, Lopez and Bryson ducking to avoid the bullets and then the assassin broad-siding his airboat in front of theirs and shooting up their engine. Ethan watched himself leap up, sprint across the deck and hurl himself across the void between the two craft to land on the metal cage on the back of the assassin's airboat.

'Jesus Christ,' Ottaway muttered at Ethan. 'The hell you think you are, James Bond?'

'Don't encourage him,' Jarvis said. 'Keep moving forward, another couple of minutes.'

They watched as the viewer caught up with Ethan and the assassin fighting on the shore, black smoke smol-dering from the crashed airboat, and then the assassin taking off into the woods with the camera.

'There,' Ethan said, 'track him from there, as fast as you can.'

The scientist relayed the command to the viewer, before trebling the frame rate of the satellite's feed. The viewer flew up to a height of a hundred feet, watching below as the assassin rushed through the forests at comi-cal speed. The image brightened and darkened every few seconds as cloud shadows raced across the landscape. The assassin reached a crumbling old jetty perhaps two miles from the crash site, where a second airboat awaited with two men aboard.

'He had back-up,' Jarvis said. 'But why didn't he bring them along?'

'To prevent any connection with IRIS in case we overpowered any of them,' Ethan guessed. 'They're probably employees of the company, whereas the assassin likely stays off the official company books. No paper trail, total deniability.'

They watched for the next few minutes as the airboat made the long journey back to civilization. The three men exited the boat and took a Lincoln from the local lot. The vehicle zipped through the fast-flowing traffic, the viewer doing a skillful job of tracking the car despite the accelerated speed of the footage.

'He's heading for the marina,' Jarvis said.

Ethan watched as the men got out of the Lincoln and boarded a small powerboat moored at Deering Bay Marina, south of Miami. Moments later the vessel raced out to sea.

Ethan checked his watch.

'Sixteen fifteen hours,' he said, and turned to the scientist. 'You got any way of tracking electromagnetic fields out of the Bermuda Triangle?'

Ottaway nodded and gestured to another screen.

'NASA's already on it. All satellites monitor or transmit as part of the electromagnetic spectrum, but they're using a few satellites in geostationary orbit right now to monitor specifically for spikes in the region of the Florida Straits.'

Ethan turned back and watched as the powerboat

soared into deep water, toward the Miami Terrace shelf. It almost looked as though it were heading out for the true ocean when suddenly a large vessel appeared on the horizon as the viewer looked up briefly to check his direction.

The powerboat slowed and pulled alongside the huge yacht. Ethan didn't need to see the name on the back of the vessel to know which one she was.

'The *Event Horizon*,' he said. 'Joaquin Abell's personal yacht.'

'You sure?' Ottaway asked.

'We've been aboard,' Jarvis said. 'Slow the frames back down and zoom in.'

Ottaway obeyed and they watched as the viewer dropped down to the deck of the powerboat, walking amongst the assassin and his two accomplices. A large access door opened vertically from the side of the yacht's hull, the door coming to rest just above the surface of the water. The powerboat was lifted via a small crane into a hangar within the yacht.

The interior of the yacht was a pixilated black mass, but as the assassin stepped from the powerboat to the very edge of the hangar, still in the sunlight, he held in his hand the camera that he had stolen from Charles Purcell.

A hand reached out from the pixilated blackness and took the camera, while another, which clearly belonged to the same man, vigorously shook the assassin's giant hand.

'Come on, you bastard,' Ethan hissed at the screen, 'show yourself.'

The big assassin was smiling broadly, his face demonically half-shadowed where the satellite camera had failed
to image his face. 'Come on,' Ethan urged.

'He's not going to be imaged,' Jarvis said.

Ethan raised a hand to indicate that the old man should
wait before abandoning hope.

Suddenly, the big assassin laughed out loud and
reached out, one huge arm wrapping around the shoulders of the hidden man and pulling him into a hug. With
a flourish, Joaquin Abell was pulled out into the sunlight
against his powerful friend as he returned the embrace.

'Freeze frame!' Ethan shouted.

The image became static, a moment of time frozen,
and Ethan thumped a fist down on the table.

'Now we've got you,' he said in delight.

'Not quite, I'm afraid,' Jarvis replied. 'This is where
our advantage ends.'

49

'The hell do you mean?' Ethan snapped and jabbed a thumb toward the screen. 'He's busted, totally.'

'Busted he is,' Jarvis confirmed, 'but nobody will ever be able to see the footage outside of this room.'

Ethan massaged his temples with one hand.

'Let me guess, national security?'

'Afraid so,' Jarvis replied. 'Release this footage as evidence in any court case and the defense will demand to know how it was acquired and from whom. Before we know it one of our greatest intelligence assets will become common knowledge and before you can say *conspiracy theory* or *human rights* we'll be sued by half the population for breaching privacy laws.'

'This guy's a mass murderer!' Ethan shot back. 'Who knows what havoc he'll create if we don't present this evidence?'

'And if we go public,' Jarvis countered, 'the detectives heading virtually every unsolved criminal case will demand access to Watchman. We'll be inundated with requests to prove that so-and-so didn't murder victim X, that accused Y didn't rob bank Z, and that naughty-little-goddamned Bobby from down the street didn't shove a stick up his neighbor's cat's ass!'

Ethan sighed as he realized the scope of what Watchman was capable of achieving. It had the potential to solve countless criminal cases, and yet could not provide evidence that was admissible in court without exposing its existence and capabilities. For the first time, Ethan gained a sense of the limitations enforced upon such technologies by the vagaries of national security; of why Jarvis could not just let him use the device to locate Joanna. The paranoia of nations, the disease of mistrust that infected all governments, ensured that rather than be used to enforce world peace and uphold justice, Project Watchman would forever remain in the shadows.

'Give us the coordinates of the yacht,' Jarvis said to Ottaway. 'It will help us to trace its current location.'

Ethan turned away and waited as the viewer on the screen zoomed out and away from Joaquin's frozen, smiling face and took in the whole of the yacht. The scientist spoke into his microphone as he reached out for a series of power buttons.

'Okay, let's shut down.'

Ethan stared at the screen and then grabbed the scientist's arm. 'Wait! Send your man down there, to the rear of the deck.'

'What do you see, Ethan?' Jarvis asked.

Ethan squinted as the viewer zoomed down toward a small knot of men, their dark suits conspicuous against the yacht's pristine white deck. As the camera zoomed in on them, Ethan realized that Jarvis had been right about Joaquin's political connections.

'I'll be damned,' the old man said beside him. 'He's not on his own.'

Although Ethan could not name all of the men now imaged so clearly by Watchman, he recognized enough of them to be sure that Joaquin was playing ball with the big boys.

'Robert Murtaugh,' Jarvis said, identifying the elderly media tycoon, 'and that's Congressman Goldberg.'

'Harrison Reed,' Ethan pointed to the man whose face was partially obscured by a broad Stetson. 'Big oil guy from down Texas way, if I remember rightly.'

'Looks like him,' Ottaway agreed, 'and the man on the end there is the governor of Florida. What's his name? MacGuire?'

'MacKenzie,' Jarvis corrected.

'Evidence of Joaquin being connected to our assassin,' Ethan said. 'Same boat, same time. Get any one of those men to turn on Joaquin Abell and we can nail him with probable cause and get the courts involved.'

'I'd better make a call,' Jarvis said, 'get this in front of the department heads before we decide what we're going to do.'

He was about to turn aside when Ethan stopped him, his eyes transfixed on another plasma screen nearby. The screen relayed information from an orbiting satellite monitoring seismometers around the globe. In the center of the screen an enormous spike had appeared.

'I think it's already gotten too big,' he said. 'Where is that coming from?' Ethan asked.

Ottaway looked up at the screen.

'Dominican Republic, on the northeast coast,' he said. 'Looks like a big one.'

Ethan looked at his watch. *Sixteen seventeen hours.*

'Right on time,' Ethan said to Jarvis, 'just like Charles Purcell predicted.'

Jarvis looked at another screen, this one showing the electromagnetic spectrum being emitted by the planet in the region of the Florida Straits.

'You got anything on GOCE yet?'

'What's GOCE?' Ethan asked.

'It's the Gravity field and Ocean Circulation Explorer satellite,' Michael Ottaway replied, as he squinted at a computer monitor filled with rolling data streams. 'It uses the concept of gradiometry, the measurement of acceleration differences over short distances. Three pairs of accelerometers respond to tiny variations in the gravitational field of the earth. Because of their different positions in the gravitational field they all experience unique conditions, and thus can provide an accurate picture of earth's gravitational field.'

'Glad I asked.' Ethan blinked laconically. 'Can you use it to pinpoint the location of Abell's facility?'

The scientist nodded, glancing back and forth from several different monitors and screens as data spilled from them in a torrent of figures, waves and charts.

'There was a massive spike in seismic levels here,' he said, pointing to one screen where a map of the Caribbean was overlaid against a chart of known geological fault lines deep beneath the seabed. 'That's the site of the earthquake now underway.'

Ethan looked at the screen and baulked.

'Magnitude 6.8,' he said. 'That's a big one.'

'It is,' the scientist agreed, 'and it's off the coast. There'll be localized structural damage, but the real threat will come from the sea when the tsunami hits.'

Ethan found himself picturing the colossal destruction wrought by giant waves strong enough to flatten hotels and bury entire cities. Nobody had forgotten what had happened to places like Aceh years before. Ethan had flown there with Joanna within hours of the event, covering the humanitarian disaster that followed, tens of thousands of people made homeless and without access to food or water. But what had angered them both the most was the speed with which major corporations swept in and claimed the prime coastal land for themselves, displacing local fishing families whose descendants had lived there for centuries, and building hotels just as fast as they could. He thought of Joaquin's plans to 'rebuild' disaster zones, and saw the same callous industrialism. Then he recalled the sheer force of the damage caused by the disaster.

'Lopez is out there,' he murmured to himself.

'She knows what's coming,' Jarvis said. 'She can look after herself.'

'Ah, here.' The scientist pointed to a screen, and tapped it with the tip of his pen. 'Very impressive indeed.'

'What?' Ethan asked, peering at a series of narrow, tall spikes, like a row of hundreds of thin razor-sharp teeth.

'These pulses,' the scientist explained, 'they're not seismic, they're gravitational. It's the signature of an object of extreme mass vibrating at high frequencies, perhaps millions of times per second. If what you've all been saying is true, and Joaquin Abell has somehow captured a black hole, then he must have deliberately destabilized it, causing it to vibrate, and then directed the resulting gravitational waves using whatever structure he's built to contain the black hole. I'd guess he'll be using a negatively charged field, so he could lower the charge in one area of the field to direct the waves. And he could control the frequency of the vibrations and therefore their range by manipulating the strength of the rest of the field, giving the gravitational pulses a sort of polarity. One set of waves goes into the earth, causing the earthquake; the other goes up into the sky, affecting nothing.'

'Except any unfortunate aircraft or boats passing over-head,' Ethan said. 'It would pull them straight down or shake them to pieces.'

Doug Jarvis considered this for a moment.

'He could point it anywhere, flatten cities, if he wanted to.'

'It would have its limits,' Ottaway said, 'but yes, he could use this as a weapon and it would be extremely difficult to stop him.'

'Do you have its location?' Ethan asked. 'The origin of these waves?'

'I do,' the scientist said, 'and it's close to where IRIS is supposed to be running a coral-conservation area.'

Ethan felt a vengeful grin spread across his features as he turned to Doug.

'Great. Send in the Navy and flatten that damned

place. If we can't use this as proof to convict him of his crimes, let's just remove the bastard from play.'

Jarvis was already nodding and reaching for a nearby phone when Ottaway shook his head.

'I wouldn't do that if I were you.'

'Why not?' Ethan asked. 'The man's a menace, he needs to be dealt with.'

'I agree, believe me,' the scientist said. 'But he's got a black hole down there, suspended in a delicate balance. You drop a bomb or something on it and one of two possible things will happen, neither of which is good.'

'Okay,' Ethan said as Jarvis lowered the phone from his ear. 'Spill it.'

'The black hole becomes exposed to its surroundings and begins dragging material into its singularity and doesn't stop until our entire planet has been consumed.' Ottaway looked at Ethan. 'Once you get too close to a black hole's event horizon, too deep inside the gravity well, nothing can escape, not even light.'

'Maybe option two?' Jarvis suggested.

'The black hole is small enough that when it destabilizes it explodes in a violent burst of gamma rays, releasing its energy into the surrounding area. There'll be a serious bang and a lot of seabed will find itself with a half-life of twenty thousand years, but essentially the black hole decays instantaneously. If this facility is deep enough underwater, the majority of the blast might be contained.'

Ethan digested what he had been told sufficiently to figure out a question.

'So which one will it be?'

'We don't know,' the scientist admitted. 'It depends

on the actual mass of the black hole. Fact is, as a species, we just don't possess the kind of technology required to contain a large black hole, so whatever he's got down there should have the potential to decay away, releasing most of its energy as what's known as Hawking Radiation. Either way, it's a hell of a gamble to go in there and level the place with heavy ordnance.'

'And you can't guess at its size?' Ethan pressed.

Ottaway sighed, thinking hard.

'It must be a relatively low-mass black hole, because if it were too large it would affect tides in the area, or even the orbit of the earth.'

'Seriously?' Jarvis asked.

'Definitely. The moon gives us our tides because its gravity produces a swell in the oceans as it orbits the earth. A moon-mass black hole would exert a significant pull on the oceans around IRIS's base, and that's not happening, so it must be smaller. That's good for us, because micro black holes that size will evaporate in a nano-second, given the chance.'

'How big would it be?' Ethan asked.

'With the mass of the moon?' Ottaway asked. 'It would have a Schwarzschild Radius of no more than a tenth of a millimeter. A black hole with the mass of the earth would be about the size of a peanut, but naturally the IRIS hole will be much smaller than that.'

'Jesus,' Ethan breathed. 'Joaquin thinks he's got a device that he can use as a weapon, but if it gets out of control we'll be looking at a global apocalypse.'

'If it starts consuming material and cannot be contained,' Ottaway said, 'then yes, it would literally be the end of the world. But an object of that mass should evaporate, although it will still be an extremely violent event.'

'Joaquin's site is in water deep enough that any radiation released by the blast should be contained,' Jarvis hazarded. 'We can ensure the area is closed off to the public afterward, although that far off the coast I doubt it will present any problems.'

'We could send in a SEAL team,' Ethan suggested to Jarvis. 'Surgical strike.'

'There's too many bodies getting involved already,' Jarvis said. 'Best we keep this under wraps.'

'In other words, you want *us* to go in,' Ethan said. 'You ever realize, Doug, that there's just the two of us, and you keep putting us in harm's way? If we get ourselves blown to pieces, who's going to do all of this for you?'

'The technology is just too sensitive,' Jarvis insisted. 'If it can be recovered discreetly it would be of immense benefit to the United States, Ethan. There's no telling what tragedies we could prevent from occurring in the future, or how many lives could be saved.'

Ethan sighed, looking at the violent spikes on the computer monitor.

'Whatever he's got down there, it'll be well protected.'

'Yes it will,' Jarvis agreed. 'But you also have something that you didn't have before.'

'What's that?'

'The element of surprise. Joaquin thinks that, with Charles Purcell dead, this case is closed.'

Ethan glanced up at the nearby television screens, and

was about to reply when a news broadcast caught his eye. A shot of a leafy residential street, a police cordon, a white car surrounded by armed police.

'That's Kyle Sears,' he said as he saw the captain in the image. And then he recognized the house. 'And that's Charles Purcell's home!'

Jarvis, Ottaway and several of the technicians watched as a limping police officer was lifted into an ambulance by his colleagues.

'It's a shot from yesterday,' Jarvis realized, 'when the police first turned up at Purcell's house.'

Ethan watched the news piece and felt a surge of anxiety.

'That's how Purcell predicted the car accident outside his home,' he said finally. 'It had to have been on the news for him to see it, and therefore to know that Captain Kyle Sears would be the detective on the scene. Joaquin might actually know when we will arrive,' he said. 'He'd only need to set up a camera at the entrance to his facility, link the feed to one of the black hole cameras recording the future, and then take a peek. If it were me, that's what I'd do. Nobody could walk into my facility without me knowing about it in advance.'

Ethan's guts were twisted with worry as he looked at the violent spikes on the GOCE's data streams and the gravitational pulses radiating away from the Bermuda Triangle.

'We might not be going *anywhere* if Lopez doesn't make it out of the Dominican Republic.'

'This is what you signed up for, Ethan,' Jarvis reminded him.

Ethan felt a surge of anger pulse within him as he glanced at Project Watchman's screen and made his decision. He turned to Jarvis and shook his head.

'We signed up to investigate crimes that the Defense Department and law enforcement had rejected as myth or fantasy. We didn't sign up to put our lives on the line day after day. You want us to go in there that badly, then you give us something in return.'

Jarvis glanced at Project Watchman.

'You don't know that they'll be able to find Joanna, or even if she's alive.'

'You don't know that they won't,' Ethan shot back and jabbed a finger in the old man's direction. 'Your call, Doug. Give me what I want and you'll get the result you want. I guess it all boils down to one simple question – whether you want your answers as badly as I need mine.'

Jarvis held Ethan's gaze for a long moment, and then he sighed.

'You get that camera, and I'll get you your answers.'

50

IRIS, DEEP BLUE RESEARCH
STATION, FLORIDA STRAITS

June 28, 16:22

Dennis Aubrey hurried down one of the corridors that joined the main dome with the ancillary structures that ringed it, heading for the communications dome. He fumbled in his pocket as he walked and retrieved a satellite phone, scrolling down through a series of numbers until he found the one that he needed.

The communications dome was normally controlled from the main hub, the two linked by optical fibers, allowing all major operations to be operated from Deep Blue's main control panel. Joaquin had ensured that Aubrey could not contact anybody on the surface, by locking him out of the communications panel. However, Aubrey knew for certain that Charles Purcell would have built redundancy measures into the system, including the ability to contact the surface directly from the communications hub, in the event of a hull breach elsewhere in the facility.

Aubrey hurried toward the hatch, a lone guard on sentry duty standing with an assault rifle cradled in his grip. He looked up with a bored expression as Aubrey approached and raised one leather-gloved hand.

'No admittance without prior clearance from Mr. Abell,' the soldier announced in a monotone military voice.

'Do you think Joaquin would have let me out of his sight if he didn't want me here?' Aubrey shot back. 'Mr. Abell is in the control center with the governor of Florida, a member of Congress and an oil man worth more money than God. If we can't ensure perfect communications with the outside world then I'll know who to blame when Mr. Abell asks why we failed.'

'I'll have to clear it,' the soldier intoned dully.

'Then clear it!' Aubrey snapped. 'Just hurry the goddamned-hell up!'

The soldier reached for his radio, keyed the microphone and droned into it. Aubrey listened as a scratchy-sounding voice replied. The soldier lowered the radio and looked down at him for what felt like an eternity before he moved away from the hatch.

Aubrey wasted no time and heaved the hatch-seal handle before shoving the heavy door open with his shoulder and walking inside, careful to seal it behind him.

The communications hub was smaller than the others, little more than a shed-sized construction that contained a desk, two computers and a bank of radios, both digital and analogue, that connected to the tethered antenna buoy some two thousand feet above.

Aubrey sat down at the desk and quickly grabbed a set of radio jacks, plugging one end into the back of the satellite phone he had stolen from the control panel and the other into a digital transmission amplifier. He glanced at the controls and saw that the buoy's transmitters had been shut off by Olaf, just as Joaquin had ordered. Aubrey smiled to himself. The satellite phone provided its own transmission – the buoy's inactive antenna would simply boost the signal when it reached the surface, much like a television aerial. Aubrey brought up Katherine Abell's number on his cellphone before dialing it into the satellite phone. He listened to the tone in his ear as the line began ringing.

'Pick up,' Aubrey whispered. 'Come on.'

The line continued to ring and Aubrey clenched his fist in frustration as Katherine Abell's cell went to voicemail. Cursing, he waited until he heard the tone at the end of her message before speaking.

'Katherine, it's Dennis. Listen to me, I don't have much time. Joaquin isn't running a conservation project down here. This is a military facility and he's developed a machine to cause earthquakes and other natural disasters. He's aiming for where you are, Katherine. I am not allowed to leave this facility. Please, if you get this message, get onto high ground until the quake has passed, and then get in touch with the authorities – the coastguard, the police. Hell, call the goddamned Navy, just get somebody out here as quickly as you can!' Aubrey paused and brought himself under control before continuing. 'I'm going to try to stop him. Please hurry, and take care of yourself, okay?'

Aubrey shut off the line and unplugged the jacks before he stuffed the satellite phone back into his pocket and turned for the door. With a heave of effort he yanked the door open and stepped out into the corridor. The guard glanced at him without interest as he pulled the hatch shut and shuffled off back down the corridor.

Aubrey reached the main corridor that ringed the central dome and branched off to each of the ancillary domes. Aubrey turned right, waiting until he was out of sight of the guard before breaking into a run. He jogged around the outside of the hub until he reached a smaller, narrower hatch that led not to another tunnel but to a small storage facility attached directly to the side of the main dome. A card-activated security panel was affixed to the wall beside the hatch, restricting access, and for good reason. The small room beyond was the armory.

Aubrey reached beneath his sleeve and slid out Olaf Jorgenson's security card. What the towering giant possessed in strength he lacked in wits and intelligence, and Aubrey allowed himself a nervous smile as he slipped the card in. It had taken only a mild sleight of hand to let the card fall into his shirtsleeve rather than drop into the box. The armory door clicked and he hauled it open. He ducked inside and looked at the racks of assault rifles, underwater pistols, knives and small arms.

Aubrey was no soldier, but he knew enough about weapons from watching television to figure out what he needed. Only the hand pistols were small enough for him to conceal beneath his clothes. He reached up and unclipped one of several Sig 9mm pistols from one of the racks, then looked down immediately below the rack to where a fully loaded clip lay.

Aubrey slid the clip into the gun's handle and slammed it into place with the heel of his hand. It slid into place with a satisfying click. Aubrey checked that the safety catch was on before he stuffed the weapon into the waist-band of his jeans at the small of his back, beneath his shirt.

Aubrey turned around and ducked out of the armory, then pushed the hatch shut behind him until he heard the electronic locks engage. With a sigh of relief, he walked back toward the main dome's entry hatch.

'What are you doing here?'

The words snapped like live current through Aubrey's body as he whirled to see Olaf Jorgenson striding down the corridor toward him, his muscular chest pulsing with each swing of his blocky arms. The giant glanced suspiciously at the armory door.

'Checking the locks on all of the hatches,' Aubrey coughed. He stood his ground as Olaf loomed over him, and conjured more mystifying terms from the vaults of his memory. 'We don't want the longitudinal-mass accelerometer to emit electromagnetic pulses that could fry the locks and blow them open, do we?'

Olaf peered down at him, the long words apparently rolling slowly through his mind like ticker tapes.

'You said nothing to Mr. Abell about the locks,' he rumbled.

Aubrey raised his chin.

'You think that Joaquin has time for a long discussion about the medium-range effects of pulsed acoustic wave signals in confined areas?' he said. 'I don't think that his guests would care for it. Do you?'

Olaf squinted down at him and then bent forward at the waist, lowering his giant angular head until his icy blue eyes were just inches from Aubrey's face. One immense and rock-solid forearm slowly pushed Aubrey inexorably backwards until he bumped against the armory hatch. Olaf's arm pressed against his chest with enough force to restrict his breathing.

'It's Mr. Abell to you,' he growled. 'You think that I'm stupid, don't you?'

Aubrey swallowed.

'Not at all, Mr. Jorgenson. But it's my job to look after this facility and if I'm not allowed to do so, we could all die down here. Mr. Abell has a machine of immense power and it requires delicate control and careful monitoring. That is what I am doing.'

Olaf glared at Aubrey for several long seconds before releasing him.

'Get back into the control room,' he ordered.

Aubrey turned without another word and marched back into the main dome, just in time to feel the immense vibrations emanating from the black hole's chamber, which were now causing the entire facility to shudder. Governor MacKenzie was backing away from the machine, but Joaquin was laughing and clapping his hands together.

'You see, gentlemen? This is *real* power!'

Aubrey walked up to Joaquin with Olaf behind him.

'Sir, the box? We'd best keep it away from the chamber.'

Joaquin glanced over his shoulder and saw Olaf lumber into view. Satisfied, he didn't even bother to look at Aubrey as he handed him the box.

Aubrey carried it to the control panel and set it down. In one smooth motion, he lifted the lid and slipped Olaf's access card back inside before shutting the lid and placing the box in plain view on the panel. Moments later, the satellite phone was back in its cradle.

51

PUERTO PLATA PROVINCE, DOMINICAN REPUBLIC

June 28, 16:25

Lopez twisted the throttle of the battered old scooter as she zipped between two carts of junk hauled by haggard-looking mules, along a dusty, winding track that led toward the Septentrional mountain range in the north of the province. The summit of Pico Isabel de Torres loomed nearly eight hundred meters above them, lost in wreaths and ribbons of cloud.

She and Bryson had landed half an hour previously at Gregorio Luperón International Airport, hiring a pair of scooters and racing away from the coast toward the interior. A brief stop at an IRIS-sponsored medical camp had gained them directions to a village in the interior where Katherine Abell had last been seen.

'It must be out this way somewhere!' Lopez shouted over her shoulder.

Bryson weaved between the two carts behind her before drawing his scooter alongside, a dressing around the bullet graze on his forearm flapping in the wind. His piratical eye twinkled in the flickering sunlight that

beamed in shafts through the canopy of palms and towering ferns.

'If she's as much of a goddamned philanthropist as you
say she is, we'll find her in the poorest village around.
People like her like to suffer for their work. They're not
happy unless their clothes are rotting and they're eating
cold gravel for breakfast. Look at Mother Theresa!'

'She's dead, Scott,' Lopez pointed out.

'That's what I mean.'

The track climbed away from the long, flat beaches of
the coast, the forests ahead cloaked in ethereal veils of
humid cloud. The engine in Lopez's scooter clattered
noisily up the hillside, a faint haze of blue smoke trailing
in her wake, and she silently prayed that the ancient
motor wouldn't give out before she reached the villages
perched precariously amidst the prehistoric-looking
wilderness.

'There!'

Bryson pointed ahead to where a few rickety shacks
peered from the tropical gloom. The clouds were directly
overhead now, the air laden with moisture that clung to
Lopez's skin like a hot, heavy blanket. The last six
months of the year in Puerto Plata were wetter than the
first, the seasonal rains regular enough to prevent any
real respite from the intense humidity. Lopez slowed her
scooter as it rattled into the center of the village, hordes
of young children in brightly colored clothes flocking
out to greet her with bright smiles that belied just how
little they possessed.

Lopez killed the engine on her scooter just as Bryson
rolled up alongside and did the same. As they stood

amidst the children grabbing at them for attention, Katherine Abell stepped out of one of the shacks that formed a circle around the edge of the village.

Lopez recognized her immediately: the square line of her jaw, the cool green eyes and the long auburn hair; but everything else had changed. Gone was the power suit and the elegant stride. Instead, she wore khaki shorts and a loosely buttoned shirt with simple sandals, and her long hair was tied up in a loose ponytail. Her clean features were scoured of make-up.

Katherine turned away the moment she saw Lopez. 'You're not welcome here.'

Lopez strode forward. 'We need your help.'

Katherine moved back into the shack without another word.

'She could be sitting on her husband's luxury yacht,' Bryson said as he followed Lopez, 'sipping a cocktail while servants manicure her nails . . .'

'It's called charity,' Lopez replied. 'Good will and all that?'

Bryson shrugged as he followed Lopez into the darkness of the shack.

The air within smelt of herbs, dried fruits and ancient soil, a haze of incense smoke struggling to conceal all other odors. Laying on a bed in the center of the shack was a girl whose age Lopez guessed at fourteen, maybe fifteen. Her belly was distended as though filled with gas, the deeply tanned skin laced with veins.

Katherine Abell knelt alongside the girl and gently drenched her forehead with cool water from a chipped porcelain bowl. Lopez eased closer and saw that the girl's breathing was erratic, her eyes rolled up in their sockets.

'What's wrong with her?' Lopez asked. 'Malnutrition?'

Katherine Abell did not look around as she replied.

'She's pregnant, but the baby is breach and I can't turn it.' Katherine scooped up some more water and spilled it across the girl's glistening skin. 'She's dying.'

Lopez winced and looked again at the girl's face.

'She looks too young.'

'She was raped,' Katherine replied without emotion, as though such a tragedy were all too common, a daily occurrence.

A thick loathing stuck in Lopez's throat as though a ghost had just joined her in the room, and her voice fell to a whisper. 'Why didn't she have a termination?'

Katherine Abell peered around at Lopez as though she were crazy.

'Because the government here outlaws abortions in all cases,' she shot back, 'including those resulting from incest and rape, even those that endanger the mother's life. They're bullied into it by Catholic dogma, made to live as though they're in the Dark Ages, so poor young girls like Isabella here are forced to carry the child or die trying. And all because of people who call themselves *pro-life*.'

Lopez stared at the wall of the hut, her eyes glazed.

'You okay?' Bryson moved to her side, one big hand resting on her shoulder as his normally arrogant features folded into something that might have been concern. 'You look like somebody's walked over your grave.'

'I'm fine,' Lopez uttered.

Bryson's eye peered at her. 'You and I both know that's women's code for "something's wrong".'

Lopez ignored him as she looked down at the pregnant girl.

At the age of fourteen, Nicola Lopez had become pregnant to a 16-year-old farm boy from Coroneo, the tiny municipality in which they lived, in the state of Guanajuato, Mexico, deep within the Vedeer Mountains. Lopez had always been a child willing to take chances, to run where other children would not, to disobey and to confront. Armed with a ferocious temper, high intelligence and a mischievous sense of humor, she had inevitably sought the company of older friends. What she could not have understood was the difference between their motives and her own.

In a tiny, musty-smelling stall on a ramshackle farm, Javier Ruben, a tall and strikingly handsome boy who had taken an interest in her, overpowered her while they were fooling around and hurt her in a way that she could neither comprehend or resolve. While she had not exactly fought her amorous companion off, nor had she realized the consequences of his actions. She had been unable to sleep for days, had wandered Coroneo in a state of shock, and had frequently found herself crying unexpectedly.

And then her *menstruación* had abruptly ended, along with her childhood. In an instant, the sleepy cobbled streets, soaring mountains and quaint churches of her homeland had become the features of an implacable, ferocious enemy.

At the time, Guanajuato, a conservative state whose

leaders were held in grim and bigoted thrall to Catholic dogma, had denied every petition by a pregnant rape victim for abortion services, and over a hundred of its residents had been arrested for seeking or providing illegal abortion. Worse, more than a dozen women had been sentenced to up to thirty years in prison for the same 'crime'. Faced with prison if her pregnancy was terminated, Lopez had no choice but to throw herself upon the mercy of her family. None had abandoned her. Her terrible secret remained exactly that, until four months later she suffered a natural miscarriage and lost the child.

Lopez knew what *pro-life* meant, and it was sure as hell nothing to do with compassion.

'Really,' Lopez said, leveling Bryson with a steady gaze. 'I'm fine.' She turned to Katherine. 'We have to leave right now.'

'I'm not going anywhere. I have work to do.'

Scott Bryson's voice cut in from behind Lopez.

'You don't move right now, you won't have anywhere to *do* your work.'

'What the hell are you talking about?'

'This area is about to be hit by an earthquake,' Lopez said.

Katherine's eyes narrowed. 'How can you know that?'

'Because your husband has built a device that can cause earthquakes,' Lopez said. 'If we don't leave in the next few minutes we might not be leaving at all. Do you understand?'

Katherine shook her head slowly.

'No, he couldn't have. He wouldn't – he knows that I'm here.'

'We wouldn't have come all of this way if we weren't pretty damned sure,' Lopez cut across her. 'We have to move, now!'

Katherine stared down at the girl.

'But Isabella . . .'

'We'll take her with us,' Lopez said.

'She can't travel, and I can't leave her here alone.'

Lopez was about to answer, when Bryson suddenly shouldered his way past and knelt down alongside Isabella's prostrate form. Lopez watched as Bryson ignored Katherine's protests, his thick and calloused hands gently probing Isabella's belly as he looked up at the ceiling, seeing with his hands.

'She's got plenty of amniotic fluid,' Bryson said, still looking up at the ceiling as he felt around. 'Baby feels fine. Do you have any anesthetics?'

Katherine blinked away her confusion.

'She's on painkillers right now, but they're making her pretty drowsy. I don't want to think what they might be doing to her baby.'

'It might help,' Bryson said. 'I'm going to try external cephalic version.'

Lopez stared at Bryson. 'The hell you think you are now, Dr. Kildare?'

Bryson grinned and winked at her. 'Watch and learn, honey.'

Bryson turned back to Isabella and leaned in, gently massaging her belly. Lopez realized that Bryson was skillfully pushing the baby back up from the girl's pelvis, then easing its head around from the top of the womb to the bottom.

Bryson ministered to the girl for several minutes, gently working his way around her body as Katherine watched, just as enthralled as Lopez. Finally, he leaned back and looked down at Isabella. The girl was no longer writhing, and some of the sweat on her skin had disappeared. Lopez realized that the girl's fluttering breath was now more even and regular.

Katherine Abell stared at Bryson. 'Thank you.'

Lopez watched wide-eyed as Bryson stood. He glanced down at her. 'What?' he asked.

'Nothing,' Lopez uttered. 'I'm just amazed, is all.'

'You think they only taught us to kill in the SEALs?' he guessed. 'Hearts and minds, honey. We were also trained to help locals in foreign countries, to win their support and friendship.'

Lopez looked at her watch. 'Shit, we gotta go, right now.'

Katherine Abell stood up.

'I don't see why I should go anywhere. This is where I'm needed.'

'No,' Lopez shot back, 'where you're needed is back in court, because only one person on earth knows Joaquin Abell's mind, and that person is you.'

'I don't know what you're talking about.'

'You're going to end up in court whether you like it or not,' Lopez snapped. 'You can either be in the witness stand or you can be in the dock. Your call.'

'I won't turn against my own husband!'

'Then why are you out here?' Lopez challenged. 'As far away from him as you can get?'

Katherine's lawyerly cool seemed to have deserted her as she flustered.

'IRIS is still a force for the good. Prosecuting it through the courts will do more harm than good to its charitable causes.'

'There *are* no charitable causes!' Lopez insisted. 'IRIS is a fraud, Katherine, and Joaquin is a megalomaniac bent on creating disasters in order to generate debt in entire countries. He knows that you're here. Don't you see? He's trying to silence you too!'

'I don't believe it,' Katherine gasped. 'I won't believe it.'

'Is that a gamble you want to take?' Bryson asked her. 'Where are your kids?'

'They're at school in Miami, far from here,' Katherine said. 'This is ridiculous. Even if Joaquin were to target me, he would never harm our children!'

Lopez was about to argue further when a deep, shuddering noise rumbled across the mountains as though some careless god were dragging their heels across the earth. In an instant the walls of the shack began swaying. Lopez reached out to steady herself.

'It's starting!' she shouted. 'Get out, now!'

52

Lopez staggered out of the hut toward the two scooters. The children were scattering toward their homes as frantic parents beckoned them inside.

The earth beneath Lopez's boots vibrated as though giant celestial strings were quivering through the bedrock deep underground. Bryson got to the scooters first, kick-starting one for Lopez in a cloud of blue smoke, before leaping onto his own and firing the engine. Lopez climbed onto the scooter as Katherine clambered onto the pillion seat behind her.

'He knows I'm here!' Katherine yelled above the noise of the engine. 'He wouldn't do this.'

Lopez kicked the scooter into gear. 'He already has! Hang on!'

Lopez twisted the throttle wide open and the scooter surged away from the village. Flocks of birds vaulted from the trees in thick clouds of wings that streaked across the lumbering clouds above, and Lopez could see millions of trembling leaves spilling droplets of moisture like a rain shower upon the track as she guided the scooter down the hillside as fast as she dared.

Bryson's own scooter growled somewhere behind her, following her closely down the trail and shouting as they went.

'Watch out for the trees!'

Lopez glanced to her left through the quivering blanket of ferns and leaves and saw the moisture-laden soil of the steep hills to her left tumbling and shifting, shaken loose as the quake gained intensity. Rivulets of earth spilled out across the track in front of her and she swerved the motorbike around the larger chunks, as from the corner of her eye she saw thick, gnarled tree roots burst from the earth like grasping skeletal hands.

'The hillside's coming apart!' she yelled back to Bryson. 'Stay on the outside!'

Lopez swerved the scooter further out toward the edge of the track, the plunging hillside vanishing to their right into a dense canopy of trees that she knew concealed a hundred-foot drop.

Katherine shouted out to her above the wailing noise of the engine.

'We can't stay on this bike when the quake really gets going!'

Lopez nodded, knowing only that they had to get off the hillside. The drenched soil and exposed flanks of the hills, eroded by years of deforestation and rain, could give way at any moment and send millions of tons of watery mud cascading down on top of them.

Lopez kicked the motorbike up a gear, sweeping it through a long right-hand bend that followed the epic curve of the mountainside as they plunged beneath a shivering canopy of trees. Cold droplets of water showered down upon them again, and Katherine's grip on Lopez's waist tightened as the scooter banked out almost to the edge of the drop. Lopez leaned into the turn as the rear wheel skipped and span on the damp track. She twisted the handlebars to the left, counter-steering against the rear wheel's grip, and letting it spin freely as she broadsided around the rest of the turn and then opened the throttle wide, the bike coming upright as the track straightened out toward the lowlands a mile away.

Bryson accelerated past them on their left as he powered out of the same corner, his motorbike quicker with only one person aboard. Lopez followed him as he leaned the bike toward the dizzying drop on the right-hand side of the track, the forest canopy whipping past as they screamed down the hillside. Lopez's shirt was drenched with water, her hair thick and heavy with moisture, but already she could feel the heat of the sun again and see ahead the vast floodplain of Puerto Plata bathed in sunlight, distant windows flickering like beacons in the haze.

Katherine yelled at her and pointed at the distant town.

'It's coming! Stop the bikes!'

Lopez squinted through the moisture dripping from her eyelids, and saw that something had changed in the town's harbour ahead. It took her brain a moment to register what it was, as a wave of fear sluiced through her.

The tide had receded more than a mile out from

where it should have been, as though dragged by some unseen force way out in the deep ocean.

A deafening crack burst the air around Lopez as though a gunshot had been fired beside her head, and in an instant she saw a spray of woodchips burst from the foliage as a tree plunged out of the forest ahead, thick branches rushing down toward the track.

'Stop the bike!' Katherine shouted.

Lopez kicked the scooter down a gear and snapped the throttle fully open. The scooter raced toward the ever-closing gap as the thick branches caught amidst the canopy above them, the heavy trunk quivering as it twisted and shook its way down toward the track.

Bryson ducked down on his bike as he shot past beneath the swaying palm fronds, and Lopez shouted out as she leaned forward and lay flat against the tank.

'Get down!'

Katherine lurched forward and Lopez felt the lawyer's head thump against her back as they plunged beneath the falling tree, damp leaves and fronds slapping across them as the scooter raced beneath the plunging trunk and out the other side. The vehicle weaved and kicked as Lopez struggled to keep it upright as they shot out into clear air.

Lopez closed the throttle to give the scooter a chance to steady itself, and that was when she heard the noise, a deep and loud rumbling like the roar of a thousand boulders tumbling down upon them. Ahead, she saw Bryson's motorbike suddenly kick to one side and then the former soldier leapt from his saddle and hit the track hard, rolling as he did so and covering his head. The earth ruptured beneath his scooter, buckling upward in jagged mounds pierced by thick tree roots, as the earthquake split the track in two. Bryson vanished from sight as the road disappeared in a chaotic explosion of dirt and debris.

Lopez shouted over her shoulder. 'Jump!'

In an instant the track beneath her shifted violently and threw the motorbike to one side. The tires lost their grip as all balance was ripped from Lopez's hands and they toppled toward the dusty surface of the track racing past beneath them.

Lopez hurled herself clear of the saddle, her arms out before her as she crashed down. The breath was smashed from her lungs as she rolled across the dusty earth with her arms wrapped around her head, the roaring still in her ears as the motorbike span past her on its side, the metal engine scraping across the rugged terrain.

She came to a stop and peered through eyes filled with damp grit. The ground beneath her was trembling with rolling seismic waves that caused the forests to sway and ripples to tear through the earth beneath her, splitting chunks off the track that spilled away into the ravine below.

'Nicola!'

Lopez whirled in time to see Katherine Abell on her knees in the dirt and the grime, balanced precariously upon a tilting slab of earth that rolled away from the track toward the plunging abyss below.

Lopez hauled herself to her feet and staggered across, reached out for Katherine's hand and grabbed it as the ground beneath her feet slid away. Katherine screamed and held on to Lopez's hand in terror as the track disappeared. Lopez's stomach lurched as she felt herself fall, saw the ground break up into a million spinning chunks of earth that plummeted away from her, and she reached out blindly with her free hand.

Her palm touched on a thick tree root exposed by the collapsing hillside. She gripped it without thought, and dense fibers sliced into her skin. The sharp pain receded as though dulled by the roar of the rending earth around her. Her hand slid down the root for almost a foot before she stopped to hang from its tip whilst Katherine Abell dangled below her. Lopez looked down and saw the top of the forest canopy some twenty feet beneath them, chunks of earth falling away from the hillside to batter the palm fronds.

The pain in Lopez's hand returned and began to spread and she felt the muscles in her arm seize up under the strain. A cascade of soil and stones spilled from the ruined track above, pouring over Lopez's head and shoulders and stinging her eyes with sand and grit. She looked down, trying to shout between teeth gritted with the effort of supporting both of their bodies.

'Climb up me, quickly! The rest of the track could go any moment!'

Katherine Abell looked up and then reached out with her own free hand and grabbed Lopez's belt, hauling herself up and wrapping her arms around Lopez's legs. Her green eyes were now muddied with terror, as the world shook itself apart around them. The canopy below them swayed and shifted, the deafening roar of the quake punctuated by sharp cracks as trees were uprooted, their mighty trunks snapping under the strain, to crash down through the forest.

Lopez grabbed Katherine's shirt and hauled her upward, forcing the lawyer to climb further up until one of her hands could reach the dense tangle of roots from which Lopez dangled.

With a last desperate effort, Lopez pushed Katherine in the right direction and finally she grasped the roots and clambered up onto what remained of the track above them. Lopez span in mid-air and grabbed the tree roots with both hands, a brief respite from the pain aching through her arm and shoulders. But now she was spent, and knew without a doubt that she did not have the strength remaining to pull herself up from the ledge.

She heard Katherine call to her, but could not hear what she was saying above the deafening noise of the earthquake that still rolled across the hillside. The cascade of dirt falling around her intensified, the shaking earth swinging her from the tree roots, and she knew that her precarious handhold was about to fail.

'Katherine!' she yelled. 'Get away from the edge!'

A weakened voice called back to Lopez from above, but she couldn't make out what it said. Lopez looked down at the forest canopy below and made her decision. There was no point in hanging on any longer, and if she was lucky the forest might just break her fall enough for her to survive. Either way, if she waited much longer the hillside would make the decision for her, and there wouldn't be much of her left to climb out from under a hundred tons of mountain dirt.

She heard the sound of a motorbike engine starting up on the track above her, and guessed that Katherine was making a run for it. With her safe, Lopez could concentrate on saving her own skin. She looked down.

All or nothing. *Do it.*

Lopez took one hand off the tree roots, timing her swaying motion and using her free arm to spin herself outward, trying to aim for one of the denser-looking trees below, with thicker branches. She was about to let go of the roots entirely when something slapped across her face.

Lopez blinked and saw the sleeve of a shirt dangling before her. She looked up, and Katherine waved down at her.

'Grab hold!'

Lopez grabbed the shirt. As she did so she swung out over the ravine and noticed that the shirt was tied to another shirt, which was tied to what looked like one leg of a pair of jeans.

The sound of a motorbike engine revved above the terrifying din of the earthquake and Lopez was suddenly hauled upward. She managed to get one boot onto the hillside as she was dragged up onto the damaged track, Bryson riding the motorbike bare-legged and with the other leg of his jeans tied to the frame.

Lopez stumbled onto the track and collapsed forward onto her knees, her exhausted arms dangling uselessly by her sides as she swayed with the churning ground. Katherine dropped down alongside her and wrapped her arms around Lopez's body, crouching down as the earthquake roared around them. Bryson let the bike fall over as he staggered back to Lopez's side and dropped onto one knee in front of her.

'Are you okay?' he shouted.

Lopez nodded, unexpectedly cold and shivering. 'I'll live.'

Bryson wrapped his arms around them both and waited for the quake to subside.

The roaring of torn earth receded after a few minutes, the swaying trees falling still around them. Lopez looked up and blinked away the grit scratching the surface of her eyes as she surveyed the battered landscape.

Dozens of trees lay across the road, which itself was rent at regular intervals by gaping chasms where the earthquake had cleaved the land in two. Beyond, she could see columns of ugly gray smoke rising from the densely packed buildings of Puerto Plata into the flawless blue sky. Sirens wailed from fire trucks and ambulances as they struggled to make their way through the carnage to those areas most affected by the devastation.

Lopez looked at Katherine, who was also caked in mud and shivering with cold.

'You still going to live in denial about this?' she challenged.

Katherine trembled as tears spilled from her eyes through the dirt staining her cheeks.

'He's ruined everything,' she whispered. 'Ruined our lives, our reputation, our future. What am I going to tell our children? That their father is a mass murderer?' She shook her head. 'He never deserved the fortune he inherited. I should have watched him more closely, should have taken control when I still could.'

'This is who Joaquin Abell really is,' Lopez said. 'Is it who you are?'

Katherine stared at the terrible carnage before them and shook her head.

'I don't want anybody's family to suffer like this, to see their loved ones vanish into an early grave.'

Lopez nodded, and then stared into the middle distance as a realization thundered through the field of her awareness. Purcell's dying words drifted ghostly through her mind. *My father took his secrets to the grave, as shall I. Time will tell, Nicola.*

'You okay?' Bryson asked, looking at her seriously.

Lopez nodded, and got to her feet.

'I know how to crack Purcell's last code,' she said. 'We've got to get back to Miami.'

They staggered to their feet and walked the last few hundred yards down the ruined road, clambering over fallen trunks and skirting enormous upturned slabs of asphalt until they reached the edge of the town. Dirty, soaking wet and with their clothes ripped and torn, they stopped walking as Bryson listened.

'You hear that?'

'Hear what?' Lopez asked him.

They looked as the sound of screaming engines suddenly roared toward them. Bryson grabbed her arm as he turned them away from the town.

'Tsunami!'

Dozens of cars and mopeds burst out from alleys and roads, all swerving to avoid each other as they raced at breakneck pace out of the town toward the hills. Behind them, a seething wall of white water surged from the ocean across the beaches and into the rows of hotels with tremendous force, battering aside everything in its path.

A chorus of grotesque screams and cries soared from the town, only to be drowned out by the crash of timber and metal as the tsunami ploughed through everything before it.

Lopez scrambled with Katherine as a roaring wall of filthy, churning water packed with debris thundered toward them.

53

CAPE CANAVERAL, FLORIDA

June 28: 17.26

'The quake struck one hour, seven minutes and eight seconds ago, magnitude 6.8.'

Thomas Ryker's monotone delivery seemed painfully inadequate, as Ethan considered the force of the seismic disaster that had slammed into the Dominican Republic's shores. A vision flashed into his mind of Lopez being swallowed by churning tectonic plates, or crushed beneath tumbling masonry. He closed his eyes and swallowed an acidic glob that had lodged in his throat.

'She'll be fine.'

Jarvis's hand rested on Ethan's shoulder. Ethan opened his eyes and sucked in a deep lungful of air.

'Anything we can get on the source of the seismic waves?'

'We're on it,' Ryker replied, having been brought down to Project Watchman to oversee the GOCE satellite's data, 'but it'll take a while for the computers to crunch the data streams and get a clearly defined picture of what happened.'

'And no word from either Lopez or Bryson?' Ethan asked Jarvis.

'Nothing yet,' the old man admitted, 'but they may well be in transit as we speak. The nearest airport is on fairly high ground, so it should have escaped the worst of the damage. If they got to it.'

Ethan nodded vaguely, staring into the distance. An image of Joanna infiltrated his thoughts once again. He had lost her and it had damned-near ruined him. Yet now, even though he might just be able to pick up the threads of his search for her, the thought of losing Lopez filled him with the same cold dread he had felt all those years ago in Palestine. Jarvis's words reached him from afar.

'Tom and I did some digging into the background of the fathers of Charles Purcell and Joaquin Abell. Interesting stuff.'

Ethan blinked himself back into the here and now. 'In what way?'

'Their connections are undeniable. They worked together on the Manhattan Project back in 1945, and afterward were effectively in direct competition with each other for government funding.'

Ethan made a swift calculation. 'So there was motive for a murder.'

'Reason enough,' Thomas Ryker said, 'depending on how seriously they took their research.'

'And there were no two more serious scientists than Abell and Purcell senior,' Jarvis went on. 'Both were committed to their causes: Purcell to the development of nuclear weapons and Abell to the development of benign nuclear power through fusion.'

'You make it sound like Montgomery Purcell was the enemy,' Ethan said.

'Perhaps he wasn't,' said another voice. Ethan turned to see Mitch Hannah stride into the room and toss his leather flying jacket across a nearby table. 'Everybody's assuming that because Charles Purcell's father wanted to develop nuclear weapons, he must be the bad guy of the story.'

'Nuclear weapons generally aren't something that good guys pursue,' Ethan pointed out. 'At least Isaac Abell was trying to do something helpful with the technology.'

'So was Monty Purcell,' Hannah replied. 'Just because he wanted to develop weapons doesn't mean that he wanted to see them used. Most everybody involved in the nuclear programs of the fifties and sixties knew how horrible the weapons were. But their purpose was mutually assured destruction as a deterrent. The Russians were building huge weapons and the only way to ensure the safety of the United States was to build an equivalent arsenal, so that neither side could fire without initiating a global nuclear exchange that would destroy everything and everyone. Essentially, there would be no point in firing as there would be nothing left to gain afterward.'

'So maybe Monty Purcell wasn't a warmonger,' Ethan said. 'That much I get. But Isaac Abell was the ultimate philanthropist. He turned down major offers of work on government weapons programs to concentrate on nuclear-power generation. It makes him even less of a suspect when it comes to Monty's mysterious death.'

'True,' Mitch Hannah admitted. 'We know from the witness statements of other people at the meeting on

Bimini Island that Isaac Abell went nowhere near Monty Purcell's aircraft on the day of the meeting, and so could not have tampered with it in any way.'

'And Purcell was also the first to leave,' Jarvis said, 'at about eight in the evening. But that doesn't mean that Abell couldn't have hired somebody else to damage the airplane for him, maybe somebody at the airfield?'

'Unlikely,' Mitch Hannah said. 'Purcell maintained his own airplane and was a seasoned pilot. It's hard to tamper with an aircraft and get away with it, because of all the checks a pilot does before committing to flight. He would have spotted anything wrong with his airplane either before or during take-off.'

'What then?' Ethan asked. 'How could Isaac Abell have possibly had anything to do with the crash?'

Mitch Hannah opened a map of the Florida Straits and set it down on the table between them, jabbing a finger at Bimini Island.

'Purcell takes off from here, and only has to fly to here.' Mitch pointed at Miami. 'About sixty nautical miles away, which in a light aircraft means a flight time of maybe thirty to forty minutes at his logged cruise-height of five thousand feet. The big clue, and what ties his death in with Isaac Abell, is the time that he took off: 8:41in the evening, on October 9, 1964.'

Ethan thought for a moment.

'He'd be flying at night.'

'On instruments,' Mitch confirmed, 'over the ocean. I checked the weather records for that night, and Monty Purcell would have been flying either in or above solid cloud, with no horizon.'

Ethan looked at Jarvis, whose face was shining with intrigue.

'So he's entirely reliant upon his instruments, and if they were to somehow go wrong . . . ?' the old man suggested.

Ethan looked at Mitch Hannah.

'When did Isaac Abell get his undersea laboratory operational?'

Thomas Ryker answered.

'October 4, 1964,' he said. 'And he'd scheduled a test of the topamak magnetic field generator at . . .' The kid's voice trailed off as he realized the connection. 'I'll be damned – nine o'clock on October 9.'

Ethan ran a hand through his hair.

'Isaac Abell deliberately schedules a test of his fusion chamber the same evening that Purcell is flying over-head. All he needed to do was keep him on Bimini late enough that his flight would coincide with the test.'

Mitch Hannah tapped his finger on the map.

'A test of a device that powerful would have almost certainly produced fields sufficient to completely destroy or otherwise render useless all of the analogue instruments in a Cessna 150B of that era, Purcell's airplane. Monty Purcell wouldn't have stood a chance – without visual references to keep his airplane in level flight, he would have lost spatial orientation within seconds and probably hit the ocean within a couple of minutes.'

Ethan looked at the map.

'You said that the test of Abell's device was at nine o'clock in the evening,' he said to Ryker, who nodded. 'And he took off at 8:41?'

'Yes,' Mitch said, immediately catching on to Ethan's train of thought. 'Assuming an average speed of maybe ninety knots over twenty-one minutes . . .'

'. . . He'd have covered about thirty nautical miles,' Ethan finished, and pressed his finger onto a spot on the map that marked the edge of the Miami Terrace reef. 'And gone down right about here.'

The four men stared at the map for a long moment.

'That's where the underwater facility must be,' Jarvis said finally.

Thomas Ryker nodded.

'If it matches the data we get from the seismic-monitoring stations and GOCE, then we've found the IRIS base.'

Ethan was about to speak when the door to the room opened and a soldier popped his head through to speak to Jarvis.

'We've had contact, sir,' the soldier said. 'A transport left Puerto Plata just over an hour ago.'

'Is Nicola Lopez aboard?' Ethan demanded, as though he'd never left the Corps.

'Unknown, sir,' the marine replied. 'American survivors of the quake are due at the airport in Miami in just over an hour.'

Ethan was walking for the door before he'd even realized it.

54

MIAMI INTERNATIONAL
AIRPORT, FLORIDA

June 28, 18:32

Ethan watched as the US Navy Gulfstream C-20D jet taxied in from the runway, silhouetted against the low sun streaming in beams across the ragged clouds in the sky. Dozens of television crews were amassed near the boarding gates, restricted from getting too close to the aircraft but able to get shots using their powerful zoom lenses.

Ethan glanced at the camera crews as they filmed the aircraft's arrival, and slowly an idea formed in his head. There was no way that he could predict which news broadcasts Joaquin Abell was using to predict the future, but it seemed likely that all of the major networks would be among them. Ethan realized that, for once, there might be a way to turn the tables on the megalomaniac.

Ethan stood with Jarvis as the Gulfstream braked to a halt just fifty yards from where they stood, its engines whining deafeningly before the pilots shut them down. Ethan had no idea how many people were aboard or how seriously injured they might be. Early reports were that the area where Lopez and Bryson had been working had been ravaged. Casualties, from multiple nations, would be in the thousands.

'She'll be okay.'

Jarvis stood alongside him, clearly aware of Ethan's agitation.

'The place got leveled,' Ethan hissed. 'That bastard Abell has killed thousands to feed his own ego and ambition. Right now, I want his throat in my hands.'

'This is not a revenge mission,' Jarvis cautioned, as the airplane's main door opened. He reached out and stopped Ethan from approaching the aircraft. 'The moment you make it personal, you become ineffective. Keep your cool, Ethan, or this'll blow up in your face.'

Forcing himself not to run toward the Gulfstream, Ethan watched as crewmen began helping people down the steps, some of them hoisted down on stretchers with saline bags held aloft. Others hobbled down onto the asphalt, their hands resting on the shoulders of the pilots or paramedics. Then three bedraggled figures, wrapped in thermal blankets, clambered out into the low sunlight.

Ethan felt a weight lift from his shoulders as he saw Lopez's thick tangle of black hair. Katherine Abell and Scott Bryson accompanied her, the big man's arm across her shoulder as they shuffled across the landing area to where Ethan was standing with Jarvis. Ethan forgot himself and strode toward Lopez, who squinted up at him in the bright sunlight and smiled.

'Enjoy your vacation, cowboy?' she asked. 'We've been busy whilst you've been sitting on your ass drinking coffee.'

A broad grin spread across Ethan's face as he wrapped

his arms around her. Lopez returned the embrace and looked up at him.

'No use getting cute with me,' she said.

'Just glad you got out okay.'

'Thanks to this guy,' Lopez said, and jerked a thumb over her shoulder. 'Rescued us from drowning when the tsunami hit. Only a SEAL could improvise a boat out of a floating garbage dumpster. I've never see him move so fast. '

Ethan looked at Bryson, whose jaw twisted into a crooked grin as he shrugged.

'What can I say? I'm a hero.'

Ethan released Lopez and strode up to him, then stuck his hand out. The big man gripped it.

'I owe you,' Ethan said without fuss, and then he leaned in close and wrapped one arm across his broad shoulder. Bryson's single eye flickered curiously as Ethan whispered quietly enough for nobody else to hear. 'I need you to leave, Scott, and make a damned fuss about it.'

Ethan released Bryson before he could respond, while Doug Jarvis gently took Katherine Abell's arm.

'You need to come with us,' he informed her. 'We don't know what Joaquin will do next and we need to stop him before—'

'I can't,' Katherine uttered, and hugged her blanket tighter around her shoulders. 'We don't know for sure if he's really behind all of this.'

'Yes, we do,' Lopez said, and turned to Jarvis. 'I know how to crack Purcell's final code. I can find the documents that prove IRIS is guilty of fraud.'

Jarvis had his cellphone in his hand almost before Lopez had finished her sentence. 'Shoot.'

'You said that his code was a cipher code that needed another code to decipher it,' she said. 'Charles told me that he and his father both took their secrets to the grave, and that *time would tell*. But his father didn't have any secrets, only Charles did. If time would tell, then I've got to assume it's the time of *death* of one of the two men. Charles's "secret" was the code on his chest. I'm guessing, but try the date of Montgomery Purcell's disappearance in the Bermuda Triangle: 9 October, 1964.'

Jarvis dialled the crypto-analysis department of the DIA immediately, and dictated the dates to them. 'Oh-nine, ten, sixty-four,' he said as he grabbed a pen and paper from the inside pocket of his jacket. Ethan turned his back, letting Jarvis lean on it and scribble whatever his contact was saying.

'Okay, got it.' Jarvis rang off, and looked at his note-pad. 'Okay, here's the code,' he said showing them the page.

frsbz racjotrl kbnq sf bpuzl mibmo yuwtez jrrwe

'And here's the cipher.'

09106 40910640 9106 40 91064 09106
609106 40910

'What do we do with that?' Ethan asked, deciding not to mention that math had never been his forte.

'You skip either backwards or forwards however many places the cipher tells you to in the alphabet,' Lopez explained. 'So f-r-s-b-z becomes . . . "first". It fits.'

Ethan watched as Lopez took over from Jarvis and swiftly decoded the message.

FIRST NATIONAL BANK OF SOUTH MIAMI SUNSET DRIVE

'Outstanding, Nicola,' Jarvis said, and immediately turned to Kyle Sears. 'Get a warrant from the DA. I want your men down there within the hour, and I want whatever documents they find in relation to Charles Purcell in police custody. No more accidents.'

'You got it.'

Ethan turned to Katherine, who stood beside him with her head in her hands, her long auburn hair hiding her face and obscuring her speech as she whispered to herself.

'This isn't happening.'

'Katherine, this is all part of his scheme,' Ethan said. 'We know that he caused this. Charles Purcell predicted exactly where and when the earthquake would strike, and he told us both how Joaquin is able to cause these disasters and why. He's been planning this a long time.'

'But why?' Katherine asked. 'He could just as likely have achieved power or influence by being himself, by helping people.'

Jarvis shook his head.

'IRIS could not have funded all that it has done

without embezzling funds from government,' he explained. 'It would have ceased to exist as an entity years ago. Joaquin has invested in charitable acts only a tiny fraction of what IRIS has received over the years from governments – the rest has gone into the construction of this device of his, something designed to gain him unassailable power and influence. He has to be stopped.'

Katherine was about to reply when a Navy jeep rolled up alongside them to collect the Gulfstream's crew for debrief. Thomas Ryker jumped out and waved them across.

'Guys, we've got something you need to see.'

Jarvis led them across to the vehicle, and as one they huddled beside the door. Ryker had a portable laptop that was sitting on the passenger seat and he turned it to face them.

'Streamed from the Robert Murtaugh News Channel just a few minutes ago,' Ryker said. 'Most of the news channels are covering the earthquake disaster already, but this one's different. It's Joaquin Abell.'

Ethan watched as Joaquin Abell's face appeared on the screen. He was standing on the quarterdeck of his yacht, the sun illuminating his face as he spoke to the camera. The news channel's scrolling text drifted past at the bottom of the screen, outlining details of the disaster.

'*It will of course be the responsibility of IRIS, as part of our charter, to send supplies, medical aid and construction materials to the Dominican Republic at this time of terrible tragedy. We cannot stand idly by after such a horrific event, waiting for the endless procrastination of world government. We must move now to prevent the spread of disease and decay and bring this beautiful part of the world back into the light.'*

Joaquin raised his hands imploringly at the camera.

'This is the chance for us to do something personal, something right. We do not need to wait for governments any longer to take these terrible tragedies and turn them into something worthwhile, like a phoenix from the ashes. I ask you now, as citizens of the greatest country on earth, to do something that has never been done before. I ask each and every one of you, every American citizen on our planet, to donate just a single dollar to the rebuilding of the Dominican Republic via IRIS. Just one dollar. Even in these hard economic times, a single dollar is something that we can all spare. Yet, combined, that equals hundreds of millions of dollars devoted to the protection, healing and future care of a people devastated by loss, by pain and by suffering. People who no longer have that single dollar to spare. Do it today to turn a crisis into an opportunity, and I give you my word, as Joaquin Abell, that your money will create a heaven where, right now, there is only hell. Thank you.'

The news channel switched to its anchor, and Ryker hit the pause button on the screen before looking at Jarvis.

'He's on his yacht,' the old man said.

'Which means that he can't have caused the disaster!' Katherine pointed out.

'Not necessarily,' Ethan said. 'He doesn't have to press the button himself to activate the horror that he's created. He's got plenty of people working for him.'

'Is the yacht still anchored out at sea?' Lopez asked.

'Right where it's always been,' Jarvis confirmed.

'Doesn't make sense if he's trying to hide his little under-sea laboratory. He's anchored within a mile of it.'

'It does if your ego is as big as Joaquin's,' Ethan replied. 'He's cocky enough to think that we don't know anything about what he's done, and arrogant enough to think that hiding in plain sight is clever.'

Ethan stared at the static image of Joaquin's face. Something was wrong but he couldn't put his finger on it.

'That was fast,' Bryson said, as though reading Ethan's mind. 'Getting a news crew out on his yacht.'

'There's no news crew,' Ethan realized. 'He's talking to a static camera.' Ethan turned to Lopez. 'We got foot-age of his yacht from a few hours ago and Robert Murtaugh was aboard along with a congressman, the governor of Florida and a few others.'

'So he's maybe heard about the earthquake,' Katherine said, 'and arranged a quick appeal, which Murtaugh has then sent to his people for broadcast.'

Ethan looked at the screen thoughtfully for a moment and then something clicked in his mind. He looked across at the Gulfstream's pilot, who was waiting patiently behind them.

'What was the prevailing wind across the Florida Straits this morning?'

The pilot replied immediately, having had the stand-ard meteorological briefing before flying that day.

'Southwesterly, eight knots, variable above five thou-sand feet.'

Ethan gestured to the computer.

'Wind that back,' he asked Ryker, 'then play it at high speed.'

Ryker frowned in confusion but obeyed nonetheless. The broadcast played at four times normal speed. Ethan leaned forward and watched Joaquin's comical babbling, but focused instead on the clouds as they raced across the sky, approaching from the horizon to pass overhead.

'I'll be damned,' Ethan said. 'Looks like our boy Joaquin's not as goddamned smart as he thinks he is.'

'You think he's lying or something?' Lopez asked.

'I know that he is,' Ethan replied. 'He's just given us our evidence to convict him.'

55

'What are you talking about?' Katherine asked. 'It's just a broadcast.'

Ethan glanced one more time at the imagery on the screen.

'The clouds are blowing toward the camera, so the camera is facing roughly west,' he explained.

'So?' Lopez asked.

'So,' Ethan said as he looked at her, 'the sun's in his face. It's in the east.'

Scott Bryson chuckled and looked at Ethan with the first signs of respect. 'Not bad for a boy scout.'

'Will somebody tell me what the hell's going on?' Katherine insisted.

Doug Jarvis turned to her.

'It means that Joaquin recorded this broadcast before the earthquake actually struck,' he explained. 'The sun rises in the east, so he must have recorded it sometime this morning.'

'And the only way he could have done that is if he

knew the quake would happen in advance,' Ethan replied. 'It's evidence enough to get a warrant for his arrest from the District Attorney.'

Lopez shook her head.

'But why would he do this? He could have waited until the quake and then shot the broadcast. Why expose himself like this?'

'Because he's arrogant, greedy and not quite as clever as he thinks he is,' Ethan guessed. 'He would have needed to get this broadcast out as fast as possible, in order to get as much money from the public as he can, to maximize his profits from what he's done. And he thinks that nobody will notice that the sun's in the wrong place because it's low enough in the sky to match the sunset, and his yacht's at sea with no coast in sight to judge direction.'

Katherine stared at the screen and Ethan could see her shoulders sag beneath her thermal blanket as she realized, finally, that there could no longer be any doubt. Joaquin Abell was behind everything that had happened, including the death of Charles Purcell and his family, and the scientists aboard the lost airplane.

Ethan turned to her.

'We need to stop him, Katherine, and we need to do it without a firefight. Joaquin is well protected and is almost certainly now in hiding. We need to get to his lab and we need you to help us, maybe even convince him that this is the wrong path that he's chosen.'

'Why me?' she implored. 'Surely you can just send the Navy?'

'Because we need to bring him to trial for what he's

done,' Jarvis said, 'and the only way that's going to happen is if he can be coaxed out of his underwater facility. Have you spoken to him since you left his yacht?'

'He called me,' she said. 'From a satellite phone aboard the facility. I didn't answer it.'

Katherine rummaged in her pocket and produced her cellphone.

'Can we listen to it?' Lopez asked. 'Right now, any information might help us.'

Katherine switched the phone to speaker and dialed her voicemail. Ethan listened as an unknown male voice began speaking, the tones touched with urgency and fear. He noted a look of surprise on Katherine's face as she listened.

'*Katherine, it's Dennis. Listen to me, I don't have much time. Joaquin isn't running a conservation project down here. This is a military facility and he's developed a machine to cause earthquakes and other natural disasters. He's aiming for where you are, Katherine. I am not allowed to leave this facility. Please, if you get this message, get onto high ground until the quake has passed, and then get in touch with the authorities – the coastguard, the police. Hell, call the goddamned Navy, just get somebody out here as quickly as you can!*' The voice hesitated. '*I'm going to try to stop him. Joaquin's already killed hundreds, if not thousands. Please hurry, and take care of yourself, okay?*'

The line cut off, and Ethan looked at Jarvis. 'You said you wanted proof.'

Jarvis nodded as Katherine stared vacantly into the distance, the phone held limply in her hand.

'Katherine, your husband needs to be stopped,' Jarvis said.

Katherine replied in a ghostly whisper.

'He's too far gone now for that.' Then she turned away from the screen and looked at Ethan. 'He told me that Dennis was a part of all this. He lied to me, again.' She shook her head, clearly angry with herself. 'I will try to help you.'

Ethan nodded and turned to Jarvis.

'We're going to need a submersible of some kind.'

'I'll talk to the Navy,' Jarvis said, already reaching for his cellphone. Then he looked at Bryson. 'You've got an atmospheric diving suit aboard your boat, haven't you?'

'Yes, I have,' Bryson nodded, 'and that's right where it's staying. I'm done here.'

Lopez turned to him.

'You can't,' she protested. 'We've almost got him.'

Bryson turned to look down at her, his crooked smile and twinkling eye almost mocking.

'No, *you*'ve almost got him. Since we met this morning I've had my boat shot half to hell, been knocked out by a psychotic Viking, been shot, caught in an earthquake and damned near drowned in Puerto Plata by a fucking tsunami.' He looked at Jarvis. 'I think you've got your seven thousand dollars' worth out of me.'

Lopez grabbed Bryson's thick forearm. 'We can't finish this without you.'

Bryson chuckled. 'You've got the Defense Intelligence Agency and the Navy right behind you. What difference does it make to you if I'm here?'

Ethan saw Lopez glance across at him, an almost embarrassed look on her face. She looked back up at Bryson.

'My chances of survival will be a lot better with you around.'

'Your chances are just fine with your little boy scout here,' Bryson replied. 'He'd just get jealous if I stayed. That right, Ethan? You're not going to let her come to any harm. You never take your eyes off her anyway.'

'Get out of here, Bryson,' Ethan muttered.

Bryson turned and without another word strode away from the vehicle toward the nearest airport gates. Neither Ethan or Jarvis made any effort to stop him from leaving.

'You're just going to let him go then,' Lopez said flatly as she glared at them.

'He's got a point,' Jarvis shrugged. 'He's done far more than he bargained for.'

Lopez ran her hands through her hair and looked at Ethan with an expression midway between anger and desperation.

'Ethan, surely you can see that we need him around.'

Ethan shrugged. 'He's not a part of this. If you couldn't convince him to stay, what chance do I have?'

'Then how do we get to Joaquin Abell?' Lopez demanded.

'We sneak up on him,' Jarvis replied, and lifted his cellphone to his ear.

IRIS, DEEP BLUE RESEARCH STATION, FLORIDA STRAITS

June 28, 19:46

Dennis Aubrey stood alone in the hub, staring vacantly at the video camera before him on the control panel. Joaquin had passed it to him less than an hour before, after it had been returned to him by that lumbering brute of his.

Joaquin's instructions had been clear: download the entire drive and have it ready within the hour. Whatever was on it would be viewed as soon as Joaquin had ensured his guests had left the hub and returned to the yacht, to be flown back to Miami.

Aubrey had obeyed his instructions to the letter, but through every excruciating moment his mind had been filled with images of the earthquake that had shattered the tranquility of Puerto Plata. The murder of Benjamin Tyler had cemented Aubrey's conviction that Joaquin Abell's sanity had been abandoned, and that had been confirmed when Joaquin had proved to his guests that he could not only predict the future, but could reduce entire populations to medieval poverty and decades of dependence on foreign aid.

When the demonstration had been complete and his guests had left for the surface, Joaquin had been elated, drunk on his own prowess, giddy like a spoilt child with yet another unearned gift clasped in its hands.

Aubrey, on the other hand, had experienced a dizzying nausea that had flooded his throat with bile and sent flushes alternately scalding and chilling his skin. Thousands of innocent human beings were dead. Thousands more would die later when the millions of dollars promised by Joaquin to aid the needy were siphoned off into IRIS accounts scattered in tax havens across the globe.

Worst of all, Katherine Abell had almost certainly perished in the catastrophe. For reasons that Dennis could not bear to admit to himself, that filled him with an anger he had rarely felt in his life.

It had struck Dennis, right there and then, that no human being on earth held any value to Joaquin Abell. Dennis had realized – too late, he now knew – that he was as likely to be killed next as anybody else. Sooner or later he would be murdered, wiped from the slate of Joaquin Abell's world like a fly swatted from a meal. An irrelevance, an irritation. A risk.

Aubrey looked again at the camera. He had hoped, desperately, that when the group of guests left for the surface he would be among them. Yet now it was clear that he would never be allowed to leave. The *Intrepid* was back at the yacht and the *Isaac* under armed guard. He was a prisoner beyond the reach of law enforcement, his family, his friends and rescue.

He pressed a button and the camera's contents played on a small screen on the panel. He sped the timeline forward until he was watching events in the near future. As he watched, his heart sank as a terrible scene unfolded before him. He doubled the replay speed, and as the seconds ticked by so he felt his bowels loosen at what he was witnessing, a terrifying future of death and destruction. Appalled, Dennis paused the footage and took several seconds to gain control of his breathing.

There was no escape. There was no alternative. The future could not be changed.

Dennis moved to a computer terminal beside the control panel and opened up a software package. He sat down and began methodically going through the camera's scenes one by one and noting specific times, scribbling them on the inside of his palm with a pen. The work took him almost half an hour, but when he was done he shut the display off and leaned back in his chair, his mind haunted both by what he had seen and what he knew he must now do.

'Dennis!'

Aubrey shot upright, a lightning bolt of fear shuddering through him as Joaquin strode into the control room. 'What news?'

'Has the governor gone?'

Dennis Aubrey watched as Joaquin approached. Olaf lumbered in behind him, wearing a shoulder holster with black straps that stretched across his broad chest. A heavy-looking 9mm pistol nestled under his left arm.

'They're on their way back to Miami,' Joaquin replied and then rubbed his hands together. 'There's no longer a man among them who will oppose us. Now, where is that camera?'

Aubrey pointed to where the camera sat on the panel beside him. He waited for Joaquin to join him at the panel.

'How long is the recording?' Joaquin asked, his eyes wide and sparkling with uncontained delight.

Aubrey took a deep breath. 'Just over four thousand hours.'

'Four thousand hours?' Joaquin echoed in wonder. 'That must be . . .'

'Six months, give or take. Six months of the future, as viewed through the lens of this camera.'

'Play it!' Joaquin almost shouted. 'I want to see it, all of it, on the big screen over there!'

Aubrey unplugged one of the jacks on the panel before him and then plugged it into a different feed. Instantly, one of the large plasma screens lit up. Aubrey reached out and pressed play.

Joaquin gasped as an image of the hub itself appeared, one of the news channels on the screens viewed through the camera's lens from within the black-hole chamber. Almost immediately, in front of the portal through which it gazed, the face of Charles Purcell appeared. The scientist gazed into the lens and then vanished. Moments later, the camera backed away from the portal and began moving along its track within the chamber, brief flares of blue-white energy flickering around the edges of the screen.

'This was when Charles Purcell retrieved the camera,' Dennis said. 'This is the past.'

'From yesterday,' Joaquin said. 'Forward it to the future!'

Aubrey span the recording forward and watched as the camera was hastily packed into a bag that was sealed shut. Blackness enveloped the screen. Aubrey span the timeline forward and all they saw was hours of blackness. He felt a little current of joy as Joaquin raised his hands to his head.

'What's he done?!' he wailed in despair.

Dennis remained silent, spinning the footage forward further. Moments later, the image returned. Aubrey's joy withered as he saw a modern family lounge, the immaculate carpets splattered with blood. The inert bodies of a blonde woman and a young girl dominated the scene. Joaquin fell silent.

'His house,' Olaf said without apparent emotion. 'He found their bodies. He must have arrived moments after I left.'

'He knew you were there,' Joaquin realized, 'and what time you would give up waiting for him and leave. He must have filmed the scene as some kind of evidence.'

Aubrey remained silent despite the fact that his blood seemed to be running cold now through his veins. He watched as Charles Purcell walked with the camera across the lounge and picked up a framed picture of himself standing with his wife and daughter, the glass of the frame thick with smeared blood. Purcell would have known that the camera had already seen this future whilst alongside the black hole's event-horizon, the information stored on its hard drive. Even if he had turned the camera off in horror or disgust at the sight of his slaughtered family, the camera would still have harbored the horrific imagery.

But Charles, ever cautious, was taking no chances.

'This is still the past,' Joaquin shouted. 'I want the future!'

'You already have it,' Aubrey said, and pointed to a different screen before playing the feed from one of the other cameras, which he'd retrieved from the chamber earlier. 'The news, Joaquin, from tomorrow. I pulled it from the chamber just a half-hour ago.'

Joaquin glanced at the screen and saw an anchor from Robert Murtaugh's news station speaking silently to the camera. Beneath her, the scrolling text revealed the nature of the story.

IRIS AWARDED FRESH CONTRACT BY CONGRESS TO REBUILD DOMINICAN REPUBLIC PROVINCE: IRIS CEO PROMISES ALL $250 MILLION TO 'PEOPLE ON THE GROUND'

Aubrey watched as the image switched from the anchor to the devastated shore of Puerto Plata, and a still image of Joaquin Abell appeared in the top-right corner of the shot. A reporter on the scene stood in front of an IRIS helicopter as food parcels, medicines and blankets were unloaded by personnel into waiting trucks.

Joaquin's face creased into a smile of deep satisfaction.

'Good work, Dennis,' he said. 'Our future is assured. Now, show me what happens here in the control room. Olaf brought the camera back here, so it must have seen what happens to us today. I want to know exactly what occurs here in the next few hours.'

Dennis shut off the newsfeed camera and sped the frames forward on Charles Purcell's recovered camera. A blur of light whizzed past the screen, then he slowed it carefully as he watched the digital time display. An image of the IRIS hub once again appeared, but this time Joaquin was standing with a pistol in his hand, alongside Olaf and several armed guards. And before them was Ethan Warner and Nicola Lopez, their hands in the air and every gun in the hub pointing at them as they stood beside the black-hole chamber, the outer hatch open.

'So,' Joaquin smirked. 'The two detectives decide to pay us a visit, do they?' He turned to Dennis Aubrey. 'Pray, Dennis, show us what happens to them both, if you will?'

Dennis carefully span the recording by several minutes, the images flashing past in a blur of color, then returned it to normal speed and looked up as the screen showed an image of Joaquin and Olaf watching as the black-hole chamber flared with bright bursts of energy and light that flickered out into the control room through the narrow portals. The two men were laughing, and Joaquin was clapping the big man on his huge shoulder.

Joaquin smirked and looked over his shoulder at Aubrey.

'Excellent, Dennis. Perhaps we should prepare for our guests' arrival? Olaf! Ready our men to welcome Ethan Warner and Nicola Lopez on their one-way trip to oblivion!'

57

FLORIDA STRAITS

June 28, 19:54

'I thought we were going to be sneaking up on Joaquin?'

Ethan Warner had to shout at Jarvis, even though he was wearing earphones against the noise from the MH-60S Sea Hawk's twin turboshaft engines. The helicopter was flying low over the ocean, skimming the waves that Ethan could see glittering with gold through the open fuselage door. The door was guarded by a serious-looking marine wearing wraparound sunglasses and manning an M-60D machine gun, the last glow of the setting sun glinting off the metal barrel.

'The aircraft carrier USS *Nimitz* is heading off for operations in the Pacific,' Jarvis explained. 'Helicopter Sea Combat Squadron 6 here are conducting work-up exercises in this area before deploying with the carrier wing. Perfect cover to get you and Lopez into position, right where we need you.'

Beside Ethan sat Katherine, her features drawn and tired. Lopez, her long black hair trembling with the engine vibrations and the wind blowing in through the open door, gestured to the six marines checking their weapons at the back of the helicopter.

'Don't suppose there's any chance we could have a detachment of troops drop down there with us? Joaquin's likely to have protection and he probably knows that we're coming.'

Jarvis shook his head.

'The fewer people know about this, the better. We're cleared to use the marines to get us aboard Joaquin's yacht using reasonable force, but beyond that we're on our own. A major military dive operation wouldn't go unnoticed, but a quick insertion onto the yacht should be simple enough. You said that none of the *Event Horizon*'s crew appeared armed.'

'Not the last time we were there,' Ethan said. 'And there were definitely submersibles aboard, large ones.'

'Okay,' Jarvis said. 'This is how it goes down. This helicopter will make a tactical descent and drop a platoon of marines aboard the *Event Horizon* to overpower the crew, whilst the helicopter jams any communications using the onboard ALQ-144 Infrared Jammer. You'll go aboard with the marines, who'll hold the yacht until you've done your job.'

'Which will be what?' Ethan asked.

'To get down there, find out what Joaquin Abell is doing and put a stop to it. Your primary mission is the recovery of the camera that Charles Purcell carried with him before he died. Your secondary mission is to find solid, court-admissible proof that Joaquin Abell is guilty of the crimes he's committed, and bring him to justice.'

Katherine Abell looked up.

'I don't want him to be hurt,' she said, speaking for the first time since they'd taken off. 'He's innocent until proven guilty.'

'He's a criminal, ma'am,' Jarvis replied. 'We already have proof that he's guilty, but it's not the kind that can be brought into the public sphere, due to national security. Ethan and Nicola are capable of taking Joaquin into custody if he is willing to go quietly.'

'And if he resists?' Katherine asked.

Jarvis reached out to a metal lock-up box beside him, opened it and retrieved two Sig 9mm pistols and four flash-bang grenades. He shared them out to Ethan and Lopez, along with two spare magazines each.

Katherine watched the exchange and then closed her eyes, but she said nothing.

'You haven't got anything with a little more punch?' Lopez asked.

'We're not sure how the facility that Joaquin has built is pressurized,' Jarvis explained. 'You go in there with heavy weapons, you might end up taking yourselves down.'

Ethan checked the mechanism on his pistol and set the safety catch before slipping the weapon into the shoulder holster he'd been given earlier. The holster lay beneath a harness that he wore, which was connected to metal clasps and thick rappel wires hooked to the helicopter's metal-plated floor. Lopez did the same, and they both watched as a red light began flashing in the interior of the helicopter. One of the marines pulled open another fuselage door and windblast buffeted through the interior.

'Ten seconds,' Jarvis shouted.

The marines all hooked their clasps up to the rappel lines and took up positions either side of the fuselage. Ethan and Lopez got to their feet and each joined the end of a queue. The Sea Hawk's attitude changed as it slowed and pitched up, and the thumping rotors hammered the air outside as the sea churned with spray beneath them.

All at once Ethan saw the elegant yacht hove into view beneath them and glimpsed a pair of crewmen staring up and pointing at the gray helicopter as it thundered overhead. Suddenly the machine slowed to a hover above the yacht's fantail.

Instantly the marines leapt one after the other and spiraled down the wires with their rifles aiming below them, ready to fire at anybody attempting to oppose their boarding of the yacht.

Ethan followed the last marine out, his gloved hands guiding him down the rappel line. Opposite, he saw Lopez matching his descent with her customary gusto, as though she too had done this a dozen times before in war zones. They thumped down onto the deck as the platoon lieutenant shouted orders to stunned crewmen standing with their hands in the air nearby.

'Get down! *Down, down, down!*'

Bodies dropped as though shot, the men totally overwhelmed by the noise, speed and force of the marines' entry. Ethan followed at a run as the marines swept through the ship toward the bridge, his pistol in his hands but held low to avoid an unintentional discharge. Plastic cuffs were hastily wrapped around shell-shocked crewmen's wrists and ankles, the gaping staff left prone where they lay until they could be dealt with later. Neutralized.

The marines burst onto the bridge to corner the yacht's officers, stopping the captain in mid-protest with the muzzle of an M-16 in his face. Ethan and Lopez stepped onto the bridge even as the marine lieutenant was barking orders to his men while standing over a cowering officer.

'Secure the fore and aft quarters, in pairs! Report in when clear!'

Ethan looked at the elderly, tall, bearded man bearing the shoulder insignia of a captain, who was standing upright with his chin raised. He stared defiantly down the barrel of the marine's M-16.

'Where is Joaquin Abell?' Ethan asked, hoping against hope that he was aboard.

The captain's eyes narrowed, refusing to be intimidated by the soldiers.

'Who the hell are you?'

The platoon lieutenant stepped in for Ethan.

'United States Marines, sir, and this vessel has been seized under the authority of the Admiral of the United States Pacific Fleet.'

The captain looked down in confusion at the officer.

'This is a private vessel, on humanitarian and conservation duties. What on earth would the admiralty want with us?'

Ethan judged the man's disbelief to be genuine.

'We think that IRIS's humanitarian activities are a shield for criminal enterprise,' he explained. 'We require yourself and your crew to stand down and let us investigate. I take it that you possess the coordinates to Joaquin Abell's facility on the seafloor?'

The captain frowned.

'Yes, but it's just a coral-reef observation hub,' he said. 'There's nothing much down there. I've seen it.'

Ethan smiled grimly.

'I doubt very much that the place you were taken to was the same one that Joaquin has been concealing from the eyes of the world.'

'Who the hell do you think you are?' the captain demanded.

Ethan was about to answer when Katherine Abell strode into the bridge.

'They're with me,' she said. 'And what they're telling you is true.'

The captain's eyes flickered in surprise. He stared at Katherine and then Ethan and Lopez in turn before making his decision. He turned to a subaltern.

'The marines have the bridge,' he said. 'Provide them with whatever assistance they require.'

The subaltern dashed away, accompanied by a soldier, and the captain turned to Katherine.

'Neither the crew nor I know anything about a second facility,' he said. 'But Mr. Abell's armed escort went down with him this morning, with a scientist by the name of Dennis Aubrey.'

Katherine nodded.

'I only learned of this myself today,' she assured him. 'You won't be detained for long, I'm sure.'

As the captain and his crew were escorted to their

quarters by the marines, Lopez gently took Katherine's arm.

'Make sure you stay behind us at all times,' Lopez warned her.

'I'm not an invalid.'

'Nobody's saying that you are,' Ethan said. 'But Joaquin's already tried to kill you once. This might sound harsh, but you're our only bargaining chip down there.'

Katherine glared at Ethan.

'If there's one thing I've realized since all of this began, it's that my husband is a coward. He isn't capable of killing for himself so he sends others to do it for him, or uses machines. I doubt very much that he'll have the cojones to kill me when I'm standing right in front of him. And maybe, if he harbors anything remotely human in that wasted soul of his, I might be able to get him to surrender without a firefight.'

Jarvis stepped onto the bridge, and looked at Ethan and Lopez.

'The Miami-Dade police gained access to a safety-deposit box registered to Charles Purcell at the First National Bank in Miami,' he reported.

'Did they find the documents?' Lopez asked.

'All of them,' Jarvis confirmed. 'Joaquin Abell is now officially wanted for fraud, and the trail of evidence will likely lead to charges of conspiracy, blackmail and murder one. If you can get him out of his lair his next stop will be jail, and after that he'll be on trial.'

58

June 28, 19:56

Ethan clambered down the entry ladder into the deep-submergence vehicle *Intrepid* and moved toward the cockpit as Lopez and Katherine Abell followed him down into the vessel. Doug Jarvis ducked his head through the hatch and called out.

'We'll lower the crane as soon as the hatch is sealed. You won't have communications with the surface due to our jamming of the underwater facility, so you're on your own.'

Lopez looked up at the old man.

'Can't you turn the jamming off now that the yacht's crew is under watch?'

'We can't be sure that Joaquin doesn't have other lines of communication with the shore,' Jarvis said. 'All he'd need is transmitters and tethered buoys and he'd be able to call in reinforcements.'

Ethan scanned the cockpit.

'I can handle these controls,' he said. 'There's enough power in the batteries for the return trip.'

'Understood,' Jarvis said, and flipped Ethan a serious – if upside down – salute. 'Good luck.'

The hatch closed, and Lopez sealed it airtight before taking a seat in the cabin behind Ethan. Katherine squeezed in alongside her and they strapped in, the *Intrepid* swaying as the yacht's crane lifted her off the deck and swung her out over the rolling waves. Moments later the hull shuddered as she was lowered into the ocean and the crane detached with an audible clunk.

Ethan opened the switches to the batteries, turned on the main engines and then pulled a lever on the control panel. The mechanism connecting *Intrepid*'s own clasps to the deck crane opened and the vessel floated free of the yacht on the rolling surface of the ocean. He grabbed both of the control columns before him and gently guided the vessel away from the yacht's hull.

'You sure you know what you're doing there, cap'n?' Lopez asked.

Ethan scanned the controls once more.

'Could have done with Bryson's help, but there's not much to it,' he replied, seeing dials registering oxygen, carbon dioxide and nitrogen levels, and others for ballast tanks, battery-charge and navigation. 'It's like a very slow airplane. This vessel is good for depths up to three thousand feet, and we'll only be going down half that far.'

'Don't remind me,' Lopez muttered, looking around at the walls of the hull. 'It's still six hundred meters. If the hull fails down there we'll be crushed like an eggshell.'

Ethan glanced at the ballast-tank controls and turned a series of dials on the panel. The air in the tanks was expelled as seawater flushed in through the open vents, and *Intrepid* sank beneath the waves. Ethan watched the ocean water slapping against the thick acrylic sphere before him and then the silvery surface of the ocean took the place of the sky. A vibrant cascade of quivering bubbles spiraled up from the underside of the hull like chromium spheres, and then the sounds of the outside world and the thumping heartbeat of waves against the exterior of the hull were silenced.

'Here we go,' he said, and pushed one of the joysticks forward.

The *Intrepid* responded smoothly, her control surfaces tilting and sending the craft down. The battery-powered engines hummed as they descended. Ethan glanced at a pair of dials and saw them registering neutral buoyancy as the *Intrepid* sank deeper into the ocean.

'How do we get up again if all the air's gone from the ballast tanks?' Katherine asked, clearly nervous.

'Compressed air,' Ethan replied, not taking his eyes off the artificial horizon that helped him to keep the vessel upright in the absence of external cues, just like an airplane flying at night. 'I open the valves, the pressurized air drives the seawater from the tanks and I then close the vents. Instant positive buoyancy, and up we go.'

The thought of an airplane's instruments punctured Ethan's mind as he considered the possibility that Joaquin Abell could cripple the *Intrepid* in much the same way as his father had destroyed Montgomery Purcell's airplane in 1964. Ethan decided not to voice his concerns, hoping that having already used his mysterious facility to create an earthquake Joaquin would be reluctant to use it again in the same day for fear of further exposing his position to passing satellites.

A small television screen on the control panel provided a computerized GPS map of their location. With communication to the outside world prevented by the electronic jamming of the Sea Hawk helicopter above, Ethan had downloaded their position into the *Intrepid*'s internal navigation computer before they'd left the ship. Now, he typed in the destination GPS coordinates: a triangulation based upon the electromagnetic pulses picked up by NASA during the earthquake and the gravitational fluctuations detected by the GOCE satellite.

'There,' he said, pointing to a small red flag on the GPS screen as Lopez leaned forward to see over his shoulder. 'He should be there, about four hundred yards ahead of us and right on the seafloor.'

'Any chance he's seen us coming?' she asked.

Ethan shrugged.

'If you mean has he seen the future, almost certainly. But I don't know if he realizes exactly how we're going to find him, or whether or not his signals to the outside world are being intercepted.' He looked over his shoulder. 'Either way, he's as much on his own down there now as we are.'

Katherine looked at Ethan.

'If he's aware of that, it might make him more dangerous, more reckless. Joaquin's arrogance has gotten worse with every passing event. He may believe himself to be invincible, especially if he's seen what's on that camera of Purcell's.'

Ethan watched the ever-darkening ocean outside as it

passed by, small fish and fragments of debris floating up past the porthole.

'Charles told us that what Joaquin sees on his cameras can often be interpreted in many different ways,' he replied. 'Even if he has seen some future news broadcast that shows his own success, doesn't mean that we won't get him in the end.'

'I hope you're right,' Katherine said, sounding unconvinced.

The beams of sunlight from the surface far above had faded, and the blue of the ocean had turned to an inky and impenetrable blackness as devoid of features as the depths of space. Ethan flipped a switch and turned on both his cockpit illumination and a series of low-intensity lights around the interior of the *Intrepid*. The soft yellow glow of the instrument panel seemed warm and inviting compared to the frigid darkness beyond the portholes.

'I can't see anything,' Lopez said, peering out into the gloom.

Ethan guided the *Intrepid* deeper until the pressure gauges were reading forces that could crush a human being like a grape. The GPS marker was now barely a hundred yards away from them, and as Ethan slowed his descent the external lights picked up the barren abyssal plain below. The *Intrepid*'s engines whipped up small vortices of sand on the surface as he leveled the vessel out some ten feet above the seafloor and glided toward where the IRIS facility should be.

Lopez and Katherine both leaned forward either side of him, their eyes straining into the blackness ahead for some sign of the base.

'There.' Lopez pointed ahead and just to their left. 'Coordinates were slightly out.'

Ethan squinted into the blackness and was just able to make out the faintest light, like a star seen from the corner of the eye glimmering faintly in an endless night. He turned the *Intrepid* toward the light, and as they closed in more lights began to appear: small, round, glowing yellow balls that penetrated only a short distance into the gloom.

Nobody said anything as the facility resolved itself before their eyes, the *Intrepid*'s lights reflecting off two large, dull metal spheres surrounded by four smaller ones. Ethan guessed that each of the larger spheres was large enough to hold an Olympic swimming pool, with the smaller spheres the size of a house.

'This is where he filtered all of that cash,' Ethan said. 'It would have taken millions of dollars to construct a place like this. The documents that Charles Purcell stole must have detailed the construction of this site and the funds to finance it.'

Ethan could see a broad, rectangular beam of light glowing from the underside of one of the smaller outer spheres, suggesting some kind of entrance, but all the rest appeared impenetrable.

'Only one way in,' Lopez observed. 'Convenient for an ambush.'

Ethan looked at the vast construction, big enough that in the darkness he could not see across its entire circumference.

Katherine Abell watched as Ethan guided the *Intrepid* beneath the outer dome toward the docking station. Her face was haunted as she surveyed the complex, clearly stunned that in all of the years that she had been married to Joaquin she had never laid eyes on the site.

'Joaquin's father was involved with all manner of secret government experiments after the Second World War,' Katherine said. 'Joaquin may have acquired and improved or extended them. And anybody else who was involved in the construction . . .'

'. . . Suffered unfortunate accidents later on,' Ethan finished, when Katherine trailed off. 'Joaquin is willing to do anything to cover his tracks.'

Ethan aimed the *Intrepid* carefully toward the opening, and as they passed underneath the dome so the glowing veil of yellow light from the interior of the docking station above filled the vessel. Ethan leaned forward and peered up through the porthole above his head. He moved the vessel into position and then reached down and flicked a pair of switches, closing the ballast vents. Ensuring that the compressed air tanks were set to 'Cross Feed' he turned the dials open for a brief moment.

A hiss of released gas filled the hull, vibrating gently through the floor panels as the seawater was expelled and the *Intrepid* rose up and broke the surface of the water into a docking bay. Light filled the cockpit as Ethan looked at the dock through the sheets of water draining across the acrylic porthole.

'Nobody here to meet us,' he said.

Lopez unbuckled herself from her seat. 'They know we're here all right.'

Ethan unstrapped, and shut down the engines and batteries to conserve power. He drew his pistol from its holster and hurried to the main hatch of the submersible with Katherine Abell just behind him. Lopez stood ready, one hand on the hatch and the other holding her own weapon.

'Ready?' she asked.

'I've got your back,' Ethan said. 'The dock exit is to our left,' he added and pulled a flash-bang grenade out, handing it to her.

'You set that off, they'll hear you coming!' Katherine said in alarm.

'We're way past that,' Lopez replied without looking at her. She holstered her pistol, grabbed the hatch and span the wheel. Moments later she shoved the hatch open and leapt up the ladder, pulling the pin on the flash-bang as she hurled it toward the dock's exit corridor.

59

The grenade arced across the dock and clattered against the deck panels as it vanished into the adjoining corridor. A terrific blast of noise and light flared outside and Lopez hauled herself up and out of the submersible. Ethan followed her with his pistol drawn as they tumbled down the *Intrepid*'s hull and leapt onto the dock.

Ethan ducked down behind one of the steel mooring bollards and aimed down the corridor through the faint wisps of smoke writhing from the flash-bang. He saw no movement, no soldiers, no gunfire. Nothing.

'That was too easy,' Lopez said from where she squatted behind a similar bollard.

'Much too easy,' Ethan agreed, and called back to Katherine. 'Clear.'

Katherine Abell popped her head out of the *Intrepid*'s hatch before climbing out and watching as Ethan grabbed a mooring line and secured the submersible.

'Tie her loosely,' he said to Lopez. 'We don't know if we'll have to leave in a hurry.'

454   DEAN CRAWFORD

'I won't be hanging around,' she replied, and looked up at the dome above her, clearly imagining the near half-mile of water pressing down upon it. 'Trust me.'

The adjoining corridor was lit by overhead panels, and narrow portholes on either side looked out into the darkness; but nothing cluttered their path as they walked into the complex.

'The other submersible must be docked off one of the other arms,' Lopez said.

'The *Event Horizon* is normally anchored to the northeast of the coral-research station,' Katherine confirmed, 'because of the strong currents in the Florida Straits. It means that although Joaquin's submersibles have to use more battery power to get here against the current, you can float out easily enough on minimum power and get back up to the yacht in the event of an emergency. My guess is that the other submersible will be docked on the southwest side.'

Ethan made a mental note.

'What's the time?' Lopez asked, as they neared the end of the corridor where an open hatch awaited, mindful of the deadline that Charles Purcell had set them.

Ethan glanced at his watch. 'Twenty eighteen hours,' he replied, 'only thirty minutes until Charles Purcell said everything would end. So there's not long left to—' He broke off and stopped in mid-pace to stare at the face of his watch.

'What?' Lopez asked.

Ethan watched in disbelief as the second hand on his watch ticked its way around the dial. He counted several ticks, unable to comprehend what he was seeing.

'My watch is ticking too slowly,' he uttered.

'Battery's running out,' Lopez suggested.

Katherine looked at her own watch, a digital one, and her jaw dropped.

'No, he's right, look.'

Ethan looked at the digital seconds counting up on the display. Even the digital watch was being distorted by something.

'It's like time has slowed down,' he said.

'It wasn't like it on the way down here,' Katherine said.

Ethan struggled to comprehend how it could happen.

'The guys at Cape Canaveral told us that black holes wrap time and space around them,' he said. 'But if that's the case, surely if Joaquin Abell really has one here, and it's exposed, then it should be consuming the entire facility around it?'

'I don't know,' Lopez said. 'Maybe he's got it contained, but somehow some of its effects are still getting out, like a leak?'

'Hell of a thing to spring a leak from,' Ethan pointed out.

'You say we've only got until 8:48 to finish this,' Katherine said to him.

'Yeah, barely half an hour until the time Charles Purcell said everything would end. He wrote a message on the wall of an apartment in Miami, then confirmed to us later that this would all end at 8:48 this evening.'

'Well then you've actually got longer, isn't that right? If time runs slower here because of Joaquin's black hole, maybe you've got forty minutes instead.'

'No,' Lopez replied. 'Purcell wrote that time on the apartment wall from his point of reference outside of the black hole's influence. This will be over in normal time on the surface or in Miami, no matter what happens to our watches down here.'

Ethan looked ahead to where another open hatch vanished into the unknown. The two other hatches to either side of it were closed and locked.

'Whatever he's got down here, it's powerful enough to slow down time for us the closer we get to it. Come on.'

Ethan led the way up to the open hatch and he and Lopez took position either side of it.

'Ready?'

Lopez nodded, and then with one swift motion they plunged through the hatch, weapons trained on the broad open hangar before them. And then they stopped, jaws agape. Ethan lowered his pistol, words piling up in his mind but unable to break through the seal of disbelief that tied his lips.

'That's impossible,' Lopez stammered. 'How could they be down here?'

Ethan shook his head, his mind devoid of an adequate explanation for what they were looking at.

Parked in what clearly was being used as a storage space, their hulls and wings sagging with age, were the remains of countless boats and aircraft.

60

June 28, 19:59

'They're inside the hangar. Shall I intercept them?'

Dennis Aubrey watched as a bank of remote cameras followed Warner, Lopez and Katherine Abell as they advanced through the complex. Olaf stood by Joaquin's side, one hand already moving toward the pistol in his shoulder holster.

'No, let them come,' Joaquin replied. 'We are ready.'

Joaquin stood with his hands behind his back and his chin held high, comfortable in his conviction that he was now entirely unassailable. Surrounding him were ten highly trained, highly disciplined soldiers. Aubrey knew that all of them were mercenaries and former members of the United States' finest regiments, who had been plucked from desolate warzones around the world to serve IRIS. Money – more even than they had been paid by various foreign governments – secured their absolute allegiance.

'We will engage them just before they reach us, in the hangar,' he decided. 'No sense in risking a wild shot breaching the black-hole chamber and dragging us all to oblivion.'

He pointed ahead and the troops jogged away in a neat phalanx toward an exit hatch that led through a bulkhead into the next sphere. As soon as the rumble of their combat boots had faded, Joaquin turned to Aubrey.

'Contact the *Event Horizon*,' he ordered the physicist, as he donned a slim microphone and earpiece. 'Have them prepare to sail. I'll need to be ashore by this evening or there'll be no spokesperson to coordinate the media response to IRIS's intervention in the earthquake crisis.'

Aubrey keyed a communication channel, opened it and selected the yacht's frequency. Almost immediately a burst of high-pitched static howled through amplifiers on the control panel.

Aubrey scrambled to turn the volume down as Joaquin whirled, his face twisted with outrage as he tore off his microphone.

'What the fuck are you doing, Dennis?!'

Aubrey shut the channel off and stared at the panel before him.

'Nothing. We're being jammed,' he said. 'Static interference from the surface.'

Joaquin looked at Aubrey for a moment, then at Olaf.

'The three of them came down here alone, correct?' he asked the big man.

'We tracked them here in one vehicle, the *Intrepid*,' Olaf confirmed. 'They are only three.'

Joaquin looked at Aubrey, the first mild tremor of apprehension in his expression.

'They must have had help, on the surface,' Joaquin surmised, realizing the extent of his sudden and unexpected isolation. 'The yacht must have been compromised.'

Olaf understood immediately and unclipped his pistol from his shoulder holster.

'We will bring Warner and his friend here,' he promised Joaquin. 'Then we will go to the surface and retake the yacht.'

Joaquin nodded, but his features had paled slightly.

'Do it, and feel free to use whatever force you deem necessary.'

Olaf's broad jaw creased with a cold grin of satisfaction as he turned and strode purposefully toward the bulkhead where the soldiers had dispersed, ducking through the hatch and shutting it behind him.

Dennis Aubrey stood still behind the control panel and looked down at Joaquin as the tycoon stared vacantly into space for a moment, no doubt considering his next move. There would be no other chance to do this, Aubrey realized. For the first time since he had been transported down into this godforsaken prison beneath the waves, he was both alone with Joaquin and had the element of surprise on his side.

He reached into the back of his jeans and felt the pistol nestled there. If he waited until Olaf and his goons returned, he wouldn't stand a chance. They would gun him down within seconds. He reminded himself that he would probably be gunned down soon enough anyway, so there was little to lose by procrastinating over—

'Dennis!' Joaquin's voice smashed through the scientist's thoughts. 'I said play that fucking camera right now, or I swear I'll have Olaf send you to the surface the slow and horrible way!'

Aubrey looked at the arrogant, self-serving, manipulative little prick of a man who, in so little time, had caused Aubrey so much grief and despair, and the possibility of vengeance sparked flames of rage within him. Aubrey felt a hot rush of anger tingle up his spine and shudder through his synapses as he stepped down off the control deck, elation and fear coursing through his veins.

Joaquin glared at him.

'What the hell are you doing, you insolent little—'

Aubrey reached around beneath his shirt, yanked the pistol from his jeans and aimed it at Joaquin the way he had seen it done in the movies a thousand times. He saw the flare of alarm in Joaquin's eyes, anger quashed by fear as the younger man threw his hands up in surrender.

'Now, Dennis, take it easy. I just need to see the—'

'Shut up!' Dennis snapped.

Joaquin's jaw clamped shut as he backed away from the gun. A flood of elation rushed through Aubrey, a heady elixir of power and control borne of the complete command of another human being. He aimed at Joaquin's chest, not making the mistake of trying to shoot the tycoon somewhere difficult like the head, where the pistol might miss and give Joaquin the chance to counterattack. And he kept well out of arm's reach, preventing Joaquin from grabbing the pistol. Aubrey knew his cop shows all right.

'This is what you really are, Joaquin,' Aubrey growled, as Joaquin backed up another pace and hit the side of the control panel. 'A coward, a bully who gets others to do his dirty work for him.'

Joaquin's jaw worked to free itself from his fear as he coughed his response.

'Dennis, there's no need for this, we can work this out together.'

'Shut it, you creep,' Aubrey snarled. 'All these years you've had it all, but you didn't earn a damned bit of it: you inherited your father's money, inherited his looks, inherited his decency, but then turned it into greed because you've never had to work for anything in your pathetic little life.' Aubrey took another pace toward Joaquin, towering over him for the first time in his life, and a confidence he had rarely felt soared through him as he shouted, 'And you took Katherine away from me! She thought you were worthy, thought you were a good man. *I* was the good man! And then you tried to murder her, like you murdered everybody else!'

Joaquin's eyes quivered with tears as he crouched down, his raised hands instinctively moving to cover his head.

'Please, Dennis, there is another way. You don't have to do this. We've almost won, it's almost over. You can go back to your family, your friends.'

'Like Charles Purcell did?' Aubrey challenged. 'Like the people that built this place did? Like the scientists who helped capture your black holes did?' Aubrey tilted his head mockingly at the man now cowering before him. 'Oh, no, I forgot, you had them all killed, didn't you, little Joaquin?'

Joaquin's trembling voice collapsed into choking noises as tears fell from his eyes.

'Please, Dennis, they were all fools. They weren't like you, Dennis. You don't have to kill me.'

Aubrey smiled, no longer afraid of this man. He aimed the pistol squarely at Joaquin's chest.

'Yes, Joaquin,' Aubrey smiled without pity. 'I do.'

Joaquin let out a howl of fear as Aubrey smiled and squeezed the trigger. The pistol clacked loudly, but nothing happened. Aubrey pulled the trigger again and the weapon clicked ineffectually. At his feet Joaquin was still howling, but Aubrey realized with a cold dread that the tycoon was not crying – his body was shaking with uncontrollable laughter. Aubrey stared uncomprehendingly at the pistol in his hand and then pulled the trigger again.

'You're more of a fool than even I gave you credit for, Dennis.'

Joaquin's delight faded away as his joy mutated grotesquely into undiluted fury. Aubrey felt a pulse of terror as Joaquin leapt up from the floor, all pretence of fear gone, and reached out to snatch the pistol from Aubrey with one hand whilst the knuckles of his other fist cracked across Aubrey's cheek.

The scientist cried out in pain at the impact as he lost his balance and slammed down onto the floor, his elbow cracking against the metal plates. He saw Joaquin follow him and a moment later the younger man's boot crashed into Aubrey's face and splattered blood onto the metal deck plates.

'You gutless fucking traitor!' Joaquin shrieked as he smashed the butt of the pistol down onto Aubrey's head, metal scraping across his scalp as the blow reverberated painfully through his brain, and thick, metallic blood spilled into his mouth.

Aubrey desperately tried to deflect the blows, his face numbed and his arms pulsing with agony at each strike of the weapon.

Joaquin suddenly stopped, his breath heaving in his lungs as he towered over Aubrey's coiled body. The scientist peered up at him through his pain and saw Joaquin chuckle.

'You didn't seriously believe that I'd let you get away with it, did you?' he asked. 'Sending those signals to the surface? Breaking into the armory? Olaf always leaves the clips there filled with inert bullets, because he always told me that one day somebody would try something stupid. They always do.' He shook his head slowly as he tossed the useless pistol to clatter alongside Aubrey, before drawing a pistol of his own from beneath his jacket. 'This one works, Dennis. Get up.'

Aubrey hauled himself off the deck as Joaquin aimed the pistol at him and then gestured for him to turn around. From his jacket pocket he produced a set of steel handcuffs.

'Put these on,' Joaquin ordered.

Dennis clipped the cuffs around his left wrist, trying to ignore the grinding fear that plagued his stomach. Joaquin stepped in and grabbed him, span him around and secured the cuffs behind his back. Then he turned Aubrey back around and looked at him appraisingly.

'Now then, Dennis, you're in luck. I'm going to let you continue your work on black holes,' he said brightly, and then leaned in close to Aubrey's face with a cruel smile. 'Up close and personal.'

Strangely, now that his doom was certain, Aubrey no longer felt any fear for himself, as though the inevitability of it had scoured the dread from his mind. His only concern now was for Katherine Abell's safety.

'What goes around,' Aubrey said, 'comes around.'

Even as Joaquin's smile withered slightly at Aubrey's unexpected defiance, the crackle of distant machine-gun fire shattered the silence.

'It would appear that my men have found your friends, Dennis,' Joaquin sneered.

Aubrey felt the last pitiful remnants of resistance trickle feebly from his body as he realized that, finally, his life was about to come to an end.

And he hoped that he had already done enough to doom Joaquin.

61

June 28, 20:06

Ethan stared up at the aircraft nearest him, the fuselage caked with the rust of ages. The undercarriage had collapsed long ago and the markings had faded, but not enough to conceal the navy-blue paint on the remaining panels or the prominent white stars painted on the tip of each wing.

'I'll be damned,' he uttered, 'a TBM Avenger torpedo bomber.'

Katherine Abell glanced at the stocky-looking Second World War airplane, the serial number FT-36 emblazoned down the fuselage beside the starred banner of the United States Navy.

'How'd you know that?' she asked.

'The Bermuda Triangle,' Ethan replied. 'Flight 19, five aircraft, all Avengers, were lost on a training mission off the coast of Florida, December 5, 1945. No trace of the aircraft was ever found. The same day, a PBM-5 Mariner seaplane sent to search for them also vanished, reportedly having exploded in midair. The last radio transmissions from the Avengers said that they were unable to find their way home. Doug's research said that Isaac Abell had been experimenting with powerful electromagnets in the Florida Straits as early as 1941 – maybe his work inadvertently caused the loss of Flight 19.'

Ethan looked past the crippled Avenger to where a more modern-looking airplane rested on its belly near a small fishing vessel.

'Recognize that?' he asked her.

Lopez nodded as she peered at the twin engine aircraft.

'November 2-7-6-4-charlie,' she read the numbers off the tail. 'Joaquin's men must have brought it here.'

'No evidence, no National Transport and Safety Board investigation and no danger of prosecution for Joaquin,' Ethan said. 'All he had to do was locate the wreck and hide it here.'

Katherine's hand flew to her mouth.

'That's the airplane that had all of Joaquin's scientists aboard,' she gasped.

'The same,' Lopez replied. 'Joaquin ensured that, after they had completed building his machine for seeing into the future, they would never be able to pass on what they had learned.'

Ethan scanned the rest of the underwater hangar. Various small fishing vessels leaned at awkward angles, their crippled hulls stained red with rust and the passing of the years, whilst a number of other civilian aircraft lay on their bellies like steel whales stranded on a foreign shore. Like a museum of past tragedies, thought Ethan, as he realized just how these long-lost vessels and aircraft must have come to be here.

'This part of the facility has been here for a long time,' he said finally. 'Joaquin built on the work that his father began, back in the fifties. His attempts to create a machine that would power the world caused accidents to ships and aircraft on the surface above, and in doing so created the legend of the Bermuda Triangle. These wrecks must have been covered up by the military at the time: they wouldn't have wanted to draw attention to their work here. This facility was shut down in 1964, and Joaquin bought it from the military when it was no longer used. Doug reckons that all of the paperwork relating to the site was handed over during the sale.'

Lopez gestured up to the domed ceiling above them.

'Those beams, they're heavyweight steel,' she observed, 'but the ones in the docking bay were newer and slimmer.'

'More modern,' Ethan agreed. 'That's how Joaquin was able to do this without attracting too much attention. Easy to say you're working on coral-reef conservation projects to cover what you're really up to, and with this dome already in place you'd be able to extend outward without the hassle of starting from scratch. Hell, I'd bet that the newer domes are some kind of prefabricated constructions, easy to transport down here from his yacht.'

Lopez was about to answer, but the voice that they heard came from speakers set into the walls of the hangar.

'Congratulations, Mr. Warner, you're absolutely right.'

Ethan glimpsed movement from behind the hull of a fishing vessel twenty yards away, and in the same moment saw half a dozen armed men break from cover, running toward them with assault rifles cradled in their grasp. Ethan hurled himself down with Lopez and Katherine behind the fuselage of one of the Avenger bombers, as a broadside of machine-gun fire raked their position. Bullets clattered through the rusting metal hulks with a spray of bright-orange sparks and burst out above them, showering them with red dust.

'We're outnumbered!' he yelled to Lopez. 'I saw at least six.'

Katherine ducked down and shielded her head with her hands as she shouted.

'Tell him to stop firing! They'll puncture the dome and kill us all!'

Ethan, sheltering behind the Avenger's brittle fuselage, looked across to the fishing vessel to their right, its hull equally aged but constructed of thicker steel. He motioned to Lopez, who was also looking at the ship.

'On three, I'll cover you.'

Lopez nodded, grabbing hold of Katherine's arm as she braced her for their planned dash across the hangar. Ethan peeked over the top of the Avenger's fuselage and saw Joaquin's men gathered in two groups of five at each end of the largest ship in the hangar.

'Three, two, one, *go!*'

Ethan leapt up and rested his arms across the top of the fuselage as he fired a rapid series of shots at the enemy's positions. Lopez and Katherine dashed out from behind the Avenger and across open space toward the fishing vessel.

Both groups of Joaquin's men ducked down as Ethan's

salvo battered their positions, bullets ricocheting off the ship's small bridge with loud cracks and twangs that echoed around the dome. Ethan fired a final two shots at each group and then rushed out toward the fishing vessel where Lopez and Katherine now crouched.

A vicious shower of bullets thundered across Ethan's field of vision, cracking the metal tiles that lined the hangar floor with bright snaking lines of sparks that leapt like electrical fields around Ethan's legs. He realized with a sudden plunging terror that the aim of their opponents was arrow straight, each bullet snapping at his heels and cracking through the air past his head, the shockwaves assaulting his eardrums. He sprinted across the hangar and hurled himself down into cover behind the reassuringly solid hull of the ship. His heart was trying to hammer its way out of his chest as he slid along the floor, and he saw stars flashing before his eyes as he gasped for air.

'Too close,' Lopez said, seeing Ethan's expression. 'These guys know what they're doing.'

Ethan nodded and blinked sweat from his eyes as he realized just how close he had come to being shot. The IRIS soldiers had stopped firing the moment he had gotten into cover: *conserving their ammunition, keeping their cool*. In fact, he decided as he regained his breath, they could not have failed to hit him at such close range.

'They aren't shooting to kill,' he said.

Katherine Abell looked at him, a feeble star of hope twinkling in her eyes. 'You think that this is all for show?'

Ethan peered carefully around the edge of the hull and shook his head.

'No, they're holding us back for some reason. Joaquin's a narcissistic megalomaniac and wants us dead, I'm sure of that. He just wants it done *his* way.'

As if in reply, Joaquin's voice echoed through the hangar from the speakers.

'Mr. Warner, Miss Lopez, you are outnumbered, outgunned and swiftly being flanked. I would ask that you surrender your weapons so that we can prevent any unnecessary bloodshed.'

Ethan smirked bitterly as he shouted out his reply.

'It's a bit late for that, Joaquin! You've already got the blood of several thousand people on your hands, not least the men that built this place for you.' He looked across at the wreckage of N-2764C, and wondered just how much Joaquin's men knew about their boss. 'I suspect that the NTSB would like to take a look at that aircraft, the one that you downed, killing the twenty-or-so scientists on board.'

Joaquin replied quietly, letting the speakers amplify his voice.

'All men must choose their allegiance, Mr. Warner,' he said.

'They had no choice!' Lopez shouted back. 'You're a murderer with a juvenile ego, Joaquin. You send others to kill for you because you don't have the guts to do it for yourself, you limp-dicked motherf—'

A rattle of gunfire drowned her out, bullets raking over their heads as Ethan wrapped an arm protectively around Katherine's shoulders and ducked down. He could tell from the blasts that the two groups were moving around the opposite edges of the hangar to flank them. Another few moments and the soldiers would be able to fire with impunity, and their cover behind the fishing vessel would be rendered useless.

Joaquin's voice echoed down to them from the speakers as the gunfire stopped abruptly.

'Surrender your weapons, or I'll order my men to finish this once and for all!'

'He'll kill us as soon as he's disarmed us,' Lopez said.

It was Katherine who replied. 'You don't know that.'

Before Ethan could stop her, Katherine stood up and walked out into the open with her hands outstretched at her sides. Ethan watched as she looked up at one of the speakers above them.

'Is this what you want, Joaquin?' she shouted out. 'A few more people to kill?'

The hangar remained silent but for the fast, light footfalls of the IRIS soldiers as they regrouped and moved into position, their weapons trained on Katherine. Ethan saw the big blond assassin at their head on his right, as the men moved from cover, no longer even trying to avoid being shot. They had the advantage of both numbers and position, and they knew it.

'That went well,' Lopez muttered as she laid her weapon down.

Ethan sighed and tossed his pistol down onto the tiles before kicking it away toward the nearest soldiers.

He stood up and placed his hands behind his head as the big man approached, flanked by his soldiers. Quickly, both Ethan and Lopez were patted down and their spare ammunition clips taken from them. Olaf walked up behind Ethan and gave him a shove in Katherine's direction.

As he joined her with Lopez in the center of the hangar, Joaquin's voice chortled down at them.

'Excellent! There, now, that wasn't so hard, was it? Olaf, please escort our guests into the control room.'

Ethan, Lopez and Katherine were shoved and prodded forward by rifle barrels that guided them past the largest fishing vessel toward a bulkhead at the far end of the hangar that was flanked by a pair of bright red fire axes mounted on the walls. Ethan briefly considered trying to make a move for one of them, but the soldiers were far too close. As they approached the bulkhead one of the soldiers, a man who looked to be in his early thirties, jogged ahead and shouldered his weapon before yanking the hatch open.

As Ethan ducked his head to move through, he glanced at the soldier.

'You know Joaquin's going to kill you, too, eventually?'

The soldier grinned without sympathy.

'The secret to staying alive,' he hissed, 'is to not ask fucking questions.'

With that, Ethan was propelled through the hatch and into the control room.

62

Joaquin Abell stood behind a raised control panel that was located on one side of the dome. Ethan saw immediately the large plasma screens arranged around the walls, and the huge metallic sphere in the center.

'Welcome,' Joaquin said, spreading his arms wide to encompass the dome around them, 'to the beating heart of IRIS.'

Ethan saw another man sitting near Joaquin. He was small and bespectacled, and Ethan guessed that he must be Dennis Aubrey, the scientist that Joaquin had effectively abducted.

Ethan, with Lopez and Katherine either side of him, was prodded to stand before the control panel as Joaquin stepped jauntily down to meet them, his face plastered with a bright smile.

'I must say,' he began, 'that I wish this meeting could have occurred under more cordial circumstances, but alas, such is life.'

'You saw us coming,' Lopez muttered.

'Of course I saw you coming,' Joaquin replied and gestured to the giant sphere nearby. 'I have foreseen everything that is about to happen here. I should thank you, both of you, for locating Charles Purcell on my behalf and providing me with the camera he stole. It has proven remarkably entertaining, I must say, to watch the pair of you die, and yet it simply cannot be as satisfying as watching it happen for real.'

Ethan shook his head.

'I think your ego is so inflated that you can no longer see where you're going.'

'Is that such a bad thing?' Joaquin wondered out loud. 'So many people are so meek, so mild. Our society has taught us to be conservative, to be magnanimous in defeat, to bow to the wishes of others. Crap, I say. Grab everything that's yours, do anything you can to achieve your goals, even if it means pushing others out of the way, because when it comes down to it they'd do the same to you in the blink of an eye. This is a dog-eat-dog kind of world, Mr. Warner, and I am a wolf.'

Lopez's face twisted into a grim smile.

'You're only a wolf in that you're a cunning animal who is brave in a pack but a coward alone.'

Joaquin smiled pityingly.

'And yet such a wise and rapid wit as yourself was not able to enter this facility and achieve her objectives without being caught by this *sly, cowardly animal,*' he said. 'You may enjoy your insults, but they will be the last you'll ever cast in this life, you little—'

'What's the point of all this, Joaquin?' Ethan cut across him. 'Your device lets you see into the future. It could have won you a Nobel Prize, changed the future of humanity for the better by foreseeing and then preventing natural disasters. You'd have been adored by millions, gotten everything you wanted. Instead, you're stuck down here on the seabed with your machine, like an overgrown teenage computer geek, planning apocalyptic disasters. Why?'

Joaquin appeared confused.

'Why?' he uttered. '*Why?* You've come all of this way to stop me and you don't even know why I'm here?'

'You're here because you're a fucking lunatic,' Lopez shot at him. 'A sane man would be using this contraption of yours for *good*.'

'For *good*,' Joaquin echoed. 'That word, it's *so* subjective. What's good for one person may be lethal for another. I'm doing this because our world is in a mess, crippled by economic fallout from unregulated capitalism, dogged by climate change, scoured by over-population. It needs strong leadership, and within a few years I, and IRIS, will be able to provide absolute control over not just government, but over our own futures. We will be able to shape this world precisely as we wish.'

Ethan chuckled bitterly.

'I doubt that very much. Life just doesn't fit into boxes, Joaquin, no matter how much control you think you might have.'

'Control,' Joaquin growled and clenched a fist between them, 'is everything.'

'You're not controlling anything,' Ethan pointed out. 'That thing you've got in that chamber, it's not a weapon: it's a force of nature, more powerful than any bomb mankind could build and capable of bringing about the end of the world. If it gets out, there won't be a world left for you to manipulate. Everything will be gone. Your control is a fantasy and you're as much at the mercy of fate as the rest of us.'

'And what would you know of it?' Joaquin snapped. 'I did a little digging of my own, after you visited my yacht. Look at you. You're a washed-out soldier and journalist, a lowly gumshoe from a two-bit detective agency buried in Illinois. What possible difference can you make to this world compared to IRIS?'

'Just preventing you from gaining a position of power would be a great service to humanity,' Ethan replied. 'That'll be more than enough.'

Joaquin's face twisted upon itself in apparent frustration.

'You don't understand. You're just tiny little people, insignificant parts of a giant machine that cares nothing for your opinion or actions. I am in a position to change this world for the better, for all humanity, and it requires such a small sacrifice.'

'Sure,' Lopez smirked, 'what's a few thousand lives here and there for your greater good?'

'Opportunity follows crisis!' Joaquin shouted. 'There is never gain without loss. I have built this, all of this, to gain the faith and trust of humanity. Mankind does not move forward in small and gradual steps. It takes a revolution to drive our progress, and I am producing one right here. This is more than just the future: this is control of the present, to bring all countries into alignment, to provide equality and safety for all.'

'And if people do not want you to control them?' Ethan asked.

'Everything I have done,' Joaquin shot back, 'every single action, has been with the intention of helping humanity climb out of its self-destructive existence and move toward a better future. Idle government will be replaced with proactive IRIS rule that protects us all against tomorrow. I built this place to *protect* humanity!'

Ethan finally got it, in a brief flash of clarity that shone through the gloom of Joaquin's warped ego. In a moment of inspiration he glimpsed Joaquin's vision and the fragile state of mind that harbored it.

'You haven't built a thing,' he said.

Joaquin sneered at him.

'This entire facility was built by IRIS, under my command, the better to—'

'You're nothing, Joaquin, nothing at all,' Ethan interrupted. 'This is all about little Joaquin living up to his daddy's name. You've spent your life trying to emulate a great man, but in doing so you've done nothing but revealed what a hugely inadequate son you really were to him.'

'What are you talking about?' Joaquin stammered. 'You never even knew—'

'Everybody has heard of your father,' Ethan replied, 'of the things that Isaac Abell achieved. But you? Everything people think they know about you is a lie, a mask. You've spent your life trying to convince people that you're some kind of great philanthropist, but in truth you're nothing but a spoilt little psychopath. Even this facility we're standing in was built by your father, not by you: all you've done is stand on his coat tails, adding little bits and pieces to what he himself created.

Everything you are is a scam, a theft of other people's ideas.' He stepped closer to Joaquin. 'Tell me, little man, of one single item in this facility that you built or invented all by yourself.'

Joaquin stared at Ethan, his jaw agape and his skin flushing red.

Ethan took another pace forward, standing just inches from him.

'Tell me, Joaquin, what's it like to be a billionaire who can see into the future, and yet to still feel so totally and utterly inadequate?'

Joaquin quivered as psychological tremors wrought havoc in his mind. The tycoon whipped one small fist up at Ethan. The blow landed on Ethan's cheek with a sharp crack, but it lacked force. Ethan barely flinched, and smiled.

'Not much weight to anything about you, is there, Joaquin?'

Joaquin trembled with fury, as though he were struggling to keep the lid on a boiling cauldron of anger.

'You've a nerve, Mr. Warner,' he uttered, 'to insult me when your life is in my hands.'

'It's not in your hands,' Ethan replied. 'Like everything else, it's in other people's hands, because you can't do it for yourself. In one way you're just like your father, Joaquin – he wasn't able to commit murder himself, either.'

Joaquin's expression fell flat, his eyes uncomprehending.

'Didn't know about that, did you, little Joaquin?' Lopez chimed in with a brittle grin. 'That your wonderful daddy murdered Montgomery Purcell all those years ago.'

Joaquin's jaw opened and closed like a beached fish as he struggled to speak.

'That's insane! You're making this all up!'

'Isaac Abell first tested the device that he built here in 1964, on the very same evening that Montgomery Purcell flew home from a meeting with him,' Ethan said. 'It was timed perfectly by Isaac, so that the magnetic fields generated by his fusion chamber would wreck the instruments in Monty Purcell's airplane as he flew overhead. The man didn't stand a chance.'

'That's bullshit!' Joaquin shouted. 'My father was an honorable man!'

'Yes, he was,' Lopez said. 'It's why he took his own life nine years later. He could not deal with the grief of having murdered a man. He killed for what he thought were good reasons, because he believed that Montgomery Purcell's mission was to make money from building weapons. But in fact Purcell simply understood that mutually assured destruction could prevent a nuclear holocaust.'

'Point is,' Ethan said, his face inches from Joaquin's, 'your father killed a man whom he thought was trying to dominate the world by using weapons against it. How do you think he would have felt about what you've done with his work since?'

Joaquin's skin flushed an unhealthy pallor, but he forced a feeble grin onto his face as he spoke.

'You'll find, Mr. Warner, that I'm made of a little more than you give me credit for.'

'Surprise me,' Ethan said.

Joaquin held out his hand past Ethan.

'My dear?' Joaquin asked.

Katherine stepped forward, and, to Ethan's dismay, turned to face them as she stood alongside her husband. Ethan saw in her features a bizarre mixture of relief and shame, as though she had been handed the secrets of the universe and then destroyed them out of spite.

'Katherine?' Lopez uttered.

'Is with me,' Joaquin said, his features locked into a smile that seemed more like a grimace. 'No matter what you may think of me, my wife has stood by my side for fourteen years and stands with me now. My dear, are they alone?'

Katherine nodded.

'It is just the three of us,' she replied. 'The other one, Bryson, quit. The marines on the yacht are under orders to stay put.'

'As I suspected,' Joaquin said. 'Your friend walked, didn't he, Mr. Warner, just as soon as you were reunited in Miami. I have been watching. The news reports on the survivors flown in to Miami – you were all in the background, standing around that truck.'

Ethan shook his head slowly, ignoring Joaquin. 'This is a mistake, Katherine, and you know it.'

'There is nothing that I will not do for my children,' she replied.

'This isn't about your children!' Lopez said. 'Thousands will die because of this!'

'And thousands more will live,' Katherine shot back. 'Criminals captured, lying politicians exposed, corporate greed slain, all by IRIS's ability to see into the future. This is the greatest opportunity in the history of mankind to cleanse the legal system of its corruption and the distorted motivations of its practitioners.'

Ethan let a bitter smile curl from his lips.

'By using fraud, corruption and the manipulation of government to get your own way?'

'What I'm doing,' Katherine uttered, barely able to meet his eye, 'is morally wrong here and now, and will cost lives. But it will save countless more in the future. The needs of the many always outweigh the needs of the few.'

'Bet you're glad that Bryson and I didn't feel that way when we got you out of Puerto Plata,' Lopez spat at her. 'Did you forget your husband tried to kill you there?'

Katherine refused to meet her accusing glare, but it was neither Ethan's nor Lopez's tortured cry that challenged her.

'Katherine!'

They all turned, to see Dennis Aubrey's face crippled with dismay and horror. Joaquin glared at the scientist but it was Katherine who spoke.

'I'm sorry, Dennis,' she said softly. 'This is the only way.'

'No!' Aubrey yelled. 'Think of what's really best for your children!'

'Our children are not your concern!' Joaquin snarled. 'Olaf, take him to the chamber. Take them all to the chamber!'

Ethan was prodded forward as Olaf shoved him toward the giant sphere in the center of the hangar.

63

'Joaquin, what are you doing?' said Katherine.

Ethan thought that he heard the first ripple of concern in her voice as they were led toward the giant sphere in the center of the dome. Nearby, he saw Dennis Aubrey being lifted out of a chair by two IRIS soldiers and dragged toward the sphere.

'It is time,' Joaquin announced grandly, 'to demonstrate the power that I hold over time itself.'

Joaquin reached the sphere just before Ethan and Lopez, and turned to face them.

'Because,' he said, 'I hold the ability not just to see into the future, but also to erase any trace of the past.'

Katherine stared at her husband. 'What do you mean?'

'The black hole,' Joaquin replied ecstatically, all of his previous rage forgotten now as he returned to his scripted plan. His mood swings were like those of a child, Ethan realized, erratic and unpredictable. 'Nothing, not even light, can escape from its grasp. Even suspended within this chamber, protected as we are from its influence, time still runs slightly slower in this facility than it does in the outside world. It's a shame for our guests, because were they not about to cease to exist I would have done them a favor. They would have aged a little less than the rest of the population of our planet during the time they've spent down here.'

'Sadly,' Lopez uttered, 'the time hasn't exactly flown by.'

Joaquin grinned, not letting her jibe contaminate his obvious enjoyment.

'But it's about to,' he said. 'As one gets closer to a black hole, so time flows more slowly. If you travel to the edge of a black hole, the famous event horizon, time will seem to flow so fast outside your frame of reference that, as you pass through the horizon, it is said that you will witness the entire future of the universe outside.'

Ethan scowled at Joaquin.

'Why don't you take a running jump into it and find out?'

Joaquin let out an abrupt burst of laughter.

'An excellent idea, except that once material is inside a black hole it can never leave. Information cannot escape the event horizon, at least not in the same form as it entered. It can be released only as pure energy over time, as the black hole evaporates. And that, my friends, will take billions of years.'

'We're in no rush to see you again,' Lopez said.

'Good, because soon you'll be lost to history,' Joaquin said. 'But let me first demonstrate to you just how efficient this process is. Olaf?'

Joaquin clicked his fingers at the giant, who turned

without a word and lumbered across to Dennis Aubrey. Olaf stooped and in one motion hefted the scientist onto his shoulder like a sack of potatoes. Aubrey began screaming and pummeled Olaf's muscular back with his feeble fists. Katherine stepped into Olaf's path, forcing him to stop.

'No, please, Joaquin, don't!'

The giant turned idly to look at Joaquin.

'This is for the best, Katherine,' Joaquin said. 'Dennis betrayed us and tried to send word to the outside world about my work. Fortunately for me, it was you he chose to contact. He has to go, for the benefit of us all.'

Katherine's features were suddenly taut with horror, as though, despite everything that Joaquin had already done, she had not imagined him doing this.

'He's innocent, Joaquin! He doesn't deserve this!'

Joaquin shrugged his shoulders, as though he were considering nothing more important than what to have for lunch.

'That is a matter of personal opinion,' he replied. 'But right now I cannot take the chance that he won't betray us again.'

Olaf waited for no further encouragement and shoved his way past Katherine with the scientist writhing on his shoulder. Ethan watched as two IRIS soldiers opened a hatch attached to a small chamber on the side of the sphere. Olaf stepped onto the edge of the hatch and pitched the screaming man inside before stepping back. The two soldiers slammed the chamber door shut and sealed it.

Joaquin turned and gestured to Ethan and Lopez.

'Make sure they see everything,' Joaquin snapped, his voice taut with excitement. 'I want them to see how they're going to die in just a few moments' time.'

Olaf lumbered up behind Ethan and with a weighty shove propelled him up against the side of the sphere. One shovel-like hand twisted his wrist up into the small of his back as the other clamped the back of Ethan's head and shoved it forcefully against a glass porthole looking into the chamber's interior.

Ethan gasped, his guts convulsing with a mixture of vertigo and fear as he looked into a sphere of endless blackness suspended within, a void of such unimaginable depth that it made him feel as though he was already falling into oblivion. Flares of plasma snarled and snapped within the chamber, flashing out toward him.

Somewhere behind him, he heard Joaquin's voice.

'Open the inner hatch!'

Dennis Aubrey lay curled up on the cold metal floor of the chamber. His guts had turned to slime within him, his bowels loosening as they gurgled and writhed, infected with a fear far beyond anything that he could have imagined possible. Every muscle in his body was locked in a spasm of primal terror, his throat constricted and his eyes wet with tears that flowed beyond his control.

Aubrey had never been a religious man. He had long considered those who leaned upon the crutch of blind faith to be crippled by far more than mere dogma. He had believed them to have forgone real wonders for mythical ones, the genuine joy of discovery replaced by the hollow promises of religion. But now, faced with the might of nature's ultimate uncaring creation, he felt a lifetime of scientific confidence abandon him. Aubrey became what all human beings were before the fury of nature's wrath: feeble, inconsequential, helpless.

'Forgive me,' he whispered into his own chest as he lay coiled upon the floor. 'If there's anybody listening, forgive me.'

A silence followed that seemed to last forever, and then suddenly he heard the hiss of hydraulics as the inner hatch opened. In a moment of morbid fascination, Aubrey peered into the darkened maw of true oblivion and then screamed with all of his might as a roar filled his ears, the gruesome song of the black hole both as deep as eternity and yet howling like a banshee as every free atom in the outer chamber was yanked toward it. The moisture in the chamber condensed into a writhing cloud of vapor and zipped toward the black hole as the latent heat energy was dragged instantly from his surroundings.

Everything else happened in a flash, every millisecond seared into Dennis Aubrey's last moment as he realized a terrible truth: he was lying with his feet pointing at the black hole. At this range and with everything happening so fast, he would literally see and experience everything before the solace of death embraced him, for his eyes and brain would be the last parts of him to enter the black hole. Even before the first electrical impulse from his brain reached his limbs in a futile attempt to turn himself around and meet his death head on, he lost the ability to move. In an instant, as the inner hatch fully opened,

Aubrey's skin and body became immobile as the temperature began plummeting toward minus 270 degrees.

The sweat on his skin turned to ice crystals as all of the air and the heat of his body was vacuumed toward the black hole at tremendous velocity. Aubrey's gaze registered tiny flares of red light as countless atoms of nitrogen, oxygen and methane were dragged in their billions across the event horizon and into the black hole. A flare of plasma appeared around the black hole like the rings of Saturn as other atoms on less direct trajectories were sent into rapidly decaying orbits around the black hole's circumference, accelerated to the speed of light and heated to thousands of degrees before vanishing beyond the event horizon.

Aubrey felt as though he were encased in a steel suit. The blood deep beneath the surface of his skin began to boil as though toxic acid were seething through every vein and artery in his body. His scream, long lost along with the air, lay frozen in time on his face as his lungs turned to stone in his chest cavity. His glasses shot away and vanished, instantly melted, into the disc of plasma orbiting the black hole.

Dennis Aubrey was lifted bodily from the floor of the outer chamber and flew toward the gaping black hole. The inner wall of the tokamak chamber flashed past as he caught a fleeting glimpse of faces pressed against the glass portholes, watching him with expressions of mute horror.

Aubrey saw the wall of the sphere glow as the entire universe beyond the black hole was shifted into the blue portion of the light spectrum. He had the briefest impression of individual atoms in their countless millions being dragged from his body as it passed through the event horizon. There was no pain, for his body was already too senseless to register any meaningful physical sensation, the nerves and pores either rock solid with cold or melting in the storm of plasma energy seething within the sphere.

His legs, closer to the black hole's singularity than his head, were stretched away from him in a nanosecond by the imbalanced gravitational field, tremendous tidal forces tearing his atoms apart as their nuclei and orbiting electrons scattered into the fiery plasma.

With his last moment of awareness, before even his eyeballs turned to solid ice, Aubrey glimpsed the outside world twist and spiral in a violent blur of colors as the light was distorted by the black hole's immense gravitational field, wrapping around it in dense coils like a light spectrum floating on the surface of a bubble.

In a blaze of energy, Aubrey crossed the event horizon. The kaleidoscope of colors turned suddenly bright blue and then plunged to black as Aubrey realized that no matter where he looked he saw the same thing: the oblivion within the black hole's dark heart, the singularity, where all paths inevitably led and where all histories were irrevocably erased.

And then there was nothing.

64

June 28, 20:24

Ethan stared in horror as he saw Dennis Aubrey's body plunge into the black hole, his face a screaming mask. He glimpsed the scientist's body stretched to oblivion around the circumference of the black hole before the man's agonized face turned a deep red as the light was shifted deep into the spectrum.

Then, he simply vanished from sight.

The writhing coil of energy around the black hole seemed to recede as it was gradually consumed, and then the interior of the chamber fell dark once more, punctuated only by the occasional flares of plasma reaching out to the chamber walls.

Ethan felt his head yanked backwards as Olaf pulled him away from the glass.

He caught Lopez's eye as they turned to face Joaquin once more. The tycoon's face glowed with malice.

'Now then,' he began, 'which one of you will be going next?'

Ethan glanced at Katherine Abell, who looked as

though she were on the verge of a breakdown. She stared with wide eyes at the chamber where Dennis Aubrey had been crushed into oblivion.

'Is this what you are?' Ethan asked Katherine, ignoring Joaquin. 'Is this what you've become, too?'

Katherine blinked as though refocusing on the here and now, and she shook her head vaguely. Joaquin walked across to her and yanked her arm, turning her toward him.

'Don't listen to them,' he crooned. 'They're not worth it, not worth the worry.'

'Is Scott Bryson not worth the worry?' Ethan asked Katherine. 'He saved your life.'

Katherine's jaw trembled as conflicting emotions warred with each other. She looked at Joaquin.

'This is wrong,' she whispered finally. 'This is all wrong.'

'This is necessary,' Joaquin insisted, 'for the greater good of us all, of all humanity. They're going to die, Katherine, I've already seen it on the camera. There's absolutely nothing that you can do to prevent that.'

Katherine shook her head.

'This, all of this, it's not about us or about humanity, is it?' she said. 'It's about you and how much power you can have over people.'

'No,' Joaquin snapped. 'It's not about that at all.'

'Then let them go, and take responsibility for your own actions instead of blaming it on the needs of a humanity that has no idea what you're doing. Let them go: it's what your father would have done.'

Katherine's challenge fell out of her lips almost of its

own accord, and as Ethan watched he realized that Joaquin had again been cornered. The tycoon opened his mouth to answer his wife, but nothing came forth. Katherine grabbed his arms and shook them as she spoke.

'It's the right thing to do and you know it,' she said. 'It's what Isaac Abell would have done. He would have seen the error of his ways and tried to prevent any further loss of life.'

'You don't know that,' Joaquin snapped.

'No?' Katherine challenged. 'Well, you tell me: would your father have released these people or would he have executed them?'

Ethan watched as Joaquin ground his jaw in his skull for several long seconds, staring silently at his wife. And then he sighed and shook his head as he turned away from her.

'Katherine, I'm afraid it's just too late for that now.'

'You mean you don't have the guts,' Katherine snarled, 'because you're not a fraction of the man your father was.'

Joaquin whirled on the spot and his fist whipped out, cracking Katherine back-handed across the cheek. She sprawled onto the floor, her hair falling over her face. Ethan tried to leap to her aid but Olaf's huge hands held him in place like a vice.

'You know nothing of my father,' Joaquin shouted, pointing down at his wife. 'Nothing!'

Katherine slowly struggled to her feet and stood before her husband with her chin lifted in defiance.

'I'm sure that he was man enough never to have hit his wife.'

Joaquin clicked his fingers at two of the IRIS soldiers standing nearby and they hurried forward to each take one of Katherine's arms in theirs.

Joaquin looked at her for a long moment and then shook his head.

'It didn't have to be this way, Katherine,' he said. 'But you leave me no choice. Put her in the chamber. Put them all in there!'

Ethan was turned and manhandled toward the chamber's outer hatch with Lopez alongside him. Katherine looked at them pleadingly as they were shoved toward their doom.

'I'm so sorry,' she said.

Ethan did not respond, instead searching desperately for some way to break free of the giant man holding him. The sphere was surrounded by cables and wires but none of them looked close enough that he could grab it, and the clinical neatness of the chamber and control platform meant that there were no weapons or implements he could use to fight his way out of trouble. The IRIS soldiers' weapons were all held at port arms and the troops were careful not to let anything get within his or Lopez's reach, all of them far too professional to make such a basic error.

There was, he concluded, nothing that he could do. He glanced at his watch. *20:26*.

'We've got about twenty minutes before this is all over. Any smart ideas?' he asked Lopez in a whisper, as they reached the outer hatch.

'Pray?' she suggested, her dark eyes flicking left and right as she sought an escape. Her dark skin seemed to have turned a few shades paler. 'Beg for mercy?'

Ethan shook his head.

'I don't think praying will help, and I'm not giving up my pride to that asshole.'

Olaf released him and walked to join Joaquin near the chamber's portholes. The tycoon called over to Ethan as his men opened the outer hatch door.

'Goodbye, Mr. Warner. I'd have imagined that a man of your caliber would put up a better fight, but it's too late now. You're literally out of time!'

Ethan ignored Joaquin and watched as the hatch beckoned, flickering intermittently as plasma energy flared violently in the chamber beyond. Katherine was shoved inside by one of the soldiers and fell onto the metal floor as her legs failed her. Lopez was turned by a soldier and aimed at the open hatch.

'Any last words, Miss Lopez?' Joaquin asked.

'Yeah, as it happens,' she shot back. 'Two of them. Fu—!'

The soldier shoved her into the hatch before she could get her parting shot out.

'What about you, Mr. Warner? Anything that you'd like to say?' Joaquin called, Olaf standing beside him.

Ethan looked at Joaquin for a long moment, aware of all eyes turning to see what he would say. Bright flares of energy flickered from within the black hole chamber's narrow portals and reflected off Joaquin's features.

'Yeah, there's something that I'd like to say,' he replied. 'I'd like to point out something that your father would have understood about this device, but that you don't. Just because you've seen into the future doesn't mean you know what's going to happen next.'

Joaquin laughed.

'Well, that doesn't seem to be the case right now, does it? It looks like your future is assured!' He turned to Olaf and clapped the giant on his shoulder as both men laughed.

Ethan was about to be prodded into the chamber when Joaquin suddenly stopped laughing, his face contorted in confusion as he looked up at Olaf. The huge man stared down at the tycoon.

'What is it?'

Joaquin stared at his own hand before speaking.

'I clapped you on the shoulder,' he uttered, 'just like in the video footage Dennis showed us.' Joaquin looked up at Ethan. 'From when you'd died in the chamber.'

Ethan said nothing, watching as Joaquin's mind struggled to comprehend what was happening.

'Dennis must have tampered with the footage,' he mumbled to Olaf in disbelief. 'He didn't spin the time-line on the footage forward to show us *their* deaths, he span it backward, to show us his own. Damn it, he must have edited the footage somehow before showing it to me. But then he must have known that he was going to die. Surely he couldn't have done that.'

'Charles Purcell did it too,' Ethan said to Joaquin. 'It's called personal sacrifice for people that you care about, something you wouldn't understand.'

Joaquin screwed his face up in confusion.

'But why would he be willing to die if he knew that I had won and—'

Ethan smiled quietly. All of the IRIS troops were watching him now as he spoke.

'Because he saw something else.'

Joaquin shook his head. 'That's not possible!'

It was not Ethan who replied, but a deep and murderous voice that thundered across the dome from the entrance hatch.

'Surprise, asshole!'

Ethan leapt sideways out of the grasp of the IRIS soldiers holding him as they all whirled to see Scott Bryson standing inside the bulkhead with an M-16 assault rifle cradled in his grip. Without any further warning, Bryson opened fire and a cascade of bullets hammered into the IRIS troops, instantly cutting several of them down. Bryson turned toward Joaquin and Olaf as he fired, chasing them with gunfire.

The hail of rounds smashed into power cables, computer terminals and ventilation channels as Bryson forced Joaquin and his remaining men away from Ethan and Lopez. Sparks showered down across dislodged metal panels as clouds of steam billowed from ruptured pipework filled the air as they dashed for cover.

Ethan hit the deck hard as Bryson's rounds slammed into the torsos of the two men closest to him, hurling their bodies like rag dolls into the side of the outer hatch. Ethan took shelter behind the hatch door and yelled in to Lopez and Katherine.

'Get out of there!'

65

June 28, 20:28

Lopez leapt out of the hatch, dragging Katherine close behind her, and they both tumbled down alongside Ethan behind the nearby wall of the control platform.

Ethan jumped to where one of the IRIS soldiers was writhing on the ground, his chest a bloodied mass of impact wounds. Ethan grabbed the man's rifle, looking down at him and recognizing the face of the young man who'd spoken to him earlier. His once-defiant eyes were now pinched with fear and he coughed a thick drool of blood from his lungs.

Ethan scurried across to another fallen soldier as Bryson laid down heavy fire on the troops now sheltering behind the computer banks on the opposite side of the dome. Ethan picked up the dead man's rifle and then dashed back to where Lopez was crouching.

'Where the hell did Bryson come from?!' she shouted above the crackling gunfire.

Ethan squatted down alongside her and handed her one of the rifles.

'You didn't really think he'd take a walk did you?' he replied. 'After what Purcell told us, I thought it was prudent to hide our assets. There were television cameras at the airport: I figured that if Joaquin saw Bryson leave, it might give us a chance.'

'How did he get down here?' Katherine asked.

'The pressure suit on his boat,' Ethan yelled back. 'It's just able to operate at this depth. The *Free Spirit* is too small for IRIS to track from down here, and they'd never be able to see Scott's pressure suit. It was the only way to maintain surprise.'

Lopez cocked her rifle. 'Now what?' she asked.

Ethan shifted position onto one knee and fired off two shots across the heads of the IRIS soldiers.

'We need to get Purcell's camera and then get the hell out of here,' he said. 'Cover Bryson. I'll work my way around the far side and flush them out!'

Lopez nodded and opened fire across the dome toward Joaquin and his men as Ethan leapt up and dashed across the open ground into cover behind the black-hole chamber's outer hatch.

The IRIS troops fired on Lopez's position, and Ethan flinched and ducked his eyes away as a volley of rounds smacked into metal panels near his head and ricocheted into the control platform. A shower of sparks fell like glowing rain onto the deck of the dome as the rounds smashed a computer monitor, and flames from an electrical fire started licking at the edges of the panel.

Ethan looked up at the enormous black-hole chamber as a new and unexpected horror breached his awareness. Bryson did not know what was contained within the chamber, and an electrical fire could cause havoc down here. Ethan peered around the edge of the hatch, and saw Bryson spraying bullets crazily across the IRIS position. One ricochet into the chamber's panels would be all it would take to cause the machine to go into meltdown, or maybe a shot that took out the power supply to one of the magnetic-field generators, destabilizing the black hole.

Ethan looked up at the control panel to his right. If the camera was anywhere, it would be there.

Ethan took aim and fired a salvo at the IRIS troops to keep their heads down, and then sprinted out across the open deck toward the control panel. Lopez saw him move, and shifted her aim to a position just behind him, firing again on the IRIS soldiers. Ethan felt the shockwaves from her bullets thumping the air behind him, and glimpsed the rounds smacking into the metal panels shielding Joaquin and his men.

A return volley smashed a pair of hard-drive units near Ethan as he vaulted up onto the control panel and hurled himself down into the walkway behind it. The unforgiving metal deck slammed into his shoulder. As he rolled he smacked the side of his head on the back wall of the walkway, a spray of sparks and plastic fragments raining down around him.

Ethan got onto his knees and peered over the edge of the control panel, then spotted the camera lying on its side near the smashed monitor. He reached out, grabbed it and shoved it beneath his shirt before crawling along the walkway toward where Bryson was sheltering behind a bulkhead on the far side of the dome, firing intermittently.

Ethan yelled out above the deafening reports echoing around them.

'Watch your fire! Don't hit the sphere!'

A clattering series of bullet impacts smashed along the edge of the control panel near Ethan's head and he crouched down, praying that the rounds were not strong enough to punch through the metal panels shielding him.

Bryson yelled back between shots.

'To hell with the damned thing! I'm almost out of ammo, we need to move!'

'Keep their heads down,' Ethan replied. 'I'll get behind them and finish this!'

Bryson nodded as Ethan turned, running back along the walkway toward the opposite end. He reached the edge, where Katherine was sheltering behind Lopez, who was still firing shots at the IRIS troops.

'I can't hit them!' she shouted at him. 'I can only keep them pinned down!'

Ethan knew that the soldiers might break out any moment, regardless of the risk of getting hit. They were doomed where they were, unless they were carrying extra ammunition and could afford to wait it out. Either way, it was a risk Ethan could not afford to take. They had to get out of here and fast.

'Just keep their heads down!'

Ethan leapt out of cover as Lopez fired off a volley, and slid down behind the chamber's outer hatch once more. He checked his magazine, counting twelve rounds plus one in the barrel, then got up and jogged round the back of the giant sphere, leaping over thick power cables and exhaust vents. Clouds of dense steam billowed up from shattered pipe-work near the black-hole chamber, the warning beacons of the dome glowing through the whorls of vapor like rising suns.

He was almost halfway round when an IRIS soldier appeared and rushed toward him through the diaphanous swirls, aiming his rifle at Ethan's head. Ethan dropped instinctively to his knees and brought his pistol up as the soldier's first shot zipped past, Ethan's sudden movement and the M-16's recoil fouling the soldier's aim.

Ethan squeezed the pistol's trigger and saw a misty spray of blood from the soldier's back as the bullet passed through his chest and exited between his shoulder blades. The soldier shuddered midstride and stumbled over the dense tangle of cables, collapsing onto his face with a thick pillar of steam blasting in billowing clouds around his body.

Ethan got up and kept his pistol trained on the motionless body as he stepped carefully forward. He saw a large exit wound in the soldier's back, already thick with blood as the man bled out internally. He wouldn't be waking up from this encounter.

Ethan stepped over the body and then saw the huge form of a man lunge at him from the other side of the pillar of steam. Ethan turned and whipped his pistol up, but before he could pull the trigger Olaf batted the weapon aside and ploughed into him like a freight train.

66

June 28, 20:32

Ethan was hurled backwards by the impact of Olaf's immense bulk and crashed down onto a thick tangle of cables. Olaf's knees dropped down either side of Ethan's waist as a huge fist plummeted toward his face, the Nordic giant's features glowing demonically in the diffuse light.

Ethan swung both of his arms sideways to intercept Olaf's punch and drive it aside. Olaf's thick knuckles cracked against the metal plates in the deck and the big man growled in pain as he grabbed Ethan's pistol and tore it from his grasp. Olaf hurled the weapon out of Ethan's reach and then plunged his hands down onto Ethan's neck, leaning forward and driving all of his weight behind his muscular arms.

Ethan's eyes bulged, his throat choked shut and his lungs swelled. Olaf, his eyes poisoned with hatred, his teeth gritted with fury, squeezed with a tremendous, unimaginable force. Stars of light sparkled and whirled in Ethan's vision, his own arms ineffective against Olaf's immense strength.

Ethan reached out and grabbed Olaf's face before driving his thumbs deep into the killer's eyes, pushing with his fingernails as he felt the soft tissue beneath the eyelids compress like a squashed orange. Olaf gagged and pulled his head back as he struggled to escape Ethan's hands, before releasing his stranglehold and smashing Ethan's arms apart to break his grip.

Ethan jerked his hips up and then yanked them down as he flicked his upper body forward and smashed his forehead into Olaf's face. Olaf's broad, thick nose collapsed with a deep crunch of shattered cartilage as a thick stream of dark blood splattered down across his vest. Ethan reached up for the pistol in Olaf's shoulder holster, but the big man gripped his wrist and forced it aside.

Olaf heaved one arm back to swing another punch, but Ethan took full advantage of the clumsy maneuver and stabbed the fingers of his free hand like lances into Olaf's bleary eyes. The giant growled and scrambled away from Ethan, releasing his wrist as he reached down for the pistol nestled in his shoulder holster and hauled it free to aim singlehanded at Ethan.

Ethan saw the pistol swing around to point at him, and in the fraction of a second before the moment of his death his marine corps training flashed through his mind and, rather than evading the weapon, he instead lunged toward it.

Ethan grabbed the pistol's barrel with both hands and clamped them down tightly. Olaf squeezed the trigger with the pistol pointed at Ethan's chest from point-blank range. The mechanism moved a fraction before jamming against Ethan's fingers as he locked its movement and then shifted one hand to ram his index finger behind Olaf's. With both of their fingers trapped behind the trigger, Olaf could not fire the pistol.

Olaf stared at Ethan in surprise but before he could respond Ethan rammed his right knee deep into the big man's groin with all of his might. Olaf's legs collapsed reflexively beneath him, and as he fell Ethan twisted and yanked his grip sideways across the pistol's barrel, twisting it against the direction of Olaf's fall.

Olaf howled in pain as Ethan twisted relentlessly aside, then crouched and drove his bodyweight into the maneuver. Olaf was forced sideways on his knees and his wrist trembled as it failed and then the pistol snapped from his grasp. The huge man scrambled away from Ethan and reached out for the discarded rifle of the dead soldier.

Ethan let himself fall away from Olaf and rolled onto his shoulder to come up the other side onto one knee with the pistol aimed double-handed at Olaf. Olaf whirled and pulled the rifle into his shoulder as Ethan squeezed the pistol's trigger.

The bullet struck Olaf just to the left of center of his chest, a neat red stain appearing as if by magic on his vest. Olaf shuddered and stared at Ethan with his blue eyes wide and almost instantly lifeless. The tiny stain on his shirt spread in moments to encompass his entire torso as his heart, grossly oversized after years of steroid abuse, spilled his lifeblood at a tremendous rate.

Olaf's huge arms trembled as the rifle dropped from his grasp, his once firm jaw hanging slack as he toppled over backwards and vanished amidst the swirling clouds of steam.

Ethan staggered, his balance uneven and his breath ragged in his damaged throat as he slowly got to his feet. He carefully picked his way forward over the cables to where Olaf lay and took the rifle from beside the man's corpse. He turned and moved to the far side of the chamber where the IRIS troops were protecting Joaquin.

It was then that he realized that the firing had stopped.

Ethan peered out through the whirling clouds of steam. Hazard lights flashed like beacons through the fog at him as though he was in some infernal subterranean nightclub, and he could hear sirens as the smoke from the fires began setting off alarms. Then, above it all, he could hear Joaquin's voice.

'Olaf? Come out, Olaf! It's over, we have them all!'

Ethan felt a crushing disappointment swamp him as he advanced a single pace to peer around the edge of the black-hole chamber. Several IRIS troops lay dead behind or beside the computer banks, many of which sparked and smoldered from multiple bullet impacts. The remaining IRIS soldiers stood in the center of the dome with their weapons pointed at Bryson, Lopez and Katherine.

Behind the soldiers, using them as a shield, Joaquin called out again.

'Olaf?! It's over!'

Ethan shouted out in response. 'I don't think your little puppy is up to replying, Joaquin!'

A long silence ensued, during which he could almost sense Joaquin's anguish.

'Where is he, Warner? Bring him out here or I swear I'll shoot Lopez dead right now!'

Ethan savored his reply.

'He's too heavy to carry,' he shouted. 'Most people are when they're dead.'

Another silence followed and this time he could hear Joaquin's voice cracking with suppressed rage.

'It's over, Ethan!' he shouted. 'Come out with your hands in the air where we can see you!'

Ethan thought hard about what Joaquin was willing to sacrifice in order to achieve his aims. It had become clear that the lives of other people, no matter how close they were, held little value for him. It was also clear that there was no way he would let Ethan, Lopez or Katherine Abell leave the facility alive, for to let them do so would bring an end to Joaquin's insane scheme. Ethan stared up at the metal sphere towering above him, and realized that there was only one thing that Joaquin could not afford to lose.

'It's not over, Joaquin,' he shouted back. 'I've still got one play left.'

From the far side of the sphere, Joaquin laughed out loud.

'You're defeated, completely,' he snapped. 'I am holding a gun to Miss Lopez's head. If you don't show yourself in the next five seconds, I'll kill her. I can afford to waste a hostage, Mr. Warner, because I have three of them. What can *you* afford to waste?'

Ethan gripped the M-16 tighter and set the fire-control switch to automatic. Then he strode out into plain view with the rifle pulled tight into his shoulder and trained ahead of him.

He saw the small knot of people turn to look at him as he appeared through the hissing steam clouds. Joaquin was holding a pistol to Lopez's head, but to Ethan's relief he saw that none of them had yet been restrained. The three remaining IRIS soldiers turned, aiming at Ethan. Bryson, standing between Katherine and Lopez, noticed instantly that there was no longer a weapon pointing at him. Having lost several men, the soldiers' professionalism was starting to crumble.

'Drop the weapon, Warner!' Joaquin shouted.

'I'd urge you to compromise,' Ethan replied, edging toward them. 'You still stand to lose. I have the camera.'

Joaquin shook his head and tutted.

'And you say that *I'm* insane,' he said. 'You are once again outgunned, four to one. Lose the weapon or Lopez will lose her head, as will you. I will retrieve the camera from your cold, dead corpse.'

Ethan smiled grimly as he glanced up at the black-hole chamber beside him.

'Then you'll have to follow me to oblivion to get it.'

Ethan whirled and aimed at the giant metal plates of the black-hole chamber. In the instant that he aimed the weapon, he heard Joaquin's terrified scream.

'No!'

Ethan squeezed the trigger, and the rifle clattered and bucked in his grip as bullets smashed into the chamber's walls.

67

The metal of the sphere buckled violently under the blows, and then two rounds ricocheted off and hit one of the giant power generators. The bullets smashed their way into radiator vents, cables, wires and mounting bolts as a shower of sparks and metal fragments sprayed down onto the deck.

Ethan flinched, stopped firing, and looked up.

The panels held firm.

Joaquin's laugh echoed around the dome and then he gestured to his men.

'Kill him.'

Scott Bryson moved before any of the soldiers could pull their triggers. He grabbed one of them around the jaw and shoulders and lifted him off of his feet before yanking his head violently one way and then the other. Ethan heard a dull crackling sound as the soldier's neck snapped like a dry twig. Holding the soldier's limp corpse against his chest, Bryson grabbed the rifle that was still in the dead man's grip and turned it toward Joaquin.

The tycoon leapt to one side, grabbed Lopez and shoved his pistol up under her jaw.

Ethan dropped onto one knee and aimed at the other two IRIS soldiers as they turned to defend their boss. In an instant, nobody could move. Bryson kept his rifle trained on Joaquin, the two IRIS soldiers held Bryson and Katherine Abell in their sights, and Ethan's rifle was fixed on the soldiers.

'Mexican stand-off,' Bryson said as he looked at Joaquin. 'Time for you to make your choice, little man. You want to die here, or in prison up top?'

'Just shoot the asshole!' Lopez shouted as she struggled against Joaquin's grip.

Joaquin sneered at Bryson from behind Lopez's long black hair.

'You've already lost. You'll never make it out of here alive and I already know that I'll be in Puerto Rico tomorrow.'

Ethan's eyes narrowed. 'What the hell makes you think that?'

'Because I saw tomorrow's news!' Joaquin shouted back. 'I was there! This is all preordained, Mr. Warner. No matter what you do the future cannot be changed! It's over for you, because you're all going to die here and there's nothing that you can do to stop that from—'

A deep cracking sound from behind Ethan cut Joaquin off in mid-sentence as it echoed across the dome. Ethan glanced over his shoulder, up at the sphere. Clouds of steam were drifting across the roof of the dome amid showers of sparks and the pulsing glow of warning beacons. From somewhere within the sphere emanated a deep humming sound, as though every atom in the facility were vibrating, and another deafening crack thundered through the dome.

Ethan saw the metal panel where his bullets had struck suddenly warp, the solid steel buckling like paper crushed in an invisible hand. A blast of steam and smoke billowed in a toxic cloud from the damaged electromagnet high above them and set off another smoke alarm. Ethan turned back to Joaquin.

'Looks like everybody's time is running out,' he said with a tight grin. 'We should all leave, right now.'

Joaquin shook his head, his face suddenly racked with panic and desperation.

'We can't leave!' he shouted. 'You're not going anywhere!'

Katherine looked at her husband.

'If you leave now, with us, then this is all over, Joaquin! There'll be no hard evidence to convict you! We can fight this, together!'

Another pair of deafening cracks thundered out from inside the sphere. Ethan flinched in shock as he guessed that the failed electromagnets were destabilizing the containment field. With the delicate repulsive balance within the chamber lost, the black hole was beginning to drag on the sphere around it. It would only be a matter of moments before the panel failed, and with it the whole facility.

'The chamber's going to breach!' Ethan shouted at Joaquin.

Joaquin shook his head and gestured to the control panel nearby.

'Widen the field from the remaining generators,' he ordered one of his men. 'Compensate for the imbalance!'

The soldier obeyed instantly and ran across to the control panel to stare at the endless array of screens, dials and instruments.

'How?' he shouted.

Joaquin jerked Lopez toward the panel, one eye on Ethan and the other on the buckling panel high up on the sphere.

'Use the touch-screens!' Joaquin ordered. 'Fourth on the left!'

More sirens began going off as the black hole began to collapse the sphere. Ethan felt the metal panels beneath his boots begin to vibrate, numbing his legs as he kept his weapon trained on the IRIS soldier still aiming his weapon at Bryson.

'We're wasting time, Joaquin!' Ethan warned him. 'We're all going to die!'

'That one there!' Joaquin shouted at the soldier, ignoring Ethan.

Everyone watched the soldier as he began pressing buttons on the screen before him. Ethan moved further away from the sphere as he glanced up at the damaged panel to see it bowed inward like a convex lens, rivets trembling under the unimaginable force.

'It's too late,' Ethan shouted. 'It's going to fail.'

The IRIS soldier finished his adjustments and Ethan felt the vibrations in the panels beneath his feet cease as the deep hum faded away. Joaquin's face illuminated with a bright smile as he laughed out loud.

'It is over! Nothing anybody does makes any differ-ence!' he cried out in delight. 'The future cannot be changed. I cannot die here today!'

Lopez stared up at the trembling panel in the dome, ignoring the pistol at her throat. Bryson, still holding the dead soldier against his chest, glanced up at it, too, just as a tiny sound tinkled above the hiss of steam and alarms. Ethan turned his head and saw a single rivet bounce down the side of the sphere to hit the metal floor plates with a high-pitched twang.

Ethan turned to Lopez.

'Cover, now!'

Joaquin's face collapsed into terror as with a final rending screech of metal torn through metal the panel imploded inward, ripped like tissue paper as it vanished from sight to be replaced by a writhing bolt of blue-white plasma that snaked from within to envelop the power generator like a ghostly hand.

Ethan hit the deck as a screaming noise wailed through the dome. He glimpsed rippling streams of water vapor and ice that were plucked from the air of the dome, flowing like a writhing river into the unimaginable blackness within the chamber. In an instant the failed power generator was torn from its roof mountings and smashed through the wall of the sphere with a terrific crash and another blaze of pure energy that seethed across the ceiling of the dome and fell like white hot rivulets of rain down toward the deck.

'The singularity's been exposed!' Joaquin bellowed above the din of rending metal and screaming alarms.

To Ethan's amazement the falling globules of energy

were snatched from midair and zipped back into the breach. Suddenly Ethan lost his balance, as though the whole dome was tilting onto its side like a capsizing ship. The previously flat deck became a shallow ramp with the exit hatch at the top and the black hole's chamber at the base. Yet despite the alarming sensation, his brain told him that the deck was still level.

Ethan instinctively grabbed at the deck plates beneath him and searched for a hand hold. He realized that the black hole's immense local gravitational influence within the facility was overpowering that of the earth, and that now the singularity in the hole's dark heart was the direction that gravity was taking.

Ethan saw the IRIS soldier behind the control panel scream as he was hauled upward from the walkway and span through the air toward the sphere, slamming into its wall with a crunch of shattered bone as his legs crumpled beneath him. The ragged breach in the chamber folded further inward in a cacophony of failing rivets, like a giant black mouth with rows of sharp metal teeth, and the soldier screamed a final horrified cry as he was dragged into the breach and vanished in a flare of energy.

Ethan felt a bitter, unimaginable cold creep toward him, saw the air in the dome vaporizing in clouds before his eyes as it lost pressure and was dragged toward the terrifying maw of the black hole still entrapped by the remaining magnetic fields within the chamber. He realized that if the field failed entirely then the black hole would be able to move freely, and there would be nothing on earth that could stop it.

'Ethan!'

Ethan turned his head and saw Lopez clinging to the edge of the control panel. Joaquin was scrambling away from her and slammed his boots into her shoulders as leverage to get away from the black hole's devastating pull. Lopez grabbed Joaquin's ankles as he struggled, and then they both were dragged off the control panel and slammed down onto the deck, Lopez sliding past Ethan toward the chamber for several yards before she managed to grab hold of the deck plates.

Joaquin cried out and grabbed at the deck plates with one hand as with the other he aimed his pistol at Lopez. Ethan shouted out a warning as Lopez scrambled to her feet, as though she were climbing a steep hillside, and then Joaquin fired.

Lopez's head jerked violently to one side, her long black hair flew across her face and her legs collapsed beneath her. She hit the deck hard and instantly slid toward the black hole.

'Nicola!'

Ethan launched himself onto his feet and was about to leap for Lopez's prostrate form when the two IRIS soldiers before him aimed their rifles at his chest. Ethan desperately tried to raise his own rifle in time but before he could take aim both of the IRIS soldiers fired, bright bursts of flame leaping from the barrels as Ethan felt a series of thumps hammer his chest.

68

June 28, 20:37

Time seemed to stand still.

Ethan had spent half of his adult life being shot at, first in Afghanistan, then in Iraq, both as a soldier and as a journalist. It had happened so many times, there had been so many close calls, that he felt he had somehow become immune, as though he knew that he would never be hit himself. It had always happened to the other guy.

But not this time.

Ethan hit the deck hard on his back, his hands flashing protectively but uselessly to his chest as the wind was knocked from his lungs and his vision starred before his eyes. The deafening roar of the chamber breach and the wailing sirens receded for a brief moment, and with a sense of terminal despair he lifted his hands up, knowing that they would be smeared with warm blood spilling from his lungs and heart.

He stared at them for a long moment, briefly wondering whether the lack of pain meant that death was in itself such a shock that nothing could be felt. He allowed himself the thought that maybe getting shot wasn't such a bad way to go after all. In fact, he realized, he felt absolutely fine.

Ethan sat up and looked at the two IRIS soldiers, who were staring past him in disbelief and backing away toward the exit, leaning back against the increasing gravitational pull of the black hole. One of them fired again, the bullets smacking the air nearby as they somehow zipped past Ethan.

Ethan turned, and felt a surge of jubilance that warred with a terrible dread that chilled his guts.

The side of the sphere was peppered with five dents, the marks of the bullets that clearly should have killed him, and several more from the second salvo now hammered the metal panels, the bullets having been dragged from their flight path by the black hole's leaking gravitational field and the huge electromagnets, to pass harmlessly by just inches from where Ethan had stood. Only the shockwaves from the bullets had hammered his chest.

But what sent fear coursing through his veins was the growing breach in the chamber. Not only was every unsecured object now beginning to drift toward the breach, but the light around the breach was beginning to bend as though it were underwater, flowing into the sphere.

Ethan recalled the words of the scientist, Ottaway, at Cape Canaveral: *once you get too close to a black hole's event horizon, too deep inside the gravity well, nothing can escape, not even light.*

He looked up and saw the power generators straining against their mounts, huge weights that would smash through the sphere from all directions and fully expose the black hole within.

'Nicola!'

Bryson hurled himself across the void past Ethan and slammed down alongside Lopez, one arm wrapping around her as the other sought a handhold to prevent them both from lifting off the deck and vanishing into the breach. Ethan scrambled to his feet, aware of the cold emanating from the black hole as it drew even the atoms in the air toward its insatiable singularity. He struggled up the steeply inclined deck toward the control panel, where dense coils of electrical cable writhed like ranks of kelp flowing in underwater currents.

Ethan reached out and grabbed the cables in one hand as he hauled himself painfully up and away from the black hole's gravity well.

Looking back toward the sphere, he had the dizzying impression of the entire dome appearing like a huge funnel, with the black-hole chamber deep inside its mouth, buried at the base of the funnel's steep walls. Bryson was clinging to the deck panels, one arm around Lopez's waist to prevent her from slipping any further toward the breach. Katherine was crawling toward Ethan along the deck nearby, flinching as bits of paper, pens and clipboards flew past her face toward the breach. He could see that the outer surface of the sphere was now a sparkling white in color, coated thickly with ice that reflected the savage bolts of plasma searing the air around it.

Alternating heat and cold, Ethan recalled from his

school days, makes metals brittle. The sphere would not hold for much longer. He could see that the swirling blur of light was growing larger, twisting around the breach as though being bent by a giant lens. He had the terrifying impression that reality was melting and pouring like liquid toward the black hole.

Ethan worked his way back toward Bryson, the deck beneath his feet tilting ever more as he moved toward the sphere, as though he were crawling on the surface of an ever-steepening slope toward the black hole's gravity well. The cold increased as he got closer to Bryson, a bitter, biting cold that condensed his breath on the air and was turning moisture to sleet crystals that swept toward the breach like a blizzard.

'Throw me some cable!' Bryson shouted. 'Hurry up or we'll be leaving our skin behind on here!'

Ethan nodded, seeing the surface of the deck frosted with sparkling particles of ice. He grabbed a handful of cables from behind the panel and pulled hard on them, yanking them free of their ties and lowering them toward Bryson. As he got closer, Ethan pinned his boots and shoulders against the deck to prevent himself from being captured by the black hole's gravity.

'The generators are failing!' Bryson shouted.

Ethan focused on getting close enough to Bryson to pass on the cables. He was almost there when a cascade of bullets crackled across the deck around him. Ethan flinched and saw Joaquin shielding himself against the black hole's gravity at the far end of the walkway, aiming one of the dropped M-16s. The tycoon was glowing blue as though enveloped in a halo of electrical energy.

Ethan blinked, his vision strangely blurred, but then he realized that the entire far wall of the dome was tinged with blue light as the black hole's increasing influence twisted time and space ever more tightly.

'Ethan!'

Bryson's cry focused his attention once again and he reached out as far as he could. Bryson stretched out for the cables and one thick fist grabbed onto them and pulled. Ethan grasped his hand and wrist, holding him steady as another shower of bullets clattered across the deck, the rounds ricocheting and zipping into the chamber breach as though plucked from midair.

'Jesus Christ!' Bryson yelled.

Joaquin, his aim frustrated as the black hole twisted the path of the bullets away from Ethan, began edging his way toward them, his boots extended out toward Ethan as he slid his way carefully on his back, aiming between his legs. Ethan realized that if he got close enough, his shots would find their mark.

'Your time is finished, Warner!' Joaquin shouted.

With an immense effort, Ethan pulled on Bryson's hand as the big man kicked with his boots and scrambled up the steepening deck plates, Lopez's prostrate body limp beneath his other arm. Ethan's guts plunged as he saw the blood smearing her temple and face, his fear of losing her suddenly dwarfing that of being dragged into the black hole's oblivion himself.

Ethan hauled Bryson the last twelve inches with a renewed sense of urgency, and the big man pulled himself to safety. Ethan rolled away just as Joaquin's voice rang out in his ears.

'Goodbye, Mr. Warner!'

Ethan saw Joaquin aiming from barely ten feet away and stared at the barrel pointed directly at him. And then Joaquin's face collapsed into agony as he screamed.

In the weird and warped blue light, Ethan saw Katherine Abell appear like a genie from the distant exit hatch, moving impossibly fast like an old movie to zoom up behind Joaquin. He realized that, where she was standing, beyond the black hole's gravity well, time was running faster. The bright red fire axe in her hand whipped down from over her shoulder and crashed through the rifle in Joaquin's grasp, shattering the barrel and smashing through his fingers with a splatter of blood.

Ethan saw Katherine screaming at her husband as she pounded him with her fists and scraped at his face with her nails as they tumbled together across the deck and into the gravity well.

Ethan reached out for Katherine as they plunged toward him. Her nails dug into the metal plates and her fingers caught, enough that she began scrambling up and away from them. Then Joaquin Abell crashed into him and smashed both Ethan and Katherine down toward the black hole.

69

June 28, 20:40

Ethan's fingers scraped across the deck panels as the metal gratings snapped at his nails and rasped across his face. His fingers caught painfully, bearing his body weight on the steeply inclined deck, and he looked up in time for Joaquin's boot to smash into his shoulder and send a lance of bright pain through his collarbone.

'Die, Warner!' Joaquin screamed.

Joaquin's boot smashed again into Ethan's shoulder and searing pain jarred his arm as he felt his grip fail, his fingers numb from the bitter cold now creeping across his entire body.

'It's over, Joaquin!' Ethan shouted. 'Give it up and we both live!'

'Fuck you, Warner!' the tycoon screamed back, his eyes poisoned with rage. 'You've taken everything from me! If I die, I take you with me!'

The dome around them was deformed now into an oval shape, with the black-hole chamber close below and the entrance to the dome far above, seemingly fifty meters away and pinched to a tiny point of light that glowed an unearthly blue.

Joaquin lifted his boot once more and aimed this time at Ethan's face, the tycoon's features shining with unrestrained malice, and then smashed it down toward him. The boot slammed across Ethan's arm, missing his face entirely, the light now so distorted by the black hole's gravity that it was warped sideways, the distant exit now not just above Ethan but also off to one side. Ethan felt his body becoming increasingly, impossibly heavy as the black hole's immense gravity finally began to overwhelm him.

Joaquin, hanging on to the deck plating with one hand above Ethan, screamed in fury and grabbed at the pistol in his shoulder holster, whipping it out and aiming it down at Ethan. With a flourish of malice the tycoon squeezed the trigger.

Ethan saw a flicker of movement in the distance far above them. In an instant Bryson's huge form surged into view like a curveball travelling at hundreds of miles per hour to smash sideways into Joaquin Abell and grab the pistol as he did so.

Ethan flinched as the sound of the gunshot crashed out, but the bullet never reached him as Scott Bryson slid down past him, his huge arms folded around Joaquin's body as they tumbled toward the black hole. Ethan saw the shot exit Bryson's lower back amid a spray of blood that shot toward the black hole and turned to crystals of ice as it vanished into the breach. He heard the big man grunt in agony as he twisted the pistol from Joaquin's grasp and sent it spinning down into the breach looming below them. Bryson twisted himself around on top of Joaquin, then grabbed the smaller man's collar in one giant fist and hauled him up onto his knees on the wildly tilting deck.

'You want to see the future, asshole?' Bryson yelled at Joaquin. 'Here it is!'

Bryson swung one huge fist back and then ploughed it through Joaquin's chest like a battering ram. Joaquin screamed out loud, his eyes wide with unspeakable fear as the blow lifted the tycoon off of his feet and he plunged down into the abyss below, his screams spiraling away with him.

Ethan saw Joaquin's clothes freeze on his body, saw his eyes go pale as the fluids within them froze solid and saw his hair turn white with frost as he plunged into the chamber, smashing a panel as he did so and opening the breach wider. Ethan saw the black hole now fully exposed, a demonic abyss ringed by searing coils of plasma.

Joaquin's body warped as it span in tight whorls around the black hole's fearsome gravitational field, bent by light and suddenly glowing brightly as it was torn apart at the sub-atomic level and ripped into ribbons of pure energy. Joaquin's image turned a deep blood red, and then suddenly it was gone.

Bryson collapsed, his fingers scraping on the metal deck plates and the shirt on his back thick with blood. In one terrible moment, as Ethan reached out to him, he knew that it was too late. Bryson's eye caught his, the twinkling light within already fading, and a brief smile flickered across one corner of his lips.

'It's your turn to keep an eye on Nicola,' he mumbled weakly.

'Don't quit, Bryson!' Ethan yelled, reaching out for him. 'Don't quit now!'

Bryson's eye glazed over. 'Don't let her down.'

The big man's eye closed as his grip failed him and he was snatched away, his body freezing instantaneously and then flaring with bright energy as he vanished into oblivion far below.

'Bryson!'

A terrible sense of loss ached through Ethan's chest as the raging storm of plasma around the black hole glowed brightly, the crackling, snarling bolts of energy reaching out for Ethan.

He tried to back away from the hole, but now it felt as though the deck of the dome was pitching almost vertically. He felt his feet slip from beneath him as he clung desperately to the deck plates, staring down toward the sphere below him and its terrifying host. The plates beneath his shirt began slipping and scraped painfully against his skin, and he saw frost forming on his boots as they slipped closer to the swirling maelstrom of light and energy.

'Ethan!'

Ethan looked up, and to his amazement he saw Lopez reaching out for him, her hand inches away and yet appearing small and stretched as though viewed through a fish-eye lens, her face seemingly twenty paces distant. Ethan reached out for her, saw his own arm extend crazily and bend sideways to his left into the distance as though twenty feet long. He blinked, nausea poisoning his innards as he struggled to make sense of the world now spiraling out of control around him, the light beginning to fold in upon itself.

He felt as though his weight were increasing with every passing second, the muscles in his arms screaming for release as he began sliding again, particles of ice forming inside his boots as his feet went numb within them.

'Ethan!'

Ethan looked back up to see the tightly coiled light curve above him and a warped face loom as though out of some terrible nightmare.

'My voice!' he heard Lopez shout. 'Close your eyes and reach for my voice!'

Ethan's arm wavered wildly from one side to the other in his vision, and he realized that it was useless for him to see where Lopez was, her image in the distance before him far removed now in time and space from where she actually was. Against every instinct in his body, Ethan closed his eyes.

'Reach for my voice!'

Ethan waved his arm left and right, focusing on Lopez's voice as she called to him, and suddenly he felt her fingers brush against his. With a final, monumental effort he held his arm still and Lopez's hand gripped his wrist and folded upon it. Ethan felt her heave, and he pushed against the floor plates as he clawed with his hands to pull himself free from the black hole's savage grasp.

Ethan felt himself being hauled upwards and away from the sphere, and as he travelled he felt the deck of the dome slowly begin to right itself beneath him, as though he were on a capsized ship that had somehow been saved from certain doom. He heard Lopez more clearly and opened his eyes to see her pulling on his arm, her free hand gripped by Katherine Abell, who was in turn hanging on grimly to the loop of computer cables stretching out from the main control panel.

Thick blood oozed from Lopez's temple into her hair as she pulled Ethan up, and he saw her eyes drooping from exhaustion and blood loss. Ethan slumped alongside her, his own body drained, yet even as he did so he felt the deck tilting beneath him, back toward the sphere.

'Come on!' Katherine yelled. 'We have to leave now!'

Ethan looked down toward the sphere and saw the remaining panels folding like the petals of a steel flower toward the dark and terrible center.

70

June 28, 20:42

Ethan dragged himself to his feet, and with Katherine they helped Lopez upright and staggered through the exit hatch and out of the dome. Ethan turned and slammed the hatch shut, sealing it.

'It won't make any difference,' Katherine gasped. 'You saw it! Nothing can stop that thing now.'

Ethan somehow managed to heft Lopez onto his shoulders. He staggered slightly, stars of light sparkling before his eyes, but he managed to move forward on his last remaining vestiges of energy.

'There might be a way to hide from it,' he gasped to Katherine. 'We have to hurry. Go ahead, get to the sub and start the batteries and engines. The controls are simple enough.'

Katherine ran away down the corridor ahead of him as he wobbled along with Lopez slumped across his shoulders. He heard her voice in his ears.

'I can walk,' she mumbled.

Ethan struggled through each painful and unsteady step and shook his head.

'If only that were true,' he managed to rasp. 'How come Joaquin missed his shot so close to you?'

Lopez's reply was weak and soft in his ear.

'The light. It was bent by the black hole, so I wasn't quite where he saw me. The shockwave must have knocked me out for a few moments.'

Ethan, his shoulders aching and his legs quivering, stepped through the hatch into the storage hangar where the aged remains of the captured ships and aircraft loomed. The lights flickered intermittently as the power began to fail, Ethan losing balance in the shuddering light and keeling sideways.

He hit the deck and gasped as his left knee cracked painfully beneath him.

'I'm sorry,' he whispered to Lopez, unable to take another step. 'I can't carry you.'

Lopez slid from his shoulders as Ethan slumped onto his hands and knees. He felt one of her small hands touch his and fold around it as, on her knees beside him, she took a deep breath.

'Just a few more paces,' she whispered, 'we can do this.'

A terrific crash echoed from somewhere far behind them, and Ethan guessed that the sphere had finally collapsed inward into the black hole, imploding and finally allowing the full force of the hole to act upon its surroundings.

Ethan hauled himself to his feet with Lopez, and together they staggered between the boats and aircraft, stumbling through the exit hatch and down the long corridor to the docking station ahead, the lights in the corridor flickering weakly. They arrived see the *Intrepid* waiting with its lights on and Katherine waving at them from the open hatch.

Scott Bryson's abandoned atmospheric diving suit bobbed in the water nearby.

'Come on!' Katherine yelled.

Ethan staggered the last few paces and let go of Lopez's hand, untying the submersible from its moorings before following Lopez aboard. He clambered down the ladder into the interior as the lights finally failed in the facility and plunged it into darkness, and the entire superstructure began trembling.

Ethan clambered past Lopez and Katherine and into the cockpit to slump into the pilot's seat. He opened the ballast vents to expel the air and the *Intrepid* sank into the inky black water, her lights piercing the deep gloom outside as Ethan turned the submersible around and threw the throttles forward.

The *Intrepid* soared clear from under the docking dome and out into the silent blackness of the deep ocean.

Behind him, Lopez's voice called out. 'We'll never get far enough away at this speed!'

Ethan shook his head.

'We're not running,' he said. 'We're going to hide.'

'Where?!'

Ethan watched as the *Intrepid*'s lights illuminated the barren ocean bed, sweeping ghostlike across endless dunes of lifeless sand, and then quite suddenly the beams were lost into absolute blackness. Ethan waited until the *Intrepid* had cleared the edge of the Miami Terrace reef and was over the abyss before he pushed the controls down and dove toward the endless depths.

The terrace dropped more than three hundred feet below the *Intrepid*, joining the abyssal plain that extended all the way out beyond Bimini Island before finally dropping off the edge of the continental shelf hundreds of kilometers away. Ethan peered over his shoulder and could just make out the edge of the reef shelf rising above them.

Somewhere behind them a bright light flared suddenly, and for an instant the entire ocean floor was illuminated as though a sun had risen across a distant horizon. Ethan squinted and saw the freezing depths glowing in the blast, saw the plunging drop before them and the abyssal plain of the Atlantic stretching away into the unknown distance. The silhouette of the *Intrepid* was cast into the brightly illuminated distance, a long shadow piercing the ocean, and then the inky blackness returned.

'Hang on!' Ethan shouted.

The submersible plunged down into the darkness over the edge of the shelf, the steep slopes rising up behind it, and then something surged past, a blast of energy that tilted the submersible almost vertically as it slammed into them from behind.

Ethan yanked back instinctively on the control column as the *Intrepid* plunged down into the deep, her engine straining to right her as the shockwave raced past. Suddenly the entire ocean seemed to surge and pull them back toward the IRIS facility and for a moment Ethan feared that he had been wrong, that the black hole would continue to consume everything around it, growing exponentially, unstoppably.

Then, as suddenly as the surge had arrived, it disappeared, and the ocean depths fell silent once more.

Ethan stared out into the gloom for a long moment and then turned in his seat.

Katherine Abell looked at him. 'Is it over?'

Ethan, utterly exhausted, nodded.

'I think so.'

Ethan looked at Lopez. She sat slumped in her seat, blood caking one side of her face and her hair matted on top of it. She stared out of one of the portholes into the empty wastes outside, as oblivious now to her companions as if she had, after all, been dragged into the black hole.

Ethan turned back to the controls, and on an impulse looked at his watch. The hands were fixed in place, the watch stopped by the electromagnetic blast that had just surged past them.

20:48, June 28.

Ethan realized that Charles Purcell's final prophecy of the future had been proven correct.

Ethan eased back on the control column, guiding the *Intrepid* up toward the surface glittering faintly above them through the gloom.

71

CHICAGO, ILLINOIS

July 3, 9:14

Ethan stepped into the office of Warner & Lopez Inc. for the first time in five days, tossing his keys onto his desk and standing in the center of the room for a long moment. His shoulder still throbbed with a dull ache from the damage he'd endured in the IRIS facility, and he had slept deeply and eaten ravenously ever since; but he knew that his wounds were superficial compared to those suffered by Lopez.

She followed him into the office, devoid of the feisty spirit and short temper that had enshrouded her like a force field ever since Ethan had first met her.

'Nothing's changed,' she said, observing the office without interest. 'It's like we never left the place.'

Ethan looked around the office, but then hesitated. A feeling that he'd occasionally experienced in his life, a sixth sense that somebody had preceded him, filtered into his consciousness. He remained still, letting his eyes soak in the office until he realized what was bugging him.

'Some of the surfaces have been cleaned down,' he said, and made his way over to the filing cabinets.

Truth was, neither he nor Lopez were much into cleaning: a little dust makes a place feel lived in, he figured. But the handles on the filing-cabinet doors were spotless. He turned and checked the drawers in his desk. They were still locked, no signs of tampering, but also looked suspiciously clean.

'My keyboard's been wiped,' Lopez said.

'Mine too,' Ethan confirmed, and then looked at her. 'We've been swept professionally enough to not have left any evidence, but they've been overzealous.'

'CIA?' Lopez hazarded. 'Shit, I don't want to have to deal with this right now.'

Ethan nodded, choosing not to reply just yet. He'd felt that Lopez needed a break after their return from Florida, and had suggested that she head home to Guanajuato, Mexico. Catch up with her family. Maybe see friends and just goof around. Lopez had thanked him for his concern but said that she was fine – and that was what had bothered Ethan. In the past she would have just told him to fuck off or something. The loss of Scott Bryson, a man whom Ethan had reluctantly realized was something of a heroic figure, had hit her harder than he'd expected, and right now he didn't have much of an idea of how to deal with it.

Ethan flicked a small television on as Lopez sorted through the pile of mail that had built up. A news article on an earthquake that had hit the Florida Straits caught Ethan's eye, and he turned up the volume as the news anchor outlined the story.

'. . . *The clean-up continues on Miami Beach today after the magnitude 6.8 quake that hit the Florida Straits just before nine in the evening on the twenty-eighth and caused a tsunami that hit the coast just four minutes later. Although there were no casualties from the wave, Governor MacKenzie has suggested that more suitable warning facilities should be installed along the Florida coastline to guard against such geological events in the future, and provide earlier warning of tsunami conditions.*'

The image of Miami was replaced with one of Puerto Plata, with a picture of Joaquin Abell in the top right corner of the screen. The news anchor kept reading from her autocue, but was not visible on the screen.

'*The governor's comments come just days after Puerto Plata in the Dominican Republic was hit by a similar quake and tsunami, killing over five thousand residents and tourists. The CEO of IRIS, Katherine Abell, has led calls for international intervention in the crisis, a plea made all the more poignant after her husband, Joaquin Abell, pictured here, was tragically lost at sea and presumed killed along with several of his employees, after a diving accident aboard his yacht, the* Event Horizon. *With currents in the Straits so strong, it's considered unlikely by the Coastguard that their remains will be found.*'

Ethan looked down at Lopez.

'That's the news article that Joaquin Abell saw,' he realized. 'Without sound on the report, he knew nothing of his own death, and with no anchor on screen there was no way anyone could have read her lips.'

Lopez nodded vacantly.

'The yacht accident's a perfect cover for Joaquin's disappearance.'

As if on cue, the image switched to a scene of the Everglades, where police and forensic teams were working amid a small knot of trees in the vast wilderness.

'*Investigators in Dade County have announced that the remains found in the Florida Everglades on June 28 are those of one Charles Purcell, a man who was suspected of murdering his family.*' The images showed Purcell's body being lifted onto a stretcher and carried from the scene. '*However, it has recently come to light that Purcell was innocent of any crime after an investigation led by the Miami-Dade police department uncovered evidence proving that Purcell was not at the scene when his family were killed but was in fact on his way home. Police remain baffled as to why he fled the scene, but believe his grief and despair at having lost his young family may have driven him to take his own life. A funeral for family and friends is to be held for Purcell in his hometown.*'

Ethan saw Kyle Sears among officers searching the scene in the Everglades, and then glimpsed both himself and Lopez in the background between the trees, talking to Jarvis.

'Sears would have been required to sign non-disclosure agreements by the DIA,' Ethan said. 'Must have driven him nuts, having so much of the case kept from him.'

Ethan turned the television off as Lopez held out a UPS package for him.

'The one Doug took from you, before we left,' she said.

Ethan took the package and opened one end of it before tipping the contents out into his hand. From within fell a single photograph. As Lopez watched, Ethan looked at it and felt a supernatural tingle ripple down his spine into the pit of his belly.

Lopez saw his expression change.

'What?' she asked.

Ethan stared down at the photograph in his hands: it showed Charles Purcell standing with his wife and his daughter in front of the sea on a bright and sunny day, their arms around each other and their smiles as bright as the sunlight beaming down upon them. Ethan turned the photograph over and felt something tighten in his throat as he read the words written there.

Looks like you made it in time, Ethan.
So sorry I could not be there in person
to say this to you and Nicola.
Thank you.

Ethan handed the photograph to Lopez, who looked at it and read the inscription, one hand flying to her mouth as she looked up at him.

'The photograph that was missing,' she said.

'From the mantelpiece in Purcell's house,' Ethan replied, shaking his head in wonderment. 'He took it with him, must have posted it along with the diary that he sent to me at Cape Canaveral. He planned everything, even his own death, knowing that to sacrifice himself was the only way to ensure that we got this photograph and that Joaquin Abell would be defeated.'

Lopez stared at the picture, and sighed.

'No less a sacrifice than Scott made.'

Ethan managed not to sound trite. 'Every bit as brave.'

Lopez looked up at him, and he saw there in her expression a desolation that unnerved him.

'Why did that have to happen?' she asked him. 'Why didn't he make it?'

Ethan had never been any good at this kind of stuff, especially with women. Most of the time a good slap on the back and a few beers in front of the game with friends was enough to snap a guy out of his misery. Most of the time it was good enough for Lopez, too.

But Lopez didn't need beer and football right now. She needed comfort, someone to talk to who wouldn't screw it up. Someone resolutely not like him. Ethan racked his brains for something profound to say in reply.

'The best people always get taken from us first, it seems.'

Ethan watched her, waiting to see how she would respond. Lopez stared at him for a few moments.

'He was alone, no family.'

'He was adopted as a baby, never knew his folks,' Ethan said, recalling what Jarvis had told them when they'd returned to the *Event Horizon* without Bryson. 'The Navy was the only family he had. Probably why he hit the bottle when he was wounded and medically unable to stay with the SEALs.'

Lopez nodded vacantly, not replying to him. Ethan sucked in a deep breath as silently as he could, and tried again.

'Look, when people pass on we end up grieving for them, but really we're only grieving for ourselves, for what *we've* lost. Scott's not in pain, not suffering, maybe he's not even alone anymore. Nobody knows what comes next, if anything. If there's nothing, then Scott's problems are over and his life was sacrificed knowing that yours would continue, something that I know would have made the one-eyed jerk very happy.'

Lopez's stony facade melted slightly. She did not smile, but Ethan glimpsed the briefest ray of light flicker behind her eyes.

'And if there *is* something after we die?'

'Then Scott's problems are still over, and he's probably sipping a stiff drink right now whilst looking down on us with both of his goddamned eyes working.'

A tiny smile flickered at the edges of Lopez's lips, and Ethan felt his own spirits lift a little. Maybe he wasn't so bad at this shit after all.

'Y'know what he said, while we were in Puerto Plata?' Lopez went on. 'He said that you probably wished he'd get lost, as he was getting in the way.'

'In the way of what?'

'In the way of us.'

Ethan's stomach did a little back-flip, like the one he'd experienced at high school when he'd been informed that a well-known cheerleader considered him 'cute'. He looked down at Lopez.

'There's an *us*?'

Lopez gave a little shrug. 'Scott seemed to think so.'

Ethan's throat felt suddenly dry. He realized he was slouching and probably looked like a slack-jawed hick. He squared his shoulders and tried to look normal.

'I don't know what to say,' he uttered, in a voice that sounded oddly higher in pitch than normal.

Lopez sighed.

'I guess I just don't know who you are, Ethan,' she said. 'I've worked with a lot of guys over the years since I moved to the US, and almost every single one of them has made a move on me. The only ones that didn't turned out to be gay or happily married. I'm pretty sure you're neither of those, so what's the deal?'

Ethan dodged the question.

'Is this about what happened to Scott?'

Lopez's inquiring face flushed and she looked away from him for a moment, before regaining her composure.

'Scott just came out with things,' she said finally. 'He was an open book. You, you're totally closed. He was all over me and you barely even reacted. I guess it just makes me wonder why?'

Ethan gathered himself together. Lopez had just suffered a great personal loss and now she was looking for honest answers from him. *Just say what you feel.* Stop being such a dick and be a man for a change. The tension drained from his shoulders and Ethan looked her in the eye.

'I guess I just haven't been able to tell you how I feel because—'

The door to the office cracked open and Doug Jarvis strode in. Lopez flinched in her chair and then glared at the old man.

'Damn it, Doug, don't people knock where you come from?'

Jarvis looked down at her in surprise.

'Sorry Nicola, but this is an emergency.' He turned to Ethan. 'Ethan, you need to come with me right now, there isn't much time.'

Ethan rolled his eyes up into his head. 'Not again?'

Jarvis placed a hand on his shoulder.

'No, it's nothing like that. There's something that I need you to see.'

'Our office got swept,' Lopez growled at him. 'Your boys been playing out of hours?'

Jarvis looked at her quizzically. 'No, not at all. I'll look into it, I promise, but right now we've got to leave.'

Ethan sighed, and looked at Lopez.

'Okay, let's go and see what this is all about, and maybe we can talk later about—'

'Just you, Ethan,' Jarvis cautioned them, as Lopez stood up. 'I'm sorry, Nicola, but this can't wait and I can only show one of you.'

Ethan looked at Jarvis. 'Where I go, Lopez goes.'

'Not this time,' Jarvis replied. 'I'll have you arrested if I have to, Ethan, but you're coming with me and you're coming alone. It won't take long.'

Lopez stared at Jarvis with something approaching contempt, but she waved them away.

'Just go,' she said.

Ethan looked at her for a long moment, and then turned to Jarvis.

'Sorry, Doug, but it'll have to wait. Nicola and I were talking about something important, and I want her to hear what I have to say.'

Lopez looked up at Ethan and for the first time in days a true smile melted her features. Jarvis looked at them each in turn, unable to decide how to respond. Lopez answered for him.

'It's all right, Ethan,' she said, still smiling. 'You can tell me when you get back, okay?'

Ethan looked at her.

'You sure?'

Lopez nodded, and seeing her still smiling provoked a gentle warmth that spread through him.

'Okay,' he said to Jarvis, grabbing his jacket. 'What's so important?'

72

DEFENSE INTELLIGENCE AGENCY ANALYSIS CENTER, BOLLING AIR FORCE BASE, WASHINGTON D.C.

Ethan had rarely received clearance to enter restricted facilities during his military service, his rank only allowing him occasional access to a narrow spectrum of classified material. Now, striding into the DIAC building alongside Doug Jarvis, after so recently being allowed into Project Watchman, he realized that he was on entirely new turf.

The large, angular building nestled close to the east bank of the Potomac, was closed to the public and contained the vast majority of the DIA's staff. Ethan followed Jarvis through the building, mindful of the offices to either side of him with their doors kept scrupulously closed, unattended monitor screens blank and password-protected, and passing operatives smiling politely but not stopping or chatting. Everybody was all business, and the business was serious.

Jarvis led him to an elevator that lifted them to the third floor. Ethan guessed that the director of the agency, Abraham Mitchell, probably resided somewhere above

him, enveloped within a force field of absolute security.
Right now, the level of protection afforded even this
floor of the building was intimidating: identity tags worn
at all times; mutual cross-referencing of people moving
between floors and even rooms; fingerprint and retinal
scanners as standard; metal detectors attuned to weap-
ons-grade materials. Cameras, sensors, fireproof and
sealable doors. Since 2001, nobody anywhere in the DIA
skimped on security. Nobody.

'Through here.'

Jarvis directed him to a door that was guarded by two
soldiers, one of whom checked their tags against a roster
before opening the door for them. Ethan stepped through
and was surprised to see a small, simple office with a
computer desk and a chair. Standing in the room was a
tall, gaunt-looking man whom Ethan recognized from
years before – a CIA man who had ordered him to sign
a nondisclosure agreement in a hidden anechoic chamber beneath a warehouse in downtown Washington DC.

'Mr. Warner,' the tall man greeted him.

'Mr. Wilson,' Ethan replied. 'Didn't think we'd be
meeting again.'

'Nor did I,' Jarvis said. 'You have a habit of appearing
in all the wrong places, Mr. Wilson.'

'As do you,' Wilson said evenly. 'The material you
have obtained is classified well above Top Secret, and
yet you intend to share it with a civilian contractor. How
do you think the Pentagon would feel about such a
breach of security, Mr. Jarvis?'

Jarvis held his ground.

'It doesn't matter, because it's already been cleared by

the director of this agency, in whose building you're standing. You got a problem, stop creeping around here and go take it to your boss at the Pentagon. Let them have the pissing contest.'

Wilson regarded them both for a moment, and then made for the door of the office. He stopped there, and looked back at them.

'We're watching both of you.'

'I'd never have known,' Jarvis replied.

Wilson turned and strode out of the office. Jarvis closed the door in his sepulchral wake and locked it from the inside.

'Nice guy, I'll guess that he's the one who had our office searched,' Ethan said.

'It's possible,' Jarvis replied, 'but right now I can't think of a good reason why the CIA would be interested in the two of you.'

Ethan looked at the spartan surroundings and the lone computer on the desk. 'You got me all the way out here for this? And there was me getting all excited.'

'This room is sufficiently sealed so that nobody can hear us outside the door,' Jarvis said. 'There are also no cameras or sensors in here.'

'What did you want to show me?' Ethan asked, somewhat confused. 'And why did I have to come all the way out to the district to see it?'

Jarvis perched himself on the edge of the desk and gestured to the computer.

'Ethan, I got Project Watchman to locate the footage of Joanna Defoe from Jabaliya, West Bank. It's on that computer.'

Ethan suddenly went cold. Memories of Joanna flitted through his mind, dragging with them years of grief and suffering that he'd tried so hard to forget. Again, the realization hit him that he'd begun to associate Joanna's memory with that grief and regret, and not the good years that they'd shared beforehand.

'Do you want to see it?' Jarvis asked, his expression pinched with concern.

Ethan sought an answer inside himself, and shook his head. 'I just don't know.'

'Closure, Ethan, is sometimes better than not knowing, even if it brings up things that we'd rather forget.' Jarvis gestured at the monitor screen. 'This footage will be destroyed as per protocol once viewed. There won't be another chance for me to pull strings like this on your behalf.'

Ethan sighed. As ever, intelligence security trumped personal emotion. He took a breath.

'Okay, Doug, play it.'

Jarvis reached out and tapped a button on the keyboard. A window popped up on the screen, with a message that read 'Video 1 of 2'. Jarvis tapped the play button, and in an instant Ethan was transported back years into his past.

A high-angle shot of Gaza City and the dangerous alleys of Jabaliya, a refugee camp crouched in the city's northern reaches. Bright daylight, angular buildings blasted dry by a thousand suns, abandoned vehicles and mangled masonry shattered by the incendiaries of Israel's fighter planes.

The camera zoomed in to an altitude of perhaps thirty

feet as, from a doorway, a tight huddle of figures burst out into the street. Masked faces aimed Kalashnikov rifles in all directions, covering their points as they advanced toward a waiting dark-blue sedan stained with dust. In their midst a woman. Blonde hair. Tall. Shoved and jostled by her captors.

Ethan sucked in a breath and leaned close to the monitor, one hand reaching out as if of its own accord, to touch the screen where Joanna stood. The gunmen pushed her toward the car, hard enough to make her stumble as she squinted. Ethan's brain went into overtime.

'She's been held in darkness,' he said quickly, his mind working faster than his mouth could produce words. 'Her shirt's fairly new. Hair's longer than when I last saw her. She's not bound or gagged. Looks fairly healthy, a bit pale, maybe.'

'Camera resolution can play with colors,' Jarvis corrected him, then conceded Ethan's point. 'But she's definitely squinting, so she's been held inside.'

The gunmen huddled in a tight circle around Joanna. One of their number broke ranks and sprinted across the street. Reached the door of the sedan and opened it. Immediately, the vehicle exploded in a violent fireball that scattered the gunmen like skittles. Ethan glimpsed the tight huddle of men around Joanna tumble as though hit by a hurricane, as a scythe of supersonic shrapnel sliced through their ranks.

Ethan leapt up out of his seat as his guts plunged inside him, one hand flying loosely to his lips as his other clenched into a fist. Thick clouds of smoke and dust swirled, obscuring his view. He stared at the screen as, through the veils of smoke, the scattered bodies of the fallen gunmen began hauling themselves to their feet, and then a burst of gunfire shattered masonry around them and kicked up tiny clouds of dust as bullets hailed down the street.

'Jo.'

Her name fell from his lips as though she had never left his life. Bullets slammed into the already-stunned gunmen and hurled them into walls or onto their backs on Gaza's ancient soil. Ethan saw a pair of Israeli halftracks advancing toward the gunmen, a large-caliber section weapon atop each hosing bullets down the street and scouring it of life.

'Shit, Doug!'

Jarvis did not move, and Ethan stared in stunned silence as the halftracks stopped firing. The street was littered with the dead or writhing bodies of masked gunmen, and framed by a thick coiling pillar of smoke from the wrecked sedan. Israeli troops spilled from behind the halftracks and advanced down the street with their rifles aimed ahead of them, kicking dead bodies and firing rounds into those that still showed signs of life.

The thick smoke from the burning car drifted clear of the street for a brief instant, and Ethan saw the tight knot of dead gunmen lying sprawled at awkward angles in the bright sunshine.

And Joanna was nowhere to be seen.

Ethan stared at the screen, unable to tear his gaze from it. 'Where did she go?'

'I don't know, Ethan. But she clearly did not die in

this raid by Israeli forces. They were looking for her, Ethan. After what happened when you worked for me there, the Israeli Defense Force has kept an ear to the ground for information leading to the whereabouts of Joanna Defoe. They even offered a reward. An inform-ant tipped them off.'

Ethan stared at the screen for a moment longer, and then he slowly turned and looked at Jarvis, his throat dry as he spoke.

'When did this happen?'

'Six months ago, Ethan.'

Ethan flopped back in his seat as sharp points of pain pierced the corners of his eyes. He dragged a hand down his face.

'Watchman could track her movements,' he said, 'find out where she went.'

'My leverage didn't extend that far,' Jarvis said apolo-getically. 'This was all the time I could scrounge. Most of it was spent finding her and then grabbing this footage.'

Ethan shot out of his seat again. 'Then get more time!'

'I had to pull in another favor for you.' Jarvis raised his hands defensively. 'I couldn't get any more than I did. If I could, you know that I would have.'

Ethan leaned on the desk and took a deep breath.

'What other favor?' he asked finally.

'Ethan, we downloaded the contents of the camera that you retrieved from Joaquin Abell before he died. We've seen all of it.'

Ethan lifted his head. 'You've seen six months into the future?'

Jarvis offered him a brief smile.

'Everything as seen through the lens of that camera,' he confirmed. 'I have to say that, for the most part, it was remarkably boring. The camera's travels did not exactly bring it into contact with much except our own agency's various buildings and offices. I suppose we should have known better: once we acquired it, the camera was in our own hands and thus would only see what we see.'

'You're saying that, after all that, after Scott Bryson and Dennis Aubrey gave their lives, all we got was six months of your office furniture and people using the coffee machine?'

'Well, it's not quite that bad,' Jarvis said. 'One of our analysts managed to obtain glimpses of future news reports, events occurring in the operations rooms of the building, that kind of thing. Of course, once we saw that footage, we knew that one way or another the camera would end up in those rooms. The point is, it caught enough information to have been more than worthwhile: most of it is sensitive enough to have been classified.'

Ethan chewed his lip for a moment.

'You likely to be able to stop any wars or anything because of it?'

'No,' Jarvis admitted, 'but the lives of a good number of soldiers and operatives working overseas will be saved and otherwise dangerous situations avoided. You and Lopez did good yet again, Ethan, and the director was delighted with what you've achieved. The unit here will continue to receive funding and you're getting more interest from the Pentagon.'

Ethan managed a faint smile of relief.

'At least we won't have to spend all of our time chasing bail runners around Illinois,' he said finally.

Jarvis nodded, glancing at the computer. Ethan peered at him.

'Is there something else on this computer you wanted to show me?'

Jarvis nodded slowly.

'Yes, there is. When we finished reviewing the footage, and despite the fact that the contents were marked as classified, the director agreed with me that, considering the lengths you and Lopez went to in obtaining the footage for us, you deserved to see the final part of it. Ethan, sit down again, please.'

A tremor of apprehension twisted through Ethan's guts.

'What's going on here, Doug?' he asked, reluctantly sitting down.

'There's no way to describe it,' Jarvis replied. 'You've just got to see it for yourself. You understand that what you are about to see will not happen for six months, and that it cannot be discussed beyond this room. It must remain absolutely classified, and between you and me. Not Lopez, not anyone.'

Ethan nodded, but Jarvis put his hand on Ethan's shoulder.

'Let me hear you say it, Ethan.'

'I understand.'

Jarvis nodded, and Ethan looked at the blank monitor before him. Jarvis reached down to the keyboard and pressed one of the buttons. Immediately, an image appeared on the screen before him. It was dark and indistinct, and he wasn't sure what he was looking at until his brain processed the scene and it leapt into life before him.

There was no sound, and the image occasionally flickered with static as coils of energy flared around the edges of the screen.

Ethan saw a forest, deep and black, impenetrable trees lining a trail that wound its way through the woods into the inky distance. The sky above was velvet black, and jagged mountain peaks towered across the horizon in the distance, their snowy peaks glowing blue beneath a brilliant white moon high above.

Ethan's eyes flicked down to the trail below as he caught sight of movement, a shadow against the shadows. A body was slumped on the trail, and as it moved he saw a thick mass of long black hair draped across damp grass. The body wearily lifted its head, and Ethan felt a bolt of electricity spasm through his chest as he recognized the face.

'Lopez.'

Ethan stared at the screen, transfixed, as Lopez looked over her shoulder and away from the camera. He saw her begin to frantically drag herself toward the camera, as though trying to escape from something.

And then he saw it.

From the dense forest blackness a huge man lumbered into view. Heavy arms dangled from broad, thick shoulders, huge legs strode cumbersomely beneath a thick fur coat. The man was wearing an oddly shaped cap that was almost conical, but it was his size that stunned Ethan. The guy must have been two meters tall, and—

Ethan's heart stopped in his chest as he realized that the

man was not wearing a coat, and was not wearing a hat. For a moment he thought that perhaps a bear had reared onto its hind legs and was tracking Lopez, but then he saw the face briefly illuminated by the moon's pale light, and the unmistakably humanoid features, a low and heavy brow with eyes sunken into deep sockets.

Thick fur hung in knotted tags as the broad, flat face looked down at Lopez as she hauled herself toward the camera. A thick, meaty hand as big as Lopez's entire head reached down and stopped her before the creature looked up, as though noticing the camera. Ethan felt fear shudder through his guts as he looked into a pair of eyes that belonged to something that was both human and animal, an unspeakable chimera of man and beast.

Ethan watched as the red eyes flared angrily at the camera, and then a huge arm flashed across the screen and swatted the camera into the air, and the image crashed into static and vanished.

Ethan sat in stunned silence and stared at the screen. Joanna was alive, Lopez was facing death and he didn't have the first clue about which problem he should deal with first. He looked up at Jarvis in despair.

'You know the future, Ethan,' Jarvis said, 'but you're going to have to deal with that yourself.'

AUTHOR'S NOTE

I often get asked by readers just how much of the science incorporated within my novels is 'real'. The simple answer is that *all* of the science within my novels is real, but some of it is stretched to embrace the extreme events that are part and parcel of thriller fiction.

As described in *Apocalypse*, we really do see back in time the further away we look, the speed of light does have a finite velocity and an endeavour like *Project Watchman* is entirely within the physical and technological capabilities of the United States' intelligence community. Their KH-11 'Keyhole' satellites are also real, and are rumoured to have optics more than capable of clearly photographing newspaper articles from orbit. Modern supercomputers could indeed crunch data sufficiently to provide a virtual replay of events from around the globe: only the storage of so many years of data might prove problematic. Quantum computers, just over our technological horizon, may resolve that issue.

The only science that I have adjusted for the sake of the plot in *Apocalypse* is the black hole itself. In reality it would take a black hole with the mass of hundreds of suns to produce the time-dilation described in the novel:

an object this massive would swallow our entire planet almost instantaneously. Time-dilation, however, is real, as is the ability of objects to travel through time via extreme velocities. If one were able to stand alongside the event horizon of a sufficiently massive black hole, then time would indeed be dilated in the manner described. Although a low-mass black hole could probably be suspended in a tokomak just like Joaquin Abell's, the gravitational field of such an object would not be likewise contained: it would continue to affect its surroundings both inside and outside of the chamber.

At the time of writing, physicists working with the Large Hadron Collider at the CERN labs in Geneva have observed what they believe to be the fabled Higgs boson, the elementary particle responsible for mass in our universe. This discovery paves the way for a greater understanding of our universe, and potentially brings the subject matter in *Apocalypse* one step closer to reality.

Dean Crawford, 2012

ACKNOWLEDGEMENTS

Since the publication of the first Ethan Warner novel, Covenant, time has flown by so incredibly quickly. The writing of new novels in the series, the rounds of edits on each of them, the new projects and the crime festivals have been a constant whirlwind of activity. I couldn't have done any of it without the fabulous support of the publishing team at Simon & Schuster, my literary agent Luigi Bonomi at LBA, my wonderful partner Debbie and our beautiful daughter Emma, and my family and friends who continue to champion my work so enthusiastically. Thanks also go to aspiring author Dean Owen, who won my blog competition to suggest the title for this book while I was writing it. Although ultimately not used by the publisher, it was an inspired choice and I'm sure his is a name you'll see on bookshelves before long.

Finally, at the time of writing, a team working at the CERN laboratories in Geneva have reportedly found the fabled Higgs boson, the particle that holds our universe together and is responsible for gravity: many thanks to them for spearheading the forward march of science and perhaps bringing the subject matter of this novel a little closer to reality.